THE
First Love
COOKIE
CLUB

By Lori Wilde

The First Love Cookie Club
The True Love Quilting Club
The Sweethearts' Knitting Club

THE
First Love
COOKIE
CLUB

LORI WILDE

WM

WILLIAM MORROW

An Imprint of HarperCollinsPublishers

Here's to all the great dads out there.
Long may you love.

THE FIRST LOVE COOKIE CLUB. Copyright © 2010 by Laurie Vanzura. All rights reserved. Printed in the United States of America. No part of this book may be used or reproduced in any manner whatsoever without written permission except in the case of brief quotations embodied in critical articles and reviews. For information address HarperCollins Publishers, 10 East 53rd Street, New York, NY 10022.

HarperCollins books may be purchased for educational, business, or sales promotional use. For information please write: Special Markets Department, HarperCollins Publishers, 10 East 53rd Street, New York, NY 10022.

A paperback edition was first published in 2010 by Avon Books, an imprint of Harper-Collins Publishers.

FIRST WILLIAM MORROW PAPERBACK EDITION PUBLISHED 2011.

Library of Congress Cataloging-in-Publication Data has been applied for.

ISBN 978-0-06-208921-2

11 12 13 14 15   ID/RRD   10 9 8 7 6 5 4 3 2 1

ACKNOWLEDGMENTS

There is a story in this acknowledgment. When I was a young nursing student, I was assigned to work in a pediatric clinic that treated children stricken with cancer. This was an extremely difficult rotation, and I saw many families split apart by the terminal diagnosis of a child. It was truly heartbreaking to watch. Most of the time it was the fathers who broke, unable to handle the pressure, and took off, leaving the mothers to shoulder the burden alone.

But there was one father I will forever remember. When his little golden-haired three-year-old daughter was diagnosed with terminal cancer, he was the one who stayed and his wife was the one who abandoned them. He'd gone to the same high school I'd attended and I recalled him as a real hell-raiser in his day. No one would have ever expected him to turn out to be such a wonderful father. He'd bring his daughter into the clinic every week and she'd be dressed in adorable clothes, patent leather Mary Janes, her hair styled in ringlets. He'd hold her in his arms and whisper tender words of comfort to her as we did wretchedly painful things to try and save this child's life.

I would love to say that we succeeded. That we saved the real Jazzy and she had a happy life with her very special father, but alas we did not.

That was many, many years ago, but the memory of that father and his daughter stayed with me. They are the inspiration for Travis and Jazzy Walker, except this time, I'm in control and they will darn well get their happy ending.

PROLOGUE

Every Christmas Eve from the time she was eight years old, Sarah Collier baked kismet cookies, slept with a handful under her pillow, and dreamed of her one true love.

She couldn't wait to fall asleep while the lights on the eaves twinkled a prism of colors through the sheer lace curtains of her bedroom window, and the piney smell of fresh-cut Douglas fir filled the house while Bing Crosby crooned "White Christmas" from her grandmother's record player.

On that most magical of evenings, in her cozy little lakeside cottage in Twilight, Texas, Gramma Mia would trot out the flour and sugar and vanilla and creamy, rich, honest-to-goodness butter (which Sarah's mother would never let her eat), and assemble the ingredients on the shiny white tiles of her kitchen counter. Even though they both knew the recipe by heart, Gramma would unfold the yellowed piece of notebook paper to reveal the faded blue ink written in spiky, cursive lettering and gently prop it up against the tea canister. Eager to get started, Sarah's excited fingers tangled the strings of her apron and pulled her wavy caramel-colored hair into a haphazard ponytail.

In seven years the dream never changed. Soft-focus, misty white lace stretched out like wedding veil trains. A dark-haired man wearing a sharp black tuxedo stood waiting at the end of a pink rose petal–strewn path, his back to her, while gentle snowflakes drifted from a gunmetal gray holiday sky.

Heart pounding, she glided closer to him until the sound of her own rushing blood was a wild cacophony of jungle drums in her ears. Then he turned, smiled, and held out a hand.

That's when she saw his face.

Travis Walker, the handsome older boy who lived next door to Gramma, but all grown up now.

Her hero.

Sarah slept blissfully, happily, her hands curled underneath her cheek, never guessing the tumult her annual dream would soon bring.

On the Christmas morning when she was fifteen years old, Sarah woke with the sweet taste of fantasy in her mouth. Smiling, she ran the tip of her tongue over her lips.

Travis.

Her budding young body felt raw and achy, and instead of jumping from the bed and running to see what lay under the Christmas tree as she normally would have, Sarah snuggled deeper into the pillow, closed her eyes, ignored the smell of bacon and waffles wafting in the air, and tried to chase down the fragments of her fading dream.

But Gramma's gentle knock at the door ruined

all that. "Sarah, honey, get up and get dressed, your folks just called. They'll be here within the hour."

Sarah sighed and sat up on the edge of the bed. It didn't seem fair that her parents barely had time for her, but when they put in an appearance she was expected to give them her undivided attention. Drs. Mitchell and Helen Collier sent her to stay with Gramma every summer and during the Christmas holidays. The rest of the year, she resided at Chatham Academy, a boarding school in Dallas. They were too busy being renowned heart surgeons in Houston and jetting around the globe as guest lecturers to bother raising their own daughter.

Stop feeling sorry for yourself. You've got more than most people.

That was true, but it didn't stop her from longing for a close-knit family. She wrapped her arms around her pillow and squeezed it to her chest, leaving a trail of kismet cookie crumbs scattered across the flannel sheet.

It didn't help that she was shy and prone to an exaggerated fantasy life. She wasn't popular at school and didn't fit in. English was the only subject she excelled at. Her parents were practical, brilliant, scientific people, and they didn't understand her at all. Sometimes, she imagined she was adopted, but she looked so much like her father, with his wild light brown hair and stark blue eyes, it was impossible to deny the lineage.

Sighing, she got of bed, changed the sheets stained with butter from the cookies, and then took a shower. She dressed in a red plaid skirt with red leggings, black ankle boots, a white silk blouse underneath a green sweater vest (with jangly jingle bells on it, which Gram had knitted for her), and just to be whimsical, she donned a headband adorned with reindeer antlers that she'd won at Dickens on the Square. Her mother would loathe the headband. Reason enough to wear it.

She wandered into the kitchen and Gramma waved her to the table. She slid a mug of hot chocolate in front of her along with a plate of Belgian waffles and thick slab bacon.

"Did you sleep well?" Gram asked with a twinkle in her eye.

"*Very* well." Sarah grinned.

"Did you dream of your true love?"

"I did." Sarah couldn't tell Gram who her true love was. You weren't supposed to tell or you'd jinx the kismet cookie prophecy.

"Same as last year?"

"And the year before and the year before that and the year before that."

Gram nodded. "Then it's for real, sweet pea. He *is* your destiny."

A happy shiver rushed over her arms and she hugged herself tight. Travis Walker. Her one true love. She hadn't seen him since she'd been back in town, even though each time she stepped out on her grandmother's front porch she glanced over at his house, hoping to see his battered Ford pickup in the driveway. She didn't ask Gramma about him. She was afraid to give away her secret crush.

Not a crush, she reminded herself. *Destiny.*

Sarah swallowed a mouthful of waffle, dripping with real maple syrup, and bit into a crisp slice of bacon. She wanted to get her breakfast eaten before her mother got there and started in on her about her weight. Gramma told her she was just the right size, but Helen Collier would whip out her calculator, tap in some numbers, and tell her that her BMI was 25.4 and that qualified as overweight. Size fourteen. Her mother would shake her head while her disappointed eyes said, *Chubby chug-butt.* Sarah took another bite of waffle and wondered if Travis thought she was fat or looked geeky with braces.

A knock sounded at the door.

"Come in," Gramma said, getting to her feet as the back door opened.

Dotty Mae Densmore, who was her grandmother's age and lived down the road, popped into the room, a basket of fresh-baked blueberry muffins dangling from her upturned elbow. "Merry Christmas!"

"Merry Christmas, Mrs. Densmore," Sarah said.

"My, don't you look festive," Dotty Mae said. "I love the reindeer antlers."

Sarah raised a hand to finger the antlers made from brown felt and stuffed with cotton batting. "Thanks."

Dotty Mae, her cheeks flushed red from the cold, set the muffins on the sideboard and turned to Gramma Mia. "So, I guess you're not going to the wedding?"

"Wedding?" Gramma wrinkled her forehead. "When is it?"

"You didn't get an invitation?" Dotty Mae pressed three fingers to her lips. "Um . . . I'm sorry, I just assumed you'd gotten one."

Gramma shook her head.

"I just got mine day before yesterday. Talk about last minute." Dotty Mae shook her head. "But seeing as how it's a shotgun situation . . ."

Sarah wasn't sure what they were talking about. What did a shotgun have to do with getting married? Surely someone wasn't planning on giving the bride and groom a shotgun for a wedding gift.

"I've been so busy with Christmas preparations I haven't even checked my mail. I hope I got an invitation. Even though it's too late to attend, I do want to send a gift. You're not going?"

"I can't. My boys and their families are driving in to spend Christmas Day with me."

"It *is* bad timing. Helen and Mitchell are on their way as well."

Dotty Mae arched an eyebrow, reached into the bottom of the muffin basket, and produced a bottle of peppermint schnapps. "Want to add a little holiday cheer to that hot chocolate, Mia?"

"I thought you'd never ask." Gram grinned and went to the tea kettle on the stove to pour hot water into a cup of powdered hot chocolate mix for Dotty Mae. "Dealing with Helen is always easier with a little fortification." Then to Sara she said, "Sweet pea would you mind running down to the end of the road and getting what's in the letter box?"

"Sure." Sarah pushed back her chair, got her jacket from the coatrack beside the front door, and stepped out onto the porch. Immediately, she peeked over at Travis's house. His pickup wasn't in the driveway. Did he still live there? He was twenty now. Maybe he'd moved out and gotten a place of his own. Hmm. She'd have to find a covert way to ask Gram about it.

She strolled along the cobblestone path leading to the road abutting the lakefront. Lake Twilight shimmered blue and shiny in the crisp, cool, early morning sunlight. She thought of the time Travis had taken her fishing off the dock. How he'd baited her cane pole with minnows and acted as if she'd snagged a giant tuna when she'd reeled in a palm-sized sun perch. She'd been ten. He'd been fifteen. The same age she was now. He always had Super Bubble in his pocket that he'd share with her, and every Fourth of July they climbed on Gram's roof together to watch the fireworks, and once he scared off some bullies who'd backed her into the alley and demanded her allowance money.

Her dream had been a little different this time. It hadn't stopped with Travis taking her hand. This time, he'd pulled her into his arms, dipped his head, and kissed her. A red-hot sizzling kiss that made her entire body tingle.

Sarah had never been kissed. Not for real. But that dream kiss. . . . Whew! It was everything she imagined a kiss would be. Firm and moist and sensual.

Remembering, she licked her lips. How long would she have to wait until she could kiss him for real? How did she make him see her for the woman she was becoming and not the little girl who wore braids and braces and begged him to tell her ghost stories? She poked at the problem with her mind, anxious to make some forward momentum on the cookie prophecy.

If he was her one true love, shouldn't he start recognizing that fact soon? Maybe she should bake him some kismet cookies and tell him to sleep with them under *his* pillow. Except that Gramma said kismet cookie magic only worked on Christmas Eve. She would have to wait another whole year. Disappointment pulled her shoulders into a slump.

Sarah reached the mailbox painted with black and white spots to resemble a Holstein cow and pulled down the flap. Only one piece of mail lay inside. It was a thick, cream-colored, square envelope. Apparently Gramma had been invited to a wedding.

She pulled out the envelope, shut the mailbox, and glanced at the address. It read: "To Mrs. Mia Martin and Miss Sarah Collier." She was invited too. A Christmas wedding. How beautiful. Then her gaze shifted to the name on the return address: Mr. and Mrs. Albert Hunt.

Huh?

Her mind did not want to process what this meant. But her hands, her treacherous hands, started shaking as they tore into the pretty cream-colored envelope and fumbled to pull out the stiff paper card. Inside was a picture of a smiling Travis embracing a beautiful young blond woman that Sarah didn't know.

The card read: "Mr. and Mrs. Albert Hunt joyfully announce the marriage of their daughter Crystal Ann Hunt to Travis Stephen Walker on Saturday, the twenty-fifth of December. Nine A.M. First Presbyterian Church of Twilight."

A cry of despair slipped from Sarah's lips as the card fluttered from her hand. Travis? Getting married? It couldn't be true. It was impossible. He was too young and . . . and . . . this woman. Who the hell was she? Travis belonged to Sarah. He was her one true love. The kismet cookies said so.

She glanced at her watch and saw that it was

straight-up nine o'clock. At this very moment, Travis was getting married.

No!

She could not let this happen. He had to know that *they* were meant to be. He couldn't marry this Crystal Hunt person. Simply *could not*.

Blindly, she turned and ran, a single thought pounding in her brain. Get to Travis. Tell him about her dreams. Stop the wedding.

Now!

She darted down Lakeshore Drive, headed for the center of town. She wasn't in very good shape and she quickly grew out of breath. The stabbing stitch in her side forced her to slow to a fast walk.

Hurry, hurry. This was an emergency.

Her mind was a mad jumble. The cold wind gusted, swirling fallen leaves across the street in front of her. This early on Christmas morning, the roads lay bare. It was ten minutes after nine when she maneuvered past the cars crowding the parking lot outside the Presbyterian church. Her heart was a cannon in her chest. *Boom, boom, boom.* Each beat jarring hard through her body.

She scrambled up the steps, wrenched open the heavy wooden door, and staggered inside.

There, just as she'd dreamed, was the drape of sheer white lace over the pews. The center aisle was strewn with pink rose petals. People packed the room. Up front at the altar, Travis stood, looking incredibly handsome in a black tuxedo. Beside him stood the twig-skinny blond from the wedding announcement photograph, dressed in a fluffy white chiffon dress. They looked like they belonged on top of a wedding cake.

Sarah's stomach reeled. *No. No!*

A minister stood in front of Travis and his bride. "Into this holy union Travis Walker and Crystal Hunt now come to be joined. If any of you can show just cause why these two should not lawfully be married, speak now or forever hold your peace."

She wasn't too late! She could still stop this.

The minister paused.

"Wait!" Sarah shouted, and sprinted down the aisle, the bells on her sweater vest jingling merrily as she ran.

Every gaze in the place swiveled off the bride and groom and onto her. A murmur of laughter rippled through the crowd, and that was when Sarah realized she still had the reindeer antlers on her head, but she didn't care. This was too important. If she had to look foolish to stop this ceremony, then so be it.

Breathlessly, she dashed to the altar.

"Young lady." The minister peered at her sternly from behind his glasses. "Do you have something to say?"

Sarah shifted her gaze from the minister to Travis.

Travis looked perplexed. "Sarah?"

"Who is this?" Crystal asked.

Sarah ignored her and stared straight into Travis's stormy gray eyes. "Don't marry her. You can't marry her."

He looked confused. "What do you mean?"

The words spilled from her in a heated rush. "I'm your soul mate. Your one true love. You're destined to marry *me*. If you marry her, it's all over. None of us will ever find the happiness we deserve."

A kind smile tipped the corners of his lips. "Sarah," he said, and reached out to gently touch her arm.

His touch set her on fire. All the air left her body.

"You're only fifteen," he said. "You don't know the first thing about true love."

"But I do! I've been dreaming of you every Christmas Eve since I was eight years old. The kismet cookies are never wrong. You and I are meant to be together."

"Good grief, are you for real?" Crystal Hunt snapped. "You're a delusional little twit who's read one too many romance novels. There's no such thing as soul mates and one true love. Don't kid yourself."

The churchgoers dissolved into guffaws, and in that horrible split-second moment, Sarah stepped outside herself, and she could see the whole thing unfolding like some hideous nightmare.

There she was, a chubby teenager with braces on her teeth and reindeer antlers on her head and jingle bells on her sweater vest, standing between a bride and groom on their wedding day, professing her love to a grown man who clearly did not love her back, while nearly the whole damn town of Twilight looked on, amused by her abject humiliation.

A jagged stab of raw pain jabbed her heart.

"Sarah," Travis murmured, "maybe you should go on home now."

Fool! He doesn't want you. You're embarrassing him.

Her face burned. Her stomach roiled. Her chest hurt. Tears spilled down her cheeks. She couldn't see. Blindly, she turned, stumbling for the door, yanking the antlers from her head, tearing the jingle bells from her sweater, ripping up all her hopes and dreams, and ran as far and fast as she could away from the raucous laughter echoing behind her.

And she vowed never, ever to put her heart on the line again.

CHAPTER ONE

"You've gotta see this, Sarah. It'll jerk your heart right out of your chest."

Ha! Too late. Her heart had been jerked out of her chest nine years ago when she was a naïve, foolish fifteen-year-old. Not that she thought about Travis Walker all that much. And if that embarrassment hadn't been enough to make her a dyed-in-the-wool cynic, the accident she'd suffered in college had sealed the deal. Absentmindedly, Sarah's hand went to her stomach, and she rubbed the scar that still ached from time to time.

She glared across the top of her computer monitor at her literary agent, Benny Gent. "I'm not doing another book tour at Christmas, Benny. Last year and the year before were—"

"Exhausting. I know. I was there." He stood in the doorway of the dining room she'd converted into an office, one shoulder slouched against the door frame, cocking his oh-so-charming grin.

He'd dropped by after a power lunch at Movers and Shakers, a hip new uptown restaurant, with her publisher, Hal Howard. In his hand Benny held a piece of notebook paper. Sarah could smell his aftershave from here, expensive and exotic, star anise and cardamom. He wore a designer suit; crisp, cream-colored button-down shirt; and a paisley silk tie. His dusty blond hair was clipped in a short, young-executive-on-the-go style, and he was perpetually bronzed courtesy of the spray tan salon in his building. Benny had the energy of a nuclear power plant, and sometimes the guy simply wore her out. Even so, he was her closest friend and confidant.

Oh, who was she kidding? He was her only real friend. Sure, she had plenty of acquaintances, but he was the only one she considered a true friend. Getting emotionally intimate with people had always been tough for her, even more so after Gram had died.

Sadness shot through her as it always did when she thought of her Gram. She'd been gone eight years, and Sarah still missed her grandmother deeply.

"I was going to say a nightmare," Sarah said. "I get all claustrophobic around strangers."

"You live in New York City."

"That's different. People ignore you in Manhattan. I like being ignored."

"Ah, so it's the celebrity factor that bothers you, not crowds."

"It's the people factor that bothers me. The thing is, you thrive on glad-handing and parties and travel. Me, I'm just a curmudgeonly hermit with a bah-humbug attitude toward Christmas. Call me Scroogetta."

"And yet you wrote a Christmas book. For children, no less. Imagine that."

"Yeah, well, everyone has lapses in good judgment."

"It made you rich."

"You didn't come out of the deal so badly yourself."

"You're in a peevish mood."

"I told you I hate Christmas."

Benny looked at her mildly. He knew her well enough not to overreact to her sweeping declarations. "You made a great decision when you wrote that book whether you know it or not. It's evergreen, and even though you'll be living off royalties into your dotage, your sales spike during the Christmas holidays. It's the logical time to do a book tour."

He always sounded so sensible. Without even meaning to do so he made her feel neurotic.

"I prefer Manhattan in December," she said.

It was October now and the leaves on the trees in Central Park that Sarah could see from the corner of her Upper West Side brownstone flared fiery autumn foliage.

"You're just being contrary," Benny observed.

"Yes, yes, I am. Isn't that my prerogative as a temperamental artist?"

"And it's my job to talk you around to what's best for the career of that temperamental artist."

Sarah sighed, leaned back in her chair, and held out a hand. Reading the letter would have one advantage. It would take her mind off the fact that she was completely stuck on her manuscript in progress. If she even could call it a manuscript.

Over the course of the last six weeks she'd rewritten the opening scene, from scratch, eighty-seven times. Not that she was counting or anything. "Let me see it."

Benny's grin widened. Smart aleck. He knew he had her. He tracked across the hardwood floor, slipped the letter into her upturned palm, and then plucked a pristine hankie from the breast pocket of his suit. "Trust me. You're going to need it."

"You mistake me for a soft touch."

Benny winked. "You don't fool me, Sadie Cool. You're a marshmallow at heart."

Sadie Cool was her pen name. She'd adopted it on Benny's suggestion after he had called her three years ago, told her she was a brilliant storyteller, and signed her on the spot. Much to her parents' dismay, in college she'd majored in English, and for her senior class project she'd written *The Magic Christmas Cookie*. Unbeknownst to her, her creative writing professor at Southern Methodist University had been so bowled over, he'd forwarded the manuscript to Benny, and his exuberant call had come as a complete shock.

Sarah had never consciously set out to become a children's author. Rather, after her abject humiliation that Christmas Day at the First Presbyterian Church of Twilight, Texas, she'd started writing as a way to deal with her disillusionment and make sense of her own shameful behavior. She'd been a young girl in love with a fairy tale and even though she'd learned the hard way that there were no such thing as fairy tales, she'd been loath to give up the dream. Even if things had not turned out happily-ever-after for her in real life, she could still make magic between the pages of her books.

Benny had sold the story for a modest advance to a big-name publisher who didn't expect much from the little book and put no muscle behind it. At that point she was nothing more than a newbie author eagerly awaiting the publication of her first book. Then somehow Benny managed to get an advance reading copy into the hands of a Hollywood producer, and the next thing she knew, Benny had sold the movie rights. Bolstered by Hollywood buzz, the book came out to great fanfare. It was hailed by critics, won several awards, and quickly gained *Polar Express*–like cult status, with bookstores throwing *Magic Christmas Cookie* parties all around the country. At the tender age of twenty-two, Sadie Cool became an overnight sensation.

Now, one year and ten months after *The Magic Christmas Cookie*'s release, her publisher was clamoring for the second book and Sarah was deep in the throes of writer's block. The pressure to top her own success was overwhelming, and to cap things off, her parents kept asking when she was going to write a *real* book. She had to hand it to Helen and Mitchell. No matter what she achieved, she was never good enough. Shaking her head at those thoughts, she read the letter written in royal blue crayon.

Dear Miss Cool,
My name is Jasmine, but everyone calls me Jazzy. I am eight years old. I am little for my age cause I been sick a long time. I love your book. My daddy reads it to me every night. I pretend I'm Isabella and get to go live at the North Pole with Santa. Cept my Daddy getsta

go with me of course, cause he's the best daddy in the whole world. I wish I could meet you some day before I die. Please write another book.

Love bunches. Your biggest fan, Jazzy.

A tear trickled down Sarah's face and she reached for Benny's handkerchief.

"Told ya."

"Shut up," Sarah said. "I'm crying because I'm getting pressured by an eight-year-old kid to produce another book and I'm hamstrung with writer's block."

"Liar."

"Don't you have somewhere else to be?"

"Nope."

"You do realize you're the bane of my existence."

"And you love that about me. I'm your contact to the outside world, Scroogetta."

"Don't fool yourself."

Benny grinned and picked up his briefcase from the floor, sat it on her desk, opened it up, and took out a manila envelope. "Jazzy's letter arrived in this packet from the mayor of Jazzy's hometown. He's inviting you to visit, giving you the key to the city, and making you honorary mayor for a week. Apparently, the town holds some kind of Dickensian Christmas festival every year and you're the guest of honor. Plus there's a local Christmas cookie club in town, and the ladies of the club have invited you to their annual cookie swap. Also, the local bookstore wants to do a signing event, throw a pajama party for the kids, and have you read from *The Magic Christmas Cookie*. They're offering to pay your way, put you up in the local B&B for nine days, and give you a four-figure honorarium. Not a bad deal. Plus getting out of this apartment might be just the thing you need to shake up your muse."

An odd tingling sensation started in the pit of Sarah's stomach and, like a brush fire, quickly spread along her nerve endings, shooting straight up into her brain. Twilight, the town where her grandmother had once lived, threw an annual Dickensian Christmas festival. They also had a Christmas cookie club, and there was a quaint little bookstore in town that loved staging children's events.

Could the invitation actually be from Twilight? What were the odds? She wrote under a pen name, for crying out loud. But it was easy enough to snoop around on Google and discover that Sadie Cool was really Sarah Collier, granddaughter of the late Mia Martin, a native of Twilight.

Sarah groaned and closed her eyes. "Please don't tell me this place is Twilight, Texas."

"Yes." Benny sounded surprised. "How did you know?"

She opened her eyes, canted her head. She'd never told Benny about Twilight or the way she'd made a gigantic fool of herself there nine Christmases ago. She'd wanted to erase all that from her memory. She was no longer that kismet-cookie-believing, reindeer-antler-wearing, chubby, metal-mouthed fifteen-year-old, and she had no desire to go back. "My grandmother used to live there."

"No kidding. Well, no wonder they're rolling out the red carpet for you. Hometown girl makes good."

"It was never my hometown."

But you spent every summer and every Christmas holiday there from the time you were eight until you were fifteen.

"Hey, your heroine Isabella is from a town just like this one. In fact, is Twilight the inspiration for your story? We could milk that angle for even more publicity."

"You do know you're a publicity ho."

"Why, thank you, Sarah." Benny looked inordinately pleased.

"Stop." Sarah held up a palm. "I'm not doing it. I have a book to write. A book, may I remind you, that my contract says I must have finished by January third. And that's after they've already granted me two extensions. I'm skating on thin ice."

"It's the middle of October. The Christmas festival in Twilight isn't until the first weekend in December. That gives you seven weeks to write twenty-five thousand words. Come on, you can do this."

"You make is sound so easy. Just snap my fingers and the words will appear on the page like magic."

"You're making excuses," Benny chided.

"I have serious writer's block!"

"Stephen King says writer's block is a myth. It's just fear."

"Yeah? Well, Stephen King can kiss it."

"I really think you ought to do this, Sarah. It would be great PR. Hal thinks you should do it as well."

Sarah groaned. "You told Hal?"

"He loved the sick-kid angle, and when he finds out Twilight is your hometown—"

"It's not my hometown."

"It would go a long way in smoothing things over if you have to ask for yet another extension." He went on as if she hadn't issued a protest. Agents.

Sarah pushed back from the desk, got up out of her chair. "You set me up, Benny."

He blinked, tried to look innocent. "I didn't."

"You shouldn't have talked to Hal without asking me first."

"I don't see what the big deal is. It's one town. One week. It's not like you're doing a four-month, fifteen-city tour or anything."

She supposed from his point of view her refusal did seem irrational. She could lie and say she had family obligations. The majority of people did during the holiday season, but she wasn't a liar, and Benny knew her relationship with her parents was strained at best, and in all the time he'd known her, she'd never spent her holidays with them. Why would she? During her childhood, they'd mostly spent *their* holidays with colleagues and/or sick people.

"Look, without getting into the details, I had an unpleasant experience in Twilight when I was fifteen and I have no real desire to return to the scene of the crime."

"There was a crime?" Benny perked up. He knew a good story when he heard one. "What did you do? Shoplift lipstick from the Wal-Mart?"

She wished. "Figure of speech."

"Think of poor little Jazzy." He pulled a sad face. "All she wants in this world is to meet her favorite author before she dies."

"Bastard."

He chuckled. "Come on, Sarah, you've got nothing to be ashamed of. You're Sadie Cool. This is your chance to go back to Twilight with your head held high as local girl done good and show those townspeople what you're really made of. I'll bet you none of them remember whatever it is that's haunting you."

"Oh, believe me, it's not something a small town like that is likely to forget." Just thinking about it made her cringe.

"I'm totally intrigued. You've got to tell me what you did."

"It was bad."

"I have a hard time seeing you doing anything that terrible."

She took in a ragged breath and as quickly as possible told him the sordid story.

"Wait, wait." Benny waved a hand. "You were wearing reindeer antlers?"

She sighed. "Regrettably."

"Ouch. That must have been really tough. So tell me, how did you manage to survive your first broken heart?"

"Believe it or not, in her own detached, clinical, misguided way, my mother actually helped me for once." Sarah rubbed her chin, remembering how her mother was the first person she'd seen after she'd come running back to Gram's house sobbing as if her life was over.

"How's that?"

"The minute we got home to Houston, my mother hustled me over to the medical school lab and took out a cadaver and showed me a human heart."

"My God!" Benny exclaimed. "Talk about adding insult to injury."

"It sounds warped, but it worked. Although Gramma Mia got really mad when she found out about it. My mother told me emotions weren't in your heart, that it was all in your head, and emotions were nothing more than transient reactions to current situations and that they could be managed and dealt with in a rational manner and there was no reason to let feelings define who you were."

"And I thought my mother was a whack job," Benny muttered under his breath and rolled his eyes.

"Not really. She made good sense when you think about it. She said I had to stop listening to my Gram and her silly notions about predestined love if I ever wanted to find an open and honest relationship based on mutual interests and shared values like her and my father." Of course, Sarah had tried that with Aidan, and look how well *that* had turned out. She put a hand to her stomach again.

Benny studied her. "This explains a lot about you."

"What does that mean?"

"It explains why ever since I've known you, you've never been in a relationship. Seems like growing up that you received so many conflicting messages about love, you don't know which way to jump."

Plus there was the issue of her self-consciousness over the scar, but she'd never told Benny about that. Some things were just too painful to dredge up. "So you can see why I'm not keen on returning to the scene of my crime."

Benny got to his feet. "But this is all the more reason you have to go. You have to face your fear.

It's the only way to put it to bed. Plus, who knows, maybe once you face your fear, you might have a breakthrough in your writing."

Sarah sighed. "Doubtful."

"Don't be such a Negative Nelly. It can't hurt."

"Easy for you to say. You weren't the one in the reindeer antlers."

"Hey, chances are that guy doesn't even live there anymore."

"Oh, he lives there."

"How do you know?"

"His family was one of the town's founders. The guy's entrenched in Twilight."

"Big deal. If you see him, you smile politely, say hi, and keep moving."

"It's not that simple."

"You're selling yourself short. Everyone is going to be looking at you as Sadie Cool. Look at all you've accomplished. A *New York Times* best-selling author, with a movie option to boot, and you're only twenty-four. C'mon," he coaxed, hooking his fingers underneath her chin and lifting her face up to his. "Think about how good you'll feel once you get this over with. No more fears to hide behind. You're Sadie Cool. You can do this."

She stepped away from him, rubbed a palm down her face. What if he was right? What if her writer's block was somehow tied to Twilight? She'd written *The Magic Christmas Cookie* as a cathar-sis. If she went back and submerged herself in the past, maybe she could recapture that angst—as painful as it might be—and tap into the creative spirit that had spurred her to create that first book.

Her gaze fell to the crayon-scrawled notepaper

resting beside her computer. *I am little for my age cause I been sick a long time.* She could feel the child's loneliness rising up off the page, and her heart wrenched. It was nine lousy days out of her life, but to this kid, her visit to Twilight would mean the world.

Sarah glanced around the room crowded with bookcases overflowing with books and thought about how her book had touched Jazzy's heart. She and the little girl were kindred spirits, bound by the written word. Books provided an escape, an adventure, a window into another world. Books didn't judge or condemn. Inside a book, Sarah felt safe. She made no mistakes, did nothing stupid. Books were her refuge, her touchstone. Books had been her friends when she'd had none. Books had even substituted for her parents' affection. Outside of books, well, she was inept, bordering on anti-social.

She didn't know how to let down her guard without taking emotional chances. She stuffed down her feelings, stayed detached. Allowing other people to see the real her was just too damn risky by half. So she kept to herself, kept her nose in a book, kept her heart walled up behind an aloof veneer, because it was the only way she knew how to survive.

But now, because of a book she'd written, she was being asked to step outside herself and bring joy to a sick little girl who might not have long to live.

"Damn you," she told Benny.

He grinned. "You'll do it?"

"Like you ever gave me a choice."

* * *

"She's coming to Twilight, she's coming to Twilight!" Raylene Pringle exclaimed as she rushed through the back door of the Twilight Bakery waving the e-mail confirmation she'd just printed off her computer.

The six other women sat gathered around the long, thick-legged oak table, laden with cookbooks, magazines, and recipe boxes. Every time she saw the table, Raylene thought of a line from the Led Zeppelin song—which someone played almost every day on the jukebox in the Horny Toad Tavern—about a big-legged woman having no soul. Thank God her slender legs were still pinup worthy, even when she was a hairsbreadth away from sixty.

Today, the group had gathered to plan the upcoming holiday events, including the annual Twilight Cherub Tree and the First Love Cookie Club swap that took place the second Friday in December. Each year the group prepared for the Christmas cookie exchange by combing through recipes in search of unique and tasty treats. Over a hundred years of cookie-making tradition imbued the festivities with lore of destiny, soul mates, and grand true loves. The mission statement of the First Love Cookie Club was to preserve, perpetuate, and celebrate the town's tradition for both sweethearts and sweet treats.

The only one in the current group who had not married her first love—mainly because she had never had a first love—was the owner of the bakery, shy Christine Noble. (Well, okay, there was Patsy Calloway Cross, who hadn't married her high school sweetheart, Hondo Crouch, but she denied he was her first love, so who were they to say she was lying?) The ladies of the club had granted Christine honorary membership when she'd offered the use of her bakery as command post central for all the upcoming holiday events the group was involved in.

The rules of the cookie club were clear. Members were women only. No men, no kids. The theory being that everyone needed a break from the stress of holiday preparation. Drink a little wine, talk a little trash, try out some interesting cookie recipes before the big swap event in December. The meetings got them in the holiday spirit in a relaxed, communal way.

Rule number two. All the cookies had to be homemade. They had to be baked, and the main ingredient had to be flour. No store-bought cookies were allowed. Period. End of story. If you couldn't fulfill your cookie obligation for some reason— the only acceptable excuse was a serious illness or death in the family—you could call upon one of your First Love sisters to make your cookies for you.

Rule number three. Whatever was said at cookie club stayed at cookie club. The ladies of the club were prone to gossip. Not maliciously, of course, simply out of curiosity and motherly concern for the people involved. But to avoid problems, they'd agreed that whatever was said during the moments of lips loosened over wine, cookies, and sisterhood stayed in the vault.

Rule number four. No chocolate chip cookies allowed. Chocolate chips are not Christmas cookies, no matter how tasty. Save them for the rest of the year.

Rule number five. Festive holiday attire had to be worn for the meetings. Halloween costumes were acceptable for the October meeting, as were harvest outfits for November.

"Who's coming?" asked Dotty Mae Densmore, the oldest member of the group. Dotty Mae was in her mid-eighties, but had the vim and vigor of a woman fifteen years younger. Her fingers flew over her knitting as she eyed the cookbook, *The Zen of Cookies*, open in front of her. She wore a sweatshirt with a grinning jack-o'-lantern appliquéd on the front.

"For heaven's sake, Raylene, close the door. It's drafty with that north wind blowing in," Patsy Cross scolded. She was on the town council, ran a store just off the square called the Teal Peacock. She wore a black pointed witch's hat and a stern look on her face.

Appropriate, the witch's hat, Raylene thought, and closed the door behind her. She and Patsy had been frenemies for fifty years, long before *Sex and the City* made the term popular. To Dotty Mae she said, "Sadie Cool."

Dotty Mae frowned. Her short-term memory wasn't what it used to be. "Who's that?"

"The author who wrote *The Magic Christmas Cookie*, Jazzy's favorite book—" Marva Bullock started, pushing aside the cornrow braid that had fallen across her cocoa-colored cheek. In concession to the holiday attire rule, her braids were threaded with pumpkin-colored ribbons held in place with black cat clips. Marva was the high school principal and the most diplomatic one of the group.

"But we found out she's really Sarah Collier," interrupted pert, zaftig Belinda Murphey, who owned the local matchmaking business and was the mother of five rambunctious kids, all under the age of ten.

"Mia's granddaughter?" Dotty Mae asked.

"That's right," said Terri Longoria. Terri was dressed in black leggings, a short black skirt, and a white knit sweater with autumn leaves patterned into it. She owned Hot Legs Gym and was married to the chief of staff at Twilight General Hospital.

Their honorary member, Christine Noble, said nothing. She sat at the end of the table wearing a Halloween apron featuring smiling skeletons, RIP tombstones, green-skinned Frankenstein monsters, and broomstick witches.

"Mia's granddaughter wrote a book under another name?" Dotty Mae looked befuddled.

"That she did," Terri assured her, "and when we found out, we invited her to Twilight to meet Jazzy. You know she hasn't been home since she interrupted Travis's wedding to Crystal Hunt."

"Oh, that's a wonderful idea." Dotty Mae smiled. "I'm glad we invited her." She looked at Raylene. "And Sarah accepted?"

Raylene nodded. "Yes."

"So," Patsy said, "Sarah's acceptance begs the question, do we tell Travis who Sadie Cool really is?"

"No," everyone said in unison.

"Why not?"

"Patsy Cross," Belinda said, "you are the world's worst matchmaker."

"We're trying to hook Travis up with Sarah?" Now it was Patsy's turn to frown in confusion.

Dotty Mae clucked her tongue. "Don't you remember that Mia told us Travis was the one Sarah dreamed of in her Christmas Eve kismet cookie dreams? They're destined."

Patsy looked skeptical. "Do we even know if Sarah is single? She could be married or in a serious relationship."

"She's not," Raylene assured her. "I asked her agent when I e-mailed him."

"It seems a bit underhanded to me."

"Well, you know how Travis is. He's sworn he's never getting married again, but he just needs a shove in the right direction. If we tip our hand, he'll be dead set against Sarah. But if he sees her first and has no time to steel himself against the idea, the magic of first love will take over," Belinda said.

"Then there's this." Raylene pulled an angel ornament from her pocket.

Every year the First Love Cookie Club sponsored the annual Cherub Tree for local children who were disadvantaged in some way. The kids were asked to fill out a wish list for Christmas and then their list was attached to an ornament and hung from the Sweetheart Tree (which in December turned into the Cherub Tree) in Sweetheart Park. Generous benefactors would adopt a cherub from the tree, pluck down their ornament, and make the child's Christmas wishes come true.

Whenever they saw what Raylene held in her hand, a sigh of wistful sadness went through the group. They all knew what was written on it. A list of Jazzy Walker's Christmas wishes. She wanted what most little girls wanted. A Barbie. New clothes. An iPod. And then there were the personalized wishes. First, she wanted to meet her favorite author in all the world, Sadie Cool, and there, at the bottom of the list, in a childish scrawl, were the words: *I wish for a mommy so my daddy won't have to be all alone when I die.*

"That poor kid." Dotty Mae sniffled into a tissue.

Marva clutched a hand to the left side of her chest.

Terri swiped at her eyes.

Belinda's lips moved upward in a forced smile.

Christine sat solemnly.

Raylene met Patsy's eyes. "Travis and Sarah are destined. We all know it. The kismet cookie prophecy is never wrong. I dreamed of Earl, Marva dreamed of G.C., Terri dreamed of Ted, Belinda dreamed of Harvey. Mia dreamed of Anthony, and Dotty Mae dreamed of Stuart. And whether you want to admit it or not, I was there the year we made kismet cookies at your sleepover and I know you dreamed of Hondo."

Patsy said nothing, but the expression on her face told Raylene the truth. Her friend was and always had been in love with Hondo Crouch, even if they'd never gotten their happily-ever-after. "Plus, Sadie Cool is Jazzy's favorite author and honestly, what are the odds of that happening? With the way Jazzy's health is deteriorating . . ." Raylene swallowed hard, waved the ornament. "This might be our last chance to make her Christmas wish come true."

CHAPTER TWO

Travis Walker looked out at the intelligent young faces of Mrs. Tilson's fourth grade class at Jon Grant Elementary and grinned. He loved career day. Heck, he loved kids. They were so open and honest and forthcoming, traits he truly admired.

"Game wardens guard our parks and lakes and shorelines and wildlife preserves," he said. "We catch poachers and enforce hunting and fishing regulations and we arrest people who break the law."

"Just like the police?" A boy sitting in the front row scrutinized the duty weapon holstered at Travis's hip.

"Yes, just like the police."

"Is that a real gun?"

"It is."

The boy's eyes widened. "Awesome. Did you ever shoot anyone?"

Travis thought about the time he'd stumbled onto an illicit marijuana field while tracking a wounded deer through the lowlands around Brazos River

Bend and found himself peering up the business end of a 12-gauge shotgun. But that story wasn't suitable for his audience.

"I've never killed anyone," he said truthfully, sidestepping the question. But he had shot someone.

Another boy raised his hand.

Travis pointed at him. "Yes?"

"How come you took my uncle to jail last week?" he asked, narrowing his eyes defiantly. "All he did was drink a beer on his own boat."

Travis knew the look. The kid had a chip on his shoulder. Once upon a time he'd been just as petulant toward authority figures. After his mother died and his father crawled inside himself, Travis had been adrift. Angry at life, he'd kicked up a fuss just to see who'd react.

"Jimmy," the teacher said, "that question is inappropriate."

"It's okay, Mrs. Tilson, I don't mind answering." Travis trod across the room toward Jimmy, who shrank down in his chair. "I arrested your uncle because he broke the law. My job is to keep the rivers and lakes safe for everyone to enjoy. Drunken boating is the same as drunken driving."

"He didn't hurt anyone," Jimmy mumbled.

"He could have if I hadn't arrested him," Travis said calmly and then went on to tell them a cautionary tale in unemotional language about the drunken boater who'd run over a skier and amputated her leg on Lake Twilight the previous summer. Travis had been the first responder on the scene, and the memory was burned into his brain.

"Wow," said the kid who'd asked him about

shooting someone. "Cool job. I wanna be a game warden when I grow up."

"Then study hard, especially in science and math." Travis glanced around the room. "Any other questions?"

"Can girls become game wardens?" asked a serious-looking young girl with solemn blue eyes and caramel-colored hair.

She reminded him of another serious, blue-eyed, caramel-haired girl he'd once known—little Sarah Collier. He wondered with mild interest where Sarah was now, what she was up to. He'd always liked her and he'd lost touch with her after her grandmother died.

"Absolutely girls can be game wardens," he said, "but remember, game wardens work outdoors in the weather. We get wet and cold or sometimes sweaty and hot. We slog through swampy terrain and often come across spiders and snakes and bugs and frogs."

The girl tilted her chin upward, reminding him even more of Sarah. "I like spiders and snakes."

"Good for you."

Just then, the door of the classroom opened and a teacher's aide popped her head in the room. "Officer Walker?" Her voice sounded tense, strained.

"Yes?"

"Could you come with me please, sir?"

Alarm swept through him, but Travis tried not to show it. "Sure. I'll be right with you."

"You need to come with me right now."

Okay, now he was really scared. "Good-bye, class, study hard." He raised a hand and followed the teacher's aide from the classroom. "What's up?" he asked once the door had closed behind them.

"It's Jazzy," the woman said.

That was all Travis had to hear. He fisted his hands, felt his pulse spurt adrenaline through his veins. He pivoted on his heel, headed for his daughter's classroom, the teacher's aide trailing behind him.

"What happened?" he barked at her over his shoulder.

"She was running—"

He stopped dead, whirled on her. "Jazzy was running?"

"She did it behind our backs, we were—"

"It's your job to watch out for her," he snarled, rage exploding inside him. "You know her medical condition."

Anxiety scrunched up the woman's features. "You're right, but Jazzy is headstrong and independent . . ."

He had no time for this woman or for anger or blame. His daughter needed him. Jazzy was the most important thing. Dismissing the teacher's aide, he strode toward Jazzy's classroom.

"Um . . . Mr. Walker . . . she's in the school nurse's office. I'll show you."

He knew where the school nurse's office was. He'd been there more times than he could count. He barreled toward his destination, pushed through the door without knocking. To hell with civility. "Jazzy!"

"Daddy." Her voice was weak, wheezy.

He shoved aside the white curtain mounted on an overhead track. Jazzy lay on the table, her lips that familiar dusky color, her blue eyes wide with fear, a thin green oxygen cannula snaking from her tiny nose. A nurse in pink scrubs, with brown teddy bears on them, stood beside Jazzy checking her pulse. Travis's heart constricted.

His daughter held out her frail arms to him and he crossed the remaining space with one long-legged purposeful stride and scooped her up into his arms. "Call Dr. Adams and have him meet us at the hospital," he barked.

"I—" the nurse said.

"Just do it," he cut her off.

The nurse nodded and hustled to the phone on her desk while Travis gently removed the nasal cannula from Jazzy's nose and then carried her toward the door. Her breathing was quick, raspy, with an elongated whistling noise at the end of each shaky exhalation. A familiar sound he knew all too well. She sounded like someone who'd smoked three packs of cigarettes a day for thirty years.

He held her tight, could feel her delicate little arm bones through the softness of her skin. God, she was so vulnerable, his tough little angel. Travis stalked from the school, headed toward the brown, extended cab pickup truck that the state of Texas issued to him as game warden.

"It's going to be okay, sweetheart," he murmured, his mouth pressed close to her ear. "Daddy's here."

She clung to him, buried her face against his neck. He could smell her little-girl scent, full of sweetness and innocence. She might be eight years old, but she barely weighed forty pounds. He strapped her into her car seat and then hustled around to the driver's side. He drove as fast as he dared, torn between getting her to the emergency room and not alarming her.

Jazzy was very sensitive and quickly picked up on the emotions of those around her. They'd been through this so many times that it was almost routine. But he could not afford to view her illness as ordinary. Each labored breath that his daughter took could be her last.

A memory hit him then, sharp and poignant, the way it often did when his daughter was in acute respiratory distress. He thought about his mother, Penelope Walker, who had suffered from severe asthma throughout most of his childhood. It had been a normal part of his life. Routine that her numerous allergies prevented her from taking him to the park like other mothers or attending his Little League games.

But in spite of her condition, his mother had been a Shiny Penny. That's what his dad had called her anyway. His Shiny Penny. Bright and true, something you could count on. She smiled every day of her life. She was an artist who used anything and everything as her medium. She drew on white butcher paper with charcoal, capturing Travis's silhouette as he grew from infant to toddler to gap-toothed kid to gangly preteen. She painted murals on his bedroom walls, trucks and airplanes and race cars. She knitted with merino wool and mohair and angora and alpaca, making scarves and mittens, afghans and sweaters, socks and caps in every color of the rainbow. Local women who lacked the talent or time to create their own crafts came to their door every week to buy the wares his mother had created.

Penelope spent most of her days in bed or on the

couch, drawing and painting and knitting in between the times the asthma stole her breath. When he crept up onto her bed as a boy, looking for affection, he had to be careful not to jab a knitting needle in his knee or snap her charcoal in half or crimp her oxygen line. Although his mother had been confined by her disease, she had not been defined by it. She had a glow about her, her whole face round and smooth as a white harvest moon. It was only later, after Jazzy got sick, that Travis realized it was the years of mega-doses of steroids that made her look that way.

When Travis reached the hospital, he thought of the night he and his dad had followed the ambulance there. He recalled how the frowning paramedics had whisked his mother inside on a stretcher, blocking Travis's view of her. All he could see of his mother were her hands. Hands that had once drawn and knitted and rubbed his back when he was tired or feeling bad, hands now turned doughy with blue-tinged fingernails, hands that would never hold him again.

He shook his head, shook off the memories, parked the truck, eased Jazzy from the backseat, and carried her through the pneumatic doors and into the emergency room bright with fluorescent lights. The front desk clerk spotted him right away and got up from his chair. Travis knew the freckled-faced man from high school. His name was Kip Armstrong.

"We're putting Jazzy in exam room three," Kip said. "Dr. Adams is on his way."

Travis moved through the double doors, past the other patients parked in the waiting room. Jazzy got special treatment. Part of it was the frequent flier aspect. They were in here so often the staff felt like family. Part of it was Jazzy's bubbly personality. Everyone who met her fell in love with her. And part of it, he knew, was pity. They felt sorry for a single father whose only child had a nasty habit of knocking at death's door. Hell, if pity got her faster service, he'd take it.

The medical staff converged around him as he laid Jazzy on the gurney in moves so habitual they felt choreographed. As if a silent director was sending out telepathic cues. Nurse One took her blood pressure. Nurse Two put a pulse oxygenation monitor on her index finger. The lab tech drew arterial blood gases, while the respiratory therapist set up the Albuterol nebulizer.

Jazzy sat upright propped on pillows, leaning forward, knees drawn to her chest, struggling to catch her breath between the coughing fits that racked her little body. Travis fisted his hands. He felt so damn helpless.

In his head, he heard his ex-wife's voice. *Face reality, Travis. She's going to die.*

Not on his watch, dammit. No way, no how. *Get out of my head, Crystal*, he growled silently to himself. *You're the quitter. You're the one who gives up on people. Not me. Never me. You forfeited your parental rights when you walked out on us because you were too damn weak to take care of our sick daughter.*

Why the hell was he thinking about Crystal? He suspected his subconscious had dredged up his ex-wife as a target for his helpless anger. He remembered standing in this same emergency room with

Crystal four years ago when Jazzy had had her first attack.

"She inherited this from your mother," Crystal had accused. "It's your bad DNA that's ruined her."

He'd never wanted to slap a woman in his life, but in that moment, he'd wanted to slap her, mainly because she'd pushed the button of his darkest fear. That he was deeply flawed and it was his fault their daughter was so ill. There had been thirty-seven more attacks that year, each one progressively worse.

They'd taken Jazzy to specialist after specialist and spent two weeks at a pediatric respiratory hospital in Austin. One quack had even suggested they remove her right lung, which seemed more affected than her left. Jazzy frequently ran a fever with the asthma attacks and no one could really explain why beyond telling them that colds and flu viruses often precipitated respiratory flare-ups. Jazzy had endured test after test as doctors searched for the asthma triggers and they'd come up empty time and time again.

"Maybe she'll out grow it," they'd said hopefully. But she hadn't. In fact, the older she got, the worse her symptoms became.

Then came the night that Jazzy had gone into full cardiac arrest following a stress test at the children's hospital and the doctors had been forced to put her on a ventilator and admit her into the ICU.

He and Crystal sat in the critical care waiting room, staring into cups of cold rotgut coffee, while the doctors worked on Jazzy. His ex-wife had raised her head and looked at him like a coyote caught in a trap. "I'm gonna go home and get a change of clothes."

He'd stared at her, incredulous. "It's a three-hour drive back to Twilight."

"I know, I know. I just need to get outta here, get some air, clear my head."

"Jazzy needs you."

Crystal had twisted her wedding ring around her finger. "You're better at this sick stuff than I am."

"You're not going off and leaving her."

"I can't take it. I need a break."

He remembered clenching his jaw and fisting his hands to keep from saying or doing something he would regret. "Fine," he muttered. "Go have your break."

She'd fled the room without a backward glance and Travis had never seen her again. When he and Jazzy got back home, all Crystal's things were gone. She'd left a note on the dining room table. *I'm sorry. I'm just not cut out for motherhood. Forgive me.*

Honestly, he'd forgiven her a long time ago. He wasn't the kind of guy who held on to a grudge. Crystal was who she was and he couldn't change her. All he could do was love Jazzy twice as much, and that was easy to do. He thought of his daughter with her wide blue eyes and her long, curly blond hair, and his heart squeezed. He'd never loved anyone the way he loved that child. That's what he couldn't understand about Crystal. How could she go away if she loved Jazzy? And how could a mother not love her own child enough to stick with her through thick and thin?

When Crystal had discovered she was pregnant, she'd wanted to have an abortion. He'd told her absolutely not, that they were getting married and having that baby. Crystal had dreamed of becoming a country-and-western singer and making it big in Nashville. She'd blamed first Travis and later Jazzy for ruining her dreams. He'd heard through the grapevine she'd made it to Nashville, but she was waiting tables, not cutting records.

Maybe he'd been wrong to insist on marriage, but he hadn't been wrong about keeping Jazzy. She was the very best thing that had ever happened to him. Without her, he'd be far less of a man.

An image popped into his head. His wedding day. He remembered the terrified look in Crystal's eyes as she stood there and then the surprising turn of events when young Sarah Collier had come bursting through the door of the church yelling at the congregation that Travis couldn't marry Crystal because he was *her* soul mate.

The memory put a momentary smile on his face.

Dr. Adams came bustling through the door, his white coattails flying out behind him. He took one look at Jazzy and the frown riding his face deepened. He tugged a stethoscope from his pocket, spoke gently to Jazzy, and then pressed the bell of the stethoscope to her chest.

Travis stepped closer, fisted his hands, watching and waiting as the physician examined his daughter. After several minutes, Dr. Adams raised his head, rattled off a list of medical jargon to the nurses, wrapped the stethoscope around itself, and tucked it back into his pocket. "Could we speak outside, Mr. Walker."

Mutely, Travis nodded to the doctor, and then said to Jazzy, "Daddy's going to be right out here in the hallway."

"Daddy," she wheezed.

He took her hand, squeezed it. "Yes, sweetheart?"

"Will . . . you . . ." She paused, chuffed in a mouthful of the nebulizer mist from the green plastic mask the respiratory therapist had slipped over her face.

"Don't talk."

"Isabella," she whispered. "Book."

"You want me to bring you Isabella and *The Magic Christmas Cookie*?"

She nodded again, asking for the two possessions that comforted her most.

"I'm on it," he said. His gut wrenched and it was all he could do to make himself leave her, even for a fraction of a second.

"What's going on here, Doc?" he asked once the door had closed behind them. "You said that last drug we put her on should do the trick. She's taking four different kinds of medication a day and showing no signs of improvement."

Dr. Adams pulled a palm down his face. "Let's go somewhere more private."

Uh-oh, this didn't sound good. Travis struggled to quell the fear growing inside him as Dr. Adams led him into the empty physicians' lounge and plunked down at the head of a small conference table. "Have a seat."

He didn't want to, but he sat.

Dr. Adams took a deep breath. "I don't know what to say, Travis. Jazzy is on the maximum dose of every effective medication we have in our arsenal."

Travis felt a chill straight to his soul. "What are you telling me?"

The physician shook his head, spread his hands. "I'm all out of tricks."

"Does this mean we have to go through another round of specialists?" he asked. He was willing to do whatever it took to make his daughter well, but he hated the thought of putting her through more tests, more hospitals, more needle pokes. Jazzy was a trouper, but the poor kid had been through so much. Where did it end?

Dr. Adams shook his head. "We could try, but I have no reason to believe the outcome would be any different than in the past."

Fear clawed at his throat. "So what are you saying? That there's no hope?"

"There's always hope. You have to believe that, Travis."

"What can you offer us?"

Dr. Adams shifted his way. "There's a new drug on the market, but—"

"Why didn't you say so before?" Travis interrupted, feeling a surge of hope.

"It's very expensive and your insurance doesn't cover it."

"I don't care. Whatever it costs, I'll get the money."

"It's twenty-five hundred dollars for one injection and she'll need a shot every three weeks."

One shot equaled his monthly take-home salary. Travis swallowed. "I'll sell my house if I have to."

"It's not just the cost." Dr. Adams pressed his

lips together. "The reason insurance won't cover the drug is because while it's been approved for treatment of another lung disorder, it's not approved for severe bronchial asthma. If a drug is used off-label, it's considered experimental. Although it has been approved in Canada for use in severe asthma."

"Fine, we'll move to Canada," Travis said, and meant it, even though he'd lived his entire life in Twilight. Hell, his father and his father's father and his father's father's father had all been born and raised in the town, and he loved the place with all his heart and soul, but he loved his daughter more. He'd leave it in a nanosecond if doing so could heal Jazzy.

"It's not that simple."

Nothing ever was. "You dangle this hope in front of me and then you snatch it away, Doc. What the hell is that all about?"

Dr. Adams met his stare. "I'm willing to go out on a limb and prescribe this drug to Jazzy for her asthma."

A tidal wave of hope hit him this time. "Thank you," he said, "thank you."

Dr. Adams held up his palm. "Before we jump into this there is a lot to consider. This medication might not even work."

"It's worth a shot."

"There are side effects."

"There's side effects with the medication she's already on."

"Yes, but this drug is still new and it has been approved for a different condition. I did some research, called some experts, and I have a tentative protocol for using the medication off-label, but essentially, we'd be flying blind. We could be playing Russian roulette with Jazzy's life."

Silence fell between them.

The reality of what the doctor was saying slowly sank in. "But this could also be the drug that controls everything, right?"

"It could. The preliminary findings are very hopeful. You need to think about this long and hard, Travis."

"I just want her well."

"I know," Dr. Adams said, "but do the risks outweigh the possible benefits?"

Travis let out a long breath and it was only then that he realized he'd been holding it down deep in his lungs. "Okay," he said. "Thanks for giving it to me straight."

"You're welcome."

Dr. Adams went back into the exam room with Jazzy, while Travis went out to his pickup truck. He drove the three miles to their cottage by the lake, found Isabella and *The Magic Christmas Cookie* book, and hurried back to the hospital.

When he went back into the exam room, Jazzy's eyes were closed and her breathing was easier. Travis took Isabella and tucked her gently in the crook of Jazzy's arm and then he sat in the flimsy blue plastic chair beside the gurney and opened the well-worn cover of *The Magic Christmas Cookie* and began to read, the ritual now so ingrained, he didn't have to think.

"Butterfly Books," he read, "a division of Jackdaw Publishing. First edition. All rights reserved." He always read the information on the copyright page to tease her, just as his mother used to do with him.

Usually, she would say, "Dad-*dy*," in a tone of exasperation, but this time, she said nothing.

Travis recited the story he knew by heart, sitting there, watching his little girl sleep. The mask was still on her face; little puffs of mist escaped from the vent slits on the side and disappeared into the air. He watched his daughter and read of magic cookies and Santa Claus and Christmas miracles a week before Halloween.

This was a scary place, where they were right now. Hung on the precipice of promise and disaster. New drug. New hope. How many times had he gotten his hopes up? How many times had they been dashed?

Jazzy turned on the gurney, opened her eyes, tugged the mask from her face. "Daddy?"

"What is it, sweet pea?"

"I'm sorry. I shouldn't have tried to run on the playground. I knew better."

"It's okay, it's all right. Don't worry. You didn't do anything wrong. You just wanted to have fun."

"Daddy?"

"Uh-huh?"

"Am I gonna die like your mommy did?"

Travis bit down on the inside of his cheek. He'd never wanted to tell Jazzy about how her grandmother had died, but Crystal had told her when she'd asked. Travis still held that against her. "No," he said, "absolutely not. I'm your daddy and I won't let anything happen to you, no matter what. Got it?"

"Will I ever be normal?" she asked.

"You're already normal," he said.

"You know what I mean. Will I ever be able to run and play like other kids?"

It was a promise he had no way to guarantee, but he made it anyway. "Yes," he declared. "One day you'll be able to run and play like other kids."

She smiled faintly, closed her eyes. "So where's Isabella now? Is she at the North Pole yet?"

"Not yet." He reached across the bed, squeezed her hand, and went back to reading about Isabella, his mind made up. They were going to try that new drug because Jazzy deserved a fighting chance at a real life.

CHAPTER THREE

By the time December rolled around, Sarah was no further along on her book than she'd been in October. Oh, she'd written plenty, but none of it had gelled. Nothing was right. She'd written, edited, discarded. She had no feelings for the work other than disgust. And disgust was not a passion on which to build a successful story.

Going back to Twilight was beginning to look damn good in comparison. That spoke to how desperate she felt, considering that she'd rather vacation in Baghdad than return to her grandmother's birthplace.

But on the first Thursday in December, as a driver guided the Town Car that had been waiting for her at DFW airport, past the "Welcome to Twilight, Friendliest Hometown in Texas" sign, and she saw Lake Twilight glimmering blue in the distance, deep nostalgia swept through her. How she missed her Gramma Mia! Even now, she could smell her grandmother's kitchen rife with the scent of fresh-baked yeast bread and the sweet taste of her homemade peach jam.

She hadn't expected the hit of sadness that fisted tight against her rib cage as the driver turned down Ruby Street with the tall, sheltering elms lining both sides of the road. The town was just as she'd remembered. Nothing had changed. Christmas decorations adorned almost every yard they passed. People smiled and nodded and waved at the car as it passed, as if they were welcoming friends.

Twilight was one of those super-adorable tourist towns frequently found parked beside rivers and seashores and at the foot of majestic mountains. Verdant green lawns lush with St. Augustine grass and white, knee-high picket fences graced most of the Victorian, Cape Cod, and Craftsman-style homes that dominated the neighborhood near the square and around the lake. Flags fluttered from rooftops, a testament to patriotism. Wind chimes whispered in willow trees. Kitschy pink flamingos and wooden cutouts of ladies bending over showing their bloomers dotted the landscape.

In the spring and summer, the flower beds were an arborist's wet dream. Planter boxes and hanging baskets hosted a range of petunias and periwinkle and pansies. Sidewalk gardens boasted daffodils and amaryllis and hyacinth in late February and early March, later to be replaced by irises and gladiolas and day lilies. Elephant ears were a favorite in the rugged Texas soil, along with hearty salvia and geraniums and begonias. This time of year it was mostly Christmas cactuses and rust-colored chrysanthemums offering a splash of color.

The sweet familiarity tasted like tears against her tongue. She clenched her purse with both hands, curling her fingers into fists around the Italian leather strap. It was all she could do not to beg the driver to spin the car around and zoom back to the airport.

The Lincoln cornered the town square with its gorgeous old courthouse erected in the 1870s when the town was in its infancy. All the buildings lining the four quadrants of the courthouse had been constructed in the same era. When she'd walked the streets of Twilight as a girl, Sarah had often half expected to see Jesse James tying his horse to one of the wooden hitching posts that still sat outside the Funny Farm restaurant. Rumors swirled that the infamous outlaw had once used the caves around the Brazos River as a hideout.

For the moment, however, Charles Dickens was being layered atop the usual Old West architecture. The first weekend in December the Twilight Chamber of Commerce threw a Dickens on the Square tourism event. At ten in the morning, workmen were busy setting up various stages around the courthouse lawn. Strolling carolers warbled in group song, practicing their vocal range. Vendors erected street stalls for displaying their wares—Victorian-inspired crafts, clothing, jewelry, and holiday decorations.

The lantern parade on Friday evening officially kicked off the event, featuring "Queen Victoria" in the lead, followed by floats filled with various characters from the novels of Charles Dickens. The last float traditionally carried Father Christmas. Out of all the festivals this festival-loving town threw, Dickens on the Square had been Sarah's favorite. Something about the pageantry of nineteenth-century England appealed to her romantic nature.

Yeah, back when you were fifteen and stupid.

She shook her head, stared out the window, and found her gaze drawn to the men in the crowd. It was only after her heart gave a strange little stutter at the sight of a tall, dark-haired man that Sarah realized she was subconsciously searching for Travis. The man turned around, and when she saw it wasn't he, the pent-up breath she hadn't even known she'd been holding slipped from her lungs in one long sigh.

The driver pulled the car to a stop outside a restored Victorian house painted a soft rosy pink. Scattered all throughout the yard were angel lawn ornaments. The sign out front read: "The Merry Cherub Bed-and-Breakfast."

She walked up the steps, but before she could ring the bell, the door was flung open to reveal a beaming middle-aged man with a graying goatee dressed in the fashion of Charles Dickens—top hat, frock coat, walking cane. He looked at once charmingly quaint and absolutely ridiculous.

"Hello, Miss Cool," he boomed, and thrust out his hand. "Mayor Moe Schebly. It's an honor to meet you."

Sarah gave him her hand and he pumped like he was trying to get her to gush water. "Thank you for inviting me, Mayor."

"We're delighted you could make time in your busy schedule for us."

"My pleasure."

"If it's not too much of an imposition, I'd like to quickly go over the details of this evening's festivities with you and your role in them before you get settled into your room." He tapped the face of his watch. "Charles Dickens has a tight schedule to keep."

"I understand."

The mayor pulled a brochure and a piece of folded paper from his dark gray waistcoat and passed it to her. "You're in the parade, of course, and you'll be riding in the final float with Father Christmas and little Jazzy. Don't feel you have to wear a costume. Although I have taken the liberty of arranging to have several gowns placed in your room should you decide to do so."

"Um . . . okay."

"If you have any questions, my cell phone number is printed on your schedule."

"Thank you."

"See you at the high school football field at five o'clock. That's where we load up the floats. I've included a map of the town for your convenience," Mayor Moe turned Charles Dickens said. "And now I must run. See you at five."

And then he was gone.

A woman who was about a decade older than Sarah had been standing behind the mayor during his rushed instructions. She too was adorned in Victorian-era clothing. The old Sarah would have sighed at the romance of it all, but Sadie Cool wondered just exactly how uncomfortable that corset really was.

"Hello." She smiled warmly. "I'm Jenny Cantrell; my husband, Dean, and I own the Merry Cherub. It's wonderful to meet you, Miss Cool. Please follow me and I'll show you to your room."

For the first time, Sarah got a good look at the interior, and all she could do was stare in stunned silence. The place was awash in angels. Angel wallpaper, thick and velvety-looking. Angel mobiles dangled from the ceiling, flying gently from the air movement of the heating vent. Angels were carved into the staircase and the impressive crown molding. Ceramic and porcelain angels sat on display inside a mahogany curio cabinet beside the front door. There was an angel umbrella stand and an angel coatrack and even an angel rocking chair. The angels came in every conceivable style and color—round, cherubic angels that looked like babies. Fun, playful cartoon angels. Tall, thin angels with windblown hair, halos, and benevolent expressions.

Rattled, Sarah edged after Jenny, who'd already started up the staircase.

Jenny stopped on the landing at the top of the stairs and took a key from her pocket. "I'm putting you in the VIP room."

The entire room—still decidedly angelic in theme—was done in various shades of pink. Egads. It looked like heaven had vomited Pepto-Bismol after eating cotton candy. She had to admit the decor took some getting used to. But there was a nice spa tub in the room and the bed looked plush and comfortable.

Jenny handed Sarah the room key. "If you need anything at all just call the front desk."

Sarah walked across the room and sank down on the mauve love seat positioned beside the window. She peeped through the lace curtain to the street below. Her grandmother's house was a few blocks over, down by the water on Lakeshore Drive. She had an urge to go see it. Her parents had sold the place after her grandmother died without even asking her opinion. Another reason there was a rift between her and her folks. But, Sarah supposed, after her big humiliation in Twilight, they'd figured she never wanted to come back here and they certainly hadn't wanted the place.

Memories tumbled in on her. Flashes of how she used to be. Shy, overweight, her nose stuck in a book so she could hide away from things that bothered her. Once upon a time, Twilight had been part of her magical escape from boarding school and her parents' impossibly high expectations of her. She'd counted the days until summer vacation, until the Christmas holiday.

And then she'd gone and ruined even that refuge.

Twilightites loved their celebrations. They never passed up an excuse for a festival or carnival or party. Part of it was due to the nature of the town's commerce, which was, first and foremost, tourism. But an element that couldn't be ignored was the community's genetic propensity for romance.

The town itself was reportedly founded on a legend about two lovers separated during the Civil War, who fifteen years later were reunited on the banks of the Brazos River where Twilight now stood. But none of that malarkey was written in the history books. According to the official version, Twilight was started as a military fort to combat violent Kiowa and Comanche uprisings that were prevalent at the time.

But reality didn't bring in the tourists.

Instead, the story of Colonel Jon Grant, sent to oversee the fort, and the woman who later became his bride, Rebekka Nash, became the preferred legend.

Not that Travis allowed himself to believe in any of that fated, destiny, happily-ever-after crap. He knew better. He believed in one thing and one thing only—his daughter, Jasmine.

Looking at her now, so robust and excited, sent his spirits soaring. She'd been on the new medication for six weeks and she'd just received her third dose. So what if the seventy-five hundred dollars had drawn his savings account dangerously near zero. He would gladly surrender every last cent he owned for her. Of course, he was already worried how he was going to afford the next round, which was due just before Christmas, while at the same time giving Jazzy the Christmas she deserved. He had a few things he could sell—an antique shotgun his granddaddy had left him, his fishing boat, a secondhand Kawasaki motorcycle that had sat in the garage since Jazzy had come into his life and changed his wild-boy ways. And there was her college fund. He didn't want to dip into it, but it was there if needed.

But what about the injection after that and the one after that?

Travis shoved the worry aside. He'd cross those bridges when he came to them. For now, he was enjoying the fact that his daughter was well enough to ride in the open-air float on a cool day without a hint of breathing trouble.

Jazzy's blue eyes were unusually bright. She was dressed like Isabella from *The Magic Christmas Cookie*—pigtails, pink pinafore, blue gingham apron. His Aunt Raylene had made the outfit after

Jazzy fell in love with the book. Over the top of her costume, she wore a pink and blue car coat with a puffy hood. In her hands, she clutched her well-worn Isabella doll, and her cheeks were flushed bright pink.

Excitement? That was okay, but what if she had a fever? He reached over to splay his palm over her forehead.

Jazzy drew back and looked irritated. "I'm okay, Daddy."

"Just checking." He smiled.

"Father Christmas." Belinda Murphey was in charge of getting everyone onto the floats in time for the parade. She had a clipboard in her hands, reading glasses perched on the end of her nose, and a whistle around her neck. "You and Jazzy can go right on up."

Travis bent down to pick up Jazzy, but she tossed her head. "I can walk. I'm too big for you to carry around."

Not really, but okay, maybe he was being overly protective. It was difficult finding a balance between being watchful and letting her do as much as she could by herself, giving her the room to be like other kids. "Sure you can, honey."

She started up the steps and he put a hand to her back. "Daddy . . ." she warned.

"Sorry, sorry." He forced himself to put his arm down.

Jazzy made her way to the sleigh centered in the middle of the float and climbed aboard with mincing, ladylike steps. Every time he looked at her his heart ached a little. He loved her so damn much, the intensity of it cut sharp as a knife. Before he'd had a kid, he hadn't known this kind of love existed. He still couldn't understand how Crystal could walk out on her.

His daughter settled into the seat, spread out her skirt all around her, and then beamed over at him. "You can come up now, Daddy."

He climbed the steps in his Father Christmas costume. In spite of the itchy beard, hc loved this, being here with his daughter, playing Santa Claus. It made him feel lighthearted again. Something he hadn't felt since Jazzy had gotten sick.

Once upon a time, he'd been the original good-time Charlie. Living only for himself, seeking adventure in all the wrong places, burying his sorrow over his mother's death the only way he knew how—by partying hard.

But one tiny little girl had changed all that.

It was a miracle really, the new medication Dr. Adams had given Jazzy off-label. How the hell had he gotten so lucky to have such a wonderful daughter, a loving community, and an open-minded doctor? He swallowed past the lump in his throat.

Dammit, Walker, don't go getting all sentimental.

He sat beside Jazzy. "Can I put you on my lap or are you too big for that too?"

She gave it some thought and finally nodded. "That would be okay."

He tucked her into the crook of his arm, felt the thrumming of her little heart through her clothes. Was it beating too fast? He took a quick peek at her lips. Nice and pink. Whew.

Travis forced himself to relax and mentally gear up for the Father Christmas gig. After the parade, he'd be inundated with short stacks begging to sit on his lap and recite their wish lists. But he loved that kind of thing and children swarmed him like bees, making *him* feel like a kid again.

He glanced around at the other floats, saw a black Lincoln Town Car turn into the entrance and pull to a stop beside the rest of the cars parked inside the stadium. The driver got out and opened the back door. A willowy woman of medium height unfolded herself from the backseat.

Immediately, people surrounded her. Travis supposed she must be Sadie Cool, the celebrity author of the children's book Jazzy loved so much. Inexplicably, he felt his own pulse rate pick up.

She moved toward the floats, the crowd parting to let her pass. Travis's gaze tracked down the length of her long, shapely legs. Defying the Christmas costumes everyone else wore, she had on a tailored charcoal gray pencil skirt, a fluffy white long-sleeved sweater, and catch-me-do-me black stiletto boots. Her bearing was regal, square shoulders, head held high. Some might mistake it for aloofness, but a strange hitch in the center of his chest told him that she was very shy and used the detached posture as a shield. He wondered if he was the only one who could see the vulnerability she struggled so hard to hide behind that polished smile.

In that moment, she lifted her head and her eyes met his. The breath left his lungs in a quick huff of air as surely as if he'd been tackled to the ground by an oversized linebacker. Longing fisted his soul, tight and painful, touching him deep. Inside his white Santa gloves, Travis's fingers curled into fists.

In his mind's eye he could see her stripped naked, lying on his bed, giving him a real smile, naughty and inviting.

Whoa, wait just a damn minute.

He stomped on his X-rated thoughts. She was a stranger. A famous writer so far out of his league it was laughable. A drop-dead beauty in designer clothes with—his gaze roved over her again, succinctly—a really nice pair of breasts.

"Daddy?"

"Uh-huh," he answered without glancing at his daughter.

The woman looked oddly familiar, but Travis couldn't place her. She had sleek, caramel-colored hair, so glossy it made him think of polished pine, that was pulled back into one long braid that fell down the middle of her back and a sweep of side fringe bangs that gave her an exotic look.

The closer she drew, the more convinced he was that he knew her. His mind nagged, but for the life of him he couldn't put a name to the gorgeous face. Did he know her? If so, how in the world could he have forgotten a woman like that?

"Daddy." Jazzy tugged on his sleeve.

He ripped his gaze off the woman, turned, and slipped his arm around her. "What is it, sweetie?"

"Is that her? Is that Sadie Cool?" Her little body vibrated like a tuning fork and her smile lit up her whole face.

"I think maybe it is."

"She's so pretty." Jazzy breathed. "Like Rapunzel with that long hair."

"Yes, she is." He looked at the woman again. She was sashaying straight toward their float, Belinda Murphey at her side.

The closer they drew, the faster his pulse raced, and when they stopped at his float and climbed the wooden steps, Travis felt his stomach vault into his throat and his tongue twist into a Gordian knot.

"Father Christmas," Belinda said. "This is Sadie Cool."

He put out his gloved hand to shake hers. "Ho, ho, ho," he said lamely.

"I'm Jazzy," his daughter exclaimed, hopping up from her seat to throw her arms around Sadie Cool's trim waist. "And I love you!"

Overwhelmed, Sarah just stood there, the little girl's arms squeezing her tightly. How did she winnow out of this embrace? Sarah was not a touchy-feely type and she didn't know the first thing about kids. Especially affectionate ones with no internal filter. Or maybe all kids were like that. How would she know? She'd been an only child, had never babysat. Benny asked her why she'd even written a children's book and her only explanation had been that she'd written it for the kid she'd once been. Overlooked and underestimated by her parents, her mind filled with a lush fantasy life. This kid, this outgoing, easily affectionate, cheery-faced, obviously much loved Munchkin took her by surprise.

"She's never met a stranger," the man in the Santa suit explained.

Geez dude, she longed to say, *ever watch the evening news? Hardly a week went by where some tragedy didn't befall a kid who was too trusting. Teach your daughter about stranger danger.* Then again, she had to remember this was Twilight. Right or wrong, people were simply more trusting here.

"Father Christmas is my daddy." Jazzy giggled and beamed up at Sarah.

Okay, all right, so the child could cure seasonal affective disorder with one of those million-watt grins. Now she knew how the Grinch felt when faced with spunky Cindy Lou Hoo. Outmatched. "My, aren't you a lucky little girl," Sarah mumbled, not knowing what else to say.

Jazzy's blond corkscrew curls bobbed enthusiastically. "He's the best daddy in the whole world."

For the first time, Sarah noticed the girl was dressed exactly like her heroine Isabella from *The Magic Christmas Cookie*. And odd feeling ran through her that was at once both comfortable and ill-fitting.

"Have a seat, Miss Cool," Belinda Murphey advised. "The parade is about to begin."

Sarah looked around and realized there was only one place to sit—beside Santa in his sleigh.

He patted the seat beside him, his gray eyes twinkling mischievously behind wire-framed Santa glasses. Gray eyes that reminded her of Travis. "Park it, Sadie."

A flippant Father Christmas? Not precisely Victorian. Reluctantly, Sarah settled in next to him as he pulled Jazzy into his lap. Underneath the float, she heard the truck engine rumble to life.

His voice reminded her of Travis too.

You're hypersensitive. Get over it. He's not Travis.

No, but sooner or later she was going to run into Travis and that's what had her on edge. Nervously, she smoothed her unwrinkled skirt with her palms and avoided looking at Santa as the float lurched forward following the other floats sliding from the football field. There were horse-drawn carriages mixed among the floats and a bagpipe band and the high school pep squad dressed in serving wench attire.

Jazzy was leaning over the side of the sleigh, waving enthusiastically at the crowd gathered along the parade route. As the sun slid down the horizon, sweetly kissing the lake, the gas lanterns, mounted on black wrought-iron streetlamps, flickered on. Street vendors hawked a variety of foods. From roasted turkey legs to steak on a stick to shepherd's pie—the air lay rich with the scent of sautéing onions and garlic and robust spices.

Many people were dressed in Victorian period costumes. Sarah spied Beefeaters and London bobbies and characters from Dickens's novels— Scrooge and Marley and Tiny Tim; Miss Havisham and Oliver Twist and David Copperfield. Children rode their fathers' shoulders. Moms carried gaily decorated picnic baskets. Teenagers, forever cool, looked bored and texted on their cell phones. "Santa! Santa!" tots cried excitedly as their float motored past.

Jazzy leaned across her father's lap to whisper in Sarah's ear. "You gotta wave."

"Huh?" Sarah looked startled.

"She's a social butterfly," Father Christmas said, waving madly to the crowd. "Jazzy knows these things. You better wave."

"Oh, yes, right." Feeling like a dunderhead, Sarah forced a smile, mentally cursed Benny for getting her into this, and waved like a Miss U.S.A. contestant.

"Perfect," Jazzy approved.

"You've got your very own Miss Manners," Sarah told Santa.

"She does keep me on my toes." He draped an arm over Jazzy's shoulder and a sense of longing so strong, it tasted like dark chocolate against her tongue, took hold of Sarah. How many times had she wished for this kind of loving, attentive relationship with her own father?

"Look, look, it's Isabella with Santa," a child in the throng called out.

How surreal, riding in a float with Father Christmas and the main character from her book. Sarah felt as if she'd stepped inside the pages of *The Magic Christmas Cookie* and she sort of liked it. Did that make her nuts?

Jazzy was standing up on the seat between Sarah and Santa, basking in the adoration of the crowd. The child was brighter than sunshine and she had Sarah wishing she'd worn shades.

Santa canted his head. "You look familiar. Do I know you?"

"I get that a lot. I must have one of those faces." What was she supposed to say? *You probably remember me as the chubby, desperate chick who embarrassed the hell out of herself at a wedding one Christmas Day.*

"No." He stroked his obviously fake white beard, patting it into place. She wondered if the thing was itchy. It looked itchy. "I've seen you before, I just can't place where."

Was she going to have to get into this now? With Father Christmas on a Dickensian float, in the middle of the Twilight town square? Talking through the spindly legs of the Shirley Temple look-alike standing on the seat between them.

Come on, just admit who you are. Someone around here is bound to recognize you sooner or later. It's going to come out.

"It's your eyes," he said. "They're an unusual shade of blue. Almost purple. The color of a mountain range."

"Why, Santa Claus, are you hitting on me?" she asked, not because she really thought he was hitting on her, but just to shift things and put *him* on the defensive.

He stared at her for so long, with a bemused expression in his eyes, that Sarah wriggled in her seat. "Why Miss Cool, what kind of Santa would do that in front of his daughter?"

"I had no idea Santa even had a daughter."

His grin widened. "They don't call me Father Christmas for nothing."

"And how does Mrs. Claus feel about that?"

"There is no Mrs. Claus."

"Oh my, got run over by a reindeer, did she?" Sarah quipped. Sometimes, when she felt out of her element, she used wit to balance the scales. Her sense of humor threw some people, but not Jazzy's daddy.

"Splat!" He shook his head, pulled a mournful face, and smacked his palms together. "Grease spot in the road. Those low-flying reindeer are hell on wives."

"Grandmas too, from what I hear."

"You better watch out . . ." His smile was purely wicked now. He *was* flirting with her.

"Because Santa is omnipotent, all-knowing, all-seeing, all-powerful."

"Precisely."

Sarah clicked her tongue. "Must be such a burden."

"You have no idea."

"Poor Santa. You're responsible for everyone's happiness."

Dramatically, he splayed a white-gloved palm over his chest. "It's my cross to bear."

"How about if you skipped one year. Took a long vacation to Fiji. Gave the world some tough love. Let them figure out the meaning of Christmas all on their own?"

"Ah," he said. "You're one of those."

"What? An independent thinker?"

" 'Grinch' is the word that comes to mind."

Sarah thrilled to the heated thrust and parry. This was too weird. She was having fun exchanging repartee with Santa. Who would have thought he could keep up? She wondered what he looked like underneath that red and white suit. "Gotta admit, Christmas isn't my favorite time of year. I've been in Fiji on December twenty-fifth, it's phenomenal. Island life, mon. You ought to give it a try sometime."

He looked as if he was itching to let loose with something snappy when he was interrupted by his daughter.

"Daddy, Daddy." Jazzy tugged on Santa's cap. "There's Auntie Raylene." She raised her voice, bounced up and down and waved even more enthusiastically, which Sarah would have sworn was physically impossible. The kid was Pollyanna, Pippi Longstocking, and Miss Merry Sunshine all rolled into one. "Hi, Auntie!"

Happy for the interruption, Sarah swung her gaze in the direction of Auntie Raylene. She had dyed blond hair, teased up big, and she wore a green skirt too short and tight for her age, but she still looked hot. Sarah realized she knew the woman.

Raylene Pringle used to be one of her Gramma Mia's friends. Once upon a time Raylene had been a Dallas Cowboys cheerleader renowned for her flashy affairs with famous football players. Later, she'd parlayed the experience into a modeling career, gotten rich, came back home and married Earl, her high school sweetheart. Gram had said that Sarah was too young to hear Raylene's stories, but whenever she'd come to visit, Sarah had lingered in the hallway trying to eavesdrop on Raylene's juicy conversations with Gram and their friends.

Then as if thunderstruck, Sarah remembered something disturbing. Raylene Pringle was Travis's aunt, and Jazzy had just called her Auntie Raylene. Did that mean . . . ?

She had no time to finish the thought because Father Christmas held up a hand and exclaimed, "I've got it. I do know who you are. You're little Sarah Collier all grown up."

CHAPTER FOUR

Travis stared into the eyes of the woman who had once professed her undying love for him. Yeah, well, okay, back then she'd been a girl. But her mesmerizing eyes made his pulse pound harder, and the earth tilted crazily on its axis. It felt like some surreal moment from those fairy tale stories Jazzy loved for him to read to her, where the guy kisses the sleeping beauty or scales an ivory tower or slays a couple thousand dragons to get the girl of his dreams.

He thought of his mother, how she used to tell him that when he found the right one, he'd know it, deep in his heart. Then she would make a small fist and lay it over the left side of her chest and stare into his eyes. "The way it is with your father and me. When you find your soul mate, you'll have no doubts."

He knew he hadn't felt it with Crystal. With his ex-wife, it had been about sex, plain and simple. But here, now, looking into Sarah's eyes, he felt . . . *gobsmacked*.

What in the hell was this feeling? He was cold and hot all at the same time. Achy and euphoric, like he had a high fever.

Her lips were temptingly close, and all he could think about was kissing her. Thank God Jazzy was there, coming between them, chattering nonstop. Or, compelled by a force he couldn't control and didn't understand, he might have actually kissed her.

When Sarah had been a teenager, Travis had never thought about her in a romantic way. He'd liked her, sure, and they'd been friends. She'd been curious and inquisitive, intrigued by things he was interested in—nature, animals, fishing—but she'd just been a cool kid.

But she was a kid no more and right now, he sure as shootin' *was* thinking about her in that way.

Little Sarah Collier had grown up very nicely. She was slimmer, but still curvy in all the right places. He liked curvy. Her eyes were sharp and smart and uniquely blue. That's how he'd finally placed her. Those unusual eyes. Her skin was lily white, as if she never went out in the sun, and her honey brown hair was thicker, longer, plaited in a braid that landed past the middle of her back. She smelled so good, like pie made from tart green apples, unexpectedly homey but with a strong sprinkle of sass. Travis felt all kinds of feelings— surprise, desire, confusion, and, let's face it, delight. He was delighted to discover that Sarah was Sadie Cool.

And here was the amazing thing.

The look on Sarah's face told him she was feeling pretty much the same emotions. They stared at each other, both breathing in short, rapid, tandem breaths.

It was a very strange moment. It wasn't every day a man discovered his daughter's favorite author was the girl who'd grown up next door to him. A girl who'd once interrupted his wedding to tell him that he was her destiny.

Destiny, fate, providence. Somehow, it felt precisely as if that's what this was.

Sarah raised a hand to her cheek. "Why . . . why are you staring at me like that? Do I have something on my face?"

Yes, an amazing pair of lips.

She made him think about soft mattresses and long winter nights, and for a guy whose mind had been centered almost solely on his daughter for the last four years, it was damn disquieting.

"No," he said in a hoarse croak. "Nothing on your face. You look great."

Her cheeks tinged pink and she turned her head away, waving to the crowd on her side of the sleigh.

And there it was again, the intense urge to kiss her. He fisted his hands, desperate to quell the sensation. Sarah was only in town for a short while. She was from the big city and he was just a small-town guy.

What's so bad about a weekend fling? Just a good time between old friends. As long as you keep it light. . . .

Absolutely not. He wasn't about to start something with her. For one thing, there was Jazzy to consider. How wrong would it be for him to get involved with his daughter's idol? And for another thing, he had a very strong feeling that if he ever made love to Sarah Collier, one long week with her would never, ever be enough.

Sarah wasn't clear on how she made it through the rest of the parade. She smiled and she waved and the entire time she kept thinking, *I'm sitting next to Travis Walker. Here sits the man I most wanted to avoid, and my shoulder is touching his.*

Travis had said nothing else to her after he'd announced that he remembered who she was. What was he thinking? She cringed inwardly imagining the scenario playing out in his head. Was he mentally rolling his eyes to discover that he'd gotten stuck on the same float as the semi-stalkery teen who had burst in on his wedding to declare he was her one true love?

Sinking lower into the seat, Sarah kept her face toward the crowd and away from Travis, ignoring her rapidly pounding heart and the sweat pooling at the collar of her sweater.

Finally after what seemed an eternity, but in actuality was only about half an hour, the parade arrived back at the high school football field. The minute their float stopped, Sarah was up out of her seat, on her feet and headed for the exit.

Which just happened to be on the other side of Travis's long, strong legs stretched out across the sleigh. She paused, dithered. Why didn't he move and let her pass? Was he teasing her?

Then she saw why and felt like a dodo for taking it personally. He was adjusting Jazzy's cap, making sure the flaps covered her ears. "There you go, sweetheart," he said. "Gotta keep those ears warm."

"Oh, Daddy," Jazzy said with exasperation. "I'm fine."

"Yes, you are," he said.

The look on his face was so tender it tugged at Sarah's heartstrings. Quickly she glanced away, saw a couple of high school boys pushing a portable staircase up to the float. Travis stood and handed Jazzy down to his Aunt Raylene, who was waiting on the ground.

Still, Travis did not climb down. She'd forgotten how slowly things moved in Twilight. She took a deep breath. Patience, patience.

He stood with hands braced to his back, eyes on the sky. "Well, hell," he said, sounding far more like the Texas cowboy he was than the Victorian Father Christmas he was pretending to be. "Will you look at that."

"What?" Sarah squinted up into the darkness.

"A little bit of Christmas magic."

"Huh?"

He raised a white-gloved palm, caught a big, fat, soft snowflake. It melted as soon as it hit his hand. "It's snowing. You know how rare that is? We only get snow once or twice a year if that, and here it is, snowing on the day you've returned home, Sarah Collier."

"Twilight is not my home," Sarah said stiffly.

"Uh-huh." Travis just smiled behind that ridiculous Santa Claus beard as a dusting of snowflakes floated around him. He looked like a scene from a Hallmark commercial.

"What's that supposed to mean?" Okay, she knew she was being difficult, but something about his smug smile rubbed her the wrong way.

"It doesn't mean a thing. How are your parents by the way?"

She shrugged. "Fine. I don't see them much. You know, same as always, important heart surgeons, too busy for family life. How is your dad?"

A clouded look crossed Travis's face, and he lowered his voice. "He passed away."

"Oh." What was she supposed to say to that? *I'm sorry* seemed so inadequate. Sarah had never been good at comforting people. Her inclination was to treat them the way she'd want to be treated. Leave them alone and let them sort things out. "Um . . . I hate to hear that."

"It was several years ago," he said neutrally as if he'd already processed and dealt with it.

"So you're good now?"

He looked down at Jazzy, who was in excellent hands with a group of doting women. "I'm good."

Sarah shifted her weight. Time to leave before they got into a full-blown conversation and it led somewhere she did not wish to go. Sarah stepped past him, angling for the stairs. He extended his hand to help her down, but she pretended she didn't see his offering and forged ahead on her own.

What she hadn't taken into account was how quickly the swirling snowflakes melted as they hit the ground. This was North Central Texas and even though it might be snowing, the rich soil was still warm. No matter how fast it fell, the snow would not be sticking around. Combine the slick wetness with metal steps and three-inch-stiletto fashion boots and you had a recipe for disaster. Which Sarah realized two seconds too late.

Her boot hit the wet patch and her foot slipped.

"Oh!" She gasped, flailing her arms to help regain her balance, but then her other boot heel caught the skid and Sarah knew she was going down.

The group of women at the bottom of the stairs all reached out for her, even little Jazzy. In her Isabella costume, she looked like Sarah's own heroine waiting there to catch her as she fell.

But she didn't fall.

Instead, two strong arms went around her, hauling her back up onto the floor of the float. Travis's hands were locked under her breasts and his warm breath fanned the hairs along her temple. She hated to think how stupid she looked. Not that it was the first time she'd looked stupid in front of him.

"You okay?" he murmured.

She tilted her head and looked into those gorgeous gray eyes that had graced many of her teenage fantasies and gulped. "Peachy," she mumbled.

He released his arms from around her waist. Thank God, because she was terrified he'd discover that her nipples were suddenly hard as little pebbles underneath her camisole. She knew *she* was terrified by this unwanted turn of events.

But his hand remained at her back, steadying her. His touch sent a ripple of sensation running up her spine. His gray-eyed gaze attached to hers in a thoroughly wicked light.

The song "Santa Baby" (the Eartha Kitt version of course; every other rendition paled in comparison) ran irreverently through her head. She sank her top teeth into her bottom lip, struggling to hold on to some semblance of self-control. But her old schoolgirl daydreams came raging back with the added fuel of adult knowledge.

She wrenched away from him, unable to handle the tumult of feelings pushing through her. *Be detached, be calm, be collected. You're Sadie Cool, act like it.*

"Well," she babbled. "Well, thank you."

Yes, that was so cool.

One side of his mouth quirked up and a mischievous expression crossed his face as if he was imagining what she looked like naked. "Don't mention it."

Sarah felt heat color her cheeks, and she ducked her head. Couldn't very well let the guy know he'd stirred a physical reaction in her. She couldn't bear it if he thought she still had a crush on him. Because she didn't. Absolutely *did not*. She was a grown woman, a successful children's book author, and he was . . .

A very buff cowboy Santa Claus with snow in his beard.

Wistful longing tugged at her solar plexus. Not good. Time to clear out of here. No more Christmas magic nonsense. Somehow she made it safely down the stairs only to be enveloped by the women who'd been waiting to surround her.

"Welcome," one of them said. "We're the members of the First Love Cookie Club and we invited you to Twilight, Miss Cool. Thank you so much for coming. It's so good to have you home."

Then they all started talking at once and she realized that many of them had been her grandmother's friends, even though she couldn't remember everyone's names. They hugged her and reintroduced themselves and hugged her some more. They smelled of Chanel No. 5 and vanilla and cinnamon and lavender soap.

Tilt!

She was on overload. Crowds made her jumpy, beaming strangers who wanted to touch her even more so. This was almost as overwhelming as being on the float with Travis. She cast a glance over her shoulder at him. He was on the ground several feet away, swinging Jazzy up on his shoulders. The little girl's head was thrown back, his daughter's delightful childish laughter filling the air.

A new emotion pushed out the wistfulness and anxiety, and in that moment Sarah experienced a loneliness so dark and stark all the breath left her lungs. She wanted to run straight back to the Merry Cherub and jump into bed with a good book.

Alas, the seven ladies of the First Love Cookie Club had other plans. Dotty Mae Densmore, whom Sarah did remember as Gramma Mia's best friend even though they'd been night and day different, linked her arm through Sarah's. "Come on," she said, "we're going to a party."

"Um, a party?"

"Tradition. The First Love Cookie Club hosts the annual Dickens on the Square gala and you're the guest of honor."

She looked around, hoping to think of a way out of this, but she couldn't come up with a decent excuse. She did, however, see Santa and Jazzy getting into a brown pickup truck.

Stop looking at him.

But she didn't, and when he turned, just before he climbed in behind the wheel, and threw a glance at her over his shoulder, Sarah's heart somersaulted.

"You're riding with us," Raylene Pringle said, coming over to take Sarah's other arm.

The rest of the group fell in behind them.

"Where are we going?" Sarah asked, feeling hijacked.

"To the Horny Toad," Belinda Murphey said, hitting the automatic start button on her key chain. A maroon minivan parked a few feet away from the floats rumbled to life.

"Excuse me?"

"You *have* been away too long"—Dotty Mae patted Sarah's hand; she smelled like peppermint and Oil of Olay—"if you don't remember that Raylene and Earl own the Horny Toad Tavern. They've closed it to the public for the party and fixed it up real festive. You're gonna love it."

Sarah seriously doubted that, but she went along for the ride. *Just get through this week, and you'll be back in New York wrestling with your book by next Sunday.*

A few minutes later they pulled up to the Horny Toad Tavern, which was little more than a roadside honky-tonk, but vehicles—most of them pickup trucks or SUVs—crammed the parking lot.

They walked through the door and were greeted by an explosion of Christmas. Holiday music blasted from the Wurlitzer in the corner. Currently, Tim McGraw was crooning "Dear Santa." A fat, seven-foot, artificial Christmas tree, overburdened with silver and red ornaments, took up an entire wall. Almost everyone was in costume. Either Victorian-era attire or some kind of kitschy Christmas getup. She hadn't worn anything remotely Christmas-related since the reindeer antler headband and jingle bell sweater vest. Delicious holiday aromas teased her nose. The pool tables had been converted to buffet tables, with one devoted just to desserts.

Sarah licked her lips at the sight of chocolate fudge cookies. Chocolate was her weakness, which was why she normally steered clear of it. A punch bowl filled with eggnog graced one end of the bar; at the other end stood martini glasses filled with a red and white drink mixture.

"Cranberry Snowdrifts," Raylene said at her elbow. "They're made with cranberry juice cocktail, crème de cacao, and white chocolate liqueur; it tastes like white chocolate–covered cranberries. Help yourself."

Sarah wasn't a big drinker, but in party situations alcohol helped take the edge off her social anxiety. She tried one of the Cranberry Snowdrifts and found it surprisingly tasty. She nursed the drink and tried to look inconspicuous, but Dotty Mae and her crew were having none of it. They told her how great it was to have her back. They talked about her grandmother. They told stories of when she was little. Terrified that someone was going to mention her extreme faux pas at the Presbyterian church, Sarah forced a smile. "I think I should mingle."

"By all means, dear, we didn't mean to hog you," Dotty Mae said.

But once she was freed from the group, she realized she didn't recognize anyone else in the room. She promised herself that she would finish her drink, make one lap around the room, and then she was out of there. She'd done enough socializing for one evening.

If you'd just give social events a chance, you

might just discover you enjoy them, Benny's voice chided.

Her agent was forever telling her that she should open herself up to life and have a bit of fun. But fun came easily to him. To Sarah, small talk with strangers was right up there with root canals on her list of least favorite things.

Okay, small talk isn't your strong suit but surely there's something here that you'd enjoy if you gave it half a chance, imaginary Benny whispered.

She thought of a certain sexy Santa with his lively gray eyes and engaging grin, and her heart did an odd little skip-hop. Who wouldn't enjoy him?

It was a stupid thought, so she shook her head to get rid of it quickly before it had time to root and grow. She was supposed to be avoiding Travis, not hanging out with him. Besides—she scanned the bar—he wasn't even here. He'd probably taken his daughter home and put her to bed.

Face it. The last thing you need is to get involved with Travis Walker.

After half an hour of kids pulling on his beard and babies bawling their heads off because they were scared of him, Travis was eager to get out of the Santa suit and take Jazzy over to the library for story hour. He vacated his seat at the Father Christmas pavilion set up on the courthouse lawn, bid the photographer good night, and rounded up Jazzy from the North Pole bounce house. Normally, he would never have let her go into a bounce house—too many germs lurking, too much jumping for a kid with severe asthma—but ever since she'd been getting the new medication, she'd been doing so well he hadn't been able to deny her. Poor kid deserved to finally have some fun.

He checked to make sure she was still doing well—no wheezing, no blue-tinged lips, no fever—and exhaled heavily. It was only then he realized he'd been holding his breath while he waited for her to crawl from the bounce house, cheeks pink with excitement, eyes sparkling.

Once he'd assured himself that she was doing well and he had her safely ensconced at the library, he headed on down to the Horny Toad for the party. Travis liked parties, even though over the course of the last four years he'd pretty well given up all that to take care of Jazzy. It was nice, knowing she was doing well and it was okay for him to kick up his heels just a little.

Feeling younger than he'd felt in a long time, Travis climbed into his pickup truck and drove toward Highway 377 to where the Horny Toad hunkered on the outskirts of town. He wondered if Sarah was still at the party, and then wondered why he wondered. She was only in town for a week. There was no point in wishing for something he didn't even know for sure he really wanted.

Of course, there was the strange coincidence that Jazzy's favorite author had turned out to be Mia Martin's granddaughter. Travis had a sneaking suspicion his Aunt Raylene and her cohorts were playing matchmaker. He found it amusing and wondered if Sarah had figured out what was going on.

This town had a way of latching on to romantic legends and milking them for all they were worth, and Sarah interrupting his wedding to Crystal was one of those stories they loved to pass around. *What if Sarah really was his soul mate?* He could just hear the ladies of the First Love Cookie Club posing that question.

He turned off Ruby Street and motored past the Twilight Cemetery where all his Walker ancestors were buried, including his mother and father. Gone way too young, both of them. His mother had died fourteen years ago at age thirty-eight. His father had followed six years later at forty-four. His folks too had gotten swept up in the sweetheart lore that permeated the town. In all honesty, the fanciful legends had been cooked up by the town's ancestors as nothing more than a publicity ploy to attract tourists to Twilight, but somehow people forgot about that and bought into it.

Here was the secret Travis had told know no one. The romantic myths scared him. His parents had been madly in love. They'd both believed they were soul mates, each other's one true love. He slowed to a stop at the traffic light, remembering his parents together, before his mother's asthma stole the best of her. They'd been so wrapped up in each other it often felt like he was the odd one out.

Then after his mother died, his father had crumpled. He'd stopped talking care of himself, stopped taking care of Travis, stopped caring about anything. He'd withdrawn into himself, withdrawn from life and finally . . . Travis had tried to get through to his dad but it had been like talking to a stone wall. Ultimately his strong love for his wife and his inability to cope without her had cost Chuck Walker his life.

Travis saw the pain his father had gone through after his mother's death, witnessed firsthand how grief could completely wipe a man out, and when he'd buried his father, he'd made up his mind he was never going to fall that recklessly in love.

In his mind, the reward just wasn't worth the price.

Chapter Five

Sarah had walked around the bar twice and was just getting ready to make good her escape when Travis walked in.

Gone was the Santa suit, and in its place he wore a starched button-down shirt and pressed chinos that in their neatness only served to call attention to his rugged, big-framed body and sharp, angular facial features. He hadn't seen her yet, hidden as she was in the shadows.

He was even more handsome now than he'd been nine years ago. His thick dark hair needed a good trim, but the unruly locks softened his steely jaw. His eyes were his standout feature, fathomless gray that seemed to stare straight into you. He shook hands with people, clapped men on the shoulders, lowered his head to whisper something to the women who laughed at whatever he had to say. Every single one of them.

The guy was a charmer. Always had been, always would be.

It startled her to realize she was breathing too

fast and she'd tightened her left hand into a fist. Irritation that she couldn't explain, didn't even want to admit, had her draining the last of her drink and setting the empty glass down on the bar.

"Want another?" asked the bartender.

Her head was already a little cloudy. "No thanks."

She turned away from the bar, looking for another avenue of escape. If she left through the front door, she'd have to go right by Travis. And if she slipped out the back exit, she'd be giving him all kinds of power over her behavior. Sarah lifted her head, shot a quick glance toward the front door again, and *bam!*

His gaze smashed into hers, eyes glittering with the promise of an indecent proposal. The corner of his mouth lifted impudently and his eyebrows rose. His gaze trailed over her with indolent slowness, causing her body to heat up.

Ah, damn, he was coming over.

She took a deep breath, bracing herself for the sensual onslaught that was Travis Walker. She was aware of every loose-limbed step he took, attuned to the magnetic aura oozing from his pores. Her pulse strummed, restless, edgy.

How she hated this out-of-control sensation.

She pretended to have a sudden hankering for food and darted over to the pool-tables-turned-buffet, picked up a red plastic plate, and circled the spread. Maybe if she didn't look at him, he'd go away.

The chocolate fudge cookies beckoned. She'd stopped eating for emotional comfort a long time ago, but that didn't mean she didn't still have the urge to stuff down her feelings with a tempting dessert.

She busied herself with studying the food selection, but from the corner of her eye she could see him following her over to the table. Crap! She stared at the cookies, willed herself into them—chocolaty, fudgy, rich and moist and crunchy with toasted pecans.

She heard his footsteps behind her and closed her eyes. *Go away.*

"You know," Travis said, coming to stand so near her she could smell his intoxicating scent, "I think we've been set up."

That was not what she was expecting him to say. She turned, jerking her gaze from the chocolate fudge cookies that were whispering, *Sarah, come eat me, you know you want to eat me.* What was it about being back in Twilight that made her want to throw Weight Watchers out the window and graze like a cow in a cornfield?

"What do you mean?" she asked.

His eyes twinkled in the glow from the colorful Christmas lights circling the dance floor. "No one bothered telling me that Sadie Cool, my daughter's favorite author, was actually little Sarah Collier all grown up."

"Would it have made a difference?"

"No," he said. "But neither was anyone considerate enough to tell you that Jazzy was my daughter."

"Why *would* they tell me something like that? It's not like it matters one way or the other," Sarah said, still determined to pretend she remembered nothing about interrupting Travis's wedding. When in doubt, deny, deny, deny.

"Would you have come to Twilight if you'd known about Jazzy and me?"

"Probably not," she admitted. In fact, if they'd told her he was Jazzy's father, she'd have been more likely to take a shuttle to the space station than come back here. "Certainly not just for a cookie club swap and a book signing. I'm not really into all the holiday hoopla. It was Jazzy's letter that made the difference."

"Those meddlesome matchmakers have got something up their sleeves. Otherwise, why not just come clean?" Travis nodded toward the culprits.

Why not indeed?

She peered across the room at the ladies of the First Love Cookie Club. The seven of them were gathered around the eggnog bowl, sliding surreptitious glances toward Travis and Sarah. Raylene winked. Dotty Mae grinned. Belinda gave a double thumbs-up.

"Oh God, you're right." She groaned. "They *are* playing matchmaker. You go out the back way, I'll head for the front door."

He leaned in closer, his mouth almost touching the top of her ear. His warm breath made her shiver. "Running away is not the way to play this."

"No?" Too bad. Escape was her favorite method of self-preservation.

"I think we should turn the tables on them," he murmured. "Are you game?"

"Why should I do that?"

"If they think we've already connected, they'll stop throwing us in each other's paths."

That got her attention. He made good sense. "What do you have in mind?" Sarah asked.

A small group of people were sliding across the

dance floor in time to "It's Beginning to Look a Lot Like Christmas." Travis cocked his head. "Shall we dance?"

"Um." A sudden heat swept through her at the thought of linking her arms through his. "I don't know how to dance."

"No worries," he said. "Just follow my lead."

"I'll trample your toes," she warned.

"I'll take my chances. Come on, let's make them think their matchmaking worked."

Before she could think of another protest, Travis was leading her out onto the dance floor, his fingers entangled with hers. It felt to her as if every eye in the place was zeroed in on them. His arm went around her waist and he pulled her to him, but he did not hold her uncomfortably close.

She stiffened, cardboard in his arms.

"Relax." He moved his hand to the nape of her neck, massaging with gentle pressure her tense muscles. Her pulse pounded viciously. "Stop thinking so much. Just let go, feel the rhythm."

"Who says I'm thinking too much?" She made a misstep, crunched his toe. Lucky for him he was wearing cowboy boots.

His laugh was a low rumble inside his chest. "It shows on your face, scrunched up, pulled inward, and your body is tight as a top."

She intentionally widened her eyes, tried to loosen her shoulders, and ended up crunching his foot again. "It is not."

He chuckled softly and pulled her closer. His proximity was so comforting she couldn't summon the energy to push away.

"Just go with the flow."

"Oh now, that's simply a hippie cliché. Sort of like love the one you're with."

He shrugged. "Clichés are clichés for a reason."

"You get a lot of mileage from that go-with-the-flow thing?"

"You ought to try it sometime," he crooned, his voice soothing enough to calm a rioting crowd. His fingers were back caressing the nape of her neck.

Sarah didn't know what else to say. His touch did feel good and she hadn't realized exactly how wound up she'd been. But it was impossible to relax when she could feel the contour of his hard, powerful body through his clothes. How was she going to get out of this?

"Don't think," he whispered. "Just dance."

"Well, duh, of course I'm thinking. How does one not think?"

"Play attention to your body. Feel the music vibrate the floor, coming up through your feet."

She tried, but it was impossible. She was too aware of him.

"You live too much in your head."

"How do you know that?"

"You're a writer. You live in your head."

"Okay, let's say you're correct in your assumptions. What's wrong with that?"

"It gets pretty lonely in there." He said it so simply, as if he could look into her eyes and see straight into her brain.

It pissed her off a little, that he thought he knew her. It pissed her off even more because he was right. Was she that obvious, that easy to read?

"Oh yeah?"

"I've read your book to Jazzy a thousand times.

And I do remember you, Sarah Collier—you can be playful and whimsical and even a little mischievous when you let yourself."

She'd forgotten about that. "That was a long time ago. I'm not that same dumb kid."

"You were never dumb. I recall you as being pretty observant and perceptive."

She felt inordinately pleased by that comment.

His grin deepened as he guided her around the floor. "Hey will you look at that."

"Look at what?"

"You're dancing. You've stopped analyzing why you can't dance and you're just following my lead," he pointed out. "You're out of your head and into your body."

Ding! He was right about that.

"How often do you exercise?" he asked.

"I don't think that's any of your business."

"I take that as never."

"I walk. I live in Manhattan."

"You walk in crowds, bustling up against people."

"So?"

"It's not the same as smooth, repetitive motion. Like dancing. It gets you out of your castle."

"My castle?" Sarah laughed. Honestly, she should break off the dancing and walk away, but she was fascinated by how he seemed to know her so well without really knowing her at all and by the way his eyes sparkled when he looked at her. Then there was the thing she didn't want to admit, not even to herself, that the pudgy fifteen-year-old buried deep inside her was wildly thrilled to be here in his arms, even if it was for just a moment.

Seriously, woman, that's so sad.

The music changed. Now "I Saw Mommy Kissing Santa Claus" was wailing from the jukebox. They were in the middle of the dance floor and suddenly Travis stopped moving.

Sarah looked at him. "What . . . ?"

He canted his head toward the ceiling. She glanced up.

Mistletoe.

They were standing underneath the mistletoe suspended from the center of the ceiling. Talk about your Christmas clichés.

Her toes curled inside her boots. It had been so long since she'd been kissed. She started to say no, she meant to say no, but when she opened her mouth, nothing came out.

He must have taken her parted lips as a full-speed, go-ahead sign, because he pulled her up closer and lowered his head.

Her breath caught and her treacherous hands rose of their own accord to link around his neck.

Travis.

She was kissing Travis Walker, the object of her teenage affections. The man whose name she'd once doodled in her high school notebook. The man she'd once dreamed endlessly of kissing.

His mouth was on hers.

Right now. And this was no dream.

She wobbled on her three-inch heels, her knees as wavy as overcooked spaghetti. The tang of pine filled her nostrils, along with something else . . . the fragrance of heated male skin, crisp like ginger snap cookies and full of sharp cinnamon spice.

He splayed a palm against her lower back and

the tip of his tongue ran lightly over her lips, sending a sweet shiver down her spine. His hand felt so big, his fingers so strong and firm. His lips teased, not taking the moment seriously. Not really kissing her, she reminded herself, but rather, showing off for the ladies of the First Love Cookie Club.

Still, she made a soft little noise at the back of her throat, encouraging him when it was absolutely the wrong thing to do at the wrong time in the wrong place. But when had Sarah's timing ever been good?

Travis deepened the kiss, but only slightly, leaving her feeling inappropriately irritated and achy. The pressure of his mouth spun her head, making her both dizzy and delirious. What was she doing? Why was she putting up with this? She should step away, smooth down her fringe of bangs, and act as if nothing had happened.

Holy schmoe, but the guy could kiss. He hadn't been the town Casanova in his younger days for nothing.

Someone in the crowded room let loose with a catcall.

Her cheeks flushed hot. She pulled back with a slight shrug, as if it was all a casual joke. Haha. Water off a duck's back. No big deal. Getting kissed underneath the mistletoe? Old hat.

She did not dare look over at the cookie club ladies. For that matter, she didn't look at Travis either. And she didn't finger her lips, which were still tingling, even though she really wanted to. She tried to act casual and distract herself by humming "I Saw Mommy Kissing Santa Claus," but then that just seemed weird.

Moving slowly so it wouldn't look like she was hell-bent on getting out from under that mistletoe, even though she was, Sarah stepped sideways off the dance floor.

Don't look at Travis. Be cool. You're Sadie Cool, remember? Act your name.

But then she couldn't stand it anymore and she felt compelled to tilt her head and pretend she was studying the revolving Christmas tree overloaded with ornaments and multicolored twinkle lights, when she was really peeking at Travis from the corner of her eye.

He moved out from under the mistletoe as well, leaned against the wall in a sexy, one-shouldered slouch. She wondered if he had any idea of the compelling figure he cut. Most probably. This was a man who'd had his share of women. He had to know the effect he had on the opposite sex.

Sarah's lungs filled with the smell of Christmas and community and her own sharp fear, but she could not peel her gaze off him.

Travis caught her eye, and the corners of his mouth tipped up into a cocky grin.

Why couldn't she just leave? Why were her feet rooted to the spot? Why did she want him to kiss her again and keep kissing her until their lips were chapped raw from all the kissing?

"Thanks for the dance," he said.

"Um . . . don't mention it."

"I had fun."

Me too. But she didn't say that.

"I hate to kiss and run," he said, glancing at his watch, "but I've got to go pick up Jazzy."

Kiss and run. For no discernible reason, Sarah shivered. "Where is she?"

"Story time at the library."

"At eight o'clock at night?"

"You've forgotten the tradition?"

A memory floated back to her then. Something she hadn't thought of in a very long time. She'd been nine or ten, a couple of years older than Jazzy was now, and Travis had volunteered to take the neighborhood kids to the story time that the library held after the Dickens on the Square parade. The librarian read *A Christmas Carol* and served refreshments. The children would circle around her in kid-sized chairs. She remembered Travis took her hand when they crossed the street and how it had made her feel so special. Later, she'd asked Gram why Travis had gone with the little kids to story time.

"His mother is very sick," Gram had said. "He just needs to get out of the house once in a while, even if it's just with little kids at story time."

She recalled feeling sorry for him. His mother had died a year or two after that. He'd lost his mother at a young age and he had a daughter who had been ill for a long time. How hard that must be for him. But Jazzy had looked pretty good. Certainly well enough to participate in the parade and then go to story time at the library. That was good news.

"Not that I would know what Jazzy normally looks like," Sarah told Travis. "But she seemed very well this evening."

"She did." The relief in his voice was palpable. "She's on an experimental medication and it seems to be working." He crossed his fingers, smiled a hopeful smile. Briefly, he told her about Jazzy's condition and her current treatment, and what had started out as smoldering looks and a red-hot kiss,

ended softly with sympathetic nods and understanding whispers.

"I better get a move on," he said, tapping the
face of his watch. "Have a nice night, Sarah."

And then he was gone. Ambling out the door,
leaving her staring in his wake, wondering what in
the hell was going on between them.

The morning after he danced with Sarah at the
Horny Toad and kissed her underneath the mistletoe, Travis woke up with her on his mind. He did
not know why he'd kissed her. He certainly hadn't
planned it, but he'd been unable to think about
anything except kissing those lush salmon-colored
lips from the moment she'd stepped onto the float
with him and Jazzy.

It bothered him, because for the last four years
the only thing he'd thought about was his daughter.
Now Sarah Collier, all sleek and cool, had swept
into his life, leaving him feeling hot and bothered
and worried.

No, he corrected. She hadn't swept into his life.
His aunt and her friends had dragged her into it.
They didn't fool him one bit. They might have ini-
tially brought her here for Jazzy, but now they were
playing matchmaker, throwing him and Sarah into
each other's paths. Well, he wasn't falling for it.

He stood in his kitchen making cinnamon toast
for Jazzy and thought about how the soft brown
sprinkles of spice were the exact same color as the
faint dusting of freckles scattered across the bridge
of Sarah's nose. Those freckles. He smiled and slid
the toast from the broiler. She might have buried
the Sarah he once knew and replaced her with the

polished guise of Sadie Cool, but she couldn't hide those freckles.

He put the toast on a plate, and then stirred a package of hot chocolate mix in Jazzy's pink sparkle princess mug. He added a handful of miniature, multicolored marshmallows just the way she liked it. Jazzy looked good, even after the excitement and activity of the previous night.

Hope lifted his heart. Had they finally found the right drug? Could this be the solution they'd spent four years searching for?

Happily humming "It's Beginning to Look a Lot Like Christmas," Travis poured himself a cup of coffee and wandered outside in his bathrobe, pajama bottoms, and house slippers to retrieve the Saturday morning edition of the *Twilight Caller* from the front lawn. He bent down, scooped up the dew-covered newspaper wrapped in clear plastic, and raised his head.

That's when he saw her.

There, at the edge of his property line, just across the one-lane road from Lake Twilight glimmering silver-blue in the spreading dawn, stood Sarah. Her hair was pulled back in a high ponytail braid and she wore black Lycra exercise pants and a plain white cotton T-shirt that stretched enticingly across her chest.

His gaze dipped downward as he took her in. It amused him to see she still wore the same black stiletto boots she'd worn the night before. When had she become such a girlie-girl? He remembered her as something of a tomboy.

That was a long time ago. She'd been a kid then. She was a woman now.

Travis eyed her curves. One hell of a woman, in fact.

He straightened, tucked the paper under his right arm, and took a sip of his coffee, trying to decide if she was really there or just a wishful apparition of his imagination. With his free hand, he cinched his bathrobe tighter, trying to cover up his bare chest as best he could, and raised his cup in greeting. "Morning."

For a moment, he thought she was going to turn and run away, but she stood her ground. He walked toward her.

She raised her chin. "I took your advice about exercising and went for a power walk."

"In those boots? You don't have any sneakers?"

"I didn't think I'd need sneakers and I don't like to check my bags at the airport, so I try to pack light. Besides, these boots are comfortable."

"For a power walk?"

"I am working on a blister," she admitted.

"C'mon in." He inclined his head toward the door. "I'll get you a Band-Aid."

"That's okay." She wrapped her arms around herself. "I'm good."

He watched her pull in, raise her defenses. "So, other than the blister, how did the walk make you feel?"

"Good . . . great . . . amazing actually." She sounded surprised.

"Fresh air clear your head?"

"Yes."

"Get your blood pumping?"

"Uh-huh."

He grinned. "Told you."

She flicked her gaze behind him and he turned to see what she was looking at. All he saw was the Queen Anne–style cottage built in the 1920s, complete with gingerbread trim, a wraparound porch, and window boxes.

"You're living in my grandmother's house," she said softly.

"You didn't know?"

She shook her head.

"Crystal and I bought it from your parents after your grandmother died. Then I paid it off with the insurance money from when my father passed away and I sold his house. I own it free and clear."

"Oh." She stayed expressionless, staring at the house.

Travis loved this house, but Crystal had hated it. "Too small," she said, "too cutesy." Crystal had dreams of living in expansive splendor far beyond the reach of Travis's pocketbook. He had to admit the place was a bit cutesy. It reminded him of one of those cozy cottages in Jazzy's Beatrix Potter books. It seemed almost magical somehow, especially when the mist rolled in off the lake.

He noticed Sarah had fisted her hands at her side and her lower lip tightened. Was she hurt by the discovery? "Your folks didn't want to keep the house for you? I know how close you were to your grandmother."

Sarah's eyes darkened. "I wasn't given the option. I was sixteen and away at boarding school when Gram had her first stroke and my parents moved her to a nursing home in Houston. I guess they didn't think it was important to let me know who bought it and I suppose I never thought to ask. My parents . . ." She shook her head and the long braid swished against her back. "We're not close. I'm a huge disappointment to them. In fact, I haven't seen them in over a year. We were supposed to get together for the holidays, but as it always does with them, something came up."

"Disappointment?" He couldn't imagine ever being disappointed in Jazzy. "You've written a book that has touched thousands of lives, my daughter's being one of them. How could they *not* be proud of you?"

Sarah shrugged. "They wanted me to follow in their footsteps. Become a surgeon. I simply didn't have the aptitude. Or the desire."

"That's because your talent lies with words."

"That's kind of you to say." She spoke in a distant tone, the way people spoke to strangers. But he wasn't a stranger and it bothered him that she was putting up a wall, pushing him away when he wanted to know everything about her.

Why? What was this strange pull of attraction? She was attractive, yes, but so were a lot of women and none of them had ever made him feel . . . What did he feel? Mesmerized? Captivated? Neither word was quite right. Spellbound?

Maybe it was the history between them. His interrupted wedding. Her heartfelt vow. She'd been completely infatuated with him at the time and he'd been pretty clueless about it. Now he was the one smitten and she seemed disinterested. Was that why he was interested? Precisely because she wasn't? How twisted was that?

Last night something inside him had come undone. Pent-up sexual desire gnawed at his insides.

Kissing her had felt so damn good, he'd wanted more. Wanted more right now, standing here on his front lawn looking into her faraway blue eyes. He ached to haul her into his bed, strip off their clothes, and thrust into her. He hungered to feel her legs wrapped around his hips, longed to feel her body quiver beneath his. He yearned to smash through the walls she'd erected around herself, shatter her resistance, and claim her as his woman.

The intensity of his desire scared the shit out of him. He'd never experienced anything like this primal pull, and it made him want to turn tail and run for his life. But Travis stood his ground, held her gaze.

A car rumbled down the lane in front of the house, a neighbor behind the wheel. He tooted his horn at them, raised a hand in greeting. Travis smiled, waved back.

"Anyway," he said, "I just wanted to thank you again for coming back home to make Jazzy's Christmas wish come true. You'll never know how much this means to her."

"You're welcome." She smiled, but it did not reach her eyes. "Well, I better head back."

He could feel her shoring up her emotions, building her walls higher, shuttering the curtains, locking him out. "Have a good day," he said.

"You too."

He watched her walk away, her head high, her steps almost a purposeful march as if she were trying to convince herself of something. And he couldn't help wondering, What would it take to break through that tough shell she'd erected and uncover the real Sarah Collier hidden away inside?

CHAPTER SIX

Raylene and Dotty Mae were waiting for Sarah in the lobby of the Merry Cherub. They stood on the guest side of the front desk while behind it, Jenny was bent at the waist, elbows on the counter, chin propped in her palms. All three were leafing through a catalogue filled with angel-related items that lay open on the counter in front of them.

"There you are," Dotty Mae exclaimed when she spied Sarah. She eyed her workout clothes. "But you're not ready to go."

"Go where?" Sarah ran a hand through her bangs, taming them down from the wind off the lake. She still couldn't wrap her head around the fact that Travis now owned her grandmother's house and no one had told her.

"You've got a full day ahead of you," Raylene said. "Didn't you get your itinerary?"

Guiltily, Sarah thought of the stack of info Mayor Schebly had given her the previous day. She'd tossed it on the bedside table in her room and never looked at it again. "Um, I'm sorry, I didn't read my itinerary . . . my agent usually handles the details of my appearances." She realized that sounded like an excuse. She hated public appearances and if Benny didn't push her, she'd never do them, but it was rude of her not to have looked at the itinerary. She'd kept them waiting. "I should have assumed responsibility for myself. I do apologize."

"Boy, that agent," Dotty Mae said, "he's sure got you spoiled."

"I suppose he does," Sarah admitted.

"It's okay, we haven't been here long," Raylene said.

"Could you ladies excuse me for just a little while longer? I need to shower and get changed."

"You go right ahead." Dotty Mae waved a hand. "I was just about to order this angel fondue set. There's Bible verses printed on the bottom of the fondue bowls. When you get done eating, ta-da, you've uncovered the word of God."

Raylene rolled her eyes. "What about your guests who don't like to mix fondue and religion?"

"Then they don't have to look at the bottom of the bowl, now do they? Sign me up for a set, Jenny." As an aside to Sarah, Dotty Mae said, "Jenny sells angelware. It's sort of like Tupperware, dontcha know, but cozier."

"Better get a move on," Raylene told Sarah. "Moe is presenting you the key to the city at nine and it's eight-thirty now."

"Yes, yes." Sarah hurried up the stairs, fishing her room key from her pocket as she went.

As much as she would like to weasel out of this thing, that didn't appear to be an option. Sighing, Sarah stripped off her clothes and got in the shower.

Fifteen minutes later, she was dressed in black slacks and a red knit sweater. She dabbed on a bit of makeup, and then wrenched her door open to find Dotty Mae and Raylene hovering in the hallway.

They left the B&B, and Dotty Mae stopped beside a faded yellow VW Bug straight from the 1960s parked at the curb and unlocked the passenger side door.

Raylene stepped ahead of Sarah, pushed aside the front seat, and folded herself into the back. "Guests sit up front. I would have brought my Cadillac, but it's in the shop and Dotty's VW is better than Earl's stinky ol' farm truck."

Sarah eased into the seat while Dotty Mae toddled around to the driver's side. The woman was eighty if she was a day.

"Should she be driving?" Sarah whispered to Raylene.

"Don't let her slowness fool you, Dotty Mae's still on the ball. I'm sure your Gramma Mia would have been just as feisty if she'd have lived, God rest her soul," Raylene said.

Dotty Mae climbed inside and started the engine. The Bug chugged to life. "So tell us, is Travis a good kisser? Last night he looked like he was a pretty good kisser."

"What year model is this VW?" Sarah evaded.

"1967."

"Ah, the summer of love," Raylene said. "I wish I could remember it better. I smoked too much damn pot that summer."

"I've heard he was a good kisser," Dotty Mae kept on. "You know he was quite the ladies' man before he got married and became a daddy."

Sarah let that slide by without commenting.

"But ever since he had that baby girl, he's done a complete one-eighty," Raylene said. "He's changed so much. Travis used to be so fearless. I remember the time he did a triple gainer off the old Twilight Bridge, showing off for all the moony-eyed girls on shore for the Fourth of July."

Sarah remembered that. She'd been one of those moony-eyed girls.

"And remember when he water-skied through the mesquite thicket at Cartwright Cove?" Dotty Mae said.

"Either time he coulda broken his fool neck." Raylene clicked her tongue. "But now he understands what it means to be a parent. You can't do the kind of stupid things you used to do when someone is depending on you."

"In a way," Dotty Mae mused, "I guess you could say that little Jazzy saved his life. Especially after what happened with Travis's father."

Sarah wanted to ask what happened to his father, but she didn't. What did she care? It was none of her concern and she didn't want to stir gossip.

"Such a shame you weren't old enough for Travis back then and he'd already gotten Crystal in trouble," Dotty Mae went on. "People don't seem to fall in love these days, the way you fell for Travis. That took some courage, interrupting his wedding like you did. I wish I'd been there to see it."

"I was there," Raylene said. "It *was* something."

Apparently so, since they were still talking

about it nine years later. *Let it go, people, move on.* Sarah suppressed a sigh.

"I've never seen any declaration of love so heart-felt," Raylene continued. "Even I got misty-eyed, and everyone knows I don't tear up easy. You were just so vulnerable, Sarah, in those reindeer antlers and that jingle bell sweater."

Please God just kill me now.

"Mmm, isn't that a stop sign?" Sarah pointed out the stop sign as they zoomed past without stopping.

"City council is planning on taking it down." Dotty Mae waved a hand.

Sarah let out a pent-up breath. "But until they do, shouldn't you still obey the stop sign just in case other drivers are expecting you to?"

"Never thought of it that way," Dotty Mae mused, turning the corner into a parking lot where an attendant was directing traffic.

They arrived at the town square just in the nick of time as Mayor Moe, a.k.a. Charles Dickens, was kicking off the day's scheduled festivities. Everywhere she looked, she saw holiday decorations. Miles of red ribbons and bows festooned the booths. Metallic garlands every color under the sun outlined the windows of the storefronts. Vast strands of twinkling lights covered every tree in sight—oaks, pecans, elms, cedars—none was spared the ebullient holiday spirit. The relentless cheeriness exhausted her, and she was surprised to see so many people standing on the courthouse lawn. Were they all waiting for her? Talk about pressure.

Moe spied Sarah and waved her up. With much

fanfare from the high school marching band playing "Deck the Halls," Sarah scaled the steps leading to the makeshift stage and joined the mayor at
the microphone.

The mayor made a speech about the universal
appeal of wish fulfillment in *The Magic Christmas
Cookie* and how proud the town was of Sarah's
accomplishments. The crowd cheered. Then the
mayor presented her with the key to the city.

The townsfolk did their best to make her feel not
only welcome, but special. Anyone else probably
would have felt honored and flattered, but Sarah
felt . . . well, that was the curious thing. She didn't
feel much at all. This was happening to Sadie Cool,
not her.

Her alter ego stepped forward, accepted the key
with a smile, and even made a short, impromptu
acceptance speech. She wished Benny was here.
He would understand the ambivalence leaking
through her. Why couldn't she accept the apprecia-
tion, the compliments?

But she already knew the answer. It was because
she'd fallen into her career completely by accident.
She'd simply been lucky, but that was the way publishing worked. It was a bit like the lottery. Write
a book, make it the best you can, send it out there,
cross your fingers, and wish on a falling star. Most
of the time you ended up holding a useless lottery
ticket, but she'd hit the jackpot on her very first try.
That didn't mean she didn't have talent or didn't
deserve the attention. Maybe she did, maybe she
didn't. It meant she was lucky. The luck was what
made her feel like a fraud. Anyone could buy a lottery ticket, spin a roulette wheel, roll the dice. And

her vicious case of writer's block seemed to back all that up. What if she really was a one-hit wonder?

The large symbolic gold-plated key rested cool in her hands.

"You do deserve this," a voice said, and for a minute she thought it was coming from inside her head. Except it was a masculine voice, accompanied by the tang of spicy cologne.

Sarah jerked her head around and met Santa's gray, comforting eyes. At some point in the presentation, Travis had come up on the stage behind her and she'd never even seen him.

How had he known about the doubts hammering around in her head? It was like he had super powers and could see straight into her brain. Dammit, how could any man look so sexy in a Santa suit? The band was playing "Santa Claus Is Coming to Town" and Mayor Moe was extending his arms to help her down off the stage. It was Father Christmas's turn in the spotlight.

Dotty Mae and Raylene ushered Sarah off to her responsibilities as honorary mayor. At nine-thirty she dug a shovelful of dirt for the groundbreaking of the library expansion that would house the new children's wing. When the head librarian told her that the town council had voted to name it the Sadie Cool Wing, Sarah had been completely bowled over. She had not expected this. It touched her and freaked her out, all at the same time. Clearly these people thought she was a much bigger deal than she really was. They had expectations, and she wasn't sure she could, or if she even wanted to, measure up.

At ten, she judged a costume contest, and at

eleven, she sat on a mattress, carried along by hunky firemen in the Victorian Bed Races. And at noon, she joined the local ladies who lunch at the Velvet and Lace Tea Room on Orchid Street two blocks south of the square. As a dyed-in-the-wool introvert there was only so much human contact she could take in one day. Being with people drained her energy. In order to charge back up, she needed her alone time. But she wasn't going to get it. Not today.

At one-thirty, Raylene and Dotty Mae took her to Sweetheart Park for the decorating of the Sweetheart Tree, turning it into the Cherub Tree for the holiday season. As the honorary mayor, Sarah was slated to put the first cherub on the tree.

They explained to her that the Cherub Tree project benefited underprivileged, disadvantaged, or seriously ill children from Hood County. The tree was decorated with cherubic ornaments containing the names and wish lists of local children. Between now and Christmas, generous donors would pluck cherubs from the tree and anonymously make a child's Christmas wish come true.

Sweetheart Park hadn't changed a bit in the nine years since she'd been away. In December, it was decorated in full splendor, filled with all manner of Christmas displays from Santa and his reindeer, to Frosty the Snowman, to an elaborate nativity scene.

A cobblestone walkway ran through the park, leading to several long wooden footbridges spanning a small tributary of the Brazos River that filtered into Lake Twilight. At the very center of the park lay the fountain featuring a cement statue of two lovers in Old Western attire, embracing in a heartfelt kiss. Rumor had it that if you threw pennies into the fountain, you would be reunited with your high school sweetheart. Sarah had to wonder what happened to those wallflowers like her who'd never had a high school sweetheart.

What about an unrequited first love? Did that count?

She was pretty certain that did not count. Either way, she wasn't wasting any pennies on a silly myth.

The Sweetheart Tree itself was a two-hundred-year-old pecan thick with sheltering branches. In the past century, hundreds of names had been carved into the trunk. The oldest name was that of the original sweethearts. *Jon loves Rebekka* had been engraved in the center of the tree in 1874, faded and weathered now, the etched lines barely visible. Many lovers had followed suit, carving their names into history. But sometime in the 1960s a botanist had warned that if the name carving continued, it would kill the pecan, so a white picket fence had been constructed around the tree, along with a sign sternly admonishing: "Do Not Deface the Sweetheart Tree."

In an uncharacteristic act of rebellion, Sarah had ignored that warning and she had indeed defaced the Sweetheart Tree. Seeing the tree again brought back the memory of her seditious graffiti. On the New Year's Eve when she was fourteen, she'd slipped from Gram's house in the middle of the night, with a penlight, a pocketknife, and a collapsible ladder. She had no excuse for her behavior other than she was caught up in the kismet cookie spell.

Briefly closing her eyes, she remembered propping the ladder beside the tree, climbing up, and finding an empty spot. Then painstakingly she'd carved: *Sarah Loves Travis 4 Ever.* Honestly, she'd forgotten all about it until this very moment. She couldn't help wondering if Travis had ever seen it. She wished she could go back in time and kick her own lovesick teenage ass and yell, *Snap out of it.*

A group of ladies and gentlemen in Victorian outfits waited for her at the old pecan. Two ladders were already set up beneath the bare branches, and a large cardboard box, overflowing with all-weather angel ornaments, sat between the ladders. The group greeted her in Dickensian speak.

If she hadn't been so worried about someone seeing the *Sarah Loves Travis* thing, she might have been swept away by the fantasy and matched the rhythm of their courtly language. Instead, she simply smiled and tried not to say too much, wanting to get this over with and get out of the vicinity as quickly as possible.

"Might I escort you to the Sweetheart Tree, Miss Collier?" asked a smooth-voiced man.

Sarah didn't have to turn around to know who was standing behind her. It was just her luck that the Cherub Tree decorating event included Father Christmas. She turned to look, purposefully keeping her face impassive. Which was hard to do since all she could think about was the kiss he'd given her under the mistletoe.

Damn Christmas anyway.

He extended his arm to her.

What could she do but take it? She slipped her hand around the crook of his elbow and he guided her over to the ladder. Two men sprang to her side to hold the ladder in place, and a woman dressed in a tattered wedding gown like Miss Havisham from *Great Expectations*, reached into the cardboard box, retrieved a pink-cheeked cherub ornament, and handed it to her. The name Ashley Duncan was painted in gold in big letters on the angel's wings; the scroll in the angel's hand detailed Ashley's wish list. Mittens (blue), coat size six, Bratz doll, Easy-Bake oven, Daddy home for Christmas.

Sarah's breath hitched and she wondered where Ashley's father was. Dotty Mae and Raylene had told her that several kids on the roster were the children of prison inmates, while others were offspring of soldiers serving in the Middle East. It didn't really matter. Either way, Ashley was missing a daddy.

"Acclaimed author Miss Sadie Cool will now adorn the Cherub Tree with its first ornament of the season," announced Miss Havisham to the onlookers in the park.

Sarah was a bit disconcerted to see that quite a crowd had gathered. But, thankfully, it appeared most of the attention was centered on Santa, who was joking with some of the kids and pretending to pull candy canes from behind their ears. Travis was such a natural with children. The guy had an easy air that drew people to him. Herself included.

Stop thinking about him. Get up that ladder, hang the cherub, and get this over with.

Clutching the ornament tightly in her hand, she started up the ladder on one side of the tree while Santa started up the other side, the width of the old pecan blocking their view of each other.

Until they reached the top of their respective ladders and a natural bifurcation in the tree trunk. Suddenly, she was looking squarely into Travis's eyes just as she realized her childhood graffiti was carved into the tree between them.

Please, don't let him look down.

He looked down.

She saw where his gaze fell.

Right where she didn't want it to go. Right on that stupid, stupid, stupid love message she'd carved in a regrettable moment of teenage, hormone-fueled madness.

Behind the Santa beard, his lips tipped up.

Look away, look away, pretend you didn't see him seeing it.

Sarah glanced away, but she wasn't fast enough. Travis raised his head and his gaze sparked off hers, just before she fixed on an inscription that read: *David Loves Debbie. See there, that's the way a heartfelt tree defacing should be done. The guy professing his love for the girl, not the other way around.*

"Hmm," Travis said.

She was not going to fall for it. She wasn't looking at him again. No way, no how. Studiously, she searched for the perfect spot to hang the angel ornament.

"Will you look at that?" Travis's voice was low so only she could hear.

Do not rise to the bait.

"It's the darnedest thing," he said.

Shut up, just shut up!

Sarah gave up looking for the perfect spot for an angel landing and just stuck the ornament on the fragile twig in front of her. "All done," she sang out to the men holding on to the ladder for her. "I'm coming down."

"Oh, sweetie," Miss Havisham said, holding the train of her moth-eaten wedding gown in one hand, standing on her one shod foot and looking more than a bit like Helena Bonham Carter. "You're just getting started."

Sarah glanced down to see one of the men was handing her another ornament.

"We've got two more boxes just like this one to go." With a flourish, Miss Havisham waved her hand at a large cardboard box.

At the same time, Travis said, "I never knew this was here."

Sarah took the ornament from the man and looped the hanger to a tree limb, then reached down for another. *Do not react.*

"*Sarah Loves Travis 4 Ever*," he read. "When did you write this?"

Play dumb.

"Huh?" Could he just let it go?

His smug smile held the wattage of the Luxor xenon light in Las Vegas. "It's carved right here in the tree."

She glowered at him. "You think I'm the only Sarah in town? You were a heartbreaker in your younger days. I bet there's a whole throng of Sarahs that could have climbed this tree and scratched their undying love for you in it."

"Uh-huh." He grinned.

"Why are you smirking?"

"I'm imagining a throng of Sarahs climbing and scratching in unison." He chuckled.

"Just hang some cherubs so we can get this over with."

"Were you in on this flash mob of Sarahs that converged upon the Sweetheart Tree one mysterious night?" he asked. "All intent on scratching my name into the bark with a pocketknife?"

"Okay, all right, I did it. When I was young and dumb and a handsome face easily turned my head, I defaced the Sweetheart Tree. I broke the rules. Happy now?"

His chuckle turned into a hearty ho-ho-ho of laughter. "You love me 4 ever," he teased in a sing-song.

"I do not."

"Hey, it says so right here and we all know if it's written down it must be true."

"Things change."

"You tell me there's no such thing as 4 ever?"

"That's right."

"Aw, I'm so disappointed. Next thing you know you'll be telling me there's no such thing as Santa Claus."

"Please don't rub my nose in this."

"What?" He sounded startled. "I don't mean to shame you. I was just teasing, Sarah."

"You didn't shame me. I shamed myself, but the past is the past, and unfortunately, while I was stupid enough to carve our names in the tree, I'm hoping you'll be big enough to forgive me."

"I think it's sweet," he said, "although I don't know how I'm going to handle it when Jazzy gets to the mad crush stage and doodles some guy's name in the tree. Maybe you can write a book about teenage angst by then and I'll just give it to her to read."

The vulnerable look on his face made up for the teasing. It had to be tough, being a single father. She couldn't imagine it. In spite of herself, she felt her heart soften. The mood between them shifted and the tension drained from her shoulders. She'd built the past up so big in her mind that she hadn't considered she'd been nothing more than a blip on Travis's radar. That was both a relief and a bit of a disappointment.

The workers below kept handing up ornaments to them, and they hung cherubs throughout the branches of the pecan. Pink cherubs and blue cherubs. Cherubs with devilish grins and cherubs with halos. Chubby-cheeked cherubs and thin little angels with their palms pressed in prayer. It was one of the latter that Sarah received next. Almost all the branches were filled with ornaments and as she searched for a spot, her gaze fell upon the wish list written in a familiar childish scrawl. There at the bottom of the list that contained the usual stuff, Sarah read: *I wish for a mommy so my daddy won't have to be all alone when I die.*

She'd seen that handwriting before and she didn't have to turn over the angel to know whose name was printed there, but she took a deep breath, flipped it over anyway.

Jazzy Walker.

Instead of hanging Jazzy's angel from the tree, Sarah slipped it into her pocket. She wanted to be Jazzy's secret Santa. Of course, she couldn't help her with the last wish, but she was going to make sure that little girl got everything else she wanted.

I wish for a mommy so my daddy won't have to be all alone when I die.

Her heart reeled and she looked through the bi-furcation in the pecan tree, saw Travis hanging a cherub of his own. Was Jazzy truly that sick? Did he know that his daughter did not expect to have a future? He looked so happy behind that Santa beard, a big smile on his face, his gray eyes twinkling. He stopped, caught her eye, winked.

Oh, Travis. Sarah couldn't hold his gaze. She looked away with a heavy heart. All this time, she'd been worried what it would be like when she met him again. How she'd react, how she'd don the successful Sadie Cool persona and pretend the humiliation of the past had never happened.

But what she hadn't expected, what completely blindsided her, was the realization this wasn't about her at all. Rather, Travis was simply a single dad with a sick kid who was in way over his head.

It was then that Sarah made peace with her secret shame. When it came down to it, no one really cared that she'd made a fool of herself nine years ago. All that mattered now was Jazzy. She could let the past go, stop living in her own narrow world, and open her eyes to the wondrous blessings of the present moment.

CHAPTER SEVEN

Following her revelation in Sweetheart Park, something shifted inside Sarah. She felt calmer, more at peace, and she didn't even tense up when Raylene and Dotty Mae broke the news that they were off to a meeting of the First Love Cookie Club.

"We start meeting in mid-October," Dotty Mae explained on the way over to the Twilight Bakery where the meetings were held. "And our last meeting is the big cookie swap event the second Friday in December."

"It takes two months to plan for the cookie swap?" Sarah asked.

"Oh, we're about more than the cookie swap." Raylene waved a hand. "We're the driving force behind all the holiday events. We bake and sell all the cookies sold during the Dickens on the Square weekend. We organize and execute the Cherub Tree event. We oversee the annual lighting of the Twilight Christmas tree the week before Christmas and bake the cookies for that as well. You can be sure that any community event you attend in Twilight, we've had our hand in it."

"Wow, you guys got a lot of power."

"Your grandmother did too," Raylene said. "She was one of us."

"And people think we're just little old ladies who knit and quilt and bake cookies." Dotty Mae winked as they walked around the back of the bakery. "If only they knew."

Raylene stepped forward to open the side entrance door. "Welcome to the inner sanctum. Command central."

A blast of delicious aromas wrapped around Sarah, teased her nose, and drew her forward. She paused in the entryway, both as an introvert nervous upon entering an unknown place and as a writer, absorbing the lush sensory experience coming at her.

The fragrance of yeast was the strongest scent. It rolled over her, thick and rich as homebrewed beer. A march of other smells trooped behind— the sharp slice of cinnamon cleaving through the yeasty envelope, the slick slap of butter, the friendly embrace of vanilla. And bringing up the rear, the subtle but undeniable whisper of almond.

Sarah inhaled deeply, swished the scents around inside her nose like a wine connoisseur savoring a bottle of 1982 Château Mouton-Rothschild, letting it linger in her head, felt the texture, sniffed the bouquet, tasted the burst of fragrance, heard the echoes of all the food prepared here with loving hands. In her mind she tasted everything the bakery had to offer; flaky scones and grainy sugar cookies, light but crispy baklava, powdery doughnuts and complicated strudel, sweet soft kolaces and puffy sopaipillas.

And cakes.

Lots of cakes. German chocolate and red velvet, carrot cake and pineapple upside-down cake. Pound cake and angel food cake. Lemon and strawberry and banana cake. It was a cascade of culinary excess and Sarah reveled in it.

Aromatic memories bubbled up inside her, transporting her back to the delights of Gram's kitchen. She could see herself with Gram, baking in that quaint little kitchen, wearing an apron too big for her, standing on a stepstool stirring kismet cookie dough. In that moment, the peace she'd felt in Sweetheart Park crested over her like a breaking wave, drowning her with emotions so strong they contracted her heart.

Feeling so much, so quickly overwhelmed her. She couldn't process the sudden rush of joy mingling with bittersweet sadness that seemed so much like a real homecoming. She stood rooted to the spot, half inside the bakery, and realized everyone was staring at her curiously.

Move, dimwit.

With a determined shake of her head, she threw off the memories, dispelled the emotions, forced a smile, and walked all the way inside.

She'd met most of the women the night before, but it had been sort of a blur and she still hadn't put all the names to faces, and she knew she hadn't met the pale-faced woman in the apron who stood at the bank of ovens with a potholder in her hand. She was younger than everyone else in the group, around thirty, with soft brown hair and even softer brown eyes, and as she moved from one oven to another, Sarah noticed she walked with a limp. Immediately, she felt a twinge of kinship and empathy. One defective woman to another. Lightly, she fingered her abdomen, felt the hard ridges of the scar through the soft material of her sweater.

"Come in, come in." A plump, smiling woman gestured her inside. Sarah recognized her as the person who'd been in charge of the floats during the parade. "I'm Belinda Murphey in case it got forgotten in the haze of yesterday."

"Hello," Sarah said. The shyness she'd battled all her life was back, nipping at her heels. Determinedly, she stiffened her shoulders and muscled through it.

"Have a seat," the woman at the ovens invited. "I'm Christine Noble, by the way, and this is my bakery. Welcome."

The back door clicked shut, sealing off the exit, closing Sarah in. "Thanks," she murmured.

Dipping her head, Sarah took the empty chair closest to the door while Dotty Mae and Raylene flanked her, going for seats of their own. The chair raked across the startlingly white tile floor with an embarrassing squawk.

The other ladies greeted her, reintroducing themselves and telling her how happy they were she'd returned to Twilight.

"I wish Mia was here." Dotty Mae sighed. "I miss her so much." Her gaze met Sarah's. "Your grandmother would have been so proud of you. Writing that beautiful children's story. Honoring her kismet cookie tradition. I hope you know that."

Sarah nodded. She missed her grandmother deeply. She could almost see her sitting at the table, laughing and joking with her friends.

"We all miss Mia something fierce," Marva said. "Your gramma was special."

"She was," Sarah agreed past the lump in her throat.

"But we're so glad you're here. In you, your grandmother lives on." Belinda reached over to pat Sarah's hand.

They made her feel like she belonged, and that scared the hell out of Sarah. Why were they so nice to her? Sure, she was Mia's granddaughter, but Gram had been gone for almost nine years. Twilight had never been her hometown. She had no real connection to these people and yet they acted like she was one of them. What did they want from her?

To settle her nervousness and get back the equanimity that had come over her in Sweetheart Park, Sarah flicked her gaze around the room. It helped to catalogue things. The exercise made her feel more grounded.

The kitchen was largely professional, filled with spotless stainless-steel sinks and appliances, but there were personal touches here and there that hinted at the personality of the owner. An old-fashioned butter churn sat in one corner next to a milking stool decorated with a blue gingham appliqué. In fact, there was lots of gingham around, from the festive red gingham kitchen curtains framing the windows to the green gingham potholder Christine held in her hand.

The antique, sturdy-legged wooden table where they were all sitting was a throwback to the farming days when large families gathered for massive noonday meals. Eight chairs fit comfortably around the table, with plenty of room to accommodate more. The wall just below the ceiling had been hand stenciled with cows and ducks, pigs and chickens, to form a bucolic border. The effect was a comfy, soft-place-to-land feel that Sarah distrusted. The Twilight Bakery felt too happy, too gentle, too cute by half.

"We're just so tickled to have you here," said a tall, muscular woman with cocoa-colored skin and attractive cornrows. "I'm Marva by the way, Marva Bullock."

"I remember you from the party last night." Sarah smiled.

"Did you have a good time?"

"It was very nice, thank you," Sarah said, and prayed no one would bring up the fact that Travis had danced with her and kissed her underneath the mistletoe. Unbidden, she reached up a hand to trace her lips at the memory, but then immediately stopped herself when she realized what she was doing.

Luckily, the women turned back to the conversation they'd apparently been having before Sarah, Raylene, and Dotty Mae had come in.

From the knitting bag Marva had slung across the back of her chair, she pulled a bridal magazine. "I brought the picture of the dress Ashton's bride-to-be picked out," she said to the group and then to Sarah she said, "Ashton's my son. He's getting married in May."

"Is this the dress she's going to trash?" A fifty-something blond who looked a bit like Debbie Reynolds asked with a disapproving note in her voice. "I hate that trend. It's so disrespectful."

"You're just getting old, Patsy," Raylene said. "Face it, this isn't the world you and I grew up in, nor should it be. Things change, keep up or get out of the way."

Patsy narrowed her eyes. "Respect shouldn't be something that goes in and out of fashion."

"I tend to agree with you, Patsy," Marva said. "But Sheniqua is going to be my daughter-in-law and I'm not about to rock the boat on something like this. You've gotta pick your battles. Her mother, who's paying for the dress, is cool with it. Who am I to dissent?"

"I don't know," Patsy said. "It seems like a risk to me."

"Risk?" asked a Latino woman with a short, chic hairdo. She looked like a contestant on a reality show Sarah used to watch. "What are you talking about?"

Patsy wagged her head. "Trash the dress, Terri, trash the marriage."

"That's superstition," Belinda Murphey pointed out.

"Aren't weddings all about superstition?" Patsy reached for a cookie from the communal plate sitting in the middle of the table. "Something old, something new, something borrowed, something blue."

"Trash the dress sounds like fun. I wished they'd done that when I got married." Terri rubbed her palms together and then grabbed a cookie for herself.

"Oh my gosh," Patsy said. "These pecan sandies are scrumptious. Rich and crispy. Who made them?"

Christine raised her hand.

"Well of course you did, you professional baker you. This is the recipe you're making for the cookie swap, right?"

Christine nodded. "Weddings are about taking risks," she said. "And Marva, you're going to make a wonderful mother-in-law. You're fair and balanced in your dealings with people. You're helpful and concerned but not nosy. Sheniqua is a lucky girl whether she knows it or not."

"Thank you, Christine, that's kind of you to say." Marva handed Terri the bride's magazine, a dog-eared page indicating the wedding dress in question.

Terri took a bite of cookie. "These are amazing, Christine." Then she looked at the magazine. "It's Vera Wang. Please tell me she's not going to trash Vera Wang!"

"Who's Vera Wang?" Dotty Mae asked.

"Just the best wedding dress designer who ever lived," Belinda rhapsodized, and spread her arms in an expansive gesture as if trying to hug the entire world. Sarah had seen Oprah Winfrey use a similar gesture on television. Belinda had a zaftig figure and an irresistible smile. Sarah could tell her relationship with food was different from her own struggle. Belinda ate from a hearty zest for life, as if she couldn't get enough. Sarah had overeaten as a way to quiet her emotions, to fill up the emptiness. Nowadays, she sublimated that emptiness with writing. But writer's block threatened to upset the balance she'd struck with food that had kept her at a size eight for over a year. She eyed the cookies in the middle of the table and her stomach grumbled.

"I bet you're getting excited," Terri said to Marva.

"It's nerve-wracking is what it is. I'm just glad I'm the mother of the groom."

Then they were off, talking about weddings and their kids.

Sarah studied the group dynamics like an anthropologist, mentally noting the subtle clues—body language, the words not spoken, the slight shifts in tone of voice—piecing together the history of these women and their relationships as an expert quilter might piece a quit. People fascinated her, even as she stood apart from them. If she could figure them out, then maybe she could understand her own impulses. She glanced around the kitchen, assessing all seven of them.

There was Patsy, the authoritarian and the group's moral compass. If she disagreed with something someone was saying—and from what Sarah could gather that was generally Raylene—she'd raise her brow and look over the top of her reading glasses in a look of domination. She had a tendency to point her index finger in a scolding gesture. Her clothes were no-nonsense: black slacks with classic lines that camouflaged her rounded middle, a white linen long-sleeved shirt, neatly pressed, a Christmas wreath brooch pinned to her collar. Everything about her said this woman was ordered, planned, and structured. When Sarah looked at her, she thought of Martha Stewart. She had the feeling that Patsy excelled at everything she did.

Raylene sat beside Patsy. Travis's aunt was the most colorful one in the bunch. She possessed all the subtlety of a freight train jumping the tracks, but you sure as hell knew where you stood with her. Raylene—as her grandmother had often said—was full of sass and vinegar. Even though she wore her skirts way too short for her age, she had the legs to pull it off. She was blunt as a club, but she made you feel like you were part of the action. Wherever Raylene went, energy flowed. She was opinionated, brash, and fun-loving, and apologized for nothing.

"We're doing too much talking and not enough preparing. Let's get this meeting back on track," Marva fretted, and tugged at her earlobe, an involuntary habit, Sarah noted, she used to reduce anxiety. Was the fact the group had wandered from their appointed agenda worrisome to her? Or was there something else bothering her? Fascinated, Sarah studied the older woman. Beside her chair she had a tote bag stuffed full. Had she once been a Girl Scout and taken their always-be-prepared credo to heart? Or was she simply a natural hoarder, loath to be caught in need. Whatever it was, Sarah had the feeling that if she was stranded on a deserted island, Marva was someone she'd want to have along.

"Were we off track?" Dotty Mae asked. "I hadn't noticed."

"If I didn't keep us in line, we'd forever be off track," Marva said, "but since you go with the flow, you're always happy with wherever we end up."

"Not always," Dotty Mae said, "but I'm not one to grumble."

Dotty Mae had been Gramma Mia's best friend and Sarah knew her better than any of the others. Dotty Mae had a tendency to go whichever way the wind blew. Her cornflower blue eyes had a sweet, faraway look that had nothing to do with her age and everything to do with her easygoing personality. She wore oversized housedresses that gave her a comfy, lived-in look. When the conversations got heated, Dotty Mae would lower her eyelids as if taking in only half the scene to soften the friction. But Dotty Mae was deeper than mere surface appearances. She also had a penchant for peppermint schnapps and clove cigarettes (which she smoked only in secret), and win or lose, she loved playing bingo. To Sarah's knowledge, Gramma Mia had never smoked or gambled, and the only time she'd ever seen her imbibe was when Dotty Mae enticed her with the schnapps.

"Well, speak up if you've got something to say." Raylene lifted her arms over her head for a catlike stretch. "Otherwise you'll get lost in the shuffle."

"Don't I know it," Dotty Mae mumbled under her breath.

"We've got to finalize the menu for our cookie exchange next Friday," Christine said. "We don't want duplicate recipes."

Christine didn't talk much, and from what Sarah gathered from the conversation, she was the only one in the cookie club who was never married.

"We're having so much fun talking, why don't we save the housekeeping stuff until the end of the meeting." Terri possessed a megawatt smile and the fun-loving attitude of someone who was always up for a party. Her sunny disposition showed in her choice of clothes, a bright yellow sweater and white slacks; never mind that it was months past Labor Day, she didn't live her life by outmoded rules.

"Okay," Marva agreed. "Let's get to our other topic of business. Jazzy Walker."

At the mention of Jazzy's name, Sarah sat up straighter and studied the faces of the women in the group.

"Jazzy has made phenomenal improvement on this new drug." Marva reached for a cookie.

"It's a miracle is what it is," Dotty Mae said. "The child is healthier than she's ever been."

"To think she was on death's door for so long, destined to end up like her grandmother." Belinda shook her head. "When I think about it, I want to rush home and hug my babies and make sure they're okay."

Marva finished her cookie and dusted the crumbs from her fingertips. "Anyway, our main concern at this point is keeping Jazzy well."

"Um, not to be obtuse or anything," Sarah ventured, "but why is Jazzy Walker's condition any of your business?"

Seven heads swiveled her way. Seven mouths dropped open. They stared at her as if she'd just committed a felony.

"Sarah Collier," Dotty Mae whispered. "Your Gramma Mia would be so disappointed in you."

Her words stung as surely as if the elderly woman had slapped Sarah. "Wh-what do you mean?"

Dotty Mae clucked her tongue. "You've been in the big city too long. You've lost your humanity, girl."

"There's plenty of humanity in Manhattan," Sarah said defensively. "Small towns don't have a lock on kindness and caring."

"Then why did you ask that question?"

Why indeed? Sarah wished the floor would open up and swallow her whole. "Some people might resent the intrusion into their lives."

"We're not intruding." Belinda looked affronted. "We're helping. Travis needs us. He doesn't have anyone else."

Great, now she was offending everyone. Sarah gulped. She didn't have the social skills to tiptoe out of this one. "Isn't that an assumption on your part? What if he didn't want your help? Travis has a lot of pride."

"Twilight isn't just any town." Dotty Mae's head quivered as she spoke. "It's a community. We help each other here. And Jazzy is Raylene's great-niece. Raylene would pay for her treatment if all her money wasn't tied up in real estate. Her plight is the plight of us all. Jazzy's new medication is expensive and it's not covered by insurance. Travis is going broke trying to keep his girl alive, and we're not going to sit idly by while that happens when we can darn well do something to help."

"You're right," Sarah said quietly. No way was she going to point out that their meddlesome behavior screamed codependency. Who was she to slap a label on them? She wasn't even spending the holidays with her parents. Just because she'd chosen to isolate herself from people didn't make others codependent. Maybe she simply couldn't understand what it was like to have so many people love you so much that you never had to hit potholes in the road of life without someone being there to pick you up and dust you off. Hell, it wasn't like she had *her* head screwed on straight or anything. "I wasn't thinking."

"You know what your trouble is?" Dotty Mae asked. Sarah didn't dare ask what, but Dotty Mae went and told her anyway. "Your problem is that no one ever rallied around you so you don't know what it's like to have a real loving community, do you, poor baby."

On the one hand, Dotty Mae was being a bit patronizing, and that irritated Sarah, but on the other hand, she had to admit the older woman was right. She didn't know what it was like to have friends you could count on for decades. Her relationship with her parents had always been one of cordial distance at best, silent isolation at worse. And the only person who'd ever made her feel like she was truly in Sarah's corner was Gram.

"We're planning a cookie bake sale, proceeds go for Jazzy's treatment. You in?" Raylene asked.

"I'll happily donate money to the cause," Sarah said.

Dotty Mae sighed.

"What?" Sarah raised her palms. Apparently there were hidden emotional land mines all over this bakery.

"Money is all well and good," Dotty Mae said, "but it's not the same as giving of yourself. I know you know how to bake cookies, Sarah Collier. Your Gramma Mia taught you."

"Okay, okay, I'll bake cookies," Sarah said. "Just tell me when and where."

"Right here, right now," Christine said. "It's why I've been heating the ovens."

"Here you go," Belinda said, passing Sarah a blue gingham apron.

The next thing she knew she was elbow-deep in

cookie dough and camaraderie and juicy small-town gossip. And she had to admit she was having more fun than she'd had in a long time. At some point, someone broke out the wine and the stories grew more loquacious, the cookies more delicious. Then somehow the talk had circled back around to Travis. She had to hand it to them. The ladies of the First Love Cookie Club were relentless matchmakers.

"You should have seen Travis after Crystal left him," Belinda said. "It was so touching. He'd be in the grocery store, toting Jazzy on his hip, pushing the cart, stocking up on juice boxes and Fruit Roll-Ups. She'd be wearing dainty little dresses and ankle socks with lace and black patent leather shoes, her blond hair curling in ringlets to her shoulders." Belinda put a palm over her heart. "Here was an ultra-macho guy with angular features and hawk-ish gray eyes, tenderly caring for this delicate child all on his own. My God, now *that's* a hero."

"Especially when you know he used to be such a rapscallion," Patsy added. "When Jazzy was born he completely turned his life around. Too bad the same couldn't be said of Crystal."

"Trust Patsy to use a word like 'rapscallion.'" Raylene rolled her eyes. "Let's call a spade a spade. He was a punk."

"Raylene," Marva scolded, "he's your nephew."

"And who would know better? He was constantly in trouble with the police for some minor infraction or another."

"He was just acting out after losing his mother." Marva leveled Raylene a stern look. "We all make mistakes."

"Honestly, getting Crystal pregnant was the

best thing that ever happened to Travis," Dotty Mae said. "I shudder to think where he'd be now without Jazzy."

"Uh-huh." The entire group nodded in agreement.

Listening to them talk, seeing how moved they were by Travis and his transformation from troubled teen to doting father, struck a chord inside her. Sarah felt a thawing of the creativity that had frozen up so solidly after the success of her first book.

It was a tiny drip at first, like the first rays of spring sunshine warming an icy tundra. But as she thought of the last wish on Jazzy's Cherub Tree ornament and how devoted Travis was to his daughter, a kernel of an idea put down roots and started to grow.

Never mind about the book she was currently struggling to get down on paper. This idea was The One. She could feel it through every cell in her body. It was the same feeling she'd gotten when she was writing *The Magic Christmas Cookie*. As if she were being swept away on a current of creativity she could neither control nor deny. She had to write *this* book and she wanted to start *now*.

"You certainly gave this town something to buzz about for a few months," Belinda was saying.

It took Sarah a minute to pull her attention from inside her head to the women surrounding her. Apparently, they'd been talking to her. Not just to her, but about The Incident. Sarah said nothing, just studiously spooned drop cookie dough onto a baking sheet.

"What was the dumbest thing you ever did over

a guy?" Terri asked the group as she carefully cut out gingerbread people with green and red plastic cookie cutters. Sarah preferred the old-fashioned metal ones with their sharp edges that cut clean.

No one spoke.

"Come on," Terri said. "You're not going to tell me Sarah is the only one who ever did something embarrassing for the love of a guy."

"When I was fourteen, I had a crush on this guy who rode my school bus. B.J. Peterson his name was. He wore a black leather bomber jacket, John Lennon glasses, and scowled a lot. Probably because he was terribly nearsighted, but I thought he was dark and moody broody." Belinda sighed dreamily. "I wanted to talk to him, but I was too chicken, plus he had a girlfriend. I'd call him up whenever I was babysitting just to hear his voice and then I'd hang up. Well, this went on for a couple of months and then one day the police came to our front door. They'd traced the call to the neighbors I was babysitting for and they put two and two together and figured out the calls happened when I was watching their kids. Everyone in school found out about it and they made fun of me for weeks. I lost my babysitting job and moody broody B.J. stopped riding the bus. I prayed the ground would open up and swallow me whole. It was awful."

"Belinda was a stalker, who knew." Terri laughed. "See there, Sarah, you're not the only one."

"I can top that," Marva said.

All eyes swung to Marva, who was painstakingly icing the cooled Santa Claus sugar cookies.

"You?" Raylene said. "The Goody Two-shoes of our bunch?"

"When I first met G.C. he was going steady with

LaDonna Dawson, the prettiest girl in school, who also happened to be a raging bitch. I have no idea what G.C. saw in her."

"Maybe she was good at giving blow jobs," Raylene volunteered.

"Do you always have to say everything that pops into your head?" Patsy scolded.

"I'm just saying . . ." Raylene shrugged. "Hand me that box of raisins, will you, Christine?" Christine handed over the raisins, and Raylene dumped them into the oatmeal batter. "So what happened with LaDonna?"

"This was really bad." Marva said. "I'm sorry for it now."

"What on earth did you do?" Dotty Mae blinked.

"I wrote LaDonna a note, pretending I was Taz Milton, the high school quarterback. Everyone knew LaDonna had a flaming crush on Taz, even G.C. In the note, I told her to meet Taz in the boys' locker room and strip down totally naked. Then I told Taz the coach wanted to see him in the locker room. And finally, I had a friend of mine tell G.C. that LaDonna had a surprise for him in the locker room. Long story short, G.C. caught LaDonna and Taz going at it in the shower stall."

Patsy plastered a hand over her mouth. "Omigod, Marva, that was harsh. Poor G.C."

Marva ducked her chin, covered her face with her palms. "I know, I told y'all it was bad."

"So," Belinda ventured, measuring out two cups of flour. "Did you ever tell G.C. the truth?"

"I came clean right after we started dating."

"And he was cool with it?"

"Well, he broke up with me, but then he realized

that LaDonna was a skank and I'd only done it because I wanted him so badly."

"Belinda was a stalker, Marva was a conniver." Terri rubbed her palms together. "This is getting really juicy. See, all you did, Sarah, was proclaim your love for Travis. Not so bad in the grand scheme of things."

"Well then," Marva said to Terri, "what did you do to embarrass yourself over a guy?"

"Me?" Terri tried to look wide-eyed and naïve. "I was a good girl."

Patsy snorted. "You were just good at covering your tracks."

"What about you, Raylene?" Terri asked. "We know you're bound to have some lusty locker room stories to share."

Raylene, who was usually the first one out with something outrageous, plunked down in a chair and pretended to be engrossed in dusting sprinkles over the sugar cookies. "Y'all've heard my stories before. Nothing new to confess."

"You've been kinda quiet this afternoon," Belinda said. "You feeling okay?"

"Fine." Raylene nodded. "Oh, will you look at the time. We've been here three hours. I'm sure Sarah's anxious to get back to the B&B. She's been on the go since early this morning."

"I am," Sarah said, although she too was wondering why Raylene suddenly seemed anxious to leave. Whatever her reasons, Sarah was grateful. She was ready to get back to the Merry Cherub and start writing the book circling her head.

"Come on, Dotty Mae," Raylene said. "Let's scoot."

CHAPTER EIGHT

After a day of squiring Sarah around town, Raylene was ready to curl up in front of the television with Earl and just veg out. Not that she minded carting Sarah around to fulfill her obligations as honorary mayor; in fact, Raylene had really enjoyed the break in her routine. But she was used to being with her husband twenty-four/seven and to be honest, even after thirty years of marriage, she'd missed the old coot.

Earl left work early on Friday nights, leaving Linc, their main bartender, in charge of the Horny Toad. This time of year, Raylene went to the First Love Cookie Club meetings on Friday evenings, but they were usually over by eight. Raylene had images in her head of curling up with Earl on the living room sofa, popping a big bowl of popcorn, and watching a movie when she got home. Maybe one of the Monty Python classics or perhaps her personal favorite, *A Fish Called Wanda*. That silly flick always tickled her funny bone. Or maybe she'd run by a Red Box and grab a new release.

She'd heard Denzel Washington's latest thriller had just come out on DVD. And Raylene loved Denzel.

Dotty Mae dropped her off after the cookie club meeting; the rattling of her ancient VW echoed throughout Woodbury Estates as she drove away. Raylene stood a moment in the darkness, smelling the rich aroma of Twilight at Christmas. The twang of wood smoke mingling with pine rode the air, and underneath that was the faint scent of the lake.

Icicles lights twinkled from the eaves of her house, changing in colors; first red, then green, then white before starting the sequence all over again. As the sound of Dotty Mae's Beetle died away, Raylene could hear other sounds. The tempestuous Scarpettis arguing next door, the mournful horn of the Burlington Northern train crossing the tracks near the feed and grain stores several miles away, the whisper of wind through the chinaberry trees on her front lawn.

She thought of the cookies she was baking for the cookie swap the following Friday. Spice cookies. The ladies of the club gave their recipes cutesy Christmas names. To rhyme with her last name, she'd dubbed her offering Raylene Pringle's Kris Kringle Spice Cookies, but the recipe had originated with her Swedish great-grandmother. Some members of the cookie club didn't like spice cookies. Too spicy, they said. Well, that's what appealed to Raylene. She liked the exoticness of spices. The tang of far-off lands mixed with plain white sugar and flour brought an extra dimension to the cookies and kept them from being ho-hum plain vanilla. That was her opinion anyway.

Arms crossed over her chest to warm her against the breeze skating in from the lake, she ducked her head and ambled up the back porch steps. She stopped in the kitchen to pour half a glass of red wine, kick off her shoes, and pad into the living room.

Earl lay stretched out on the couch underneath a blue and silver Dallas Cowboys afghan she'd knitted for him. The television was on, tuned to ESPN, and her husband was snoring soundly. But the house was cleaned, the floor freshly vacuumed, the tables dusted. Earl kept a better house than she did.

She stood in the doorway, one shoulder leaning against the wall, and studied him. Earl had a friendly, lived-in face that smiled often, laughed a lot, and angered slowly. He'd gotten a bit paunchy over the years, but he wasn't overweight, and while his hair had slipped off the major part of his forehead, he looked good bald. Not Yul Brynner good, but attractive nonetheless.

Everyone liked Earl. He was the kind of guy who'd not only give you the shirt off his back but his pants and shoes too, if you needed them. He was nonjudgmental. A man you could tell a secret to and no one else would ever find out.

She'd known Earl Pringle since he'd pulled her pigtails on the playground in first grade. He was as much a part of her life as her own siblings had been. Carrying her books home from school, declaring he was going to marry her one day, giving Raylene her first kiss underneath the Sweetheart Tree on Valentine's Day when she was eleven. He was her first boyfriend, her first lover, her first everything. And he was her last, but he hadn't been her one and only.

Raylene took a swallow of wine, hitched in a deep breath, and wandered back forty-one years when she'd just turned eighteen and received the news she'd been selected as a Dallas Cowboys cheerleader. It had been one of the defining moments of her life, and the first person she'd wanted to tell was Earl.

She'd tracked him down where he was stocking shelves at the local mom-and-pop grocery that had long since been replaced with a Super Wal-Mart. She'd been so excited it never occurred to her that Earl wouldn't share her joy.

"I'm happy for you," he said with the woeful face of a kicked puppy.

"You don't look happy."

He'd struggled to smile. "You're gonna leave me. You'll be around professional football players. They've got everything I don't. Money, power, fame."

She'd swatted his shoulder. "Don't be silly. I love you, Earl Pringle, even if you do have the same name as a potato chip. I'm not going to leave you."

But she had.

He'd been right. When those football players had flirted with her, she'd melted like a bee into honeysuckle. She'd hurt Earl. Hurt him badly.

On the television, the program shifted to a prerecorded talk show with Roy Firestone sitting behind a desk musing on the Cowboys' possibility of making it to the playoffs as a wild card team. Their season had been a mixed bag. In Raylene's opinion the Cowboys hadn't been the same since Tom Landry retired.

She took another swallow of wine and almost choked on it when Roy Firestone's guest sauntered on stage. Lance Dugan, former Dallas Cowboys running back, was still drop-dead handsome at sixty-something with his salt and pepper hair and lean, muscular body. Once upon a time, he'd stolen her breath. Now, looking at her ex-husband stole her mellow mood.

Because Raylene had a secret so big that in thirty-six years she'd never told another living soul. It ate at her sometimes, in spite of the carefree attitude she projected. The things she'd done. The lies she'd told to the dear, sweet man sleeping on the sofa. The man she'd loved since she was six years old.

Feeling suddenly blue to the bone, she poured herself another half glass of Merlot and walked to the sliding glass door that led out onto the back patio. She plucked her cell phone off the kitchen table where she'd dropped it when she came in and took it outside with her, along with the glass of wine.

The night air had a slight nip to it, but it wasn't bad since she was wearing a thick Aran sweater she'd knitted for herself when she was pregnant with Earl Junior. She plunked down in the chaise longue and dialed the number of the only friend she was certain would be up at this hour. Patsy had insomnia as bad as Raylene. Damn menopause. They were both fifty-nine. You'd think that crap would be over with by now.

She hit the fifth number on her speed dial, took a swallow of wine along with a big sigh, and looked up at stars sprinkled across the night sky. "Hello, Patsy."

"Um . . . is that you, Raylene?"

"Don't pretend that I woke you. I saw your lights on when we drove past your house."

"No, I wasn't asleep," Patsy said, but she sounded weird.

"You okay?"

"I'm fine. Why?"

"I was just wondering how you were holding up since Jimmy died," she said, referring to Patsy's husband who had recently passed away after a long bout with Alzheimer's.

"It's been almost a year. Why did you really call?"

Why indeed? Mainly because she just wanted to talk but she wasn't about to admit her loneliness to Patsy. "What do you think about Mia's granddaughter?"

"Sarah turned out very pretty."

"I'm not talking about her looks."

"She was always a serious girl."

"Pretty standoffish if you ask me."

"We can't all be as gregarious as you, Ray."

"Is that a jab?"

"Only if you take it as one."

"Why don't you like me?"

"I like you fine."

"No you don't."

Patsy paused.

"You still there?" Raylene took another slug of the wine.

"I'm here. I might not always like you, Raylene, but I always love you. You know more about me than anyone walking the face of the earth today."

"Except for Hondo."

Patsy said nothing.

"Do you think we made a mistake bringing her back to Twilight?"

"You're talking about Sarah?"

"Who else?"

"No, I don't think we made a mistake. Did you see how happy Jazzy was at the parade last night?"

"I saw how Travis kissed her at the party. He's moving way too fast. I never expected him to move this fast."

"Raylene?"

"Yes?"

"Finish your wine and go to bed."

"How did you know—" In the background, Raylene heard a masculine voice murmur something low. "Omigod, you've got a man over."

"I don't," Patsy denied.

"You're lying through your teeth." Raylene sat straight up in the chaise.

"It's the television."

"Oh, don't even try pulling that bullshit on me. Is it Hondo Crouch? Patsy Calloway Cross, do you have the sheriff in your bedroom?"

"I'm hanging up now."

"Yes, you hang up and go make love to Hondo. This reunion has been forty years in the making."

"It's not a reunion it's just—"

"So it *is* Hondo," Raylene crowed. "I knew it. Oh Patsy, I'm so happy for you."

"Put the wine down, Ray, and go to bed."

"Patsy's got a boyfriend."

"This is it, I really am hanging up now. Good night."

Raylene sat there, shivering in the darkness and

drinking her wine. A part of her wanted to go inside, shake her husband's shoulder, wake him up, and tell him what she should have told him thirty-six years ago. But when you'd hidden a secret this long from the one person you loved most in the world, how did you go about revealing it? And if you brought it out into the light, that meant you had to do something about it. She wasn't prepared for that step. Not by a long shot.

Still, she couldn't shake the guilt. Talking with Patsy—who served as Raylene's conscience—hadn't helped. In fact, she felt worse. Her heart ached for the mistake she'd made, for her wrong choices.

She picked up her phone again and punched into the keypad a number she hadn't called in a very long time. A sleepy male voice answered on the fifth ring.

"Hello," she said, "it's me. I hate to call so late, but I've been thinking about the past. It was thirty-six years ago today."

"I know," the man said.

"So tell me, Lance, how is she?"

Sarah's mind churned with a story idea about a little girl with a terminal illness who was given a magical toy soldier just before Christmas by a mystery stranger—an angel actually—who told her that if she just believed strongly enough, then the toy would grant her most heartfelt wish on Christmas Eve.

After Dotty Mae and Raylene dropped her off at the Merry Cherub, she hurried up to her room with a bag of assorted cookies tucked under her arm and went straight to her laptop. The need to write was an urgent, driving force as primal and basic to her as the need for food or sex. She felt that if she didn't write soon, there was a very real possibility she might die. Desperately, hungrily, she kicked off her shoes, curled up in the middle of the bed, and began to work.

Her fingers flew over the keyboard. She could barely keep up with the thoughts, phrases, and images pouring from her head. Jazzy and Travis and the women from the cookie club and the town of Twilight had kicked her muse into high gear.

On and on she wrote, working far into the night, eating cookies and getting swept up into the story playing out like a movie in her mind. Inside her head, Sarah became the little girl she'd named Lillian and called Lily for short. All Lily's emotions welled up in her own heart. Seized by the power of the narrative surging through her like blood through her veins, Sarah tasted heaven far beyond the goodness of the cookies. When she wrote like this she felt completely free. No restraints, no restrictions, just a wild happiness like catching lightning in a jar and illuminating the whole world for one vivid flash of inspiration.

Dawn was peeping through her window when she finished two-thirds of the first draft. She needed more noodling time before she could write the ending. Her process had been like this with *The Magic Christmas Cookie* as well. She hit a wall just before the ending and that's when uncertainty set in.

Time to put it aside and get some rest.

When she woke up, she'd call Benny and tell him

to relax, that this time she would be making her deadline.

Smiling, Sarah turned off her laptop, slipped underneath the covers, and then realized she hadn't checked her itinerary for tomorrow. She got out of bed and crossed the room to retrieve the schedule from her purse. Reading it, she groaned. In three short hours, she was expected to be master of ceremonies for the children's activities including pony rides, jugglers, magic acts, mural painting, and a Scrooge scavenger hunt.

Clearly, the citizens of Twilight expected her to earn that four-figure honorarium.

At five minutes to nine on Saturday morning, Travis waited in line with the rest of the parents at the Piccadilly Circus façade set up in Sweetheart Park. Jazzy was holding on to his hand, wriggling with excitement.

"Settle down, jumping bean," he said tenderly. "You don't want to get the asthma acting up."

"But Daddy," she protested. "I feel grrreat."

"So now you're Tony the Tiger?"

"Yep." She bobbed her head. "I can't wait for the scavenger hunt."

"Maybe you should try something a little less strenuous than running around hunting for treasure. How about mural painting?"

"Treasure hunt, please Daddy. I promise I'll stop if I start getting wheezy."

"But by the time you start getting wheezy it'll be too late."

"I've got my inhaler." She held it up for him to see. Although she hadn't needed it since she'd started on the new drug.

He wanted to tell her no, but how could he refuse a face like that?

Especially when she'd been missing out on the fun for so many years. Who knew how long their luck would hold? He might as well let her have a good time while she could.

"Okay," he conceded, "but the second you feel winded you come and tell me."

"Deal," she said in that jaunty Jazzy way of hers, and held out her hand to shake on it.

Ahead of them in line waited a family of four including a teenage girl who giggled for no discernable reason, while behind them, two college-age guys reeking of beer roughhoused. They were punching each other repeatedly on the upper arms. Once upon a time, he'd been that stupid, but Travis had to wonder why the young men—who were clearly still drunk from a wild Friday night—were hanging out in Sweetheart Park where all the children's activities were being held. Then he saw one of them wink at the teenage girl, who giggled anew, and it all started to make sense.

"Hey," he said sharply to them. "This activity is for kids, beat it."

"Oh yeah?" slurred one of the young Turks. "Says who?"

Travis opened up his jacket and quickly flashed his badge. They didn't have to know it was a game warden badge. "Says me. You're prime for a public intox charge."

The young man held up his palms. "Dude, no offense, we were just hanging out."

"Well, hang out somewhere away from the children. Don't spoil their fun."

The guy shot a lingering look at the teenage girl.

The age difference between them and the girl was about equal to the age difference between Travis and Sarah. What was a huge gap between fifteen and twenty shrank from twenty-four to twenty-nine. What a difference a decade made.

"You're too old for that," Travis chided.

Just then a woman came hurrying up to the makeshift gate set up to cordon off the park for the events. Immediately he recognized that long blond braid and those black stiletto boots.

Sarah.

"Dude." One of the teens nudged his buddy in the ribs with his elbow and eyed Sarah with interest. "Check out the hottie. I call dibs."

"Now you boys are too young for a woman like that," Travis drawled. "I think it's time you went on down the street."

The taller one looked like he was going to challenge Travis, but something in his eyes must have warned the kid off, because he shrugged and said, "Who cares. This is lame anyway."

"Hi Sadie!" Jazzy waved at Sarah.

Sarah, who looked rushed, stopped to smile at his daughter. "Hi, Jazzy, are you here for the Scrooge scavenger hunt?"

"Uh-huh." His daughter bobbed her head. "I wanna win the grand prize."

"What's the grand prize?"

"Four tickets to Six Flags Holiday in the Park."

"I'll keep my fingers crossed for you," Sarah said, and crossed all her fingers.

"Morning," Travis greeted her.

"I've got to go." She gestured toward the platform in the center of Piccadilly Circus. "I'm the master of ceremonies."

He raised a hand, but she'd already turned to trot off. Hmm, had she just given him the bum's rush? She could have at least said hello.

Sarah took her place at the microphone. It was clear she wasn't a natural at public speaking. She read from a script welcoming visitors to the Dickens event and explaining the rules for the scavenger hunt. The participants had their choice of three lists to complete. They could do a nature hunt in the park, a store hunt at the shops on the square, or a photo hunt where they were to have their pictures taken with various people and landmarks around town. They had until three P.M. to return with the items on their lists.

"Which one do you want to do?" he asked Jazzy, hoping she'd go for the nature hunt.

But his daughter knew how to really make memories. "Photo hunt, Daddy, so I can get my picture taken with people."

"Okay," he said. "Go grab us a purple list."

Jazzy went up to the attendant passing out the different colored lists that corresponded with the various hunts and she came back with the items for the photo hunt. The first item on the list read: *Have your photo taken with a local Twilight celebrity.* The participants could choose from Emma Parks, the actress who'd recently married local veterinarian Sam Cheek; Mayor Moe Schebly; Sheriff Hondo Crouch, Vietnam War hero; or author Sadie Cool.

"Sadie's the one we want. C'mon, Daddy." She took his hand and started dragging him toward the stage.

"We have to wait until the hunt officially starts," he said.

Patsy Cross, one of the event organizers, took the microphone from Sarah. "We don't want to make things too easy for you," she said, "so since Miss Cool is one of the items on the photo hunt list, we're going to give her a head start to hide or disguise herself. Don't worry, she can't get too far away. She's restricted to the park and town square area, as are all the people on the photo list. But they can put on costumes, so take a second look at everyone you pass on the streets."

Sarah slipped down off the stage and Travis watched her cross the street and go in through the back door of the Buffalo Nickel, a quaint little curio shop filled with antiques and Texas-themed souvenirs.

"Okay, participants, are you ready?" Patsy asked the crowd.

"Yea!" Jazzy hollered.

"On your mark, get set . . . . go!"

Everyone moved at once, racing off in different directions. Travis grabbed hold of Jazzy's hand so she wouldn't get lost in the stampede.

"Where'd she go, Daddy?"

"She went into the back door of the Buffalo Nickel, but I think I know where we can find her."

"How do you know?"

"Sadie . . . Sarah . . . and I used to be friends when she was just about your age."

Jazzy's eyes widened. "Really? How come you're not friends now?"

"Well . . ." He stalled, trying to think of a way to explain the complicated situation between him and Sarah. He put his hand to his daughter's shoulder, guiding her down the sidewalk. "It's not that we're not friends, it's just, well . . . I'm a bit older than she is, and when you're young it's hard to be friends with someone who's not the same age as you."

"Like me and Mitchell Addison."

Travis peered down at his daughter. "What about you and Mitchell Addison?"

"Well . . . ," she said, mimicking his stalling tactic. "Mitchell has a crush on me, but he's only six and I mean I know I look six, but I'm not and I read on an eighth-grade level and he likes comic books and . . ."

"You like Mitchell too."

"Yeah, but he's just a kid."

Travis smiled.

"He bought me a ring," Jazzy said.

"What?" He was surprised at the protective alarm that went off inside him. She was only eight. No reason to get worried about a kid with a crush on his daughter, but he had a sudden flash forward to the future. Jazzy was blond-haired and blue-eyed and cute as a bug, and friendly, friendly, friendly. Honestly, he'd never thought about what it would be like once she hit puberty. He'd been so focused on just getting through each day. One downside to living in the moment, the future was just around the corner waiting to blindside you.

"Okay, I don't think he really bought it. I think he got it out of one of those claw machines. He loves to play the claw machines at the bowling alley but he tried to give it to me in front of my friends so I had to tell him I didn't like him and didn't want his ring."

"Jasmine Dawn Walker, were you mean to that little boy?"

Jazzy hung her head, toed the dirt. "I tried to tell him gently."

"You hurt his feelings."

"Daddy," Jazzy said miserably, "his bottom lip started trembling. I was scared he was gonna start crying. I didn't know how to handle it."

Travis felt sorry for both his daughter and poor little Mitchell Addison.

"It hurt me too," Jazzy whispered. " 'Cause I really do like him, but I can't be friends with him. Is that how you feel about Sarah?"

"Sort of."

Jazzy cocked her head and looked up at him. "Do you like her?"

"I do."

"But you didn't like her when you were a kid?"

"I did, but it was like you and Mitchell. She was too young for me."

"But she's all grown up now."

Travis nodded. "That she is."

"Well," Jazzy proclaimed, "I like her and I like her book. Now let's go find her and get my picture taken so we can win this scavenger hunt. I've always wanted to go to Holiday in the Park."

Something told Travis that Sarah had slipped from the Buffalo Nickel into Ye Olde Book Nook. His strongest childhood memory of Sarah was that she always had her nose stuck in a book, just like Jazzy. Although he had a feeling that if Jazzy hadn't been sickly, she would have been a lot less bookish. His daughter was a natural extrovert, whereas Sarah was introverted.

"Let's go in here," he said, pushing open the door to the bookstore.

Sarah's book was on display in the center of the store, surrounded by the best-loved books by Charles Dickens set out to take advantage of the festival crowd—*A Christmas Carol, Great Expectations, David Copperfield, The Adventures of Oliver Twist, A Tale of Two Cities*. He'd read them all to Jazzy. *A Tale of Two Cities* was his favorite. He loved the opening line. That pretty well summed up the paradox of his life with a sick daughter. *It was the best of times, it was the worst of times. . .*

But now, with Jazzy looking so radiantly healthy and Sarah back in Twilight, for the moment it felt like the very best of times.

They searched through the book stacks, but didn't come across her. Just when Travis was beginning to think he'd guessed wrong, he saw the tips of a familiar pair of snazzy black pointy-toed boots, peeking out at him from the curtain patterned with a lush tapestry of books that separated the main part of the store from the back room where the overflow was stored.

Travis laid a finger to his lips, took Jazzy by the hand, and pointed at the boots. "That's her," he silently mouthed.

Jazzy stepped forward and pushed aside the curtain.

There sat Sarah in an old but plush overstuffed chair made from the same bookish material as the curtain. In her hand, she held a copy of *A Wrinkle in Time*. Her long caramel-colored braid was pulled forward and it fell fetchingly over one breast. Travis didn't mean to stare, especially not in front of his daughter, but his gaze zeroed in on that breast, shown off so well by the blue fuzzy sweater she wore, the same color as her eyes.

"Gotcha!" Jazzy crowed. "Get out your cell phone, Daddy and snap our picture." Without waiting for an invitation, his gregarious daughter flounced over and plunked herself down in Sarah's lap.

Sarah had a critter-in-the-headlights-on-a-dark-stormy-night look on her face. "Get in here and close the curtain quick before we're mobbed," she said to him.

Travis stepped inside the cozy nook and pulled the curtain closed. Jazzy snaked an arm around Sarah's neck while he got out his cell phone. "Say cheese," his daughter instructed and smiled big.

After he snapped the picture, Travis turned the phone around so he could see what it looked like. There was Jazzy looking as cute as always nestled in Sarah's lap. But what took him by surprise— hell, what took his damn breath—was the tender maternal expression on her face as if she was completely smitten with his child.

"How'd it turn out?" Sarah asked.

"Good." He stuffed the phone back into his pocket; for some odd reason he did not want her to see the photograph.

They were in a cramped little space surrounded by books. He looked in her eyes and she looked back into his and Travis felt the crackle of something he'd never quite felt before. He kept thinking about that kiss he'd given her underneath the mistletoe and how much he wanted to do it again.

"Well," he said.

"Well," Sarah said right back.

He rubbed a palm along the back of his neck and ducked his head. "Guess you're tied up for the day."

"That's my assumption."

He shifted his weight, knowing they should go, but wanting very much to stay here in this quiet cramped little corner that smelled of books and Sarah's airy cologne.

"Was there something else?" she asked.

"Um, no." *Go.* But he just kept standing there.

Jazzy was still in Sarah's lap, thumbing through *A Wrinkle in Time.* She seemed to have forgotten about the scavenger hunt and looked perfectly content to spend the day here.

"Well, we better go hunt down more photographs," he said.

"Photographs. Right."

"We better hurry because . . ." He jerked a thumb over his shoulder. "People are, you know, really competitive about things like this."

She nodded.

Damn, it was easier having a conversation with a Mason jar. Why was he trying so hard?

"I remember this story. It's a good story. Will you read it to me sometime?" Jazzy asked Sarah.

"Sure," Sarah said.

Jazzy snagged Sarah's gaze. "When?"

"When?"

"Yeah, when will you read it to me?"

"Um . . . I don't know."

"How about Christmas Eve? We could make those cookies from *The Magic Christmas Cookie.* You know, the one Isabella and her grandmother make."

"Kismet cookies."

"Yeah, we could make kismet cookies and then you could read *A Wrinkle in Time* to me."

"*A Wrinkle in Time* is a long book, Jazzy," Travis said. "You can't read it in one night. And Sarah's not going to be in town on Christmas Eve. You and I can make Christmas cookies together and we can spend the week between Christmas and New Year's reading *A Wrinkle in Time*."

Disappointment tugged at his daughter's mouth. "Yeah, okay, I guess that will work."

"Maybe we could make kismet cookies another time," Sarah suggested.

Travis's gut tightened and he glanced at Sarah, sending her a message with his stare. *Don't make promises you can't keep.*

Jazzy shook her head and her mouth dipped down sadly. "The kismet cookies only work on Christmas Eve."

"You know the kismet cookies are only a fairy tale," Sarah said gently. "Right?"

Jazzy looked like Sarah had just told her there was no such thing as Santa Claus. "Yeah, sure, I knew that. I just thought it would be fun . . . you know . . . pretending it was true."

This wasn't good. Jazzy liked Sarah way too much. The last thing he wanted was for his daughter to get hurt. He put his hand to Jazzy's shoulder. "We gotta get going, kid."

"Okay." Jazzy hopped up.

Travis drew back the curtain, looked out to see a mob of people rummaging through the store.

"Oh look," a woman shouted. "There's Sadie Cool."

"Now I know what a deer feels like in hunting season," Sarah muttered.

The next thing Travis knew, a herd of photo-seeking treasure hunters were muscling him and Jazzy out of the room.

"Wow," Jazzy said. "I guess we were just standing in her way."

Out of the mouths of babes, Travis thought, and guided his daughter from the bookstore.

CHAPTER NINE

Thankfully, Sarah's duties as honorary mayor ended on Sunday evening along with Dickens on the Square. But even as she was happy to be off the hot seat, she had to admit she felt wistful watching workers tear down the little kiosks and sweep up the scattered debris. The fantasy of Victorian-era England was gone with the whisk of a few brooms, the knocking down of a few boards. How easy it was to dismantle a fantasy.

From the window of her room at the Merry Cherub Sarah could see the east side of the square. She sat at in the window seat with her notebook computer in her lap, watching Twilight transform itself as she wrote. The town was a chameleon, she had to give it that. Changing with the seasons and the holidays, donning whatever persona helped reel in tourists.

From Monday until the First Love Cookie Club cookie swap on Friday, her schedule was finally her own again. She could relax and stay holed up in her room and drink the delicious raspberry green tea Jenny brewed, and write. Solitude. It was Sarah's idea of paradise.

To her delight, the book continued to flow like water, ideas pouring from her. She still didn't have an ending, but she was confident it would come.

Besides the writing, there was another project that required her attention. The wish list on the back of Jazzy's angel ornament that she plucked from the Cherub Tree. She went shopping and got everything Jazzy had wished for, except, of course, the part about a mommy for her daddy. Only Travis could supply his daughter with a new mother. Because she wouldn't be there for Christmas, Sarah planned to wrap the packages and leave them with one of the First Love Cookie Club members to distribute with the other cherub gifts.

Sarah had to admit that Jazzy had burrowed under her skin and made a home there in the way no one else ever had. She didn't make friends easy and she normally wasn't comfortable around kids, but there was something about this little girl. It was in Jazzy's sweet smile. As if she perpetually expected sunshine and rainbows and spring flowers.

On Wednesday evening, after spending the entire day writing, Sarah had planned on grabbing takeout from the Funny Farm restaurant on the square and bringing it back to her room as she'd done the previous two nights. She'd finally gotten out of her pajamas—which she'd been in all day, a luxury afforded to writers—braided up her hair, and then pulled on a pair of jeans, a red sweater, and her black high-heeled boots. In Manhattan she wouldn't have bothered with makeup just to go pick up takeout, but in Twilight she was bound to run into someone she knew and she had her Sadie Cool image to uphold. In concession, she put on lipstick and mascara, and then shrugged into a jacket.

She went downstairs and just as she entered the lobby, Travis and Jazzy walked in, the jingle bells attached to the front door jangling merrily. Jazzy's hand clung to her dad's.

"Hello," Travis greeted her. "Just the woman we came to see. Jazzy has something to ask you."

Jazzy stepped forward, looking like a pint-sized seraphim in a green and white velvet dress, and black patent leather Mary Janes, her hair falling in perfect ringlets to her shoulder. Her skin was alabaster, her lips and cheeks strawberry red. All she needed to complete the angelic image were wings and a halo. "Can you come to the Christmas pageant with us at our church tonight?"

"If you don't have other plans that is," Travis amended. "It's only an hour long and we can grab a bite afterward at Pasta Pappa's."

"They got really good pepperoni pizza," Jazzy added.

Sarah hadn't been to a church Christmas pageant since . . . well, since Gramma Mia had taken her all those years ago.

"We understand if you're too busy." Travis put his palm to Jazzy's back. "I know we sprung this on you at the last minute—"

"Please come," Jazzy pleaded.

How could anyone say no to a face like that? Sarah said, "I'd love to."

"Thank you." Travis met her gaze.

"Well, c'mon then." Jazzy reached up and took

Sarah's hand and started trolling her toward the door.

Sarah threw Travis a helpless look.

"She's a force of nature." Travis laughed and scooted around to open the door for them. "My daughter."

Sarah's shoulder brushed softly against his as she went past. Instant warmth seeped through her body and she quickly turned away before he could see the attraction she still felt for him etched on her face.

Still felt?

Who was she kidding? This surge of desire was ten times stronger than what she'd felt for him as a teenager. Back then, all that had been involved was her silly, infatuated heart. But now, all grown up, the sexual chemistry blew her away.

So what? She was going back to Manhattan on Sunday and he had a life here with his daughter. It wasn't as if anything could happen between them. *Unless. . .*

No. She was *not* going to have a one-night stand with him. That was totally out of the question. Because she feared one night with Travis would never ever be enough and she didn't have the mental energy to deal with having her heart broken again.

They walked the short distance to the First Presbyterian Church of Twilight. The evening air was crisp, but not cold. Christmas lights twinkled from almost every storefront and house they passed. As a tourist town, Twilight had a warm image to uphold. All visitors welcome. In spite of her natural cynicism, she succumbed to the whimsy of it, breathing in the scents wafting from the businesses on the square—fresh-baked bread, simmering cinnamon potpourri, pumpkin pie. If Twilight was a taste, it'd be a richly layered strudel, as sinful and sweet as gossiping at an old-fashioned coffee klatch.

People were piling into the church. Most smiled and waved. Several said hello.

When Sarah looked up at the regal one-hundred-year-old building, she hesitated. Nine years ago she'd rushed up these same steps, hell-bent on stopping a wedding by declaring her love to Travis Walker. She felt the old flush of embarrassment well up inside her and she balled her hands into fists at her sides.

Travis's hand went to her upper back, the heat from his fingers leeching through her light jacket. He bent his head to her ear, and she could smell the intoxicating scent of him, all masculinity and zesty soap. "You've got nothing to be ashamed of."

She resisted his comfort, stiffened her back. It was like he was tromping around inside her brain and knew exactly what she was thinking. She didn't like that. It felt too personal. Too intimate.

He got the hint, moved his hand, and then she wished it was back. Oh, what the hell was wrong with her?

"C'mon." Jazzy, completely unaware of her past trauma with this particular building, reached down to grasp one of Sarah's clenched fists. "Don't be a slowpoke."

Sarah glanced at Travis.

He shrugged.

"Force of nature," they said in unison, and laughed.

It felt good to laugh with him. Good and strange. Very strange. It seemed as if she'd stepped into one of the fantasies of her fifteen-year-old self. She and Travis going to the church pageant with their adorable little daughter.

You're not a couple and Jazzy isn't your daughter and hell . . . you don't even want to go there, so why are you?

The blond force of nature didn't give her much time to dither. Jazzy hauled Sarah up the steps and through the front door. "Hurry, hurry, we want to make sure we get good seats up front. If you don't hurry you have to sit in the back and then you can't see the costumes very well. I like seeing the costumes up close. The costumes are the best part."

"What can I say? My daughter loves dress-up."

With Jazzy in the lead, they almost raced to the front of the church and managed to snag the three remaining seats in the front row. "Was this perfect or what?" Jazzy asked. "Three of us, three seats left."

"Pretty perfect," Travis said.

"It's like they knew we were coming." Jazzy smiled, clearly satisfied, and leaned against the back of the pew.

Sarah saw the expression that crossed Travis's face whenever he looked at his daughter. It was pure, unadulterated love.

"You don't know how amazing this is," he said. "A few months ago she couldn't walk across the room without wheezing and that's the way it's been for four years. Until this new miracle drug." He shook his head. "I'm still stunned at her transformation. She's making up for lost time."

"I'm so happy for her," Sarah said. "She deserves the very best the world has to offer. And for you. There's no way I can begin to imagine what you've gone through."

Travis rested his arm on the back of the seat in a casual gesture. He was so easy with his own body, so comfortable around other people. Did it mean anything special? Or was he simply stretching out? Why did she have to analyze everything to death and drive herself crazy?

After a moment, he leaned in closer and whispered, "Don't look now, but we're being watched."

"Don't tell me not to look now. Now I have to look precisely because you told me not to. Don't you know how this works?"

"Apparently not." He grinned.

"You roused my curiosity. I have to satisfy it or go mad."

"Okay then, go ahead and look now."

"What a minute." She canted her head. "Is this a trick to get me not to look now? You know, reverse psychology?"

"What do you think?"

"I think so." Sarah turned to glance over her shoulder. Practically the entire congregation was staring at them. Bug-under-a-microscope staring. Ulp. They should have sat in the back.

"Yipes." She turned back around. "I see why you said not to look."

"Told ya."

"This is a lot of pressure. I can feel them all breathing. Staring and breathing."

"The play will be starting soon, don't think about it."

"There you go again, telling me what not to do. Now I'll have to—"

"Think about it," he finished for her.

"Right."

"It's okay."

"It's not. They're staring and drawing conclusions and judging," she whispered.

"It's the downside of small-town living. Everything you do is gossip fodder."

"They're going to read more into this than there is."

"Granted."

"They're probably already starting to write the legend of Travis and Sarah as we speak."

"We'll be right up there with Jon Grant and Rebekka Nash."

"You think?"

"Famous author rekindles spark with devastatingly handsome single dad?" he teased. "Oh yeah, this is the stuff of serious legends."

"Rekindles? There's no rekindling going on. Something has to be kindled in the first place before there can be rekindling."

"You're nervous."

"Hell—" Sarah shot a glance at Jazzy. "Heck yes," she amended.

"You talk a lot when you're nervous. Mostly, you're pretty quiet, but when you're nervous—"

"I babble. Got it. Nervous babbler. That's me." If she kept babbling maybe he'd stop talking about their gossip-worthiness as a couple. Because they weren't a couple. They were just sitting next to each other at a church pageant. That was it. Nothing else involved.

"I'll remember to make you nervous the next time you clam up." He said it like there were going to be lots of next times. Like she wasn't leaving for home in four short days.

"Shhh." Jazzy placed an index finger over her lips. "They're getting ready to start."

The crowd was still sifting in, but everyone grew quiet as the curtains parted and the play began. Sarah tried to concentrate on the Christmas story, but she was distracted by the pressure of Travis's forearm against her shoulders and his crisp clean fragrance. The guy smelled entirely too good. An intriguing combination of outdoorsy pine and the fresh-laundered aroma of fabric softener. Not to mention there was the not so small fact that his muscular thigh was pressed right up against hers.

She darted a glance over at him. Both his hands were on his knees, his fingers splayed loosely. Everything about him was loose. His ubiquitous smile (at some time she was going to have to ask him how a guy with as many troubles as he had could smile so much), his hair that was just a tad past the point of needing a trim and draped casually over his forehead, his slow, natural breathing. He was a walking antidote to her own tense, rigid way of being in the world. How did a person get so relaxed without pharmaceuticals? She supposed you had to be born that way. Able to see the moon and stars and rainbows and sunshine while ignoring the potholes and litter and brambles and sharp poky pebbles underfoot. Or maybe he was on pharmaceuticals. Maybe SAM-e was the key to his effervescence.

"You still up for pizza?" Travis asked when the play was finished and the crowd filtered out.

"Um, maybe we shouldn't add fuel to the gossip mill."

"Ah, who cares? It's only gossip. We've come this far. What's a meal and another hour? The only question is, are you hungry?"

Sarah was about to say no, to beg off, but then her stomach growled loud enough to wake the dead six counties over.

Jazzy burst out laughing. "She's starving, Daddy."

And that settled that.

One minute she was at the church planning her escape back to her room, and the next minute she was sitting at a booth at Pasta Pappa's, the table clad with the traditional red and white checkered tablecloth.

The place was a total cliché in Italian decor, right down to Dean Martin on the jukebox singing "That's Amore" and the candle in the Chianti bottle in the middle of the table. But the air smelled deliciously of garlic and onions and basil. And the pizza, when it appeared, was warm and gooey with generous portions of mozzarella cheese. They drank Coca-Cola from red and white glasses with red and white straws and noshed on pepperoni pizza while Dino sang about love, and damn if it didn't feel like a *Lady and the Tramp* moment.

"What's your favorite candy?" Jazzy asked around a mouthful of pizza.

Travis tapped his mouth with three fingers. "What's good manners?"

Jazzy swallowed. "Not talkin' with your mouth full. Sorry."

"Hmm, what's my favorite candy?" Sarah mused. "Let me think on that. There's so many good ones."

"Mine's Reese's Pieces. Chocolate on the outside, peanut butter on the inside. Yum." Jazzy rubbed her tummy.

"How about Reese's peanut butter cups?"

Jazzy canted her head as if this was a matter for very serious discourse. "I like them, but they're just not as good as Reese's Pieces. Reese's Pieces are crunchy."

"I get what you're saying."

"So have you thought about it? Do you know what your favorite candy is? Daddy's favorite candy is Tootsie Pops, right, Daddy?"

"That's right." Travis nodded.

"Tell Sarah how come they're your favorite."

His eyes met Sarah's across the table. "They're hard on the outside and while that might throw some people, I like how you have to lick and lick and lick to get to the soft, chewy Tootsie Roll in the middle. It's two different candies in one."

Sarah had the strangest feeling he wasn't talking about Tootsie Pops. "You know, I've always had a weakness for Tootsie Pops myself," she confessed, and wondered if it had anything to do with the time he cut across her grandmother's front lawn after coming back from the grocery store, pulled a cherry Tootsie Pop from the sack he was carrying, and tossed it to her and said, "Here you go, squirt."

"You know what we should do?" Jazzy asked.

"I'm getting an inkling," Travis said.

"What's that?" Jazzy feigned innocence.

"It means you're dropping hints."

"Who me?"

He ruffled his daughter's hair. "You want to go by the Candy Bin on the way home."

"Well, now that you suggested it," she said, "I think that's an excellent idea, Daddy."

Travis's eyes met Sarah. He cupped one hand around his ear. "Hear that?"

"What?"

"That's the sound of me being wrapped tightly around someone's pinkie finger."

"She's a master charmer." Sarah grinned. "Takes after her father. I've heard payback is wickedly just."

"Does this mean we're going to the Candy Bin?" Jazzy asked.

Travis gave his daughter a rueful smile. "Was there ever any doubt?"

They walked from Pasta Pappa's to the Candy Bin, which was right across the street, and picked out their selections. Reese's Pieces for Jazzy, a grape Tootsie Pop for Travis, a cherry one for Sarah.

The walk back to the Merry Cherub was a quiet one. Jazzy was intent on Reese's Pieces and Sarah was no longer so nervous that she felt the need to babble. The clock in the courthouse chimed nine times. When they reached the porch of the Merry Cherub, Travis stopped on the bottom step.

"This was fun," he said.

"Even if we jump-started grapevine gossip?"

"I'm not worried about my reputation," he said. "Are you?"

"No. I had a nice time."

They stood looking at each other, Jazzy happily humming "Santa Claus Is Coming to Town." And the moment felt completely and utterly perfect. It was so perfect, in fact, a hard knot of longing lodged itself tight against Sarah's rib cage.

"Well," Travis said. "Good night."

"Good night." Sarah raised a palm and leaned her head against the porch column, and as she watched them walk away she couldn't help thinking it was the best date she'd ever had.

"Daddy?"

Travis kept his hand at her back, feeling the steady rise and fall of her breathing, reassuring himself that the exertion wasn't too much for her as they walked home. "Uh-huh, sweetheart?"

"How come Sarah has two names? I thought she was Sadie Cool?"

"One name is her real name," he explained. "The other is a pseudonym."

"What's a . . . pseudonym?" Jazzy said the word slowly, trying it out on her tongue.

"It's a name that people like writers or actors take for their public image."

Jazzy wrinkled her nose. "So it's a fake name?"

"I suppose that's one way to look at it."

"But isn't that lying? If you say it's your name, but it's not really your name?"

"No, it's a business name. Like the people who run the Candy Bin are named Hollister."

"Yeah, but the Candy Bin isn't a person's name."

"But you can have a person's name for a business name like Sarah does."

"Why doesn't she just use Sarah as her business name? It's a pretty name."

"For privacy reasons I imagine."

"What does that mean?"

"So if people go looking for her, they can't find her."

"She doesn't want to be found?"

"Not by bad people."

Jazzy turned her head to look up at him, alarm written on her face. "Bad people are after her?"

Why had he said that? It was a stupid thing to have said. "No, no, I didn't mean that. Not bad people . . . just, well . . . sometimes when someone is famous like Sarah is, there are other people who want to be around them all the time and the famous people don't even really know them and wish they'd go away."

"Oh, like Sarah was hiding from people at the scavenger hunt?"

"Yes, like that."

"Sarah doesn't like being famous?"

Travis paused, considering it. "No, I don't think she does. She's the kind of person who enjoys being by herself a lot."

"Like Mommy?"

Travis snorted. That's what Crystal had told Jazzy when she'd left. That she just needed to be by herself for a while. Well, four years was a long-ass while. "Did you eat all those Reese's Pieces already?" he asked, trying for the misdirect.

"Yep." She grinned up at him. "You know, if I was famous, I would never hide from people. I like people. Even the weird ones."

"I know you do, sweetheart. And they all like you."

"Except for Mommy. She didn't like being around me."

"No!" Travis said. Jazzy looked startled, and he realized he'd spoken too sharply and lowered his voice. "Mommy loves you very, very much. She just wasn't ready to be a mommy."

"But you were ready to be a daddy."

"Yes, I was very, very ready to be your daddy."

"How come you were ready and Mommy wasn't?"

"People are different, Jazzy, that's all. Not everyone is alike."

They were walking up Lakeshore Drive now and the wind coming off the lake was chilly. He should have brought the car. Why hadn't he brought the car? Jazzy might be doing well right now but something as slight as a cool breeze could cause her to start coughing. He stopped, crouched down. "C'mere."

"What is it, Daddy?"

"Let's do your coat up tight and tie the hood under your chin. We don't want you catching cold."

"I'm fine." When she moved her head, the all-weather material of her pink and blue car coat made a swishing sound.

"Indulge your old dad, okay?"

"You're not old." Jazzy giggled as he pulled the zipper all the way to the top of her throat and secured the hood under her chin with the pink tie string.

"Thanks for that." He kissed the tip of her nose and she giggled again.

They arrived at the house a few minutes later. Jazzy took a bath and got ready for bed, then he came into her bedroom to perform the ritual he performed every night—reading his daughter a bedtime story before tucking her in. Tonight, she asked for *The Magic Christmas Cookie*. Travis had read it so many times he knew it verbatim. He recited the story of a lonely little girl who wished on a magic Christmas cookie for a family of her own and got whisked away to the North Pole by a beautiful golden sleigh. Once there she found the love and happiness she'd always been searching for with Santa and Mrs. Claus and all the elves.

When the story was finished, he tucked the covers around Jazzy, gave her a good-night kiss on the forehead, and got up.

"Daddy?"

He paused at the door, his hand on the light switch. "Uh-huh?"

"Do you think maybe Sarah is ready to be a mommy?"

CHAPTER TEN

Do you think maybe Sarah is ready to be a mommy?

Jazzy's question ate at Travis as he got ready for bed. He'd hemmed, he'd hawed, he'd hedged, and finally he'd just told her good night and turned off the light without really answering her question.

It wasn't the answer to the question that bothered him so much. Honestly, he had no idea if Sarah was ready for marriage and motherhood. He barely knew the woman. Yes, he'd known her years ago, but to him she'd just been the kid next door, although to her, he'd clearly been her adolescent fantasy. But he was a different person now and so was she.

No, what troubled him about Jazzy's question was the implication that his daughter saw her as mommy material. Not just that, but he could tell she was charmed by Sarah. Jazzy fell in love with people quickly and absolutely, and he was scared she'd fall in love with Sarah only to have Sarah go back to New York, leaving her just as Crystal did.

He didn't blame Sarah, of course. She couldn't help it that Jazzy was enamored. No, he blamed himself. He was the one who hadn't seen this coming. He shouldn't have invited Sarah to the Christmas pageant. Shouldn't have taken her to eat pizza at Pasta Pappa's or for Tootsie Pops at the Candy Bin. And he shouldn't be feeling the things he was feeling for her. He was physically attracted to her, big time. Plus they had fun together. He enjoyed her quick-witted banter, and obviously Jazzy had picked up on that. But his job was to protect his daughter, and exposing her to Sarah on more than a superficial basis had been a huge mistake.

Sarah was only in town until Sunday. All he had to do was get through the pajama party at the bookstore on Saturday night and then he'd be home free. Until then, he'd do his best to just stay out of her way.

It was only a few more days. How hard could it be?

The First Love Cookie Club started their annual Christmas cookie swap at three in the afternoon and the party usually went on until nine or ten at night. Over the years, they'd learned if they started the party at six or seven, then everyone would linger until the wee hours of the morning, so they hit on the idea of starting in the afternoon and it had worked so well, they'd adopted it as their ritual.

Or rather that's what Christine told Sarah when she arrived at Christine's house at two fifty-five with the peppermint cookies she'd baked in Jenny's kitchen at the Merry Cherub. The cookies were wrapped up in a cheery blue box decorated with snowflakes. Jenny had made the box for her when she realized Sarah intended on simply using a paper plate and plastic wrap.

"Oh my, those smell delicious," said Belinda, coming up the sidewalk behind Sarah. She wore a blue denim skirt and a thick Santa Claus sweater with a blue jean jacket over it, and she carried a huge festive holiday tin featuring Santa's elves at a bowling alley.

"So do yours," Sarah said, catching a whiff of cream cheese and apricots.

"They're Winter Wonder Land Cookies. My great-grandmother's recipe. Aren't family traditions wonderful?"

Christine ushered them into the foyer, took their jackets, and hung them on the coatrack beside the door. From where she stood, Sarah could see into the living room. A large, fresh-cut pine tree sat in front of the window, tastefully decorated with red and white lights, candy canes, and red and white cooking-themed ornaments. There was a tiny red stand mixer, a Tom Thumb–sized carton of eggs, Mrs. Santa in an apron holding a platter of cookies, a curtsying gingerbread woman, and a red and white refrigerator with the door standing open and a little light inside.

The furniture was French provincial, the main color scheme sage green and eggshell with yellow accents. A big orange Maine Coon cat lay curled up in front of the gas fireplace. From the music system the sound of Bing Crosby crooning "White Christmas" sent Sarah rocketing back to a childhood memory she'd all but forgotten. In that moment she was thirteen again on the cusp of womanhood, but still excited by Christmas.

She was at Gram's and her parents were supposed to arrive that Christmas Eve. She hadn't seen them since Thanksgiving holidays and she was anxious to tell them about the straight A's she'd gotten in English. The cookies were baked, the presents she'd picked out for her parents and wrapped herself were tucked under the tree. And then they'd called at the last minute. Hospital emergency. They weren't going to make it to Twilight for Christmas.

Gram had been more upset than Sarah. "I'm proud of my daughter," she'd said. "She came from working-class people who were lucky to graduate high school and she studied hard and pulled herself up by her bootstraps and became a heart surgeon. But she doesn't know the first thing about being a mother. And on that score, I'm ashamed of her. She's got something missing. Helen just doesn't have the maternal gene."

Sarah had pretended not to care as she stared at the packages underneath the tree. She'd withdrawn inside her head and started telling herself a story about a magical place where parents never stood their kids up on Christmas. Finally, when they had shown up two days later, they'd given Sarah a suture kit, a microscope, and a certificate of deposit with the money in it earmarked for medical school. What she'd wanted and specifically asked for was *Harry Potter and the Sorcerer's Stone*, a CD by the Backstreet Boys, and a Mickey Mouse watch. She'd gotten none of those things.

Gram had picked up the wrapping paper off the

living room floor, looked at Sarah's unhappy face, and muttered, "She doesn't have a clue."

"Sarah?"

She blinked, realized Christine had been saying something to her. "Yes?"

"Come on into the kitchen. Would you like red wine, white wine, or eggnog, or would you prefer something nonalcoholic?"

She didn't normally drink at this hour of the day. In all honesty, she rarely drank alcohol at all, but a cup of eggnog or a glass of wine might help her relax a bit. Benny was always telling her she needed to let her hair down once in a while and enjoy herself. The thing was, she found it hard to relax when she had to be "on" socially.

"Eggnog sounds nice," she said, trailing Christine into the kitchen.

Belinda had bustled in ahead of them and started laying out her cookies on the sideboard already laden with various nibbles. Artisanal cheeses—Stilton, Garroxta, Brie, smoked Gouda. Elegant crackers—sesame, pumpkin seed, cracked black pepper. Crudités—celery, carrots, cucumbers sliced long, cauliflower, and broccoli spears. Dips—hummus, French onion, black bean, avocado. Unexpected to find such a chic spread in a small country town.

The centerpiece was a floral mix of white and red poinsettias surrounded by sprigs of holly. Twinkle lights were strung around the inside of the windows, and on the kitchen counter, vanilla-scented candles flickered. In a silver tin beside the candles, several dozen iced sugar cookies lay nestled.

It was all so nice it made Sarah's head hurt.

The doorbell rang and Christine went off to answer it. A minute later she came back with Raylene, Patsy, and Dotty Mae, carrying bags and packages. All three wore Christmassy outfits. Dotty Mae was dressed in a green crushed velvet pantsuit so much like something Gram would have worn it made Sarah nostalgic. Raylene had on one of her infamous short skirts (today it was red leather), topped with a white silk blouse under a holiday-themed knitted sweater vest. Patsy wore a sparkly burgundy top over tailored black slacks, with a diamond-studded snowman brooch pinned to her collar.

"Y'all ready to party?" Raylene asked and held up a bottle of peppermint schnapps.

"Marva and Terri aren't here yet," Christine said, but just then there was a knock on the back French doors.

Sarah looked over to see Marva and Terri standing on the patio.

"Gang's all here," Dotty Mae said.

Christine waved them in.

The French doors opened and Marva and Terri popped inside. Terri carried brightly colored, lunch-sized paper bags with handles and a clear plastic case stuffed with art supplies—green and red glitter, bottles of Elmer's glue, pipe cleaners, construction paper. The wind scooted in with them, blowing autumn leaves, now crunchy and brown, over the threshold.

"Get back," Terri said, and kicked the leaves back onto the patio. "You're not invited."

"What's with the art supplies?" Patsy asked Terri.

"Vivian asked me if I'd decorate bags for the party favors for the PJ party tomorrow night at the Book Nook. Gerald is so excited. He can't wait to wear his new Spider-Man pajamas in public."

"Who's Gerald?" Sarah asked Christine.

"Terri's four-year-old son. He's cute as a button, but be forewarned, he's hell on wheels," Christine whispered. "You'll see for yourself tomorrow at the pajama party."

"And you brought these paper bags to our party why?" Raylene eyed the art supplies with disdain.

Terri smiled brightly. "I figured if we got bored—"

"Honey, I'm gonna be drinkin', you don't want me anywhere near scissors," Raylene said. "Speaking of which, hook me up with some eggnog, Christine."

Everyone laughed and dived into the drinks and food.

On the island counter in the center of the kitchen, Christine had busily arranged the cookie selection. Eight different types, eight dozen apiece—Raylene's spice cookies and Christine's pecan sandies and Sarah's peppermint cookies and Dotty Mae's fudge cookies and Patsy's thumbprint cookies and Belinda's cream cheese and apricot cookies and Terri's molasses cookies and Marva's lemon squares. It was a kaleidoscope of smells and colors and textures. An embarrassment of riches.

Food porn, Sarah thought, and then she noticed what was missing. No kismet cookies. No one had made her grandmother's recipe. Out of respect? Or because they thought Sarah was going to make them? She'd thought about it, but she hadn't had the heart.

Once they were all seated around the room Christine picked up a little silver bell and shook it to produce a melodious tinkling sound. "Okay," she said. "Who wants to go first?"

"Go first?" Sarah raised an eyebrow.

"It's a tradition at the First Love Cookie Club for the members to tell stories about their first loves—both with cookies and with romance," Belinda explained. "So at every cookie swap each December, we all tell a story about our first loves. And it's got to be something we've never told before."

Sarah shifted uncomfortably. She didn't want to talk about her first love. Not to a roomful of people she barely knew. Especially a roomful of small-town people who liked to swap stories.

"Since I've never had a first love," Christine said, "I'll go first just to get us started and talk about the first time I realized the healing power of cookies."

"Do tell." Terri crunched a celery stalk loaded down with red pepper hummus.

"It was just after the accident." She waved at her leg. "And the doctors had told my parents I would probably never walk again, much less run track. My dreams of Olympics glory were over. And Marva here . . ."—she paused to smile at Marva—"who was my math teacher at the time, came to see me in the hospital. She baked me a batch of cookies to cheer me up. I was sobbing my heart out because the only thing I'd ever wanted to be was an Olympic sprinter. Marva told me to stop feeling sorry for myself, that there were plenty of people much worse off than I was and if I couldn't run anymore, I needed to find something else I loved just as much to take the place of running."

Everyone swung her gaze to Marva.

Marva looked humble. "It wasn't me. It was all you, Christine. I just pried your eyes open a bit."

"That wasn't all. After you left, I bit into one of those cookies and it tasted like heaven in my mouth. Butterscotch pecan, I remember it so clearly. Those cookies made me feel better. You put your love and concern for me into those cookies and it transformed me. Knowing that I could bake cookies like that and put all my love and devotion into them and now look where I am . . ." Christine swung her arms expansively, a beatific glow on her face. "Owning my own bakery, serving the community every day with my personal expression of love. I've forgotten all about running, but I damn sure walked again."

"Um . . ." Marva said, "I don't suppose this is the time to tell you those cookies were store-bought?"

"What?" Christine exclaimed.

Marva laughed. "I'm kidding."

"Oh whew." Christine pantomimed wiping sweat from her forehead. "And here I was thinking my whole career was based on a lie."

They all laughed then, the room filling up with the sounds of their pleasure.

"So who's next?" Christine asked.

"I'll go," Terri offered. "Did I ever tell you guys about the first time Ted kissed me?"

Everyone shook her head and Terri was off, talking about how Ted had kissed her underneath the bleachers after her team won the regional soccer tournament.

"Ooh," Belinda said. "First kisses from our first love. That'll be this year's theme."

The stories continued, and Sarah knew they'd soon get around to her. But she didn't want to play the game. Didn't want to admit that she'd been kissed by her first love just last week under the mistletoe at the Horny Toad.

Sarah sat watching it all unfold, the detached observer, not part of them, but feeling the warmth like a fringe dweller sitting on the outskirts of a campfire. In fact, she was sitting closest to the exit, a bit apart from the rest, a visitor to this fine world. That lonely, distant feeling she often felt in a room crowded with people pushed at her. Pushed her back, pushed her away, until it felt as if she was standing in the corner all by herself. Everyone else was laughing and talking and eating.

And as usual, she was on the outside looking in. An ill fit no matter where she went.

Observing the others, she felt herself sinking into the dark spiral that had plagued her since early childhood. A dark spiral she oftentimes found oddly comforting in its bleakness. It crept upon her like a cold, black hole whenever she tried to fit in where she didn't belong. It was easier, preferable to just separate, detach, disengage.

In that moment her feelings were too big to process. Her need to belong, her fear that she never would. The childish, all-consuming love she'd once felt for Travis; the new feelings for him stirring inside her that she could not face.

The darkness surrounded her on a cellular level, pulling in, bunching up, protecting her from the shiny glow of the outside world. It was too bright— this light they generated with their stories and their friendship and their love—it felt like an assault. An assault of the cheer and warmth and camaraderie she was not a part of.

She remembered a time when she was small. Maybe three or four, playing alone in the darkness of her bedroom closet, having a tea party with her imaginary friend, Sadie. It was near Christmas, maybe just after Thanksgiving.

Downstairs, her parents were having a party of their own. The air smelled of roasted meat and exotic spices. The sounds of laughter, jokes, and heated debate drifted up the stairs. In her isolation, in the womb of that room, Sarah felt incredibly safe. If she could just stay here, with Sadie, in the dark, in the closet, far away from the noise and activity, she became convinced nothing bad would ever happen to her. But as comfortable as that sweet notion was, she knew if she gave in to that impulse she wouldn't make it. Her whole life seemed one huge struggle against that urge she'd first recognized at such a tender age. As much as she might want it, she could not afford to surrender to the imaginary world, because being swallowed up completely was worse than the raw, achy vulnerability she was experiencing right now.

Sitting here in this homey room with them, the smell of cookies in the air, the taste of eggnog on her tongue, the smiling faces all around her, caused tears to well up behind Sarah's eyes. How could she process all this without losing herself? Her shell was too hard, Rapunzel's tower too tall.

She fisted her hands, fighting back the feeling that she was going to explode into a thousand pieces and not be able to find her true self among the scattered debris. She felt yanked in two divergent directions. One part of her that pulled away because it was the only way she knew how to survive, and the other part of her, yearning, craving for connection, for wholeness, for a place to belong.

People were up, moving around, getting more food, pouring more wine, telling more stories. In that moment, she lost her battle against her instincts. Quietly, she got to her feet.

No one noticed.

Patsy and Raylene were arguing good-naturedly, everyone else was taking sides, throwing in their comments. Sarah didn't even know what they were talking about. She'd stopped listening, swept up in her own emotional turmoil. "I'm going outside for some fresh air," she mumbled.

No one even glanced over at her, confirming Sarah's suspicion that she was basically invisible. She hitched in a breath, eased toward the door, praying no one noticed, no one said a word to her, even as she wished for that very thing.

To be noticed. To be included. To be one of them.

By the time she grabbed her jacket off the coatrack and slipped out the door, her heart was pounding as if she'd run a hundred-yard dash. She'd made good her escape, and with it came a rush of euphoria.

But what she was escaping to or from, Sarah had no idea.

The sun hung low on the horizon, but the temperature was a mild fifty-eight degrees. Sarah thought about going back to the Merry Cherub, but the thought of traipsing through the lobby filled with guests and a cheery Jenny dissuaded her. She was in the mood to be alone. Jamming her hands into the pockets of her jacket, she scurried away, headed for the walking path around the lake.

Passersby smiled and nodded, forcing her to smile and nod back. Missing the anonymity of Manhattan, she ducked her head and quickened her pace. A few minutes later, she was at the marina.

She hadn't actually intended on taking out a pedal boat—she'd had no intent at all except to get by herself and examine the mix of emotions churning inside her—until she saw them bobbing at the pier. Six of them, painted bright red, with white Merry Cherub lettering that identified them as the B&B's boats. She remembered that on the day she'd arrived, Jenny had told her the pedal boats were stored at the marina for use by her guests and she'd given her the combination.

"You can't forget it." Jenny had laughed. "The combination matches the word LOVE on a telephone keypad. Five to the left, six to the right, eighty-three to the left."

Armed with that information, Sarah clattered down the wooden-plank decking to where the pedal boats were docked. She unlocked the chain from around one of the boats, secured the padlock back to the chain, and in a spur-of-the-moment jaunt, slid into the seat and started pedaling the boat backward into the slough. Water churned up behind her and once she was free from the dock, she reversed her pedaling and took off.

The wind kicked up, blowing against the back of the boat, propelling her swiftly out onto the lake. Around her, fish jumped up, grabbing for in-

sects, their tails splashing as they broke the surface. Pedaling the boat helped free her mind. The
darkness lifted and she felt a rush of exhilaration
as the boat bobbled over the waves. The air swirled
fresh and crisp and the cooling temperature added
to her sudden sense of euphoria. Free. She was free.
Alone and moving her body, paddling the boat on
the lake, her mind free to roam.

The euphoria lasted until her legs grew tired and
she tried to turn the boat back to the docks.

But the pedal boat wouldn't turn.

She kicked harder.

The water churned noisily, but the boat stayed
in one spot. She tried backpedaling, but that didn't
work either. A pedal boat was navigated solely by
using the legs. There wasn't any other way to steer
the damn thing. Then she noticed that she wasn't
staying in one place. The gusting wind was sending
her out into the middle of the lake as easily as if she
was a water bug. No matter how hard she kicked,
the current was stronger.

Okay, she was mildly concerned. She was adrift
on a lake that encompassed over eight thousand
acres with a depth of eighty feet and she wasn't the
best swimmer in the world. She didn't have a life
jacket because Jenny kept them stored at the Merry
Cherub, and the sun was about to set. Still, the craft
was intact and with the rate the wind was gusting,
it would eventually blow her to shore. Hopefully,
someone would come along before then.

She glanced around the lake, and that was when
she realized she couldn't see the shore, nor did she
recall having seen any boats on the lake. In fact,
the only cars she remembered seeing at the marina

were parked in front of the attached bar and grill. Surely, though, someone was out here. A diehard fisherman or two. There had to be.

"Cell phone," she reminded herself, and fished it from the pocket of her jacket. She flipped it open and turned it on, waiting patiently while it powered up, only to discover she had just a single bar. It might not be a strong enough signal for a phone call, but she could at least send a text message.

The dampness of gathering dusk seeped into her fingers. Her normally nimble thumbs felt stiff. Who should she text? Good thing she'd gotten all their phone numbers.

Travis?

God, she hated looking like a dumbass. The cookie club ladies would no doubt have their feelings hurt that she'd run out on them. Jenny was surely busy. And Travis . . . well, the last thing she wanted was for him to see how stupid she'd been. That left the police.

Did she call 9–1–1? That seemed a bit drastic.

She paused, fingers poised over the keypad.

A fresh burst of wind slapped against the boat, rocking it hard, catching Sarah unprepared. She fumbled the cell phone. It slipped from her hand and tumbled headlong into the water.

She stared in stunned disbelief and then laughed at how preposterous this whole thing was. Lovely. Well, that solved the problem of whom to call.

One good thing, even though she wasn't much of a swimmer, she'd never really been afraid of water. And as long as she stayed on the boat, everything would work out. Or so she told herself to keep from freaking.

She pedaled and felt water spatter her face. At first she thought it had started to rain, but a minute later, when a second splash of water hit her cheek, she realized it was coming from below, not above. Looking down, she saw water filling the pedal well. The wind must have blown the water in and now whenever she pedaled it was flying up to douse her.

Fine. She'd just bail it out.

Except there was nothing to bail out the water with and it was getting colder by the minute and the sun was playing peek-a-boo with the gathering clouds. Not the best situation she'd ever been in, but certainly not the worst either. She was smart, resourceful. She could think her way out of this.

The gale—because it truly was a gale now— rushed over the water with startling ferocity. It spun the boat three hundred and sixty degrees. Cold sliced through her, clean as a machete through sugarcane. In a matter of seconds, she was completely disoriented. She had no idea which direction she'd come from.

"This was not one of your most brilliant moves, Sadie Cool," she muttered, more to hear her own voice than anything else.

The boat was listing to the right, the side she was on. The water in the well of the boat was even deeper now.

Time to start bailing.

Setting her jaw, she leaned over, made a cup of her hand, and began to scoop. Her fingers, already stiff from the cold, tightened as they touched the icy water. She ignored the pain shooting up her nerve endings and scooped for several minutes, but then realized to her dismay the water level in the well was going up not down.

That's when she saw it. The tiny, but deadly hairline crack in the hull.

Wind hadn't knocked the water in as she'd surmised. It was seeping through a breach in the fiberglass. No amount of bailing was going to stop the boat from sinking.

"Just your luck, Collier, you grabbed the one leaky pedal boat."

How had this happened? In the span of forty minutes she'd gone from warm and safe and comfortable in a roomful of kind and loving women, to spinning in the wind in the middle of the lake, making like Kate Winslet in *Titanic*.

As the right side of the flat-bottomed boat dipped lower, water ran over the front. Her pulse pounded a hard, thready rhythm. She could hear it beating against her eardrums. She let loose with a couple of choice swearwords and it made her feel a little better, but didn't change the situation.

Move. You've got to move.

With her feet on the pedals, the water in the well came up to her ankles. Good thing she had boots on or her feet would be soaked.

A crow flew overhead, crying *caw, caw, caw* as if laughing at her.

"You're right," she said, "I deserve to be mocked."

Stop talking to the crow and move.

She pushed against the pedals with her feet while at the same time scooting her butt to the left side of the boat.

For an instant, the unseaworthy craft seemed to

right itself with the shift of her weight, and for one dumb moment she thought maybe water hadn't come in through the hairline crack in the hull, but had indeed been blown in by the wind. That hope was short-lived as the boat quickly started listing to the right again.

She scooted as far left as she could, maintaining the balance a little longer. Her one hundred and thirty pounds against whatever the water in the well weighed. The sun crouched on the horizon. Soon, very soon, it would be dark. She gulped and stopped pretending she was even remotely in control.

The silence—interrupted only by the rush of wind and lapping of the water—stretched out like doom. The air smelled of impending rain and stinky fish. Great. It was going to rain on her and then she'd sleep with the fishes.

She laughed nervously. The water kept encroaching, slipping farther over the bow, first over the right side, then the left. The pedal boat tipped forward. Sarah sat balled up on the left side, her knees drawn to her chest, her wet boot heels dampening her bottom.

On the upside, the boat was sinking slowly. On the downside, slow wasn't a particularly positive thing in reference to the end of your life.

Closer and closer the water crept. Lower and lower the sun dipped. Colder and colder, Sarah shivered.

Desperately, she scanned the lake, but all she saw was dark blue water. No shoreline, no boats in sight. Not even a buoy to swim toward. Before long, the water was over the entire front of the pedal boat. It was sinking faster now. At this rate, she'd sink along with the sun. She had nowhere else to go but the back of the seat. Carefully, she eased herself upward until her butt was resting on the back of the seat, her legs in the seat.

Eventually, the water claimed the seat and swirled around her ankles. She drew her legs up beside her, perching like a bird, shoulders drawn in, arms wrapped around herself, all out of options. In a matter of minutes, she'd be in the water. Sarah, who barely knew how to dog paddle, was going to drown. She imagined the headlines: *Antisocial Children's Author Drowns on Lake Twilight.*

This was it. It was all over. This was how she was going to die.

Chapter Eleven

Sunset, like most things on the winter lake, settled in a slow, easy slide. The sharp yellow edges of sunlight slipped into a dreamy haze of purple-tinged blue, the same spectacular color as Sarah's eyes, which deepened in indolent stages, progressively blurring the edges between the shoreline and the water, muting the details of bare tree limbs reaching skyward, smudging the outlines of ropes mooring boats to the dock. That evening, a fine mist and strong blowing wind hastened the drawing close of dusk's curtain, casting the lake in a fog of gray wool and the marina in a milky rinse of rusty orange. The upshot was a sudden rush of silence, comforting as a hand-knitted sweater, tasty as a freshly baked cookie, reliable as a grandmother's hug.

Travis breathed in the moment. Being the father of a chronically ill child had taught him how to live in the now. How to fill his lungs with the split-second instant, hold it tight in a long caress, and savor the uniqueness. He loved winter in general and the holiday season in particular. But this year was extra special. This year, for the first time in four long years, Jazzy was no longer a slave to her asthma. It was a Christmas miracle indeed, one he would never forget.

Unexpectedly, he found himself wishing Sarah was here with him. He tried to squelch the feeling as soon as it arose. There was no point wishing for what he knew he couldn't have, but he just couldn't stop thinking about her.

Travis wished he could enjoy her like the sunset, take pleasure in her company while she was here. But he had Jazzy to think about. He couldn't do that. Nor could he in good conscience start something with Sarah he knew they couldn't finish. She deserved more than just a momentary fling, and honestly so did he. He'd done the casual sex thing before. He knew that while it might feel good at the time, in the long run it could leave you feeling empty inside. No, he was ready for something more substantial in his life and maybe, now that Jazzy was doing so much better, the time was finally right. But Sarah was leaving town on Sunday. There was no time to explore this thing, see if it could grow into something more.

Honestly, he didn't quite know what to make of his strong sexual attraction for her. Especially given the history between them. She'd been infatuated with him once and he'd been too old for her. Now he felt like he was infatuated with her and she was too big-city cool for this simple country boy.

He took in another deep breath, filling his airways with the scent memory of her—along with the smell of the lake—murky sweetness combined with womanly allure. Thinking about her sent a hot tingle of electricity running like a string from his head to his feet. Then he reminded himself what was at stake. He couldn't let his desire get the better of his common sense. He'd been there before. Rash lust could cause a lot of problems.

The wind kicked up, skimming fiercely across the water and sending a fresh battalion of white-capped waves licking against the shoreline. There'd been a wind advisory issued for the local lakes and waterways so Travis didn't expect to see any other boats on the lake as he maneuvered his game warden's boat through the choppy waves, heading toward home. Since he lived on the lake, he took the boat home with him, docking it at the pier at the end of his private wharf.

Part of his job entailed going out in bad weather, looking for folks who hadn't been prudent enough to check the weather conditions before venturing out onto the water. Most of the fishermen in the area knew better, but there was always a tourist or two in the mix and there was no telling what they'd do.

Today, he'd been out here for several hours and hadn't seen a soul.

He thought of Sarah again, remembering the times he'd taken her fishing when she was just a kid. He'd done it as a favor for his next-door neighbor Mia Martin, who'd mothered him after his own mother died, but also because he'd liked Sarah.

She'd been a quiet kid, but curious. When she asked questions, they'd been intelligent and well-thought-out. Like why did fish bite more readily in cooler weather than in the heat of the summer?

Or why was it that crappie preferred bushy, deep water, while catfish skimmed along murky slough bottoms? If she'd kept coming to the lake, he could have made a real angler out of her. She'd loved fishing almost as much as he did.

The cold wind gusted, ruffling his hair, nipping at his ears. He did up the top button on his coat and increased the boat's speed. He was looking forward to getting home and diving into the big bowl of stew he'd started in the crockpot before he left for work that morning. He loved the way the house smelled of simmering chuck roast and earthy root vegetables. He'd pick Jazzy up from the sitter who kept her after school until he got home from work.

No wait, Jazzy was spending the night with her best friend, Andi. Although he was a little uneasy about the whole thing. She'd never spent the night away from home except with his Aunt Raylene. He didn't want her far from him in case she got sick, but since she hadn't had an asthma attack in almost two months, he'd agreed to let her sleep over at Andi's when she'd begged. It was hard to let her go, but he knew she needed to expand her horizons. Already, she seemed much younger than her age.

The sun was almost gone by the time he entered the main part of the lake. He was only a few minutes from home now and his focus was on the familiar landmarks guiding him in—the old dead tree that poked from the water, the grinding sound of machinery at the rock quarry a mile north of the lake, the cluster of bats that flew from the underground caves every evening about this time. His stomach grumbled, anticipating that stew. He was so wrapped up in the simple ordinary splendor of the end of his day that he almost did not take one last look around the lake.

But a spidery prickling at his neck drew his attention to the right when he was headed left.

At first he saw nothing but the mix of sky and water merging into one wash of deep majestic blue, but then he heard a soft, reedy sound and the hairs on his arms stood up. It was a human voice, crying out for help in the darkness.

He slowed the boat, cocked his head, and listened as he scanned the water. There, several hundred yards away, he spied her. A woman crouched atop what appeared to be a sinking pedal boat. The listing craft was almost completely submerged. In a matter of minutes, maybe seconds, the woman would be in the water.

Alarm had him yanking his boat around. He barreled straight for her. She should be okay, even if she ended up getting wet, since he'd seen her. But he hated to think what would have happened if something hadn't told him to take one last look around.

The woman spotted him and began waving her arms.

When he got closer, he recognized the sinking pedal boat as belonging to the Merry Cherub, and when he saw the woman had long caramel-colored hair pulled back in a single braid, his mouth went dry.

Sarah?

Could it be? What in the world was she doing out on the water in a pedal boat at dusk in the middle of December?

He felt at once both angry and concerned. Hadn't she listened for wind advisories before taking the boat out? Why hadn't Jenny warned her against it? Sarah was from Manhattan. Yes, she spent a few summers here as a kid, but she was ill-equipped to take a pedal boat out on the lake alone in high winds and she should have known better.

When he was within a few feet of her, he killed the engine so the wake from his boat wouldn't be the thing that sent her into the drink and he went for the life preserver. She was now standing on the back of the seat of the pedal boat, the water lapping at her boots, her balance impeccable. He decided against the life preserver, hoping that he could do this without her ending up in the water, and instead picked up an oar from the bottom of the boat.

"Steady, steady," he called. "I'm going to row over and if we gauge this correctly you can just step right into my boat."

Calmly, she nodded.

How in the hell did she stay so calm when he was an experienced boater and his pulse was thundering through his veins? Maybe she didn't fully understand the danger she'd put herself in. He wanted to yell at her, *What in the hell were you thinking?* But the minute he saw the quiet fear in her eyes, he knew she'd been through enough and she didn't need him jumping down her throat. Thank God she was okay. His gut squeezed when he thought of the alternatives.

Once he was near enough, he tossed the oar back into the boat and held out a hand to her.

She started to inch toward him, but the wounded

pedal boat sank deeper. Startled, her eyes widened and she raised her arms to leverage her balance. The water swirled at her calves.

"Easy now."

She paused, took a deep breath, tried for another step. The pedal boat made a gurgling groan. It was finished, no buoyancy left in it. Time to make a move or she was going in all the way.

"Jump!" Travis commanded. She hesitated for a split second. He met her eyes, cemented her to him with one long, hard look. *Come on, sweetheart, you can do this.* "Jump!"

Clutching hard to his gaze with her own, Sarah jumped.

He caught her in mid-air, dragging her into his boat, while the lake swallowed her boat in a watery embrace.

The force of her momentum knocked him off balance and they ended up on the bottom of the boat. The wet oar was pressed into his back and Sarah Collier, the awkward girl next door who used to have a crush on him, turned famous children's novelist, was lying on top of him. They were both breathing hard—from fear, from exertion, from raw animal attraction they'd been dancing around for a week—and in perfect tandem rhythm, as if inhaling the same single breath of air.

They stared deeply into each other's eyes.

His heart thundered. His mind spun. Every place her body touched his, he felt completely and utterly alive. This was the closest he'd come to sex in so long he'd lost count.

And that's when Travis Walker knew he was in serious trouble.

* * *

"I've got you, sweetheart, you're safe," Travis murmured.

Sweetheart. He'd called her sweetheart. That much got through her numb terror.

"Travis," she whispered, still unable to believe it was he, that he'd pulled her foolish hide from the water's cold embrace just in the nick of time. Okay, so the utilitarian brown boat with the hopped-up motor wasn't exactly a valiant steed, but at this moment, he sure looked like a knight in shining armor to her. And that made her babble idiotically, "You came for me."

He laughed, not making fun of her, but low and comforting. "I imagine it feels that way right now, but honestly, I was just on my way home. If I hadn't turned my head when I did, I probably wouldn't have seen you."

"If you hadn't seen me . . ." She left the rest unspoken.

"But I did and everything is okay now. You're one tough cookie, Sadie Cool."

"I don't feel the least bit tough. In fact, I feel very, very stupid."

"Most people would have completely lost it by now," he said. "Instead here you are worrying about looking stupid."

"I have lost it," she said around her chattering teeth. "This is me losing it."

"Kudos, then, on the dignified hysteria."

He was trying to reassure her. Travis's MO hadn't changed over the years. He grinned and teased to put people at ease. His arm was around her, his hand holding her steady as he reached for a woolen blanket that lay folded on the seat beside him. He tucked the blanket around her, the backs of his knuckles accidentally grazing her breasts.

She heard his quick intake of breath. Her nipples, already painfully hard as pebbles from the cold, constricted even tighter at his touch. Sarah huddled on the edge of the seat, shivering underneath the blanket he'd thrown over her shoulders. It smelled like horses. She felt embarrassed and completely stupid. She'd almost gotten herself killed simply because she hadn't possessed the social skills to mix it up with the ladies of the cookie club.

"Let's get you back to shore. Hang on, I'm opening the throttle." He pushed on the gas and the boat surged, skimming over the water, rushing cold air over her even colder body.

She hunched deeper into the blanket and tucked her head down. Her teeth clattered like castanets.

He stood at the wheel, the wind whipping around him, his hair blowing back. He wore a brown uniform topped with an all-weather coat that was a slightly darker shade of brown. What a virile man.

Her emotions were a wild tumble—fear, regret, gratitude, foolishness, joy at being alive. She could have died on that lake. But one strong, throbbing emotion beat out the rest.

Raw desire unlike anything she'd ever experienced clawed at her. Need stoked by danger, near death, and sudden rescue demanded attention. She looked at Travis and saw the same need reflected in his eyes. She couldn't deal with the tumult of it and ducked her head, pretending to shield herself from the wind.

Swiftly, he docked the boat at the back of his house, tied it up, and then helped her to climb gingerly onto the wooden pier. He sheltered her from the wind with his body, drawing her up against him, ushering her up the jetty, onto the deck, then into the house.

The minute they were through the door, he broke away. "I'll draw you a hot bath. You need to get out of those wet clothes immediately."

He hurried to the bathroom and she heard the water come on. Slowly, she stripped off her wet clothes. The house smelled of stew. She wrapped the blanket around her nakedness and glanced around. Once upon a time her grandmother's overstuffed fabric couch and love seat sat in this living room. Her lace curtains hung from the windows. And beige Berber carpet covered the floors. Now, the couch was leather and blinds covered the windows and the floors were hardwood. The flower-print wallpaper had been replaced. Now the walls were textured and painted a warm honey color.

Beside the window stood a Christmas tree decorated with multicolored lights, handmade ornaments, and candy canes, just like the illustration of the Christmas tree in *The Magic Christmas Cookie*. Jazzy and Travis had decorated their tree in the likeness of her book. It brought a lump to her throat. Was this some kind of sign?

Don't read anything into it. They didn't even know you were Sadie Cool.

Which made this even more special.

One thing in the room remained the same—the bookcase sitting in the corner. It had been Gram's. Her heart gave an odd little thump and Sarah moved across the room to run her hand over the polished oak.

Travis cleared his throat.

She jumped and spun around to see him standing behind her. She reached to pick her wet clothes up off the floor, still clutching the blanket tightly around her.

"Leave your clothes," he said. "I'll put them in the dryer. Get in the bath. Get warmed up. I put my bathrobe on the back of the door for you to wear until your clothes are dried."

She obeyed because there was no reason to argue. She was cold and he had saved her from drowning after she'd done a very foolish thing.

The bathroom must have been Jazzy's, for it had been redone in a mermaid theme. The walls were painted Indian summer blue. Fishing net sprayed with sparkle glitter dangled from the ceiling with plastic starfish and turtles and sand dollars caught in it. Sticky appliqués of mermaids cavorted around a mirror shaped like a ship's portal. The shower curtain was dotted with mermaids as well. The room made her smile.

Sarah dropped the blanket and caught sight of her disfigured torso in the portal mirror. She started to quickly avert her gaze from her reflection as she usually did when she got in or out of the shower, but this time, she made herself take a good, hard look. How would Travis view her body?

Tentatively, she ran a hand over her abdomen and fingered the irregular border of the reddish pink burn scar that began just below her rib cage on the right side of her body, swooped down under her navel, and ended at the top of her left hip. Her skin was puckered, stretched, and even after three years, still looked unsettlingly raw. No bikinis for Sarah Collier. Ever.

No getting around it. Anyone was bound to be thrown by the scar the first time he saw it. Aidan sure had been.

Sarah moistened her lips with the tip of her tongue, remembering the first guy she'd dated after the accident. Aidan Hartley. Tall, thin, dark-haired, intense, and introverted, and just as un-emotional as Sarah. He restored rare books and they'd shared an interest in foreign films. She'd thought they were a perfect match even though his kisses left her lukewarm.

It wasn't as though she hadn't warned him about the scar in advance. Aidan had claimed it wouldn't bother him. But when they'd started making out on their fourth date and he'd slipped his hand under her blouse and felt the scar, he'd abruptly shifted gears, told her it was getting late, he had to get up early, blah, blah, blah. Then he'd hustled out of her apartment and never called her again.

And Aidan was the second guy to dump her because of the scar.

Her gut clenched at the memory. She'd told herself not to let that jerk-off affect her self-esteem, but she hadn't been out on a date since and that was over a year ago.

What if her scar disgusted Travis too?

What was she worrying about that for? It wasn't like she was on a date with Travis.

No, but she was naked in his bathroom.

Purposefully, she shook off the thoughts and stepped into the warm sudsy bathwater. A box of

Mr. Bubble sat on the edge of the tub. She smiled. He'd made her a bubble bath. She eased into the hot water and laid her head back against the wall. Instantly, the heat began to relax her tense muscles. She closed her eyes and took several long, slow, deep breaths.

It was odd, being here in Gram's house with Travis owning it. And what felt even odder was being naked in his tub with only one thin wall separating them. Sarah gulped and her eyes flew open. She had no business luxuriating in here like it was a spa. Her goal was to get warm and get the lake stink off her.

She pulled open the drain and hopped from the tub and then rinsed it out behind her. After she dried off, she slipped on Travis's navy blue terrycloth bathrobe and secured the belt tightly around her. It smelled like blue spruce and sunshine. Quintessential Travis.

She had no bra, no panties, not even socks. All her clothes were in the wash. But he'd also left her a pair of navy blue house slippers. Apparently they were his as the slippers were four sizes too big. She pushed her feet inside the house shoes, draped the wet blanket over the shower bar to dry, and then padded out into the hallway.

Pausing, she stood with one hand holding the neck of the bathrobe closed high at her throat. If she tilted her head to the right she could see him from there, crouched on the braided rug, stoking a small flame he'd started in the fireplace.

Compelled by a force she could not deny, Sarah canted her head and studied his brilliantly muscled buttocks encased in those brown work pants that shouldn't have looked sexy, but on him they did.

Travis turned then and caught her staring. He got to his feet with a grin and she quickly looked away. Her pulse was hammering and her mouth was dry and she felt hot all over. Who needed a fire? One look from him and her body was ablaze.

"Um," she said. "Where's Jazzy?"

"At a sleepover. It's her first."

"Are you nervous?"

"You better believe it."

"You're a great dad."

His grin widened. "Who would have thought it, huh? Bad boy Travis Walker turning his life around over a tiny little blond?"

"She's an amazing kid."

"I think so, but then I'm prejudiced."

She chanced slanting another glance directly at him. He was backlit by the fire that had sprung up, and it cast him in a devilish orange glow. He had become a paradox, this rebellious youth turned responsible single dad. It was a compelling transformation. A lock of hair fell across his eyebrow giving him a rakish look, whispering that he wasn't one hundred percent tamed.

Water trickled from her hair, slid coolly down her temple. His grin disappeared and his gray eyes darkened. Slowly, he stepped across the room toward her, the hardwood creaking underneath his weight. He reached out to touch her with the tips of his calloused fingers, his eyes fixed on hers, pinning her in place.

She couldn't move, couldn't breathe.

Tenderly, he brushed the water from her skin. "Sarah . . ." he said hoarsely, then didn't say anything else. He turned his palm, ran his knuckles down her cheek.

Everything stopped in that moment. She could no longer hear the ticking of the mantel clock or the snap of wood in the fireplace. She couldn't feel her legs or see anything beyond those glorious gray eyes. How many times had she dreamed of a moment just like this? She and Travis Walker alone in a room together, desire for *her* reflected on his face.

Travis was touching her and she was naked underneath his robe and the air smelled of stew and wood smoke and they were in her grandmother's house where she'd once dreamed those dreams of him.

He stepped closer, lowered his head, but then just stopped and studied her. His hand was still on her face, his thumb tracing over her chin. Her heart started pounding so loudly she could hear nothing else, was certain he could hear it right through her chest. *Thump, thump, thumpety-thump.*

"Ever since I kissed you underneath the mistletoe, all I can think about is touching you, holding you, making love to you," he said in a husky voice.

"This is insane," she murmured, but tilted her head back, exposing her neck to him. They were moving too fast, she was in over her head. She hadn't even told him about the scar yet. She didn't want it to come as a complete shock. She simply wasn't ready.

"Yeah, it's insane. But you're driving me crazy, Sarah. I want so much from you. Maybe too much. All I know is that I haven't felt like this in a very long time."

She wanted to tell him she'd never felt like this. Desperate, hungry, completely out of her mind with need.

"Are you sure it's me that you want? Maybe you're just horny, and it's not really me. I could be anyone, I—"

His mouth came down on hers in a hard kiss that made her gulp. Then he pulled his mouth away and rasped, "It's you."

"How can you be so sure?"

"Because I can't stop thinking about you. The way you smell, the way you move, the cool, self-contained look in your eyes that says you know the secrets of the world and you're not telling anyone. It snowed on the day you arrived. Do you know how rare that is in early December in this part of Texas? You looked so damn beautiful standing on the float with the snowflakes caught in your hair. Hell, who knows? Maybe those kismet cookies were right. Maybe there is such a thing as destiny."

Her heart swirled at the possibilities, but her head shoved this explanation away. She didn't believe in any of that stuff. Not anymore. "I came back to Twilight because of Jazzy."

"And Jazzy is my daughter."

"Precisely. Another good reason why this is a bad idea." She took a step back, away from his arms, and then for good measure, took another.

"Okay," he said. He came forward; gray eyes glittered in the firelight. "But it doesn't change how I feel. I want you so badly right now I can barely breathe."

He couldn't breathe? She couldn't remember the last time she'd taken a full breath. Not since she'd set foot in this house that had once been her only real home, not since he'd pulled her from the lake just in the nick of time.

She put her palms up to stop him and connected with the honed ridges of his muscular chest beneath his blue plaid flannel shirt. But her hands seemed to melt, turn to putty. They slid around his rib cage to hug his back. Dammit! What the hell was wrong with her?

"Sarah," he murmured.

There's no such thing as destiny, no such thing as kismet, no such thing as fate.

And yet, here she was.

If this wasn't destiny, then what was it?

CHAPTER TWELVE

She didn't protest when he kissed her again. In fact, she even pursed her lips. This time his kiss was soft, as when he'd kissed her underneath the mistletoe, but more inquisitive. She reached up and cupped his face between her palms, holding him steady, and touched the tip of her tongue to his. There. She was taking control. She wasn't leaving anything up to destiny. If this happened, it was because they made it happen.

No quirk of fate. No stars aligned. No magic cookies.

Sarah gazed into his eyes, tumbled into them. Normally, she kissed with her eyes closed, but she wanted to see everything—his thick eyelashes that curled almost to his eyebrows, the way his dark hair lay across his forehead, how the muted light glinted off his angular cheekbones.

He deepened the kiss and closed his own eyes and she followed suit, letting her other senses take over. Taste, touch, smell, sound. He tasted of Christmas, splendid and redemptive. Peppermint candy canes. Had he eaten one from the tree while she'd been in the bath? His breath came out in a hearty rasp. Just one spicy sweet sip from his lips and her mind spun crazy with daydreams of brightly colored packages and sleigh bells and roasted turkey.

The texture of his tongue was incredible, the feel of his masculine palms slipping up the sleeve of her bathrobe divine. The scent of him slipped into her nostrils, rising up hot with their growing passion. The rich smell of earthy man tinged with her own fragrance—the aroma of Mr. Bubble. It rolled over her, lighthearted and heavy, a ferocious mixture that stirred her blood.

Here she was, with the man of her dreams, and she couldn't wrap her head around it.

Hold up. She wasn't going to romanticize this by making it into anything more than it was. She was just going to go with the flow, stay out of her head, and be in her body. Speaking of which, her body was achy, raw in lust with him. She might not be able to stop this headlong hormonal rush shooting through her, but she could most certainly keep her heart from getting tangled up in this. She wasn't going to let herself get hurt again.

Sarah pulled back, splayed a palm against his chest. "We need to talk."

"I'm listening," he said, leaning in close to run his hot, wet tongue along the outside of her ear.

Sarah shivered. "This is just hormones, chemistry, lust. That's all."

"You can tell yourself that all day, but we both know differently," he said, his husky voice coming out like Sam Elliott on steroids. "But I don't want to do anything that you don't want to do. I don't want to confuse or upset you."

"Excuse me?" She sank her hands on her hips and glowered at him. "You think I've been doodling your name in my notebook for nine years just waiting for the chance to jump your bones?"

"No, of course not. But once upon a time you did believe I was your soul mate."

"Once upon a time I used to believe in Santa. You give yourself too much credit, Travis." She notched her chin up. "I'm a big girl. I know how to distinguish sex from love. Let's not mistake sexual attraction for anything more than it is."

He stared deeply into her eyes. "Is that the way you really want it?"

She nodded. "Yes."

Slowly, Travis reached down to untie the sash of her robe, but she moved her hand to block his. She wasn't ready for him to see her scar.

But she was too late. Already his hand had slipped in between the folds of the robe and her scar tingled underneath the brief brush of his knuckles.

Sarah stared into his face, tremulous and scared of his reaction, but nothing registered on his face. It was as if he'd touched normal, soft, supple female skin. She stood frozen, not knowing what to do or say.

His left palm stayed splayed across her bare belly. With his right hand, he tilted her chin up and brought his mouth down on hers for another long, lingering kiss.

Okay, apparently touching the scar hadn't freaked him out. What would happen when he saw it?

This thing isn't going that far, she assured herself, but then he started doing this incredible thing with his tongue and, helplessly, she melted against his hard-muscled body.

Wrapped up in each other, glued together by contact at the shoulder, hand, leg, hip, and chest, Travis and Sarah stepped forward together into a brave new world of sensation.

Sarah fell into the well of his heated embrace, his life force filling her with an electrifying energy she'd never felt before. His male vigor washed over every square inch of her in magnificent waves.

He stoked in Sarah a need so hungry she feared there was no sating it. She wrapped her arms around his neck, deepening the kiss, exploring him with her tongue, and barely noticed when he lifted her up off the floor, carried her to the couch, and laid her down on the soft, supple leather.

Eyes gleaming with desire, he looked down at her, his gaze stroking her face as deftly as fingertips, and inhaled deeply. "You look so beautiful in firelight. I want to see you naked."

She felt her cheeks heat. The look in his eyes fried her senses. "I . . . I'm not ready."

"Okay, I'll go first." His fingers went to the buttons of his shirt, he worked them furiously, and once they were all undone, he stripped off his shirt.

Sarah bit down on her bottom lip at the sight of his muscular bare chest.

Honed and smooth, hard and ripped. Glorious! The reality of him put all her fantasies to shame.

He sat down on the couch beside her, pulling her into his arms again, raining kisses on her face.

She was getting sucked in, she could feel herself falling, but she couldn't do anything to stop it. All the old emotions she'd tucked away, locked down tight, came bubbling to the surface, and she knew at once that sex would never, ever be enough for her. She couldn't do this. Could not take it one step forward. There was so much at stake, so much holding her back. Their past, her scars, the precarious future.

"Travis . . ." she said, knowing she should put a stop to this, but simply unable to find the words. They needed to wait, but dammit, she did not want to. "There's something . . . I have to . . ."

She couldn't find the words, so she just stood up and dropped the robe.

Travis stared at her and his eyes widened. Audibly, he sucked in his breath. Doubt squeezed her hard. What was he thinking? Was that a look of disgust on his face?

Outside in the driveway came the sound of a car door slamming and then voices. Children's voices.

With lightning speed, Travis was up off the couch and at the window, peeking through the blinds. In an instant, he whirled on his heels and ran from the living room.

Confused and more than a little dazed, Sarah reached for the robe, but before she could get to it, there was Travis thrusting her not-quite-dry clothes at her. "Go! Now! You've got to get out of here."

"What is it?" she asked, jamming her legs into her panties, then struggling to get her bra on.

"Jazzy. No time. You have to go now." He scooped up her boots from the floor and stuffed them—along with the remainder of her clothes—

into her arms. He placed a forceful palm at her back, scooting her across the living room floor and past the kitchen to the back door. Sarah heard the front door open just as Travis shoved her out on the porch decking.

"Daddy, I'm home!"

"Gotta go," Travis said, and slammed the door in Sarah's astounded face.

The second he closed the door on Sarah, Travis knew he'd made a terrible mistake. She was going to think this was about her scar, not the fact that Jazzy had come home unexpectedly.

He almost yanked the door open and pulled her back inside and told her how sorry he was for treating her like his dirty little secret, but then his daughter was in the kitchen, canting her head at his bare chest.

And Andi and her mother were standing in the doorway behind Jazzy.

"What's going on?" Jazzy asked.

"Um . . . nothing," he said, resisting the urge to cover his bare chest with his hands. "It just got hot in here with the fireplace going, so I . . . um . . . took my shirt off." God, he was a horrible liar. "What's going on with you? Why are you home?"

Jazzy looked chagrined.

"She got homesick," Andi's mother, Sandy, said. "And since we're all going to the slumber party at the Book Nook tomorrow evening, we just decided it was best if Jazzy came home tonight. We are all still on for the pajama party, right?"

Travis plowed a hand through his hair, suddenly realizing that Sandy was eyeing his bare chest like he was a piece of chocolate cake. Sandy was newly single, having just gone through a divorce, and before Sarah had come to town, before he'd realized she was Sadie Cool, he'd made plans with Sandy to take their daughters to *The Magic Christmas Cookie* pajama party together. That seemed so long ago now. So much had changed.

"We are still going, Daddy, aren't we?" Jazzy sounded alarmed.

"Sure, sure, of course we are." He smiled at his daughter, and Sandy beamed at him. "Thank you for bringing Jazzy home."

"No problem." Sandy lowered her eyelids and slid him a speculative glance. "Since I have the minivan, do you want to come by the house tomorrow and we'll all ride over to the bookstore together?"

"I think we'll just take our own vehicle," Travis hedged. "I've got some things to do tomorrow." *Like go tell Sarah how sorry I am.*

"So we'll just see you there?" Sandy said brightly.

"Yeah." He nodded.

Sandy and her daughter left. Travis turned to Jazzy. "So you got homesick, huh?"

"I missed you."

"I missed you too, princess." Playfully, he tweaked her nose.

Jazzy cocked her head and studied him for a moment. "You seem . . . different."

"Different? Nah, I'm not any different." He knew his daughter was very intuitive, but how could she possibly know that he was *feeling* different? Trying not to look self-conscious, he trailed into the living room to retrieve his shirt from the floor and shrugged into it.

Jazzy tapped her chin with an index finger. "Yep, you're different."

"I'm your same old dad." It was unnerving, the way she was looking at him. As if there was nothing he could hide from her. Then he realized this was the first thing he'd ever hidden from her. That was probably it. He looked guilty.

"Are you hungry? Have you eaten? Why don't we have some stew?" Travis made a beeline for the crockpot, took a couple of bowls from the cabinet.

"What's that noise?"

"What noise?"

"It sounded like someone on the back porch."

"Nah, there's no one on the porch." Was Sarah still out there?

"I think there is." Jazzy headed for the back door.

Swiftly, Travis darted in front of her, a bowl of stew in his hand, blocking her from the door. "Food's ready."

She eyed him and muttered, "Something is very different."

"Sit down, young lady, and eat your dinner."

Thankfully, Jazzy sat, and as he settled the bowl in front of her, he leaned his head back to stare out the rear window just in time to see Sarah disappear around the corner of the house. He couldn't help feeling like the crud on the bottom of the lake. One way or another, he'd find the perfect way to apologize.

In the aftermath of being thrust out on Travis's backyard deck in her underwear, Sarah stuffed her arms inside her shirt and tugged it down over her head, then zipped up her jeans. She tried to convince herself that it was okay. It was better to know right up front that her burn scar was a deal breaker. It wasn't as if they were even dating or anything.

This was good. It was a good thing he'd shoved her out the back door when his neighbor had brought his daughter home. No one would blame him. How could she blame him? His daughter came first. She got that. It's just she couldn't help thinking what might have happened if Jazzy hadn't returned home when she did. Would Travis have been able to overlook her scarred body? Their chemistry was strong, but was it strong enough to overcome that?

So, whew, she wasn't going to brood or feel sorry for herself. The foreplay had been good—oh, who the hell was she kidding—the foreplay (as much as they'd gotten to) had been fabulous. Which sort of only made things worse.

She stabbed her feet into her boots, jammed her arms into her coat, and stumbled down the red-wood steps, ducking her head in the process so if Jazzy was inside the kitchen she wouldn't see her passing by. What a lovely new take on the prover-bial walk of shame, slinking nefariously away so as not to get caught by your almost-lover's eight-year-old daughter. Her heels clattered on the pavers as she headed for the back gate.

She swept past a rose bush bare of vegetation. It clutched at the hem of her jacket with old summer thorns. Without a backward glance at the house that had given her so many wonderful holiday memories, Sarah hunched her shoulders against the wind rolling off the lake and headed for the Merry Cherub feeling broken in so many ways.

Her nose burned and tears pushed against the backs of her eyelids, but dammit she was *not* going to cry.

The farther she walked, the shittier she felt. She pretended not to stare enviously at the people she passed—lovers strolling along the shoreline holding hands, couples lining up two-by-two for festive horse-drawn carriage rides around the square, happy families ambling along the sidewalk, brightly colored shopping bags and gift-wrapped packages in their arms.

A tear slipped down her cheek. Then two. Now three.

Bah-fricking-humbug.

At six P.M. the next evening Sarah arrived at Ye Olde Book Nook on the square to find a line of people queued up to get into the bookstore, many of them clutching well-worn copies of *The Magic Christmas Cookie*, wearing pajamas and carrying sleeping bags.

Usually, at these types of affairs, there was a publicist assigned to help guide her. In Twilight, that turned out to be Belinda Murphey, who was outside working the crowd. She was a dynamo, dressed up like Mrs. Santa Claus, an Isabella doll tucked underneath her arm. She had the group singing, "It's Beginning to Look a Lot Like Christmas." The minute she spied Sarah, she broke off in mid-song and hustled over to escort her into the bookstore.

"Sadie Cool coming through," Belinda announced. "Make way, make way, there'll be time to get to know Sadie once we're all inside. We have all night!"

Earlier in the week, Sarah had dropped by to introduce herself to the bookstore owner. Smiley-faced Vivian Jones was a wizened senior citizen with a startlingly deep voice and sharp green eyes. Belinda handed her off to Vivian and went back for crowd control.

Ye Olde Book Nook was one of those rare independent bookstores that didn't sell used books. That told Sarah that Vivian had some money of her own. Independent bookstores had a tough time keeping their doors open in the current publishing climate. But Vivian seemed to have carved a niche for herself targeting the tourist trade, by offering a large section of regional titles dealing with the legend and lore of Texas.

"I can't tell you what it means to have you here," Vivian enthused, sounding like Barry White with a bad cold. "The kids are so excited. Heck, I'm excited too. We've advertised the dickens out of your appearance. I took out an ad in the *Fort Worth Star-Telegram* and at the radio station in Weatherford, where they run a Saturday morning talk show about books and authors. They've been mentioning your appearance for weeks."

"It is an honor to be here," Sarah said, and meant it, even though she was nervous about the whole thing.

"I knew your grandmother," Vivian went on. "She was a dear friend and I'm sure you don't remember me, but I remember you. I was at Travis and Crystal's wedding when—"

"So this is where we're having the pajama party," Sarah interrupted, surveying the cordoned-off area.

This section of the store was covered in quilts and blankets. In the middle of the floor sat a rocking chair decorated with red bows and holly. Stacked behind the rocker were copies of the re-released *The Magic Christmas Cookie*, packaged with Isabella dolls. Set up on the opposite side of the area were tables laden with Christmas cookies and fruit punch and other snacks.

"Oh, yes, yes. First we'll have the book signing out front." Vivian waved toward the front of the store. "Then those lucky few who made their reservations early will be escorted back here for the pajama party."

Sarah forced a smile and resisted the urge to slip out the back door. Okay, so she wasn't fond of crowds, but these were her fans. She could do this. It was only one night. Right? She took a deep breath and slowly let it out. The butterflies in her stomach settled a bit.

Vivian glanced at her watch. "Oops, it's after six, we better let them in before they knock Belinda down. You have no idea how popular you are with my readers, Miss Cool."

"Please, call me Sar . . . — um, Sadie," she invited.

"Sadie it is. Now take your position at the table and I'll go let them in." Vivian beamed and waved to the table where she had books, a pen, and a glass of ice water set out.

Sarah sat there feeling awkward and vulnerable and not really sure what do with her hands as the doors flew open and the crowd flooded into the store. People surrounded her, chattering and shoving books at her to sign. She felt her mind detach from the hubbub, and mentally she pulled back. It was almost as if she was standing outside her own body, watching it all happen from a safe distance. She smiled and signed books and made small talk and then looked up to see Travis standing in front of her, tall and heartthrob handsome. But it wasn't just his good looks that had feminine heads whipping around to stare at him. There was that charming way he smiled, the relaxed, self-confident way he walked, and that greatest-single-dad-on-Earth thing he had going on. He was the only grown man in the bookstore thronged with women and children and he was holding Jazzy's hand and looking completely irresistible.

He wore a black polo shirt, starched blue jeans, and chestnut-colored cowboy boots. A five-o'clock shadow had sprouted around his chin, and his hair was windblown. He smelled of lake mist and candy canes. Her stomach did a stupid roller coaster loop-de-loop, sliding up into her throat before plunging back down where it belonged.

"Hi, Sarah!" Jazzy grinned. She wore pink fuzzy bunny pajamas with a pink car coat over the top. "We just had peppermint cocoa at Rinky-Tink's, with pink marshmallows. I wanted to invite you but Daddy said you were too busy to come with us, so now here we are. We're staying for the pajama party."

Sarah blinked at Jazzy. "Your Daddy is staying too?"

"Yep," Travis drawled, and flashed his deadly lady-killer smile. "Daddy too."

What was he smiling at her for? Last night, he'd tossed her out his back door. Did he think she was just going to act like that hadn't happened? Be all giggles and grins? But of course that's precisely how she should act. As if his behavior hadn't affected her at all. As if she didn't care.

His gaze lowered to take in the V-neck of her flannel pajama top and then slowly roved back to her eyes.

Crap! Why had she worn a push-up bra? "Um . . ." she said, "there's a line of people behind you."

"Oh, don't worry," he said, and pointed with his thumb in the direction of the area cordoned off for the PJ party. "We'll wait for you over there until there's a break in the action."

"The line's pretty long. It might be a while."

"The store closes at eight," he said. "That's when the party officially begins."

"And you're going to wait the whole time?"

"Wouldn't have it any other way."

Was he trying to irk the hell out of her? Why was he acting as if nothing had happened? Well, if he could be blasé, so could she. "Suit yourself."

"I will."

"Good."

"Great."

"Splendid."

"Terrific."

"Oh, Travis," simpered a pretty young mother zooming across the room. She linked her arm through his. She was wearing a zebra-striped negligee with matching dressing gown and fussy bedroom mules. Her hair was freshly coiffed and her faux nails looked newly painted. Sarah knew a woman on the hunt when she saw one. "Andi and I were hoping you and Jazzy would be here. Come on over, we've commandeered a table in the corner."

The woman whisked him to the back of the store.

Do not look. Who cares where they're off to? It's none of your business.

She glanced in their direction and saw Travis peeking over his shoulder at her as he was being trolled away like a bass behind a fishing boat.

Ha! Served him right. So why the twinge of jealousy biting into her?

The traffic finally slowed just before Ye Olde Book Nook closed up for the night. Vivian made a big deal of starting the pajama party and introduced Sarah with much fanfare.

Belinda had stuck around to help serve the cookies and punch and get the kids settled in their sleeping bags and on pallets. While all that was going on, Sarah grabbed a small plate of veggies and dip from the hors d'oeuvres buffet. She hadn't thought to eat supper before this thing and she was starving. She'd positioned herself out of the way of the fray, but then turned around to see Travis sauntering over to where she stood nibbling a broccoli floweret dipped in ranch dressing.

"You look like you'd rather be having a root canal," he said.

"No, I love broccoli."

"I'm not talking about the broccoli."

"Whatever gave you that idea?" She wished he'd just leave her alone. She only had to get through one more night and then it was hasta la vista Twilight.

"You're hiding out in the corner by yourself and you keep looking at the clock."

"So, you and Little Miss Zebra Print." She nodded to where the woman in the black and white striped negligee was sitting with Jazzy and another girl about Jazzy's age.

"Sandy?" Travis looked over and Sandy wriggled her fingers at him. "What about her?"

"Does she know you shove your dates out on the back porch in their underwear when they get inconvenient?"

"We weren't on a date."

"Oh, excuse me. I didn't realize that was a technicality." She didn't know why she was being bitchy. She understood why he'd done what he'd done.

Travis shoved a hand through his hair. "Look, I'm really sorry about it. I must have made you feel—"

"You didn't make me feel a thing," she cut him off. "Other than cold. It was pretty cold on the porch. In my underwear."

"I freaked," he admitted. "Panicked. I didn't know what to say to Jazzy if she found you there. I've never had a woman sleep over."

"Seriously?" Sarah arched an eyebrow and looked around the room. Half the women in the place were staring at him like he was a big, thick slice of filet mignon. "I find that difficult to believe. You were always such a player in high school. One girl after another." She sounded jealous. She could hear it in her voice. Hell, she *was* jealous.

"Believe it. You were the first since Crystal."

"Lucky me." She stared at Travis's neck so she

didn't have to look him in the eyes. The pulse at his throat was jumping visibly. "Does Sandy know that?"

"I didn't feel a need to share that information with her."

Even though she didn't want to, she dragged her gaze to his face and felt a profound craving for something she was afraid to want. A craving that went against all reason.

"Please forgive me," he said. "I was very rude."

He held her gaze and she simply could not look away. She studied his handsome features in the fluorescent lighting that should have made his skin look sallow like everyone else's, but instead lent a burnished glow to his complexion, and waited for her breathing to slow. This was not the time or place for a lusty stare-down.

"I should have stuffed you in a closet instead of pushing you out the back door." He winked.

She had to laugh at that, although the sound came out rushed and breathless. She glanced at his broad, masculine chest and then flashed back to his eyes. They were gentle, apologetic. Quickly, she looked back at his chest again, remembering how it had looked stripped bare of clothing. A lump knotted up in her throat. She raised her chin, grinned, forgiving him for anything and everything.

"I brought a peace offering," he said. "I hope you'll forgive me."

"Oh?"

"Hang on." He disappeared into the back of the store and returned a minute later with a huge bouquet of cherry Tootsie Pops tied up with red Christmas ribbon.

"They were out of roses?"

"You're too special for clichés. Besides, you can take Tootsie Pops on the plane. The roses would go to waste."

"Handsome, contrite, and practical." She laughed again and accepted his Tootsie Pop bouquet.

His answering smile hijacked what little breath she had left. "Am I forgiven?"

"Uh-huh." She couldn't think of anything else to say, so she popped a carrot in her mouth and tried to deny how shaky her knees felt.

Travis stood looking at her, not moving, breathing the same air.

Sarah heard the clomp of mules on the laminated faux wood flooring, smelled the scent of Chanel No. 5, caught a flutter of zebra print from the corner of her eye.

"I snagged us some spiced apple cider," Sandy oozed.

Travis smiled, at her, not Sandy. "Thanks."

Sandy beamed. "Great, I'll just take the cider back to our spot."

"You do that," he said, not once breaking eye contact with Sarah.

Sarah suppressed a smile and when Sandy was out of earshot, she said, "You're leading her on."

"How's that?"

"Sitting with her. Letting her fetch and carry your cider when you're not interested."

"Her daughter and Jazzy are friends. That's all."

"Zebra Print Sandy has other ideas."

"You think?"

"I know. She's over there licking her chops right now."

"Watch out, your eyes are turning green."

"I'm not jealous."

"Now your nose is starting to grow."

"You're incorrigible."

"And you love that about me." He winked. "I shake you up."

Boy, did he. This was the Travis she remembered from her youth, teasing, fun-loving, relaxed.

Suddenly his smile disappeared and his features sobered. "So," he said, "you're leaving town tomorrow."

She nodded.

"Do you think you'll be coming back this way anytime soon?"

Sarah met his gray-eyed gaze. "I really don't have a reason to come back."

"Oh." He stepped back, splayed a palm to the nape of his neck. "There's no way we can persuade you to stay a little longer? Maybe until after Christmas. We've got the annual lighting of the town Christmas tree on the square, that's always a lot of fun."

Sarah shook her head. "I've got a book due . . ."

He forced a smile, but there was no longer a light in his eyes. "It's okay, I get it."

"It's just that my home is in New York."

"You're wrong about that, Sadie Cool," he murmured. "Whether you want to acknowledge it or not, Twilight is your home."

"I've never even lived in this town."

"Doesn't matter." Now his smile was sad. "Twilight is still in your heart."

That pulled her up short. Was he hinting that he wanted a relationship? "What are you saying,

Travis? If you've got something to say to me, then just come out and say it."

"This town is going to miss you. Jazzy is going to miss you . . . I . . . I'm going to miss you. Last night was . . ." He glanced around. "Well, this isn't the time or place to discuss the implications of last night. That's why I was hoping you could stay in Twilight a little longer."

How she wanted to say yes! She felt something inside her loosen, like the bracings on a river dam threatening to give way against the swell of heavy rains. She wanted to tell him this, but she was so afraid of the consequences. She'd never been emotionally close to anyone and she didn't know how. It was easier, safer, to just pretend last night had been a lark and she was on to the next adventure.

"Look you're off the hook for last night." Sarah held up the Tootsie Pop bouquet. "Honestly, Travis, it's okay. Last night was great, especially the part where you saved me from drowning. That was my favorite part. The ending was regrettable, but hey I understand. Don't feel that you owe me anything at all. Your priority is your daughter, as she should be. Take care of her and just let it go at that."

He scowled. "I—"

But he didn't get any further because Vivian scurried over. "It's time to start the story, Miss Cool."

Sarah took her place in the middle of the circle and started to read. The rapt children sat mesmerized by the story. She slipped inside the book and let herself be carried off, blocking out everything around her except the words on the page—withdrawing, tucking in, escaping the intensity of emotions she'd never learned how to deal with beyond burying them. The words she knew so well tumbled over her, ran through her, came out of her.

As her tongue flew over the words, her body coiled tighter and tighter, until she was outside herself. It was like she was hovering above her own body, watching herself perform. Watching Travis watching her.

A shudder ran through her but she didn't feel it. She was that out of touch with the feelings balling up inside of her. She wanted him so badly but she was so afraid to let herself go, to take the emotional risks necessary. What if she took a chance and things didn't work out? No, much easier and safer to back away now before things got really sticky.

Her mind swirled with images of the night before. Travis's lips on hers, his hands on her body, the look in his eyes. Then stupidly, for one whisper of a second, she raised her head and her gaze met his and she realized three important things.

One, she was a woman with an emotional wall so tall she had no idea how to go about knocking it down. Two, Travis was a single father with an ailing little girl who wished desperately for a mommy. And three, she had fallen madly in love with them both, but she was scared of showing it. Terrified that if she did, she'd have her heart broken right in two.

Chapter Thirteen

Travis studied Sarah. She was so wrapped up in reading to the children, it was as if nothing existed for her except the inner world she'd created. Her eyes lit up with passion and she took on the voices of the characters, becoming each one in turn. When she was Isabella, the heroine from her book, her voice grew higher, reedy, and her eyes widened. When she was Santa, her voice dropped and her shoulders broadened and she laughed from deep in her belly. The children were transfixed, caught in the spell of the story and Sarah's expert telling of it.

This was Sarah's world and the only connection he had to it was through the book his daughter loved.

The rest of the time, when she wasn't immersed in her fictional world, Sarah was guarded and cautious. His father had been like this—quiet, withdrawing, hard to know, difficult to access. He'd often made Travis feel alone even when they were in the same room together. Maybe that was one of the reasons he went a little overboard lavishing attention on his daughter. His father had often looked down on him for making decisions based on his feelings. Was Sarah the same way? So logical that she was Spock-ish when it came to emotions?

Did he really want to try so hard to be with her? Never mind that he wanted her so much it made his bones ache. There were those feelings again, illogical, but powerful. How did she manage to turn them off and lead with her brain? So what if when he looked at her he felt as if they were destined. There were some things love just couldn't fix. His gaze traveled over to his daughter. He knew that firsthand.

Love.

The word tap-danced in his head. Was he really in love with Sarah Collier or was it just gratitude for all she'd done for his daughter masquerading as love? Or maybe it was simple lust. Not destiny or kismet at all, just intense physical attraction of which he'd never felt the like.

In that moment, she raised her head and looked him in the eyes, then quickly glanced away again, and Travis knew he was doomed to love a woman who might never be able to love him the way he needed to be loved.

Once she was back in Manhattan, amid the honking of taxis, the crush of crowds, and buildings so tall they obscured the sky, Sarah couldn't write. Gone was the smooth muse who'd sat on her shoulder in Twilight and whispered fragments of brilliant story into her ear. All she could think about was Travis and Jazzy and everything she'd left behind.

"Come on, we're getting you out of this apartment. You need sunshine," Benny told Sarah on the Tuesday after she'd returned from Twilight. "Let's go for a walk in Central Park."

Sarah stayed slouched in her seat, her gaze pinned on her computer screen. She stretched the sleeves of her sweater past the ends of her fingertips and stared at the blinking cursor. Where had the rush of inspiration gone that had seized her in Twilight? How could it have just disappeared?

"Hello." Benny knocked on her cherrywood coffee table. "Anybody home?"

"I can't think. My mind is blank."

"It's just jet lag. You've only been home a couple of days. Get on your feet, get out of your chair."

"A walk isn't going to fix this."

"How do you know?"

"I've already taken three walks today."

"Ice skating at Rockefeller Center?"

"Forget it. This block is exercise proof."

He took her coat from the hook beside the door and held it out to her. "I don't think you have writer's block."

Sarah groaned and shambled over to poke her hands into the coat. "Please don't quote Stephen King to me again."

Benny opened the door and ushered her into the hall. "I wasn't going to quote King. I was going to say you seem homesick."

"Twilight isn't my home," she protested as he took her elbow and guided her toward the elevators.

"Maybe not geographically, but in your heart, I think it is." They got in and he punched the button for the ground floor.

"What on earth makes you say that?"

"When you talk about the town, your whole face lights up. The cookie club women, the town square, Jazzy."

"It doesn't." She touched her cheek.

They went through the lobby, pushed out into the rush of cold December air. "The rest of the time you mope and you sigh a lot and you keep staring out the window lost in thought and it's not the good kind of lost in thought like you're working on a book. You're either homesick or lovesick." Benny paused, and narrowed his eyes. "You didn't fall in love while you were away, did you?"

Sarah walked faster, outdistancing him, headed straight ahead toward Central Park.

"You did!" Benny exclaimed, rushing to catch up with her.

"I didn't."

"Don't tell me it was with that guy you were hung up on back in high school."

Blindly, she nodded and swallowed back the lump welling up in her throat, then explained how Jazzy had turned out to be Travis's daughter and the ladies of the cookie club had been playing matchmaker. All around her, New York throbbed with energy, but she couldn't help comparing the stimulating pulse with the serene pace of Twilight. One place revved you up. The other calmed you down.

"Wow."

"Wow is right."

"So what happened?"

Sarah shrugged. "Nothing happened."

"Oh, don't lie to me. Something happened."

"Okay . . ." Sarah inhaled deeply. "We might have almost made love."

"What stopped you?"

She touched her stomach, felt the ridges of the burn scar through her clothing. "My fears, his kid, our doubts. Oh, and he shoved me out the back porch in my underwear." Her breath came in frosty puffs and she snuggled deeper into her coat.

"What?"

Sarah waved, and then jammed her hands into her pockets. "It's not as bad as it sounds. His daughter came home unexpectedly and he didn't want her to see us like that."

"He's ashamed of you."

"No, not at all. He just doesn't want Jazzy to get too invested in me."

"And why is that?"

"Because . . . well, you know me, Benny. I've never had a real romantic relationship. I don't know how to go about it. And while being with Travis was a dream come true, I can't trust my feelings. Are they real? Or is it simply wish fulfillment? I don't know if I'm capable of seeing him through any lenses other than those rose-colored glasses of my youth."

"You're scared to trust your emotions."

"That about sums it up."

"But in the meanwhile, your writing has stalled."

She nodded.

"I've read what you sent me," he said. "That's why I dropped by in the first place. To tell you that the story absolutely blew me away. It's got so much more pathos than *The Magic Christmas Cookie*. But three-quarters of a story doesn't cut it. You've got to have that power ending."

"I know." She groaned. "And I've hit a wall I can't find my way around."

"Wrong."

"What?"

"There's a way around it, you just don't like it."

"What's that?"

"If you want to get your inspiration back you have to return to where you found it in the first place."

"Twilight?"

"Twilight," Benny confirmed.

He made it sound so easy. Just get on a plane and go back.

And see Travis again. He was bound to think her return meant something more than the need to recapture her vanishing muse. Which begged the question, was her disappearing creativity simply a way for her devious subconscious mind to get her back to Twilight?

"I don't mean to put the screws to you," Benny said as a group of runners jogged past them. "But I had lunch with Hal again today."

She stopped walking and looked at him. The air smelled of snow, and somewhere someone was roasting chestnuts. "I don't like the look on your face."

"It's not good news."

A chill pushed through her that had nothing to do with the nippy air. "Oh?"

"He says if you don't get it turned in on schedule

this time they're canceling your contract and you'll have to pay back that quarter of a million advance. If that happens, your writing career is as good as over."

Travis tried to tell himself that it was probably all for the best that Sarah had gone back to New York. She wasn't ready for a serious relationship and because of Jazzy he couldn't afford anything casual.

Who was he trying to kid? He didn't want anything casual from Sarah. He was serious about her, which sucked considering she was on the fence about him.

How had this happened? How had he gone from minding his own business and taking care of his daughter to being crazy about a woman who clearly had commitment issues?

On the Wednesday after Sarah had left, he was out in his boat on the lake, pondering these questions, when his cell phone vibrated. When he saw on the caller ID that the message was from Jazzy's school, a cold sweat broke out on his neck.

"Yes," he barked into the phone.

"Mr. Walker, this is the school nurse at Jon Grant Elementary."

A spike of fear drove down his spine. "What is it?"

"I don't mean to alarm you sir, it's just since Jazzy has been so improved, I simply wanted you to know that she's having a little trouble catching her breath this morning. It's not nearly bad as it used to be, but I thought you'd want to nip this in the bud."

"I'll be right there."

Twenty minutes later, he and Jazzy were in Dr. Adams's office. As the nurse had said, Jazzy's wheezing really wasn't as bad as it had been in the past, but in light of her miraculous response to the new drug, this setback concerned him. Had the drug stopped working? Were they headed back to square one?

Jazzy sat on the exam table, her head down, while Dr. Adams listened to her lungs with a stethoscope. When he was finished, he called the nurse in to help Jazzy get dressed and pulled Travis into his office.

"Jazzy's progress on the new drug has been remarkable," Dr. Adams said. "She's far exceeded our expectations."

"Okay, so what's this little episode of shortness of breath all about?"

"It appears that she's having some breakthrough issues."

"What does that mean?"

"The drug isn't holding her three weeks this time."

Travis waited. He'd been so afraid to hope that this medication was indeed the thing that could fix Jazzy once and for all. He'd gotten his hopes up before, only to have them dashed. For the last two months, he'd never seen her so energetic and pink-cheeked, so full of life. But today, she'd taken a step backward. He fisted his hands.

Dr. Adams steepled his fingers. "It means the drug isn't lasting three weeks. Remember, we're experimenting here to titrate the dosage. I think we need to increase the frequency of her injections to every two weeks."

Travis gulped. "That's five thousand dollars a

month instead of every six weeks. So roughly that increases the cost from forty thousand dollars a year to sixty thousand."

The doctor nodded.

"I've got to be honest. Today's injection is going to wipe out my savings. The only money I have left is Jazzy's college fund and there's only enough in there to last for another six weeks."

"Now that we know the drug does work, we're going to have to figure out a way for you to afford it until the FDA approves the medication for the treatment of severe asthma."

"How far off is that?"

"It's hard to say," Dr. Adams hedged. "I could front you a couple of doses and I'll willingly waive my fee—"

"You don't have to do that," Travis said. "I'll get the money."

In his head he was frantically trying to think of ways to make five thousand a month. He loved his job as game warden. It was the only job he'd ever wanted, but the pay, while good enough to support him and Jazzy comfortably, wasn't enough to cover medical bills like these. He knew the town would rally around him, throw fund-raisers. They'd done it ever since Crystal had left him, but he didn't want to ask for donations. That felt too much like begging, although if it came down to it, he wasn't too proud to beg. Not where Jazzy was concerned. He knew his Aunt Raylene could pitch in a little, but she and Earl had taken a big financial hit in the economic bust because most of their fortune was tied up in real estate. He'd rather provide for Jazzy on his own if he could.

The cottage was the only thing he had left to tap

for cash. No way around it, to keep his daughter healthy, he was going to have to sell the house.

Sarah stared at the blank screen, sweating metaphorical blood, attempting to will words to magically appear on the page. She'd been frozen like this ever since Benny had left. She couldn't remember when she'd last eaten and she was a bit fuzzy on what day it was. She'd fallen into the well of writer's fugue and it was an ugly place indeed.

It wasn't so much that she'd have to pay back the advance. She'd received only half of it on signing anyway and the money she'd gotten for the movie option would pay that back. Plus she had a small trust fund her father's parents had left her and there were still plenty of royalties rolling in from *The Magic Christmas Cookie.*

What paralyzed her was the thought of losing her career. Never mind that her quick success had made her feel a bit fraudulent. When it came down to it, writing was all she'd ever wanted to do. It was all she really knew. If she wasn't a writer, then who was she?

Something her Gram had once said rose in her mind. "Your mother has never learned that a career is just a career. It doesn't define who you are."

Sarah let out a sigh. Imagine that. She and her mother had something in common.

The phone rang, but inertia had such a strong hold on her that Sarah didn't move from the chair. She just kept sitting and staring at the empty computer screen and listening to the phone ring.

The answering machine picked up.

"Sarah, are you there? If you're there, please pick up. It's Travis."

Impulse rocketed her out of her seat and launched her to the phone. But discretion held her back, her hand hovering over the receiver. Elation warred with caution. Joy that he'd called her did battle with her logical, detached mind. Fear arm-wrestled with hope.

Be careful.

"I know I'm not the person you most want to hear from right now, but please pick up. This is about Jazzy."

Sarah snatched the cordless phone from its cradle. "What's wrong?"

"Don't panic," he said. "Jazzy is okay, but we do need your help."

She didn't know what to say, so she kept quiet.

Travis exhaled audibly. "Listen, Jazzy had a little episode and when I took her back to the doctor he said she was going to need the injections twice a month now. In order to afford it, I have to sell your Gram's house." He paused. "I thought I'd give you first crack at buying it. I know how much you love this place and if you'd like, we could rent it from you and I'd keep it up."

In her mind's eyes she could see Travis standing there, cap in hand, his game warden badge at his chest, looking exactly like what he was—a loving father in need. And Sarah wanted the thing he was offering. She'd been bereft when her parents had told her they'd sold Gram's cottage. Bereft and angry. Now, she had a chance to get it back.

But at what cost? If she bought the house, Travis would be her tenant. It would cause a shift in their relationship. All the power would be hers.

What relationship? She didn't have a relationship with him. He was someone she'd known nine years ago, that was all. A guy who treated her as a little sister because she was just a goofy kid with a dumb unrequited crush. Why not become his landlord? Better her than someone else owning Gram's place.

This time, she wasn't able to squelch her impulses. "Yes, of course I'll buy it. I'll call Jenny and make reservations at the Merry Cherub and fly back to Twilight tomorrow."

On Friday, Travis took a personal day off so he could pick up Sarah at the airport. When he saw her step into the baggage area at the American Airlines terminal at DFW airport, his heart hammered hard. She wore a long-sleeved, knee-length, wine-colored dress, and he could see the outline of her curvy body beneath the soft material. He crossed the floor to the carousel and reached down to grab her bag just as she went for it.

Simultaneously, their hands closed over the handle. They looked into each other's eyes and he felt the world settle in with a click, as if it had been spinning out of orbit and he hadn't known until now.

Riding a wave of impulse, he took her into his arms and kissed her. She kissed him back like she'd been holding her breath the entire five days she'd been away. Had it been only five? It had felt like five hundred.

The next thing he said was completely spontaneous and he meant every word. "Welcome home, sweetheart."

Coming back to Twilight was far different than she expected. Sarah had anticipated awkwardness, but there was none. It was as if she and Travis had been together for years and it surprised her how easy things were between them.

As soon as they arrived in town, they reclaimed her room at the Merry Cherub, booking her in through New Year's Day. Then they went to the courthouse to see a lawyer to draw up papers for the sale of the house. Because Travis owned the property free and clear and Sarah was paying cash, the transaction could be completed by the following Friday, which happened to be Christmas Eve.

The only issue they had was agreeing on a price. Travis was asking far less than it was worth.

"It's your grandmother's cottage," he said softly.

"It's lakefront property," she argued.

"My asking price is what Crystal and I paid for it."

"That was nine years ago and my parents sold it so cheaply because they just wanted out from under the responsibility of it. The place is worth fifty thousand more than you're asking."

"You're inflating the price because you want to help me out with Jazzy's expenses."

"So what if I am?"

"I'm not going to let you pay more than fair market value."

"It's fair market value," the lawyer interjected. "Just at the high end."

"See there," Sarah said.

"It's only twelve hundred square feet."

"With its own pier and dock."

"It needs some renovating."

"You'll be renting it from me, do whatever you have time to do."

The lawyer shook his head. "I've never seen anyone argue to pay more for a piece of property."

Sarah reached over and took Travis's hand and looked him squarely in the eyes. "Take my offer. For Jazzy's sake."

She could tell he had to swallow a big chunk of his pride, and she knew only love for his daughter could make him do this. "All right," he finally agreed. "But I am paying you rent."

"Of course." She didn't have to tell him she was planning on putting his rent money into a money market account in Jazzy's name.

"This will be a Christmas present to us both," Travis told her as they left the courthouse.

"Yes," she agreed.

"Miss Sarah," Mayor Moe called out as he sauntered over to them. "You're back."

"Hello, Mayor." Sarah nodded, and didn't elaborate on why she'd returned, but she could tell Moe was dying of curiosity.

"How long are you staying?" he asked.

"I'm not sure."

"Well, it's wonderful to have you back for however long you're here." He beamed, and then shifted his attention to Travis. "Just wanted to tell you Frank Jennings left the back pasture gate unlocked for you. He says you've got plenty of great ones to choose from this year."

"Thanks, Moe."

"Plenty of great what?" Sarah asked.

"Christmas trees. Travis is the official lumberjack for the town Christmas tree. He harvests a big native Texas cedar every year from a local ranch."

"Oh, that's right. You still have the tradition of

lighting the Twilight Christmas tree the Sunday before Christmas."

"You remembered." Moe looked pleased. "Hey, why don't you go along with Travis tomorrow? He could use a woman's touch in picking out the perfect tree." Moe winked at Sarah. "Make sure he gets a big one. At least fifteen feet."

"Are you saying my trees haven't been perfect?" Travis joked.

Moe slapped Travis on the back. "You kids have fun."

And just like that, Sarah had a date for the following morning to go chop down a Christmas tree.

CHAPTER FOURTEEN

In North Central Texas, winter was a most fickle creature. Things could heat up to seventy degrees one morning, then by that afternoon, a norther could sweep in from the Panhandle and by dark temperatures could sink below freezing. North Texans knew to keep a heavy coat stashed in their cars just in case the balmy weather turned vicious. The prudent among them also kept blankets and emergency supplies in their trunk, just in case a razzle-dazzler of an ice storm struck. It happened at least once or twice every winter and it always blew in like a freeloading uncle showing up on the doorstep, unexpected and unwanted.

The Saturday morning that Travis and Sarah set off to find the perfect Christmas tree dawned warm as April. She could almost hear the buds on the peach trees ringing the grounds of the Merry Cherub, plotting an early debut. Texas peach trees had notoriously poor timing. A couple of warm days and they were itching to burst out in blooms, completely ignorant of the calendar and those sly Panhandle northers.

"It's such a glorious day I decided to walk over," Sarah said as she strolled up into Travis's yard where he was putting covers on the outdoor faucets.

He pushed back his gray felt cowboy hat and eyed the sky. "Don't trust it. Bring a heavier coat."

"I'm already burning up in this jacket," she said. "Besides, we won't be gone that long. A couple of hours at most, right?"

He looked like he was going to disagree, but then he shrugged and started his pickup truck. "Have you forgotten about North Texas winter weather? It can change in the blink of an eye."

"Even when it's cold here, it's still warmer than it is in New York."

He arched an eyebrow, stepped to the back door, and held it open for her. "Suit yourself, but don't say I didn't warn you."

"So how does this choppy down tree thingy work?" she asked as they stepped into the kitchen.

"'Choppy down tree thingy'? What is that? Writer-speak?"

She laughed. "It's just me showing my vast ignorance of proper holiday traditions."

"You've never gone with your family to chop down your Christmas tree?"

Sarah let out laugh that ended up sounding sort of like a bark. She was trying to picture the doctors Mitchell and Helen Collier cutting down Christmas trees and failed miserably. The only cutting they liked to do was in an operating room. "Hardly. I can't imagine my dad chopping down a tree. It could hurt his surgeon hands. I spent my holidays with Gram, remember? And she was a bit past the age of cutting down Christmas trees. It was a good year if my parents managed to show up on Christmas Day."

"You've been sadly deprived."

"Shocking, I know; get out the violins."

"So," he said, his eyes twinkling mischievously, "I'm going to be your first time."

"Yeah," she countered quickly, "that's a lot of pressure. A girl has expectations. She wants her first Christmas tree cutting to be special."

He grinned and then looked down at her feet. "You're not wearing those boots."

She wriggled her toes. "What's wrong with them? They're warm."

"We're going to be walking through pastures."

"I don't mind getting them a little muddy."

"They're stilettos, for crying out loud," he said. "You'll break your neck."

"They're all I have."

"Hang on. I'll be right back." Travis darted into the garage, leaving her standing in the kitchen that had once belonged to her grandmother. She looked around, remembering. In the corner cabinet on the far side of the stove was where Gram used to keep her canisters. That's where Sarah once stood on the step stool and sifted the flour Gram had measured out into a big yellow bowl for mixing up the kismet cookies. Now, this kitchen was going to be hers.

"Here we go." Travis burst back into the room carrying a pair of women's black rubber boots.

At the sight of them all the breath left her body. "Those . . . those are my Gram's."

"I found them in the gardening shed when we moved in here."

Nostalgia winnowed through Sarah. She re-membered watching Gram slip on the boots to wade out in the garden to pluck her harvest after a summer rain.

Travis held the boots out to her and their fingers brushed. A wildfire of sensation shot through her the way it always did when he touched her. Sarah's stomach lurched. Oh, this wasn't good. She had no business going off with him to some isolated ranch on a Christmas tree hunt. She should be back at the Merry Cherub writing the ending of her book.

"All set?" he asked when she'd slipped off her Italian leather boots and plowed her feet into Gram's rubber work boots. They felt solid, reli-able, and very comfy.

"All set. Do we need a saw or anything?"

"Everything is loaded up in the toolbox in the back of my truck," he said.

Of course, he was Mr. Wilderness Man. She fol-lowed him out to his pickup with a long flatbed trailer attached for hauling the Christmas tree. He opened the passenger side door for her. She planted one foot on the running board for a boost up into the high seat and he held out a hand to steady her. He made her feel cherished and it was a dangerous feeling indeed.

He got in and took a pair of scruffy-looking work gloves from the glove compartment.

"Hey, look," she said, "you actually keep gloves in your glove compartment."

"You don't?"

"I don't even own a car. I live in Manhattan, remember."

He tossed the grubby gloves into her lap.

"Ugh, what did you do that for?"

"Put 'em on."

"I have gloves, thank you. She tugged a pair of delicate leather kid gloves from her coat pocket.

"Trust me, you're gonna want these."

She picked up one of the offending gloves by its pinkie finger. "They've got gunk on them."

"That's because they're work gloves. Those girlie things you've got won't protect your hands. We're going to the back pasture of a working cattle ranch, there's no one there to impress with your great fashion sense."

"You think I have a great fashion sense?"

He started the truck. "Stop fishing for compliments."

"You think I look good?"

Travis grinned. "Sin-sational."

"Thank you."

"Now put on the work gloves."

"It kills the look."

"The look died with the rubber boots."

"You've got a point." She wriggled her fingers into the gloves. They were way too big. "Look, Paul Bunyan hands."

He laughed. "It's fun to see you like this."

"What, buffoonish?"

"Lighthearted. You're usually so serious."

"Hey, life *is* serious."

"Which is why we so desperately need those lighthearted moments to get us through the crappy ones."

"You're a flaming optimist, aren't you?"

"When you've got a sick kid, you have to be."

"Jazzy's been doing really well though, right? Even with this setback."

"Yeah." He nodded. "But even an optimist is sometimes afraid to hope too hard. She's been sick for so long and has been through so much, it's difficult to believe this one drug has made such a difference. Thank you for agreeing to buy the house and letting us rent from you."

"Thank you for offering the house to me before just selling it to someone else."

He looked at her for a long moment, then murmured, "You're one awesome woman, Sadie Cool."

Travis turned off the main highway onto a one-lane dirt road and bumped over a cattle guard. All around them was grassland dried yellow in winter. They drove for fifteen minutes without seeing anyone or anything except a few head of Angus cattle, over rough Texas terrain—gullies and washes—until they came to a fenced-off area. Travis stopped his four-wheel drive pickup truck and got out to open the gate. Sarah sat in the cab watching him. He cut a ruggedly handsome figure in his gray cowboy hat the color of his eyes, blue flannel shirt, faded denims, and scuffed boots.

Once the gate was open, he came back toward the pickup and caught her watching him. He cocked his head and leveled her an insouciant grin, making her knees so weak she was happy she was sitting down. He could have been a bull rider with that wiry frame. The way his eyes caught hers sent a current of electricity running straight to her heart.

He got back into the pickup, bringing the smell of the outdoors with him, grass and cedar and earthy Texas soil. Her insides turned to jelly. Every time she was around this man, she lost her ability to think calmly, rationally. Desire rushed over her.

Emotions ambushed her. She was feeling too much and she was giddily afraid.

He drove clear of the gate, got out, and reversed the process. They traveled for a time, seeing mesquites, scrub oaks, cactus, and pecan trees, before they arrived at a small log cabin in a clearing. Beyond the clearing was a huge cedar thicket.

"What's this place?"

"It's a hunter's cabin Frank Jennings sometimes rents out. I don't think he's running a deer lease this season, so no one else should be here."

Travis killed the engine and got out of the pickup. Sarah followed suit. He went around to the bed of the truck and removed a long-handled axe, ropes, and bungee cords.

"What can I do to help?"

"Pick out the perfect tree."

They walked through the forest of cedar, the air heavy with the Christmassy smell of them. Sarah eyed the trees, searching for one that was the right height that still had a good shape on all four sides.

"How long have you been the official Twilight Christmas tree lumberjack?" she asked, tromping over the briars and tall dead grass. She was grateful now for the rubber boots he'd made her wear. Gram's boots. She wriggled her toes, thinking of Gram, feeling closer to her than she'd felt in years.

"About the time Crystal took off. I wanted to do everything I could to make Jazzy's holidays special and she loves it that I cut down the town Christmas tree."

"How come we didn't bring her with us?"

"My Aunt Raylene wanted to take her to see *The Nutcracker* at the Bass Hall in Fort Worth.

She's wanted to do it for years, but I've always been afraid to let Jazzy get too far away from home. Now that she's doing better, I couldn't keep denying her. They're going to make a day of it. Tea at the Worthington, shopping, all that girl stuff."

"It must have been really tough for you," she said, "with both your parents gone. Alone with a sick kid."

Travis shrugged. "I manage."

"You do much more than manage. Jazzy is an amazing child. Positive, upbeat."

"Sometimes I wonder if she feels she always has to put on a happy face for me," he said, "because I always try to put on a happy face for her."

Sarah's breath tangled up in her lungs. Even though it made no sense, even though they were nothing alike, she felt a bond with him that she couldn't explain. They were so dissimilar. He was gregarious. She was shy. He liked the country. She'd made a home for herself in New York City. She kept people at a distance. He would embrace the whole world if he could. But they'd both suffered. He more than she. He'd lost his parents and could just as easily lose his child. Sarah couldn't begin to imagine what that was like.

But she'd suffered too. She'd never really been able to connect with her parents. She'd lost her beloved Gram. And then there'd been the disaster that had scarred more than just her body. She'd allowed fear to hold her back and keep her from taking emotional risks, while Travis couldn't afford to gamble on anything.

They'd both been changed by what they'd experienced, Travis growing from a reckless young man into a responsible father, while Sarah had gone from wide-eyed romantic to total cynic. As kids, their lives had intertwined during the holidays when she'd come to visit her Gram, and now, years later, they'd intertwined again over his daughter.

Her gaze followed the line of a tall cedar standing majestic green against the background of troubled blue sky, suddenly knotted up with gray clouds. The wind had changed directions, now gusting in from the north. She shivered and raised the collar of her jacket. These were the conditions Travis worked in every day as a game warden, nature in the raw—beautiful, exciting, powerful. The morning sunlight dimmed, went bright, then dimmed again as it played tag with the broody clouds marshalling across the western horizon.

"Cumulonimbus squall lines," Travis said.

"What?"

He nodded at the sky, tilted back his head, and inhaled deeply. "Storm's closing in. Smell the wind?"

"Um . . . no . . . not really."

"Ice," he said. "Those clouds are carrying ice."

"How do you know that?"

"I've seen it, smelled it. We need to cut down a tree and get back to town before it hits. I hope Raylene is watching the sky. I'd hate for her and Jazzy to get trapped in Fort Worth in this mess. Hurry and pick a tree."

"There's so many."

"Tall and fluffy will do."

Feeling the pressure, Sarah circled several trees. "Ooh, ooh, this one!" she exclaimed, and pointed to the perfect tree, which she hadn't seen before.

Travis went to work on the tree, chopping it

down with just a few expert whacks. She helped him drag the prickly-branched tree to the flatbed trailer and load it up. Good thing he'd made her wear the work gloves.

By the time they got the tree securely strapped down and covered with a big blue tarp, the wind was gusting icy cold across the pasture and the sky had darkened considerably with the gathering squall line. He rubbed his palms together. "Let's get the hell out of Dodge, Miss Kitty."

She grinned at his teasing and climbed into the passenger side of the pickup truck while Travis slid behind the wheel. He paused a moment to pull his cell phone from his pocket. "Just going to call Aunt Raylene and tell her to cut the trip short," he explained.

Sarah listened while he contacted his aunt and from the one-sided conversation gathered that Raylene had already checked the weather and canceled the trip.

"Hello . . . ?" Travis pressed the phone closer to this face. "Can you hear me? Aunt Raylene?" He paused, pulled the cell phone down, and peered into it. "Dammit."

"What is it?"

"The battery's dead," he said. "Here, let me plug it in to recharge." He plugged it in. They waited, but the battery did not recharge. Travis frowned. "It's gone. Do you have your cell with you?"

"No, I lost it in the lake the day you rescued me and I haven't gotten around to replacing it. I'm sorry."

"Not your fault, although how do you get by without a cell phone?"

She shrugged. "I'm not a phone person."

"Yeah, but you need one for emergencies. We're buying you a new one when we get back to town."

"Yes, sir."

He blew out his breath. "Anyway, Jazzy's safe and snug as a bug in a rug on Aunt Raylene's couch watching *The Little Mermaid* for the two millionth time, so I don't have to worry about them getting trapped by an ice storm in Fort Worth."

"That's good."

Through the windshield, Sarah watched the sky turn the color of a fresh bruise and the wind viciously slap the treetops. In just a few hours the temperature had plummeted dramatically. She had forgotten how erratic and unpredictable North Texas weather could be. Travis turned the pickup truck around and checked the trailer in the rearview mirror.

He headed in the direction from which they'd come. The pickup truck crested a small rise but on the other side was a deep gully rutted in the road. The truck slammed down hard, followed by a loud bang, and the impact rattled Sarah's teeth.

The truck stalled.

Travis gave it gas, but a loud clanging and grinding noise had him easing off immediately.

He swore colorfully.

Sarah frowned, alarmed. This didn't sound good. "What is it?"

"Stay in the truck," he said, getting out. "It's too damn cold for you to be out here."

"What happened? Can I help?"

"Just pray it's not what I think it is."

He shut the door and disappeared from her view as he bent down to check underneath the truck. A couple of minutes later he was back inside, a grim expression on his face.

"I take it my prayers didn't work."

"It's a busted axle," he muttered.

"What does that mean?"

"It's gotta be towed in. My cell phone battery is kaput and . . ." He trailed off just as the heavens opened and spat out an avalanche of icicles.

CHAPTER FIFTEEN

"So this is a hunter's cabin." Sarah glanced around the tiny one-room log structure that was in severe need of a good dusting. Cobwebs dangled from the corners, looking all Halloweenesque. A camp stove that had seen better days in the 1950s crouched next to the rough-hewn pine table. Battered pots and pans hung from pegs on the wall. The soot-covered fireplace gave off an I'm-a-serious-fire-hazard vibe and across from it sat a double bed piled high with faded quilts.

Travis flicked on the light switch but nothing happened. "Power must be off since Frank's not leasing this year."

"Just you and me and cabin makes three."

"Yep."

"Well," she said.

"Well," he echoed.

Oh great, now that they were trapped in here together he was going to turn into monosyllable man. Lovely. Feeling a bit claustrophobic, she peered out the window. The ice was coming down in swift, gray sheets, making *clink, clink, clink* noises as it hit the panes.

"You know," she said, "I'm not really a wilderness girl."

"No kidding. The stiletto boots you wanted to wear were a big tip-off. And the fashion gloves for tree chopping. That was a giveaway too. Oh, and your tiny designer purse."

Sarah clutched her little Dooney & Bourke to her chest. "What's wrong with my purse? It holds all the essentials. Makeup, money, credit cards, driver's license, breath mints, tissues. What else do you need?"

"It's fine for a day in Manhattan."

"Exactly."

"Except we happen to be in a back pasture on one of the biggest ranches in North Texas in an ice storm. Do you at least have some matches in there?"

"I don't smoke."

"Don't worry. I'll handle it."

"Oh, so the big he-man is going to take care of poor, ill-equipped city girl?"

"I didn't say that."

"You implied it."

"Don't drag out the big words. I'm not going to get into a verbal fencing match with you."

" 'Implied' is not a big word."

"It's a fancy word."

"No, it's not."

"You're a writer, words are your weapons, I get that. When you're feeling vulnerable it's only natural that you'd whip them out."

"Weapons? What are you talking about?"

"You use your intellect to keep people at a distance," he said mildly.

Did she? Probably. "Oh, please. That argument has at its core a central fallacy."

He smiled, almost to himself, as if he found her infinitely amusing.

The smile irritated her. "What?" she snapped.

"Fallacy?"

"What's wrong with 'fallacy'? It's a legitimate word."

"Fancy."

"All right, if that's the way you want to play it, so what if I use fancy words? It's who I am. Deal with it."

He folded his arms over his chest and didn't speak, but the smile had turned into a smirk. One look from him and she was wound up like a pound puppy on adoption day. She wanted to walk out on him, except there was nowhere to go.

"So what if I got straight A's in school and graduated with a 3.8 GPA from college? I would have had a 4.0 if it hadn't been for that required statistics class. I hate statistics. What's the probability that it will sleet on a day that starts out sixty-four degrees and sunny, right? Statistics would tell you that the chances are slim to none, but does statistics take berserk Texas weather into account? No indeedy. And that's what's wrong with statistics."

"You're nervous," he said.

"What makes you say that? Why would you think I was nervous? I'm not nervous."

"You're prattling."

"I am?"

"You told me you prattle when you're nervous."

"Did I? No, no, I said I babble when I'm nervous."

"What's the difference?"

"Babbling is nonsensical. Prattling is going on and on and on . . ."

"Which is what you're doing."

Sarah wrinkled her nose, raised a palm to her mouth. Gosh, where had she learned to prattle? Surely not when she was in her apartment diligently writing. Then again, maybe that's precisely where she had learned to prattle. All those hours alone, talking to imaginary characters, trying to coax them to talk to her on the page.

"I'm sorry. Am I getting on your nerves?"

His smile was kind. "Never. And don't worry," he said, not only brave in the face of her prattling, but easily sliding into macho-male protector mode. "We're going to be fine."

He opened up the backpack he'd dragged in from the pickup truck with him and started going through it. "Water," he said, slapping several bottles down on the table. "Turkey jerky." He tossed the fat package beside the water bottles.

"I hope you have dental floss with that," she said because she was definitely feeling outgunned. He had been prepared, where she'd been relying on the statistical probability that it would not sleet.

"Toothbrushes too." Miraculously, he extracted new toothbrushes, toothpaste, and dental floss from the backpack's side pocket. "I'm a big believer in dental hygiene."

"Oh yeah, your dad was a dentist. I remember. No wonder you have such sexy teeth."

"You find my teeth sexy?"

She flicked a gaze over him. "Don't get all ego-y about it."

"Ego-y, huh? Is that anything like 'choppy down tree thingy'?"

"It's exactly like that." She giggled.

He gazed at her tenderly. "I love to hear you laugh."

She felt her cheeks flush. She loved to laugh, Sarah realized.

"Apples," he continued. Four large Red Delicious joined the water and turkey jerky.

"Impressive, Officer I'm Prepared for Any Disaster."

"Hey, I've gotten trapped in the wilderness before. This is experience talking here."

"Lucky me, I'm iced in with Daniel Boone."

"Thank you for the compliment." Travis grinned and kept digging. "Nuts."

"What? Did you forget the kitchen sink?"

"No, actual nuts." Out came three small plastic sacks. "Pecans, cashews, walnuts."

"Cashews, yum, my favorite."

"Club crackers and string cheese."

"You truly are a wilderness man."

"Two cans of chicken noodle soup." He held them up. "With round noodles because that's Jazzy's favorite kind."

"If you have chocolate chip cookies in there I'm marrying you." The minute she said it, she could have bitten off her tongue.

"Chocolate chip cookies move you that much, huh?"

She shrugged, laughed. "Well, you know . . . chocolate."

"Makes even a rational woman lose her head?" Travis tilted his chin and slanted her a sideways glance that sent a delicious shiver sliding down her spine.

"Um . . . something like that."

"You're cold," he said.

She crossed her arms over her chest. Crap, were her nipples showing through her bra and sweater? "No, I'm not." Fact was she was hot, hot, hot.

"I'll get a fire going."

He'd already started a hellacious fire inside her. "I thought you didn't have any matches."

"No," he said, "*you* didn't have any matches. I always carry them."

"Show-off."

"Come on, admit it, you like that I came prepared."

"You're way too self-assured for my own good."

"I'm not nearly as confident as you think." The raw honesty on his face took her by surprise. "Truth is, I'm as afraid of being stranded here with you as you are of being here with me."

"Really?" she whispered.

"Sarah . . ." He stepped forward and she didn't back up. "Ever since that night I pulled you from the lake all I've been able to think about is making love to you, really making love to you. When you left Twilight, I thought, Well, that's it, but then you came back—"

They met in the middle of the floor, his arms going around her, pulling her up tight against his chest while she entwined her arms around his neck.

She inhaled him, pulled his bottom lip into her mouth and nibbled lightly.

He groaned and closed his eyes. "Woman," he growled. "Keep that up and you're in serious trouble."

Sarah stepped back. He was right. This was headed only one place. Did she really want to go there? Was she ready to take that leap?

"Let's take it slow," he said, reading her mind. "Real slow. We've got all night. Nobody's going to be able to get out here to rescue us in this ice storm. I'll start a fire. We'll be safe and warm."

As if to prove his point, the wind gusted outside and sent a fresh pelting of sleet knocking against the windowpanes.

It was true. He did make her feel safe in a way she'd never felt before. She'd spent so many years taking care of herself that this was heady stuff. Knowing he could and would take care of her, come what may.

"Promise not to throw me out on the porch half naked when it's over?" she quipped.

"Sarah," he murmured, cupping her face between his palm. "I'm so sorry about that."

"I'm teasing."

"Only partially," he said, seeing straight through her. "I hurt you."

"I understand. Jazzy comes first."

"She does, but I had no right to make you feel embarrassed or ashamed."

"Seems to be my MO where you're concerned."

"I think it's time we got you a new MO."

"Oh? And what would that be?"

"What if you assumed the role of my girlfriend?"

"Why, Officer Walker, are you asking me to go steady?"

"What would you say if I was?" His gray eyes drilled into her.

Her heart thumped and her mind filled immediately with lovely fantasies. But she'd learned a long time ago you couldn't put your faith in daydreams. "I'd say that long-distance relationships rarely work out."

"And I'd counter that writers can work anywhere. In fact, seems you work better right here in Twilight than you do in New York."

"Are you asking me to give up my place in Manhattan?"

"You got anything keeping you there?"

She dared to hold his steady stare. "Do I have anything waiting for me here?"

He hesitated. It was just for a fraction of a second, but it was enough to extinguish the flicker of hope that fluttered in her chest. "You've got a lot of friends here."

"Yes," she said, stamping on the rush of sadness and forcing a smile. "I do have that now."

"Sarah, I—"

"Don't feel like you have to apologize for not being able to make me any promises. It's okay. I get it. You're a good father who has to make sure his personal decisions don't adversely affect his child."

"Sarah," he whispered, "you are the kindest, most understanding woman I know."

"It's not that," she said. "I care about Jazzy too."

"So we take it one step at a time?"

"Hey, the longest journey begins with a single step, right?"

"Right."

"Um . . . before we take this any further, I have one question," she said.

"What's that?"

"Do you have any condoms in that backpack?"

He laughed. "What do you think?"

"Oh? You were that sure of yourself?"

"No, I just didn't want to be caught unprepared."

"You know, they really should consider you as director for FEMA. You're much better prepared than some of the people they've had in charge."

"Speaking of being prepared, I need to get that fire going," he said.

"Are you hungry? I could heat up some of that soup for lunch."

"Sounds good."

Sarah retreated to the gas camp stove to heat the chicken noodle soup while Travis braved the elements in search of firewood. Whatever happened tonight in this cabin, she was going to take it at face value. Just enjoy the moment. No fantasies. No expectations. No hopes of happily-ever-after. She was simply going to have a good time.

While the soup heated, Sarah stepped into the adjoining bathroom—such as it was—to freshen up. She brushed her hair and applied fresh lipstick. When she emerged, she found a crackling fire in the fireplace and Travis bent over, feeding in more logs.

Unbidden, her gaze tracked down the length of his muscular back to take in the curve of his butt underneath his jeans. She tilted her head, fully enjoying the view.

He straightened, turned, and visibly sucked in a deep breath. "My God, but you're gorgeous."

The tops of her ears flushed. "He can predict the weather, pack one hell of a backpack, and start a fire with ice-cold wood. What more can a girl ask for?"

"If you don't know," he said, reaching out a hand to draw her closer to the fire, "I've got my work cut out for me."

"I'm looking forward to benefiting from your expertise." She went up on tiptoes to nibble his earlobe.

Travis groaned and buried his face in her hair. "If you don't stop that right now, the soup is going to burn to the bottom of the pan and I won't give a good damn."

She giggled, amazed at her own exuberance. "Down, tiger, I'll go ladle us up some soup."

To take advantage of the warmth, Travis dragged the table and chairs over, positioning them in front of the fireplace. They sat down at the table across from each other, the bowls of soup between them adding steam to the already sultry air. The way he looked at her as they ate sent heat seeping through her body. Nervousness suffused her along with the heat. Nervousness and excitement. They were iced in together with no place to go and nothing to do. . .

Unbidden, her gaze tracked over to the bed.

He saw where her gaze went and a grin tipped his lips. Quickly, Sarah yanked her attention back to her soup bowl.

"So tell me, what was your favorite story as a kid?" he asked, clearly searching for a neutral topic to put her at ease.

"*A Wrinkle in Time* by Madeleine L'Engle."

"The book you were reading the day we found you at the scavenger hunt."

"Yes. Madeleine helped me through some tough times as a kid."

In particular the time I embarrassed myself over you. She gave me hope that I could disappear into a black hole and come out sane on the other side.

"You associated closely with Meg," he said.

"You know the main character? You've read the book?"

"Don't sound so surprised. I do know how to read."

"I didn't mean it that way."

"It's one of Jazzy's favorite books too. But *The Magic Christmas Cookie* is still number one on her list. You helped her cope with life the way Madeleine L'Engle helped you." Travis cocked his head and studied her for a long time.

"What?" she asked, unnerved by his stare.

He shook his head. "I still can't get over the fact that you're Sadie Cool. It's just so—"

"Unbelievable?"

"I was going to say impressive."

She shrugged. "No more impressive than raising a child on your own."

"Do you ever want to get married? Have kids?"

Did she? Sarah shrugged. "Honestly, I've never thought about it." That wasn't really true. She'd thought about it, she just figured she might never find a man willing to look past her scars and personality quirks. "I'm only twenty-four."

"I was married and the father of a three-year-old when I was twenty-four."

"I know," she said. "Some of us bloom later than others."

"Some might say that you knew what you wanted from a very early age."

Was he talking about writing or him? Sarah shifted in the chair, focused on her soup.

A long silence ensued, then Travis said, "How come you came with me to cut down the town Christmas tree?" He reached out to run a finger over the back of her hand, gently tracing the blue-tinged vein that ran from her index finger to her wrist. "I mean, don't get me wrong, I'm really glad you did, but I thought you weren't really into all the holiday hoopla."

She shrugged. "Moe kind of drafted me."

"You could have said no. I expected you to say no."

She lowered her eyelashes, shrugged against his chest, felt a fresh surge of warmth radiate through her. "I don't know. I guess I just . . ."

"What?"

"Wanted to be with you," she admitted.

His fingers kept moving from her wrist to her elbow and back again in lazy strokes. "I really am glad you came."

"Guess what I found in my purse when I was freshening up," she said, changing the subject, looking for an excuse to move her arm away from him before she burst into flames.

"What?"

She reached over for her purse and pulled out a couple of Tootsie Pops from the bouquet he'd given her. "Dessert."

He laughed and she passed him a sucker.

"Why do you suppose they call them suckers?" she pondered, unwrapping her cherry Tootsie Pop. "I mean why not lickers? Some people lick them, right? And what about the people who simply let them melt in their mouth?"

"Then there are the crunchers who just bite down and to hell with their teeth. They want at that chewy middle," Travis drawled, and lowered his eyelids in a way that made him look all lusty and seductive.

"Which one are you?" she asked, relieved he'd left his question about romantic relationships alone. "A sucker, a licker, or a biter?"

"A licker all the way." His devilish eyes sparked. "What about you?"

"A melter. I'm a melter." God, why had she said that?

"Hmm. That's good information to have. You never know when it might come in handy." He winked.

A shiver arrowed down her spine and she felt . . . What did she feel? That was the thing. She was never sure if her feelings were real or just something that would fall away if she gave it time and distance. Mostly she'd found the latter to be true. Emotions always changed. They weren't something you could count on to stick around for long.

"So how come you're not spending the holidays with your folks?" he asked, slowly licking his sucker.

Her gaze was transfixed on his mouth. "They're not holiday kind of people."

"Not particularly family-oriented."

"To say the least.

The tip of his tongue curled around the raised ridge of the Tootsie Pop. Oh, the slow care he took with it. "That sounds like the short version," he said. "We're not going anywhere for a while, you might as well tell me the long version."

"They're brilliant surgeons. Among the top heart surgeons in the world. They live it, they breathe it, they never should have had a kid."

"I for one am damn glad they did." He stopped licking the sucker long enough to drill her with a steady stare.

Sarah gulped, overwhelmed by his intensity. "I felt so utterly abandoned by my parents, but I didn't fight it. I didn't try too hard to win their love. I simply accepted my fate and learned not to expect anything from them."

He reached over to squeeze her hand. "I hurt for that little girl."

"Honestly, I'm okay with it. What I remember most from my childhood is the silence in that big house. Mostly, it was only me and the housekeeper. My parents were always at the hospital or on lecture tours. Even when my parents were there it was like we weren't really a family. It was the two of them and me alone, as if we were spinning in separate orbits and there was no way our emotional paths could ever cross. My parents are so in sync with each other. Their conversations are always about medicine. I felt like I was an observer, put there to simply watch them and not really interact. I don't think they quite knew what to do with me. When they did try to engage me, it was as if we were speaking different languages. I suppose that's why they shipped me off to boarding school as soon as they could. I reminded them of their failure as parents."

"I can't imagine sending Jazzy away." His voice

cracked with emotion. "What was it like for you at boarding school?"

"It was okay. I didn't like sharing a room with someone else." She made a face. "Privacy is very important to me and I was socially awkward. I spent a lot of time in the library, but when I had to interact with others, I would imitate their facial expressions and mannerisms and speak like they spoke to fit into the scene. I watched and I learned and I mimicked. What about you?"

"Me? When I'm around people I get charged up, energized, and I think about what I can do to make things more fun for everyone," he said.

"Now *that*, I can't imagine."

"So . . ." He paused. "What's it like for you when you're in a romantic relationship?"

How could she begin to explain to him that for the most part she was happy without a romantic relationship? Odd as it might sound to some people, she took pleasure in abstinence because it freed her from personal entanglements.

Okay, yeah, sometimes when she was out on the street and saw people holding hands or kissing she would feel lonely and she'd start to hate her isolation. But whenever she was with someone she discovered that the real joy only came afterward, when she was alone again and could go over what she'd felt and really process the experience. It was as if remembering the encounter was more rewarding than the actual relationship. In the long run, in the past, she ended up feeling lonelier with a partner than without one. It made her wonder if she would be able to feel something spontaneous, on the spot when something intense was happening, rather than disappearing into her own mind.

You did once. With the very man sitting across the table from you.

Yeah, and look how that turned out.

But it was happening to her again; in spite of all her resolve not to fall, she was in love with him. Maybe she'd never stopped loving him, she'd just tucked his memory away for nine years while she waited.

"You want to tell me what it is you're really afraid of?" he asked.

She shrugged. "Who me?"

"Well?"

Sarah glanced down at his hand and aimlessly traced her index finger along the sturdy muscles. A log in the fireplace snapped, shooting a shower of sparks upward into the chimney. She peered into his eyes, suddenly understanding that this feeling was every bit as unnerving for him as it was for her. She took courage from that realization and smiled softly.

"I'm afraid . . . because, well, I don't know where this is going. I don't know where I want it to go. And I'm scared because I want you more than I should." She paused, glanced away, stared into the fire, unable to keep looking at him.

"Yes," he said. "I can see how the thought of being with me would frighten you."

Was he being sarcastic? Had she hurt his feelings? "You aren't what scares me," Sarah said. "*I'm* what scares me. I've never had a real relationship. I don't know if I'm even capable of one."

"You're afraid of feeling too much."

He nailed it. Nailed her. Sarah frowned.

"I shouldn't have brought you along on this trip. Or I should have insisted we wait. I knew a storm was coming. I just thought we could beat it and I thought . . ." His eyes were enigmatic. "Who the hell am I kidding? Part of me wanted to be iced in this cabin with you."

"You did?" she mumbled, and looked away again.

He let out a pent-up breath, ran a hand through his dark, shaggy hair. "Not consciously, but on a subconscious level. It seemed like the only way I could pin you down."

"But now," she said, "you're pinned down too."

"Yeah." His smile was wry. "If I was smart, I'd just take off walking and head for town and come back to rescue you with the de-ice truck."

"Please don't do that. I don't want you to go."

"Which is probably why I should, but I can't go off and leave you alone, and not just because it would be unchivalrous. I'm enjoying your company."

She took a deep breath and tentatively dared to murmur what she was feeling. "I'm enjoying your company too. I want more."

"Are you sure?"

She swallowed. "I haven't been able to think about anything else for days, Travis."

He took her hand, turned her palm up, and slowly traced his fingers up and down. The movements were innocent but the sensations they aroused in her were wholly erotic. "Before we take this any further, I think you need to tell me about that scar."

She froze, felt herself pull back mentally. He kept stroking her palm and she tried to take that back too, but he speared two fingers around her wrists and held her hand in place.

"No," he said. "No more running away. If you want this as much as I do, we're going to have to be open and honest with each other about everything. No secrets. That's how intimate relationships work."

"Is that how it was with you and Crystal?" She was taunting him and she knew it. She formed a fist between his fingers.

"No," he said. "That's how I know what doesn't work. If we want to take this to the next level we're going to have to knock down a few walls first."

"That's the question," she said. "Do we want to take it to the next level?"

He unfolded her fingers, opened her hand again, and this time traced letters into her palm. He held her gaze as he did it, looked deeply into her eyes. It made her feel both uncomfortable and exhilarated.

I want you, he traced.

"Are you sure it's me you want and not Sadie Cool? She's just a persona. My alter ego. She's not who I really am."

"With that statement, you underestimate both of us," he growled. "I know who you are, Sarah Collier. I've known you since you were eight years old."

"I'm afraid," she whispered.

"Of what?"

"Once you really see it . . ." She hauled in a deep breath. "That you won't be attracted to me anymore."

"There you go, underestimating me again," he said, his big strong fingers curling around hers.

"You say that now—"

"I mean it. You are the sexiest thing in the world to me, and it's not just about your looks. It's in the regal way you carry yourself and how composed you are. Take getting iced in, for instance. You didn't even blink when you realized we were going to have to spend the night in a hunter's cabin. Let me tell you, Crystal would have bitched up a blue streak."

"I've never found complaining about something I have no control over to be a very effective strategy."

"Exactly." He held her gaze captive and she couldn't look away. Didn't want to look away. "I'm going to tell you something I don't talk about much. It's a scar you can't see. It's a scar on my soul and I'm going to show it to you."

CHAPTER SIXTEEN

Travis hadn't intended on getting into this, but he understood her self-consciousness over that scar was one of the things standing between them, and until he got her to talk, they weren't going to get past it. Tit for tat. If he told her his dark secret, she'd owe him hers.

"You know my mom died of the severe asthma when I was fifteen."

Sarah nodded.

"It's the same condition that affects Jazzy, except until recently she was even worse than my mother."

"Travis, you don't have to talk about this."

He raised a palm. "I was pretty messed up after my mom died. I did a lot of things I shouldn't have."

"Like getting Crystal pregnant."

"Yeah," he said, "but I can't regret that. I got Jazzy out of the deal. But I do regret putting my dad through hell. He was a wreck after my mother died. My parents were high school sweethearts who'd never been apart a day in their married lives.

My dad sank into a deep depression and he didn't have the heart or energy to discipline me." Travis spread his palms. "I've got to be honest, I was a total shit. I didn't care about anything or anyone but myself."

"That's not true," Sarah said. "You were lashing out because you were in so much pain over your mother's death. Gram saw it. She understood."

"Your grandmother was really good to me. She helped a lot after my mother died."

"I wish I'd been older. That I could have helped you."

Travis stared down at his hands. "My mother used to say she and my dad were soul mates. That they were destined to be together. After she died, my dad told me that destiny was a living hell because when your other half dies it's like someone reached into your chest and yanked your heart out and yet you continue to live." He raised his head, met her gaze again. "That's why you completely freaked me out with that destiny talk at my wedding."

"Travis . . . I was just a dumb kid with a fanciful imagination."

He reached out his hand again and she rested her palm against his. He interlaced their fingers. "You weren't and that's what scared me so damn much. But you were fifteen and I was twenty. I couldn't have thoughts like that about you, so I shut them down."

Outside, the wind howled as sleet continued to pelt the cabin. Travis got up to put another log on the fire. When he turned, he looked at Sarah, cast in the glow of firelight, and he burned for her in a way he'd never burned for anyone. He quickly glanced away. He had to get this story out while he still had the courage to tell it.

"After my mom died, I was basically all alone except for your Gram, my Aunt Raylene, and their friends. It's why I got into trouble. I was searching for something I couldn't find. Nothing made sense. My world was upside-down and everything I'd ever believed in was gone. I went looking for love in all the wrong places. I didn't know any better. I hooked up with Crystal because she made me feel something again. In hindsight, I can see clearly that I was trying to put together a family of my own to replace the one I'd lost."

Sarah said nothing, tamped down the tears that wanted to spill for him.

"I was still a bit of punk after I married Crystal and before Jazzy was born," he admitted, stirring the embers with a poker. "I'm ashamed of the way I acted back then. I'd go out, leave Crystal home alone, get drunk. One night I got into an accident. Hit a car with a family of five in it. Thank heavens no one was hurt, but it was a serious wake-up call. I know my dad felt like he'd failed me. I wish . . ." His throat tightened and he had to force himself to keep on speaking. "I just wish he'd stuck around to see Jazzy born. To see how she changed me for the better."

"I'm listening," she murmured.

Travis put down the poker and sat on the hearth. He rubbed his palms over his jean-clad thighs. "My father was more depressed than I ever guessed. He was a reserved guy who didn't talk about his problems. He withdrew from people. Kept himself closed off." Travis was finding it even harder to say the words than he expected.

"What happened?" Sarah gently prodded after a few minutes.

Travis met her gaze. "The depression won." He paused, bit down on his bottom lip.

"Please, you don't have to talk about this. I can see it's still very painful."

"No, I want you to understand. I'm an open book, Sarah. With me, what you see is what you get. The good, the bad, the in-between. I want to share it all with you."

"Okay," she said softly.

He pulled his palm down his face. "Two months before Jazzy was born, my father took a bottle of nitrous oxide from his dental practice, drove to a Wal-Mart in another county, and parked in the far corner of their parking lot. He climbed into the backseat of the car, locked all the doors, turned on the nitrous, and inhaled the gas until he stopped breathing. They didn't find his body until five days later."

Silence filled the room. Sarah kept her face expressionless, but he saw that her breathing had quickened, that she was biting the inside of her cheek.

"Could it have been accidental?" she asked. "Maybe he just wanted to feel better?"

Travis shook his head. "The medical examiner ruled it as an accidental overdose, but I think he was just being kind so Dad's insurance would pay out. That's how I ended up paying off the cottage. But me, I know he did it on purpose."

"I . . ." She raised a hand as if to touch him, com-

fort him, but then dropped it in her lap. "Travis
. . . I'm so sorry."

He shrugged as if it didn't matter. He'd learned
the best way to deal with sorrow was to put on a
brave face and keep putting one foot in front of the
other until finally, finally the pain began to ease a
bit. "Scars are just evidence of where you've been,
they're not markers of where you're going. I swore
I was never going to be like my dad and isolate
myself from the people who loved me. That was
my father's downfall. He kept to himself. He didn't
let anyone help him. He never told me what was
going on in his head. He withdrew even from me.
He kept his dark secrets and I had a lot of trouble
forgiving him for that."

"Not everyone can embrace being with people
the way you do," Sarah said. "Some people just
need to be alone in order to make things right in
their own heads. It doesn't mean they're hiding.
We're all different. Your father just had a different
way of coping than you did."

"Well, it wasn't a very damn successful method,
now was it?" Travis heard the anger in his voice.
Yeah, he was still mad at Dad.

"He probably wanted to connect with you very
badly, he just didn't know how. Especially if he
was clinically depressed." Tentatively, she reached
out and put her hand over his.

"You know what it feels like, don't you?" he
said.

"What?"

"Not being able to fully connect with people
even when you want to."

She inhaled audibly. "I do."

"Help me to understand."

"I can't speak for your father."

"No, but as someone who withdraws when you're under stress, you might give me insight into my dad's behavior."

She paused and he thought for the longest moment she wasn't going to tell him, then finally she said, "This is how it works for me. The world feels like an invasion. Everything is coming at you so fast. Cell phones, text messages, pagers, traffic noises—"

"Then why do you live in New York?"

"Because there is an odd peace in the chaos. You can be in your own little bubble in New York in spite of all the people."

"You need to come fishing with me sometime," he said. "I'll show you real peace."

"I don't know why I'm the way I am. Maybe I was just born this way. Maybe it was because I was alone so much of the time as a kid. Maybe it's because I basically parented myself except when I was here with Gram. Whatever the reason, I feel safe when I'm alone and off balance the rest of the time. I live in my head a lot and I love details and information."

"But you just said information was an assault."

"It is, if I don't have a time and place to process it in private."

"Okay, I can respect that. You need your space and you need a soft place to land."

"I don't expect much from life. In fact, I like it better when there's not a lot of expectations. The success of *The Magic Christmas Cookie* caused problems for me. Public appearances are a night-

mare. The only way I get through them is by pretending to be Sadie Cool. There's intense pressure
to produce a second book as good or better than
the first."

He nodded, waited. Let her go at her own pace.

"It's not that I'm commitment-phobic or that
I don't want a relationship. It's just very hard for
me to reach out, and a lot of people don't get this.
They see me as distant, aloof, and I suppose I am."
She sighed. "The scar doesn't help matters."

He looked at her, looked into her, and told her
with his eyes that it was all right. That her secret
was safe with him.

"I've never been very good at relationships. My
parents and I barely talk. My agent is my best
friend and honestly, I don't mind. I had a boyfriend
in college, sort of. It wasn't a love match, but he
was cute and I was feeling the need for compan-
ionship. We hooked up over a mutual love of jazz
music and for a little while things weren't bad. We
went out a couple of months and then he started
pressuring me to socialize more. Get out. Go to
parties. To me that held the appeal of slamming
my finger in a car door, but for him, I agreed to try.
We went to a new jazz club that had opened up in
a rather rundown part of Houston."

A thought flashed into Travis's head. A news
story he'd heard about three years back. A fire
in a jazz club in Houston that hadn't been up to
code; several people had been severely injured. One
person had died. His gut tightened.

"The club was very crowded and the music was
too loud. I asked him if we could leave and he got
really angry. Called me a hermit and recluse, said

I'd end up an old maid. So even though every instinct in my body told me to leave, I stayed." She reached for a bottle of water, twisted off the top, took a long drink before continuing with the story he knew was going in a horrible direction.

"A fire broke out. Someone had been freebasing cocaine in the bathroom. There was a stampede. I got knocked down." She spoke in a clear, detached, calm manner as if it had happened to someone she didn't even know.

"Sarah," he whispered, but her expression never changed.

"A burning beam fell across my waist. Someone—not the guy I was with—lifted it off of me and carried me to safety. I spent three weeks in the burn unit with third-degree burns. But I was lucky. It was over less than ten percent of my body. I've had some skin grafts. I could have more to reduce the scarring if I wished, but I haven't had the mental energy to deal with that, especially in the wake of my literary success."

"What happened to the boyfriend?"

She shrugged. "He broke up with me while I was in the hospital."

"Sounds like a real prince," he growled.

"That was nothing compared to the next guy I went out with," she said. "I told him about the burns. He said he was cool with it. Until it came time to take off my clothes. One look and suddenly he remembered ten dozen other places he needed to be."

"He ran out on you after you let down your guard and showed him your scar?"

"Hey, what can I say? It looks pretty bad."

"Asshole." Travis clenched his fists.

"That's just the way it is."

"Are you lumping me in the same category with those guys? You think I'm gonna take off on you if you pull off your shirt?"

Sarah glanced out the window and laughed. "Hey, this is my big chance. Captive audience. It's the only way the burned girl is going to get laid." Her laugh was rough, humorless.

"Don't . . ." Travis raised a finger. "Don't put yourself down that way, Sarah. You're a fine, gorgeous woman any man would be lucky to have."

"In spite of the scars and personality quirks?"

"Because of them," he said firmly. "They make you who you are. Strong and independent. Perceptive and calm. Curious and objective. Wise and kind and trustworthy."

Her cheeks flushed red.

"Those two losers are fools. You know that."

"So is Crystal."

"Yes she is. She left the most fabulous child in the world behind." Travis got to his feet and crossed the short distance between the fireplace hearth and the table. He reached for Sarah, drew her to her feet, and she let him. He gazed into her eyes, just looked and looked and looked. She held her own and felt the power of their connection. It was beyond anything he'd ever experienced in his life.

He was in love with this woman, but he didn't know if she was ready to hear him say it. But he knew she was his destiny as surely as he knew his own name and she'd known it before he had.

He was attracted to her quiet self-possession.

She made him feel restful and steady, as if her calmness granted him permission to take internal solitude seriously. She was like the lake he loved, deep and serene, and she evoked in him the same sense of peace.

Whenever he was with her, he felt as if he was truly at home. He didn't have to scramble around to find his identity in meeting the needs of others. In fact, until he was with her, he'd never recognized that he filled his life up with other people so that he didn't have to take stock of what he'd neglected—himself.

She gave him permission to find out who he really was. Between taking care of his mother, then coming to terms with his father's suicide, and finally looking after his ailing daughter, he'd shoved aside his own needs to do what needed to be done, but it left him feeling a little hollow inside.

He loved how Sarah was free to go her own way; independent of what others expected of her. But this quality also gave him pause. How could she ever put down roots? How could he ever really connect with her permanently if he was always afraid she would simply wander away?

Travis thought of how his father used to withdraw. He'd stay in bed and sleep for days on end, barely waking up, not eating, not caring about anything. He'd given up on life.

Sarah wasn't depressed as his father had been. He knew that. But the potential was there. It worried him, the way she isolated herself at times. Did he really want to get involved with someone who kept people at arm's length? Especially when he had Jazzy to think about.

Except he couldn't deny the bond his daughter had forged with her. He'd never seen Jazzy this happy. Sure, part of it was due to her renewed health, but the way her face lit up whenever Sarah came into the room did strange and wonderful things to him.

And around Jazzy, Sarah opened like an unfurling rose. They seemed to feed off each other in a way he could not comprehend. They talked of magical cookies and fairy tales and castles and princesses and once-upon-a-time in way he didn't get. It was like they created their own little world. He might think that was a bad thing, except when they were together, they laughed in a way neither one of them laughed when they were apart.

"I've waited a long time for you, Travis Walker," Sarah said. "Don't disappoint me now."

Travis fell into those amazing blue eyes, darker now with a sheen of desire. All traces of the girl next door were gone. She was a grown woman in every sense of the word. He reached to cradle her chin in his palm and felt the pulse under her ear skitter beneath his fingers like a wild thing desperate to escape a trap.

He lowered his head and kissed those sweet salmon-colored lips. A tender kiss that contradicted the savage urges raging inside him. It was all he could do not to yank her clothes off her and tug her down on the hardwood floor. But he didn't surrender to the blood pounding through his veins, surging hotly through his body. At least not completely. Instead, he just kept firm pressure on her mouth while he stroked the side of her neck with his thumb.

Her lips parted on a soft sigh and she sank against him, her breasts pressing against his chest, her warmth seeping through his skin, stoking the blaze growing inside him. His erection jumped, demanding attention, but Travis held on to his control. Being a father had taught him the value of patience.

He could wait, no matter how painful. He had to take care with her. She was precious cargo and she'd just entrusted him with her darkest secret and he wasn't about to disappoint her.

Sarah's heart pounded. She was scared, yes, but she wanted this more than anything in the world. They'd been building toward this moment since that day on the parade float. No, longer than that. Since the day she'd burst into the church and told him he was her destiny. This was the moment she finally revealed her secret to him.

Even though he'd said it wouldn't matter to him, that no matter what, he would think she was gorgeous, she worried it wasn't true. *What if. . .*

No. She wasn't going there. She was going to live in the moment, experience everything he had to offer her, and let the future take care of itself.

She looked at Travis, saw the nervousness in his eyes, and knew he was feeling just as vulnerable as she was. He was taking a big risk too. Going out on a limb for her, trusting that she wouldn't abandon him as most everyone else in his life had done in one way or another.

He trusted her, made her feel safe, and she had to trust him.

She reached for the hem of her sweater, intending on pulling it up, pulling it over her head, exposing her scarred, fire-ravaged body to him, but he reached out to still her hand with his. "Let me."

Trembling, she dropped her arms.

His touch was cautious and incredibly gentle. Slowly, he raised her sweater, but his eyes stayed on hers. He didn't look away as his hands touched her feverish skin and his fingertips skimmed along her sides. Like a blind man, he explored the ridges of the scar that fanned out across her belly from her ribs to her pelvis. Then his fingers reached up to remove her bra.

Emotion clogged Sarah's throat as she stared into his face and never once saw a flicker of anything but tenderness and caring. Outside the ice storm raged, but in her head she could hear Bing Crosby crooning "White Christmas" and she was fifteen again, innocent and unscarred and madly, truly, deeply in love with this man.

He pressed his face into her hair and inhaled deeply. "God, you smell so good, Sarah. You smell like home."

Finally, he tugged the sweater over her head and flung it over the chair. She tensed, waiting. But he didn't look down, just kept looking at her. She reached up to splay her palm over his chest, felt his heart thumping hard and steady.

He kissed her; long, lingering, sweet. Then he lowered himself to his knees, eye level with her damaged belly.

Fresh fear flashed through her. What was he seeing? What did her body look like to him?

He pressed his warm lips to the scar, kissing her

where no man had ever kissed before. "Beautiful," he crooned between each kiss. "Beautiful, beautiful, beautiful."

As he kissed and crooned, he undid the snap on her jeans, eased them down—along with her panties—over her hips, to her ankles. She kicked them off and stood naked before him.

After he'd thoroughly kissed her, he got to his feet again and removed his own pants. They stood naked together and she saw nothing on his face but admiration, respect, and—did she dare hope?—love.

"Sarah Collier, you're beautiful inside and out and no scar is ever going to change that and I want to make love to you more than I want to breathe." He stripped off his own shirt and tossed it beside hers.

He took the elastic band from her braid and slowly unwound it until her hair was a wavy cascade around her body. "Jazzy calls you Rapunzel. Rapunzel, Rapunzel, let down your hair so I may climb your golden stair."

"You know your fairy tale princesses."

"I have my daughter to thank for that. Come down out of your ivory tower, Sarah, and be with me."

She kissed him this time, and in her head Bing switched to her second favorite Christmas song, "Christmas Canon" by Trans-Siberian Orchestra. The smooth romantic music tugged at her heartstrings. She tried to block it. Tried to detach and stop feeling, but all her defenses were gone. In his arms, she was fully, completely exposed.

And then Sarah just started to cry as she'd never

cried before. This moment was too beautiful to be believed. Every dream she'd ever dreamed, every hope she'd ever dared hope about Travis Walker was coming true and her heart filled with more love than she could ever express. It leaked from her in great rolling sobs.

Travis's eyebrows rose in alarm and he enveloped her in a tight hug. "Sweetheart, what's wrong?"

"Nothing," she blubbered through the cascade of tears. She wanted to stop, but she couldn't, and that scared her because she'd never had much problem detaching. But with Travis, there was no detaching. She felt him everywhere.

"Sarah, you're scaring me."

"I'm fine. Everything is wonderful, perfect." She swiped at the tears with the back of her hand.

"Please, Sarah," he said, his voice raspy, "please don't break me."

"Never, Travis, never," she pledged.

"C'mere." He took her hand, guided her across the room, and sank down onto the cool blankets, pulling her with him. The white winter sunlight glinted off the icy wonderland outside, spilling the bright white color through the window, slanting over the bed. Sarah realized she'd never made love in the daylight. Before, no afternoon delight. But now, everything was pure delight. How had she gotten here, to this most exalted place?

They were belly to belly—hers scarred, his flawless—gazing into each other's eyes.

He rolled her over in one fluid movement until he was on top and she could feel his body heat radiating over her. "Like it or not, Sarah, this means something," Travis murmured.

"Yes," she said, wondering again how in the world she'd gotten here, to this cabin in the woods with the man of her dreams.

"This isn't like the night I pulled you from the lake. That was hard, frantic—"

"Lust."

"This is different." He stroked a finger down her cheek and briefly she closed her eyes against the intimate feel of his work-roughened skin. "We're both going to be different after this."

"I know," she whispered.

She felt the head of Travis's penis expanding against her thigh. Gazing into his eyes, she could feel the shift start, subtle in the beginning, but definite, concrete, something you could bank on. It was like the unexpected ice storm, slipping into the midst of a warm winter morning, inconvenient and sharp, but exciting and dynamic, a blast of frisky freshness upsetting the languid status quo. It made her feel incredibly alive.

"I'm going to make love to you now, sweetheart," he whispered.

The rising wave of her desire swept her along as if she was a grain of sand sucked into the undertow and carried out to sea.

"Make love to me," she murmured, and ran her palms over the hard plains of his masculine shoulders, his muscles tensed with holding his weight above her. She wanted him so desperately. Even more than the night he'd saved her from drowning in the lake.

He kissed her then. Each kiss growing sweeter and sweeter.

She felt his erection stretch and tighten. Just

thinking about having his cock inside her made her arch her pelvis upward. But, simultaneously, he arched his back, pulling away, teasing her.

"Hey, no fair," she whispered, and reached up to splay her palm against his beautiful ass.

He laughed. His penis hard as cement jutting into her scarred belly.

She pushed his ass down with her palm, letting him know where she needed for him to go.

He lowered himself down, but did not enter her. Instead he moved against her, rubbing the head of his penis against her straining clit, a perfect rhythm building. Then suddenly he stopped and looked deeply into her eyes. "You are an incredible woman, Sarah."

He was totally into her. She could see it in the hotness of his gaze. He made her feel like she was the center of his universe, cherished, admired. A heated flush rushed up her chest to her neck to burn her cheeks. How she'd once fantasized about a moment just like this one!

Everything in her universe dissolved except for this man—the bed, the cabin, the storm. Nothing existed but the two of them, floating on the updraft of something monumental.

And then slowly, he eased into her.

She hissed in her breath on a sigh and let her legs fall fully open to him. His strokes were easy, tender, careful, but sliding in deeper with each controlled thrust. A groan of pleasure slipped from his lips and Sarah smiled up at the ceiling, her heart overflowing with joy.

"Oh my, this is . . ." She had no words to describe what she was feeling. Phenomenal, sensational, extraordinary, no superlative seemed accurate enough. Instead, she reached up to thread her fingers through his unruly locks and gave a gentle tug.

He laughed. "I feel it too, sweetheart," he said huskily, and kept the rhythm unhurried and deliberate.

She spun on the specialness of the moment. Appreciating every movement, every sound he made, the way her body responded to his. It was as if he was the sun and she was a budding flower soaking up his rays, expanding in his warmth. She squeezed at him with her internal muscles, clamping down, drawing him in.

"Whoops," he said. "What was that?"

The look on his face was wild, feral, and it yanked at something primal inside her. She loved watching him lose control, loved knowing she was responsible for his headlong rush to ecstasy.

She did it again.

"You keep up that little trick and I'm done for, darlin'."

She laughed.

"God, I love to hear you laugh." He buried his face against the curve of her neck and nibbled lightly.

Sarah moaned softly.

"Ah, so you like that?"

"Uh-huh."

He kept nibbling while he picked up the pace, his body sliding in and out of her as his tongue did wicked things to her neck.

Her breathing shot from her in heavy gasps. He was driving her berserk.

But she wasn't the only one going berserk as she rhythmically squeezed and released him. "That's right, I'm giving it right back to you," she murmured.

She felt a fine sheen of perspiration slick his back and the air filled with the smell of his masculine scent. She loved this, loved the way he was pushing into her.

"Drive into me," she coaxed shamelessly. What was it about him that brought out the animal in her? "Come on, give me all you've got."

He did as she asked, ramming into her so quick and hard that his balls slapped against her. She curved her body upward, getting as close to him as physically possible. She clung to him, doing her best to keep up with his delirious sprint. "That's it, babe, give it to me good."

Travis was coming undone, she could feel his hold slipping, but that was okay, because she was losing it too.

No, no, she was already lost. Gone, swirled away inside the tempo, caught up in the vortex of sensation, rising higher and higher. She gave a strangled cry, a sharp, keening sound as if she'd been hurt. But it wasn't a cry of pain, rather one of most supreme pleasure.

She squeezed. He pushed.

Higher and harder and faster until the bed was banging against the wall . . . and then just when she was on the verge, when they both were so close they could taste it, Travis stopped.

He posed over her, every muscle in his body tensed; sweat breaking out on his skin, every nerve cell quivering hotly. He held them both on the razor's edge, knowing instinctively when to stop and still having the ability to do so. The man's control was beyond astounding. He stayed buried deep within her, his penis a constant throb at her womb.

Waves of undulating energy flowed through her feminine core like ripples in a lake dotted with rain. They were pressed so close together, the fire between them raging. Sarah felt as if she was melting, dissolving into him and he into her, mingling together in a sticky, wet pool.

"Please," she whimpered, "please."

"Not yet," he whispered with his mouth pressed against her ear. "Not yet."

He kissed her gently, his cool mouth belying the inferno surging through them both. He slid his mouth down her body, his tongue skimming her skin. Slowly, he eased out of her and she whimpered again at the loss of him.

"Easy," he murmured. "Easy."

She slanted a glance downward. The head of his engorged penis was swollen and discolored. It must hurt him to be so close and not yet come. She reached down a hand to touch him, and he let out a long hiss as if her fingers had burned him to the bone.

"No," he said, "don't touch me or I'm doomed."

She studied his face and slowly drew her hand away. He dipped his head to kiss her again, then moved his lips down her chin to her neck and leisurely tracked his way down the column of her throat. He found her breasts and paid equal attention to each nipple, beaded hard and jutting upward, begging for his notice.

By the time he made his way to her belly, she was

fully charged up again. The sweet spot between her legs wet, hot, and achy. He trailed his fingers over her skin, lightly tickling her and raising goose bumps all over her body.

And then he was there, a place she wanted him most. His head between her thighs, his tongue—oh, that damnable tongue—driving her completely insane.

She shifted her hips, letting his mouth pull her into the maelstrom again. She couldn't hear anything, couldn't smell or taste or see. All she could do was feel. This man. His mouth. On her most vulnerable area. She'd never allowed anyone to go there before. Not that anyone had tried. She was sensitive about giving up this part of herself. But not with him. Not with Travis. With him, she reached nirvana.

CHAPTER SEVENTEEN

Later, they lay in bed together listening to the crackle of the logs in the fireplace, snuggling in the sweet afterglow of lovemaking.

"Thank you," he whispered into her ear and then softly kissed her forehead.

"What for?" she asked, combing her fingers through the dark hairs on his forearm.

"For being you."

"I am who I am; it's not something you have to thank me for," she said, feeling wildly pleased. Sarah couldn't get enough of looking at him, charmed by the happily-ever-after fairy tale of having this handsomely naked man in bed with her.

Whoa, don't get ahead of yourself. No one's said anything about what comes after this.

Still, she couldn't stop the joy from wriggling through her. She clasped the moment to her breasts, held it close, savored it.

From where they lay, cuddled together under a pile of quilts, they could see out the large plate-glass window. Light from a full moon reflected off the icy wonderland outside. Everything was frozen. The grass, brittle and crunchy, the bare-limbed trees reaching up like bony ghost fingers toward the dark broody sky, the power line wires heavy with blue-white icicles. The air stretched silent, empty of sound.

Nothing moved.

Inside, the reflected light gleamed off Travis's chiseled cheekbones. She reached up to trace an index finger over the smooth plane, feeling the warm elasticity of his skin.

He closed his hand around her finger, brought it to his lips, kissed it. Then kissed the next finger and the next and the next. His hot, damp lips sent a demanding thrill running through her.

She'd never been much for outward displays of affection. The casual arm thrown over her shoulder, a hand at her waist, a kiss in public. It ruffled her need for privacy, for distance, for personal space. But with Travis, she found herself craving his touch, unable to get enough, and it was joyous indeed.

He put his arm around her, pulled her closer, and she snuggled against him completely at peace. He'd taught her how to be fully inside her body and it was a whole new world of pleasure and sensation. She felt like a kid at Disney World for the first time—awestruck and amazed. He seemed to know right where to touch to set her off. Knew things about her body she didn't even know herself. What a grand discovery!

Sarah ran a palm over his chest, taking delight in the small patch of wiry dark hair, tangling her fingers in it. She kneaded his skin, felt the firm, sculpted muscles beneath. Her fingers grazed over his nipple and it hardened instantly while a carpet of goose bumps rose on his flesh.

"Like what you see?"

"Mmm," she purred lazily, and followed the trail of hair from his chest to his navel.

Travis kissed her softly, but the kiss didn't stay soft. Neither did Travis. Intensity rose off him in radiant waves, a sharp contrast to the frosty cabin air.

Sarah shivered with delight.

"Cold?"

"Not in the least, but would you warm me if I said yes?"

Travis laughed. The woman's smile lit him up from the inside out.

Jazzy was the only other person who had the power to make him feel so happy. He couldn't help kissing her again, tasting her, holding her. He couldn't help himself. There was no escaping this feeling. She was all around him, filling his nostrils with her earthy, womanly scent. The sound of her quickened breathing hastened his own intake of oxygen. He couldn't get enough of her.

Desire ignited, surged through his blood, snatching him up on a thick swelling of love. He should have been filled with worry and apprehension, but he wasn't. This felt too right. Too good. Too damn vital to be wrong.

She began doing incredible things with her devilish tongue. He groaned.

His penis was an aching beast, hard and taut and hungry, surging in anticipation of her next move.

With her clever tongue, she licked a heated path from his throat to his chest, then moved down to playfully nibble at his nipples. Every cell, every nerve fiber bundle inside him vibrated like a tuning fork.

His balls tucked up tight against his body, craving her attention. He could barely catch his breath. Sarah must have read his mind, because she reached down to gently stroke the head of him with a whisper-soft touch. He arched his back, thrust his pelvis forward, praying for more.

When she pressed her sweet, sweet lips to his erection, Travis came totally undone. Her tongue was a weapon of exquisite torture, hot and wet. How had he ever lived without this? Without her?

It didn't take long until he felt his climax rising, pushing up through his shaft. Sarah must have sensed it too because she pulled her lips away and sat up. He wanted to sob at the loss, but then she smiled seductively and boldly straddled him, her hair a soft cascade around her face.

Travis drank her in with his eyes. He could see her scar flash silver in the moonlight, a testament to her courage and resiliency. He was honored she felt comfortable enough to fully expose herself to him, scars and all. He felt like he'd won a blue-ribbon prize, been bestowed a great honor.

He started to say something, but then she leaned down to cover his mouth with hers. He raised his trembling hand and curved it around her breast. The weight of it felt glorious against his palm. In a languid up-and-down rhythm she rode him. Halting her upward momentum only when it seemed he would fall from her velvet clutches. Down and up. Down and up again.

He thrust upward, egging her on. She increased the tempo, until they were galloping together to one absolute conclusion. He felt the riptide of biology dragging him under. He felt her muscles tighten around him. They moved together, breathed hard, and came in one rippling heated explosion.

Sarah collapsed against his chest, shaky and perspiring. He wrapped his arms around her as their hearts slammed against their chests.

He wanted to tell her he loved her. He almost told her he loved her, but something held him back. Travis had never felt as vulnerable as he did in this moment, or as invincible. She made him feel like he owned the world, while at the same time he was deathly afraid of saying or doing the wrong thing that could ruin it all.

So he just stayed quiet and held her tightly until they both fell into a deep, dreamless sleep.

When they awoke again it was mid-morning. Bright sunshine slanted through the window. The storm was gone, the temperature had risen, and the icicles on the eaves had already started to melt. The nonsensical weather of North Texas at its most insane.

They made a breakfast of beef jerky and cheese and crackers, and honestly, Sarah was so ravenous that filet mignon and scrambled eggs couldn't have tasted any better. Her body was sore and achy in all the right places and she just couldn't seem to stop grinning. It was a glorious day and all was right in her world.

Wearing nothing but his jeans, Travis went to stand in front of the window and scowl out at the ice. Sarah got up and threaded her arms around his waist. Such a spontaneous gesture was out of character for her, but she couldn't seem to stop touching him. She'd told him her darkest secret and he'd told her his. They were on equal footing, no more secrets between them. It tasted like freedom.

"Are you worrying about Jazzy?" she whispered.

"How did you know?" He put his hands over hers.

"Because you're a good father. She's with her Aunt Raylene. You know she's safe."

"What if she gets sick?" he fretted. "And I'm not there?"

"She's not going to get sick."

"You don't know that."

Sarah had never been one to sugarcoat things, so she was torn between honesty and wanting to make him feel better. "Okay, she said, "I'll play devil's advocate. Let's say she does get sick. What's the worst that could happen?"

"She'd die and I wouldn't be there."

"Statistically, how likely is that?" She kissed his bare back. God, the man had muscles to spare.

"A one percent chance is one percent too much."

"We need to get back to Twilight," she said.

"Yes."

"What's our best option with the truck axle broken and your cell phone battery kaput?"

"Start walking. I wish we hadn't got such a late start of it. I wasn't thinking clearly when we slept in."

Caught up in their mating, neither one of them had been thinking at all. "How far is it into town?"

"Twenty-two miles or so."

"Even walking four miles an hour, which is a pretty quick pace, it would take us over five hours and that's without taking a break."

"We only need to make it to the highway. We can catch a ride from there."

"If anyone happens to be out on the icy roads, especially in this out-of-the-way place."

"It's our only option."

Knowing he was right, they packed up their things and went outside. Much of the ice was melting now, turning to wet mucky slush. Carefully they picked their way over the slick terrain and headed for the highway. They'd been walking for over an hour and had barely gone a mile when they heard the sound of a heavy machine engine.

A few minutes later a large yellow bulldozer rumbled into view with Mayor Moe behind the controls.

"Will you look at that." Travis grinned and started waving. "Here comes the cavalry."

Raylene and Jazzy and Patsy were just leaving the Funny Farm restaurant on the square after lunch, when Moe Schebly bulldozed into town, pulling a flatbed trailer behind him. Raylene hadn't felt like cooking and Jazzy had wanted chicken fried steak. Earl was manning the Horny Toad. Business always picked up during icy weather, so she'd asked Patsy along for company.

"Will you look at who's in the cab of that dozer with Moe," Patsy said.

"Daddy!" Jazzy exclaimed as her father climbed out of the bulldozer, then turned to help Sarah down. Jazzy broke loose from Raylene's hand and ran across the street to launch herself into her father's arms.

"Best father in the whole damn world," Patsy said. "He's had to work hard to make up for that piece-of-crap mother."

"Do you have to always be so judgmental?" Raylene asked.

"What part of that isn't true?"

"No matter what she did Crystal is still a human being."

Patsy cocked her head and shot Raylene an odd look. "Since when did you start championing Crystal Hunt?"

"She's not the devil personified. She just made a mistake."

"Hmph. A pretty damn huge one if you ask me."

Travis had Jazzy on one hip and an arm around Sarah. Sarah was looking up at Travis as if he'd hung the moon. Raylene knew at once they'd gotten stranded in that hunter's cabin on Frank Jennings's ranch, and it didn't take a biology major to figure out what had happened last night.

For some strange reason anger and alarm and anxiety tangled up like a ball of knotted yarn inside her. "My nephew and the novelist look pretty damn cozy," Raylene groused.

"What are you complaining about? I thought that's why you and Dotty Mae lured Sarah back here in the first place. To play matchmaker for Travis."

"Who are we to meddle in someone else's life?"

"You're acting weird." Patsy sank her hands on her hips. "Just look at how happy they are."

"Maybe he shouldn't be happy with Sarah. Maybe he should mend fences with his ex-wife so his daughter could get to know her mother." Raylene thought about the terrible mistake she'd made. She simply couldn't let Crystal make the same mistake. Maybe Sarah was good for Travis, but the important thing here was Jazzy. A little girl deserved to grow up with her real mom. Jazzy had wished for a mommy for Christmas, and who better than her own mother? It was wrong not to give Crystal an opportunity to make things right while she still had a chance.

If the other members of the cookie club had any inkling what she was up to, they'd have a hissy fit. Particularly Dotty Mae, who'd always had a soft spot for Sarah. Not that Raylene had anything against Sarah, but Crystal deserved a second chance. She was the child's biological mother. She deserved to know this was her last opportunity to get her family back.

"I'm cold," she told Patsy. "I'm going to my car."

"You wouldn't be so cold if you'd stop wearing those miniskirts."

Raylene blew a raspberry. "Yeah? You're just jealous 'cause I can still get away with it."

"Ha! Dream on."

"Just tell Travis I'll call him later."

"Did you forget to take your estrogen today?" Patsy scowled.

Raylene flipped her the bird, turned and headed for her pink Cadillac Earl had bought her for her fifty-fifth birthday along with a Bruce Springsteen

CD with "Pink Cadillac" on the track list. Earl loved making out in the backseat with Springsteen cranked.

Shivering, she got in, slammed the door, and started the engine. Raylene had been just like Crystal. Had stars in her eyes and thought she was too good for the likes of Twilight. She'd done unthinkable things and hurt people just to further her career. And she'd paid a very big price, just like her nephew's ex-wife.

Empathy, tinged with bitter regret, pushed through her. In the rearview mirror she saw Travis sling one arm around Sarah's shoulders in a loose, relaxed gesture, and tousle Jazzy's hair with his other hand. They looked the picture of a loving family. Sarah tilted her head toward him, a radiant smile on her face, and when their eyes met, Raylene could feel the sparking heat all the way across the street through the windshield of her Cadillac.

Uh-oh, she might already be too late.

She knew a well-satisfied couple when she saw one. Those two had been intimate. No doubt in her mind.

What surprised her was her own emotional reaction. She'd orchestrated this whole thing. Found out that Sadie Cool was Sarah. Told the cookie club. Got them to rally around her matchmaking plan. Pushed Travis and Sarah into each other's path. Babysat Jazzy. All in an effort to make the last item on her great-niece's wish list come true.

It was what Raylene thought she'd wanted for him.

But when Travis bent his head to give Sarah a

deep, soulful kiss on the courthouse lawn, a kiss that said he was falling in love, Raylene knew this wasn't right. A terrible sense of panic that honestly had little to do with the pairing of Travis and Sarah, and everything to do with the dark secret she'd hidden for thirty-six years, rushed over her. She thought of another motherless little girl and her stomach roiled.

She had to end this relationship before it got out of hand. Raylene liked Sarah. She liked her a lot. But she wasn't right for Travis and most of all, she wasn't the mother for Jazzy.

Driven by an impulse she could not quash, even though a part of her was screaming, *Butt out and leave your nephew alone*, Raylene dialed directory assistance. She had a very important call to make. She could only pray that she wasn't too late.

A minute later, armed with a Nashville phone number, Raylene made the call.

"Hello?" a woman said. Raylene could hear country-and-western music twanging in the background.

"Crystal? Crystal Hunt?"

"Yeah? Who's this?"

"This is Raylene Pringle, Travis Walker's aunt."

"I know who you are. What do you want?" Crystal sounded truculent and Raylene wanted to just hang up the phone and let it go, but she simply couldn't. This was her way of making amends for her own sins.

Then she blew out a hard breath and for the first time in thirty-six years, she confessed the awful thing she'd done.

* * *

The following evening, promptly at six P.M. on the Sunday before Christmas, Mayor Moe gave the word for the official decorating of the Twilight Christmas tree to commence. The crowd that had gathered on the courthouse lawn surged forward enthusiastically, armed with plastic ornaments and gaudy garlands, silver tinsel and shiny ribbons, colored bows and peppermint candy canes.

Sarah looked up at the tree they'd chopped down together. The beautiful Christmas cedar that the entire town was decorating. The lights twinkled with breathtaking beauty. Snow flurries danced in the air. Carolers broke into a chorus of "Let It Snow." She was holding hands with Travis on her left, Jazzy on her right. It was an incredible moment, totally sublime. When she was an old lady in her rocking chair looking back over her life, she'd dredge up this perfect memory of a time when she was completely happy.

Travis reached over to run his hand through her hair. The familiarity of the gesture lifted her heart. He touched her like they were officially a couple. "I still can't believe you went and cut your hair."

After they'd gotten back from being iced in at the hunter's cabin the previous afternoon, Sarah had marched right into the nearest hair salon and told them to whack off her waist-length locks to her shoulders. Rapunzel had been hiding in her ivory tower too long. She'd changed, and a change of hairstyle seemed to go with the new Sarah.

She tilted her chin, raised a hand to her head. "It was weighing me down. Holding me back."

"I like it . . . You look . . . freer, lighter." He fluffed it. "It's still long enough to be sexy, but not so long that it gets tangled up in everything." The spark in his eyes left "everything" open to interpretation.

"Ah, so I looked restrained before."

"A bit," he said. "Controlled. That's not a bad thing, it's just . . . this is different. You look different."

"That's what I was going for."

"It's working." He winked.

"I think it's pretty," Jazzy declared.

"Thank you." Sarah smiled.

"Sarah," Jazzy said, reaching up to take Sarah's palm. "Now that you're back, can we bake kismet cookies on Christmas Eve?"

"You better ask your father about that."

"Daddy, can we? Please, please, please?"

Travis looked at Sarah, sent her a do-you-really-want-to-do-this expression.

She nodded. "I'd love to pass along Gram's tradition."

"Great!" Jazzy beamed. "Christmas Eve, our house, don't be late. Now I gotta go get me some tinsel before it's all gone."

Sarah and Travis laughed as Jazzy raced over to the booths where volunteers were passing out decorations.

"I'd forgotten what this was like," Sarah said. "Such a jovial madhouse."

He had his arms crossed over his chest, and a proud smile hung on his face. He wore a red and green striped sweater and starched blue jeans with a sharp crease running down the legs. Jazzy had already joined the crowd with a fistful of candy canes to hang on the tree. The sound system set up for the

Dickens event was still in place and the strains of the Burl Ives's version of "Holly Jolly Christmas" filled the square. The air smelled of mulled wassail and simmering cinnamon and crisp pine. The temperature hovered around forty-five, challenging anyone to guess which direction it was headed next.

"What?" He turned to meet her gaze.

"This town at Christmas. It's surreal. I feel like I'm trapped in *It's a Wonderful Life*."

His steady gray eyes held her gaze. "But it is a wonderful life, Sarah. We should celebrate every chance we get."

The optimism on his face was touching. He actually believed it was true. Even after everything he'd been through. Maybe it was *because* of everything he'd been through. How did a person develop such a hopeful attitude toward life?

He rested his hand across her shoulder and drew her closer to him. "You're just afraid to believe," he said, eerily reading her mind.

That was true. She'd believed once so deeply in the power of the kismet cookies and she'd been hurt just as deeply by reality. She couldn't get her innocence back no matter how hard she might try.

"Are you trying to tell me that there *is* such a thing as happily-ever-after?"

His eyes were enigmatic, his expression mild. "You're the writer. You tell me."

"It's just fiction, a fairy tale."

He chucked her under the chin. "Then why do you write it?"

"Because I keep hoping—"

"There you go. Right there. Hold on to that hope. You've gotta have hope."

"You're not going to burst into an encouraging song are you?"

"If it would help." He grinned. "Listen, Sarah, I'm not always so optimistic. Not long before you came to Twilight, things were so dire with Jazzy, I feared she wouldn't make it to her ninth birthday. But look at her now . . ." He waved to his daughter, who was running around hanging candy canes on the Christmas tree, a huge smile on her sweet face. "See that right there? Hope."

Hope. Such a lovely word. Why did it feel so out of reach?

"Here's some tinsel," Travis said, passing her a handful of shiny silver strands. "Let's get in there with everyone else and enjoy our wonderful life."

Travis watched Sarah delicately drape a strand of tinsel over a branch of the Twilight Christmas tree.

You could tell a lot about people by the way they put tinsel on a tree, Travis decided. There were the chunkers, eager and impatient, who didn't sweat the small stuff. They lived for the experience and simply lobbed the tinsel and let it fall where it may. Jazzy was a chunker. She liked to watch the tinsel slither down the needles and she laughed whenever it stuck in a clump.

Then you had minimalists who were stingy with the tinsel or eschewed it altogether as simply too much tree bling. His father had been like that. He'd wanted plain white lights, a few ornaments, and that was it. No garlands, no cranberries and pop-corn strung together on a strand, no candy canes. In fact, after Travis's mother died, he'd refused to put up a tree at all. Maybe that's why Travis loved decorating Christmas trees. He'd been short-changed.

And then there were the artists who positioned each strand just so, stepping back to assess their handiwork, moving forward again to futz until it was perfect. Sarah was a futzer.

Which, considering that this was a group decorating project, was an exercise in futility. No way was the tree going to come out perfect.

The way she tilted her head and studied the tree without recognizing that probably some rough-and-tumble kid was going to horse around and knock it off just as soon as she carefully finished threading the boughs with tinsel, made her seem incredibly vulnerable.

Deep within his chest, Travis felt a tugging, a sudden sadness combined with a powerful urge to protect her at all costs.

In the twinkling lights from the Christmas tree her blue eyes glistened. She wore a blue coat the color of an ice floe and black woolen slacks with those high-heeled boots he couldn't seem to break her of wearing. He had to admit she looked damn good in them. On her head was perched a jaunty white cap with a tassel over the sexy new hair-cut. She looked like a snow bunny, at once both naughty and innocent.

Sarah had a calmness about her that soothed him and made him feel as if everything really would be all right. But his life had been in turmoil for so long, Travis was afraid to trust the calm.

And yet, she stabilized him. She made him feel as if the sky wasn't perpetually on the verge of fall-ing, as if he wasn't always waiting for the other shoe to drop. She took things in stride. She was a good listener, and when she was with him she made him feel as if he was the only person in the world. Her focus was phenomenal and her ability to detach from her emotions gave her a wisdom most people lacked.

He enjoyed seeing the positive effects he'd had on her. She'd blossomed under his attention, opening up in ways he'd hoped for, but hadn't fully expected. Whenever he made her smile, it felt better than sunshine on a cloudy winter day. Travis wanted to tell her how attractive she was, but every time he tried, she'd brush aside his compliments as if she didn't believe them. She still thought of herself as an ugly duckling, or a burn victim. He saw it in the aw-shucks way she blushed when he told her she was beautiful.

But it was more than that and he knew it. She couldn't believe that he was interested in her. In her teenage mind she had built him up as some kind of romantic hero without ever really knowing who he was inside. She'd had a crush, an infatuation, and now that he was returning the feelings, she didn't know what to do about it. Particularly since she'd stuffed those feelings away and moved past that stage of her life. Had she outgrown him?

That unsettling thought had eaten at him since their time in the cabin. She'd seen things, been places. She'd wined and dined with celebrities. She lived in one of the biggest cities in the world and she was rich and famous. He was just a country boy who loved his quiet life with aspirations no bigger than to dance with his daughter at her wedding. How could Sarah ever be happy with a man like him, in a place like this?

Sarah turned to him as if she'd sensed he was fretting about her. "You're not decorating the tree."

"I'm having fun just watching you and Jazzy."

"Come on, you got me into this, you're getting into the mix." She grabbed his hand and tugged him over.

Her touch—as it always did—unraveled him. Hoping it didn't show on his face, he dived right in, mimicking her tinsel-draping techniques. On one side of them, tying red bows to the branches, were Belinda Murphey; her husband, Harvey; and their five ankle biters, Kimmie, Kameron, Karmie, Kyle, and Kevin.

On their other side were Jesse Calloway and his new bride, Flynn. They were canoodling more than decorating. Jesse owned the local motorcycle shop and Flynn was going to school to become a primary school teacher. Jesse had his arm around Flynn's waist and kept kissing her temple while she tried to clip reindeers made from candy canes and pipe cleaners onto the tree.

Travis felt jealous; he wanted to canoodle with Sarah but he'd already gotten the message that she wasn't keen on public displays of affection and he wondered why. Maybe she didn't want people to know they were as intimate as they were. But the entire town knew they'd been snowed in together, and even if they hadn't made love, everyone's mind would have been running there.

"You know," she said, "this is the first time I've actually enjoyed Christmas in years."

"You should come back every year," he said, and then he dared to add, "Or maybe you should just stay. You are in the process of buying a cottage."

"Can't do that," she said. "I have tenants."

"Maybe you could just stay with the tenants," he blurted, then immediately regretted it. With Sarah he'd learned you had to move slowly. This wasn't the right time or place to suggest they move in together. He hadn't even realized how much he'd been thinking about living with her, and now that the words were out of his mouth, they hung there like a solid thing in the air between them.

They stared at each other. He couldn't read what was in her eyes, but an uneasy expression settled on her face. His stomach reeled. He shouldn't have said that. He was moving too fast for her. Hell, he was moving too fast for himself. "What's on your mind?" he ventured.

A sad smile tugged at her lips. "Whenever I'm in this town I feel like I'm holding a snow globe in my hand. Inside is this magical world I can't reach."

That startled him. "You may feel like you're on the outside of a snow globe looking in, but sometimes I feel like I'm inside the insular world of that snow globe and I can't get out. Sure, it's warm and cozy and welcoming, but I might forever be a caterpillar stuck in his cocoon, never able to spread my wings and fly. Don't get me wrong, I love my town and I love my daughter more than life itself, but my wings were clipped the day Crystal got pregnant. For me, with all your knowledge and sharp observations, you bring the outside in. When I'm with you, I don't have a sense that anything is missing. You're the piece of the puzzle that makes me whole, Sarah, and I hope I do the same thing for you."

She didn't answer. His sphinx.

"We can stay apart and stay on our separate

sides of the snow globe. You in silence on the outside, me safe but crowded on the inside. Or we can be together and have both worlds."

Someone jostled into him. "Oops, sorry, I tripped over a sprig of holly."

It was his Aunt Raylene giving him an odd look. Had she overheard him ask Sarah to move in with him? Hell, was that what he'd just done?

Travis had a sudden thought. "Could you keep an eye on Jazzy for a few minutes, Aunt Ray?" he asked.

Raylene shifted her gaze to Sarah. "Sure, go on."

"Thanks." He took Sarah by the hand and tugged her away from the Christmas tree throng.

"Hey," she said, holding up a fistful of tinsel, "I wasn't finished."

"Here." He took the tinsel from her and thrust it at Moe, who was strolling by. "Hang some tinsel, Mayor." He pulled Sarah toward Rinky-Tink's. "Let's go get some hot chocolate."

"I'm sure Jazzy would like to come too, I—"

"Don't worry, I won't bite," he said, and then teasingly added, "unless you want me to."

CHAPTER EIGHTEEN

Sarah and Travis sat in front of the wide plate-glass window at Rinky-Tink's, drinking whip cream–laden hot chocolate from thick Santa Claus mugs and sharing a small plate of chocolate chip cookies. The place was mobbed with tourists and they'd been lucky to get the prime sightseeing table just as someone had vacated it. She was still trying to decide if he had actually asked her to move in with him out there by the Christmas tree or if she'd been imagining it. She didn't want to jump to conclusions, but the lovelorn fifteen-year-old lurking inside her had already taken a header off Mount Everest.

His dark hair was combed back off his forehead, giving him a regal appearance, and his broad fingers were curled around the handle of his mug. She remembered what those fingers felt like curled around her and a shiver shimmied down her spine.

"Well," she said, "this is nice. You, me, hot chocolate."

His grin was wolfish. "It would be nicer if we were alone instead of in a crowded ice cream parlor."

She lifted her mug to her mouth, took a long swallow, felt the hot chocolate warm her up all the way down. Or maybe it was the look in his eyes that was doing the warming. She nibbled a cookie and tried not to read too much into it.

"Before we talk about what I just said out there . . ."—he jerked his thumb in the direction of the Christmas tree—"I want to give you something. I was going to wait until Christmas, but the time seems right."

"You got me a Christmas present?" She felt flustered, flattered. "I haven't gotten you anything yet." Actually, she'd had no idea what to get him that struck the right tone. What gift said, *We've been intimate, you didn't flip out at my scar, but I don't know where the heck this is going*? Now she was about to find out.

He leaned over to his coat that was draped over the back of the empty chair and pulled a package from the big front flap pocket. It was wrapped in shiny green paper and tied up with a silver bow. Their fingers touched when he passed it to her. She raised her eyes and he stared right into her.

"What is it?" she asked.

"Open it."

Self-consciously, she plucked at the silver ribbon, slowly unraveling it. Sarah peeled back the wrapping to reveal a well-worn hardback copy of *A Wrinkle in Time*. Her heart rate quickened.

"It's a first edition," Travis said.

"But how? I just told you it was my favorite on Friday night and by Sunday evening you have a first edition?"

"Express mail."

"Cost you a fortune."

"I wanted to make sure I got it before Christmas."

Gently, she opened the book, reverently ran her fingers over the pages.

Looking up, she saw he was nervous. He shifted in his chair and leaned forward, his voice had gone up just a hair, but she noticed the difference. It was touching.

"I love it," she said honestly. "It's the most perfect gift anyone ever got me."

"I wanted to get you something special to remember us by, me and Jazzy," he said.

Carefully, she laid the book down. "And here I thought you'd just asked me to move in with you."

He splayed a hand to the back of his neck, looked sheepish. "That didn't quite come out the way I intended it."

"I was going to say you were moving kind of fast."

"After what happened between us at the cabin, we've been moving very fast, but I can't think only of me. Jazzy and I are a package deal and she so badly wants a mother . . . I can't . . . we can't . . . rush into anything." He reached out to lay his hand over hers. "We have to be sure."

Sarah wasn't sure of anything except the way her heart jumped whenever she was in the same room with him. It always had. She supposed it always would. No matter what happened. But he was right. This *was* moving way too fast. There was so much potential for hurt on both sides. She was afraid to believe that fairy tales could come true, and Travis . . . well, Jazzy would always be his first priority and she understood that. She wouldn't love him as much as she did if he were any other way.

"I have to go back to New York," she said. "My book is due after the first of the year."

"And after that?" He stroked the backs of her knuckles with his thumb.

"I could return for a visit."

"Jazzy and I could find a new place to live, let you have the cottage."

She shook her head. "No, I want you to stay in the cottage. It's the only home she's ever known."

"We can move. She'll adjust. She's a strong kid."

"That she is."

In unison they turned to look out the window to the Christmas tree on the courthouse lawn. Through gaps in the passersby, they could see Jazzy with her Aunt Raylene at a festive kiosk, stringing cranberry and popcorn garlands.

"But do you think there's a possibility that something deeper could develop between us? Something permanent?"

Sarah held her breath. This was her every childhood fantasy come true. Why couldn't she just say, *Yes, yes, yes, I love you, Travis Walker.* She wanted to say it so badly that it hurt, but she was so afraid of taking that emotional leap, of laying her heart on the line and getting it shattered. She thought of the pain she'd felt when she was fifteen and knew that this would be a hundred times worse.

Honestly, she feared that once he really got to know her, he wouldn't be so enchanted. Her preference for disappearing inside books for long stretches at a time might get old for someone who preferred having lots of people around. The novelty was exciting, and while opposites did attract, when it came down to it, were they simply too different to make a good match?

Maybe your differences are the very thing that will bind you together. You complement each other. Each one strong in attributes where the other is not.

How she prayed that was the case, but they needed time to find out. She parted her lips to express that very thought when suddenly, Travis jumped up, knocking over his chair in the process, and said, "Son of a bitch!"

His skin had blanched pale and he was staring out the window and his body was trembling all over. He looked like he'd just received an electrical shock.

Sarah brought her hand to her mouth and followed his gaze, trying to see what had alarmed him. "What is it? What's wrong?"

"It's Crystal," he said, "and she's got Jazzy."

Travis stormed out of the ice cream emporium, barely aware that Sarah was trailing after him. He had one thing on his mind and one thing only. Getting his daughter away from his ex-wife.

He hadn't seen Crystal since she'd walked out on him. He'd filed for the divorce and received full custody of Jazzy and she hadn't contested it. He hadn't pursued child support because he didn't want her damn money. What he wanted was to know why she was here.

"Crystal," he barked, balling his hands into fists.

She was seated beside Jazzy at the garland-stringing kiosk; his Aunt Raylene was nowhere in sight. Both his ex-wife and his daughter glanced up as he approached.

"Daddy!" Jazzy exclaimed. "Look! It's a Christmas miracle. I prayed for a mommy and look she came back home."

All the anger left him in one long *whoosh* of air. Seeing the utter joy on his daughter's face was his total undoing. She was *happy* that her mother was back.

Crystal looked gorgeous with her long blond hair flowing down her shoulders and her tight red sweater and equally tight blue jeans. Once upon a time he thought she was the most beautiful girl he'd ever seen. Back when he was young and dumb and horny and hadn't realized just how superficial that beauty was. Now, he much preferred Sarah's simple elegance to Crystal's artifice of heavy makeup, teased hair, and snug-fitting clothes.

"What are you doing here?" he asked tightly, moving across the sidewalk. He'd always had a deep-seated fear that Crystal would change her mind about not contesting the custody agreement and try to snatch Jazzy away from him. He used to have nightmares about it, but the anxiety had lessened with the passing of time. Now, it all came rushing back like a water faucet turned on full blast.

Crystal had her arm around the back of Jazzy's chair. "I came to see my daughter for Christmas. Is that okay?"

Travis didn't know how to answer that. He wanted to say hell no, but he knew he could not. Curtly, he nodded.

"Can she stay with us, Daddy?" Jazzy asked. "She can sleep in my bed with me."

Tersely, he asked Crystal, "Could I speak to you in private?"

"Sure." Crystal rose to her feet, using the flats of her palms to smooth out her jeans.

He took her elbow and yanked her behind the kiosk. "Okay, out with it. Why are you really here? If you're looking for money, think again. I'm completely tapped out."

"I know." Crystal was having trouble meeting his eyes. "I heard you had to sell the house to pay for Jazzy's medicine."

"Where did you hear that?"

She shrugged. "You know this town."

"Gossip sure gets around," he said sarcastically. "If you know so much about what's going on around here, how come we're just now hearing from you?"

His ex-wife picked at imaginary lint on her sweater. Travis could have sworn her boobs were bigger. Had she gotten implants hoping it would help in her quest for a music career? Trust Crystal to pick enlarging her breasts over actually getting better at her music.

"I was ashamed," she said, "and I figured you and Jazzy were better off without me." Now she was pulling her poor-me stunt. Just another way Crystal vied for attention.

"We were," he said, knowing it was cruel but saying it anyway. The woman had put him through hell.

"I'm not asking for anything more than to spend some time with my daughter." She raised two fingers. "I promise. And if you could see it in your heart to let me crash at your place, I'd appreciate it. I'm pretty well tapped out myself."

He folded his arms over his chest and glowered at her, but said nothing.

She crossed her arms over her chest, mirroring his body language. She used her chin to point in Jazzy's direction. "She's looking really good. Not a hint of wheezing even though she's out in the night air."

"The medication is working."

"It's pretty expensive, huh?"

"Twenty-five hundred dollars a shot and she has to have one every two weeks."

"Insurance doesn't cover it?"

"No, it's off-label." He explained what that meant.

"Well, you have to keep doing it."

"Of course. Which is why I sold the house."

"But you're still living there?"

"I'm renting it from the new owner."

"Oh."

They stood there staring at each other, but she was a stranger to him. She always had been, he realized. He'd never understood her. She'd had a desperate yearning to be famous. He wondered if she still did.

"How's Nashville?" he finally asked, not knowing what else to say.

She nodded. "It's okay."

"Any movement on the recording career?"

"I've got some irons in the fire," she said, and he knew she was lying. Whenever she lied she rubbed the bridge of her nose.

"Where you working?"

"I'm waiting tables at the Opryland Hotel."

The small talk petered out.

"So." She took a deep breath. "Can I stay with you during the Christmas holidays?"

He was going to say no. Yes, he'd let her see Jazzy, but he wasn't going to let her bunk down at his house. She'd given up that right when she'd abandoned them.

"Daddy?"

He turned his head to see Jazzy standing behind him. "Yes, sweetheart?"

"Please let Mommy stay with us, Daddy. Please, please, please. It would make this the very best Christmas ever."

The minute she saw Crystal and Travis together, all Sarah's old fears of intimacy kicked her squarely in the teeth and she did what she'd always done when relationships got complicated.

She retreated.

With the first edition copy of *A Wrinkle in Time* that Travis had given her clutched in her hand, Sarah set off across the courthouse lawn, zigzagging around revelers, headed for the Merry Cherub.

Don't feel, don't feel, don't feel.

But no amount of chanting to the contrary could stop the burning deep in her heart. Too late. She'd fallen for Travis Walker all over again and just when she was about ready to admit that to him, here comes Crystal with the timing of a Swiss watch.

Tears she did not want to shed pushed at the backs of her eyelids. She would not cry. She could not cry. She was not a crier. Teardrops fell from her eyelashes, dropped to her cheeks, and rolled wetly to her chin.

God, she hated this. Feeling so deeply. It was horrible, the torture of being in love. She was so affected by the emotions tearing at her, but it was her habit not to feel at all. To stay emotionally in balance. Or so she told herself. Was it simply that she preferred to be emotionally closed off? Feeling nothing at all. How did she get back that armor that had once kept her so safe?

Fool! She'd known better than to come back to Twilight. And yet here she was. Feeling and hurting and caring too damn much. She could kick her own ass.

Tears clogged up her nose. Did she have a tissue? She jammed her free hand into her coat pocket to see and instead of a tissue, her fingers brushed against a harder object. What was this? She pulled it out.

Jazzy's angel ornament with her Christmas wish list attached. The lump in her throat swelled. Through the mist of tears, she read the last item on the little girl's list.

I wish for a mommy so my daddy won't have to be all alone when I die.

Had some stupid part of her secretly been wishing she could be the mommy to fulfill Jazzy's wish? The tears ran hotter, faster. Sarah could scarcely see where she was going. All the same, she quickened her pace, escaping from the noise of the celebration behind her, escaping into the darkness beyond the friendly lamplights.

"Sarah, Sarah." Travis was grabbing her elbow,

spinning her around, pulling her into his arms.

"No." She jerked against his restraining arm. "Let me go."

Immediately, he released her, stepped back. In the soft glow from the porch light, she could see he was breathing heavily. She kept her gaze averted, not wanting him to see her red-rimmed eyes and tearstained cheeks.

"You're crying."

"No I'm not." She sniffled. "Allergies. Probably that cedar tree."

They stood there for a moment, neither speaking nor looking at each other, and then finally Travis said, "I had no idea Crystal was going to show up."

She believed him. The look of shock on his face had been real when he'd glanced out the window of Rinky-Tink's and seen her with Jazzy. But that wasn't the issue.

"Talk to me," he pleaded.

She shrugged, held *A Wrinkle in Time* up to her chest. She hadn't even gotten the chance to thank him for the gift. Now didn't seem the time. "What is there to say? Your ex-wife is back."

"So? What does that have to do with you and me?"

Quickly, she peeked at him. He looked as miserable as she felt. "Travis, there is no you and me. Yes, maybe we were working on getting something started, but it never got off the ground. Better to let it go now—"

"Bullshit!"

She blinked, stepped back, stuck her hand in her pocket.

"You're using Crystal as an excuse because you're afraid of what you're feeling."

"That's not it." She fisted her hand around Jazzy's angel ornament. A girl needed her mother. Even if she was a lousy one. Sarah thought of her own mother, how she would have done anything for just a little more attention from Helen. If Crystal was back to make amends with her daughter, she should be allowed to do so without Sarah getting in the way. "You have to give Crystal a chance."

"I do not."

"What if she's really changed? People do change."

"I don't care, I don't love her."

"Maybe not, but Jazzy does."

"What are you saying? That I should take my ex-wife back even though I don't love her and she sure as hell doesn't love me, just for Jazzy's sake?" He looked baffled.

"I'm saying you owe it to Jazzy to let her mother spend time with her. It's the adult thing to do."

He shook his head. "I can't believe you're quitting without even giving us a fighting chance. We're good together, Sarah, and you know it. Both of us are better people when we're around each other."

"How's that?"

"When I'm around you, you show me how to be independent, objective, and detached when I need to be. And when you're around me, you're more outgoing. You get out of your head into your body."

"Oh, don't even bring up sex."

"Why not?" He stepped closer, desire flicking

in his eyes. "I've never experienced anything like it with anyone else and I have a feeling it's the same for you."

Sarah feared terribly that he would try to kiss her. "There's more to life than just sex."

"That's true, but great sex is what puts the shine on life."

"You could try Turtle Wax," she quipped inanely.

Travis threw back his head and laughed. "See there, that's what I love about you, your wry sense of humor."

Love? He'd said the word "love."

Don't read anything into it.

Normally, she could have been cool about this, detached and observant without getting involved. But he'd ruined all that. He'd pulled her back to her fifteen-year-old self where she felt everything so intensely and didn't yet possess the skills to bury her feelings deep. Damn him for that.

She squeezed the angel ornament inside her pocket and drew in a constricted breath. "It's for the best. We might have temporarily brought out the best in each other, but in the long haul we werc sure to get on each other's nerves."

"That's it? You're waving the white flag before we've even begun?"

"I'm saying let's take a big step back. You have Jazzy and now Crystal to think about."

"Baggage," he said. "That's what this is about. I've got too much baggage for you."

"You can't deny that your life is complicated."

"And you live for simplicity."

"My needs are very basic," she said, not only because it was true, but to get him to back off. He did owe it to his daughter to give her mother a second chance, and he couldn't really do that if Sarah was standing in the way.

"If she stays here, Crystal's going to try to win me back," he said. "You have no idea how seductive she can be."

"I can guess," Sarah said dryly.

"So are you really saying what I think you're saying? It's over?" He looked so hurt, but he couldn't be feeling one-tenth of the pain she tamped down inside her.

"I'm saying we need to put this in the deep freeze."

"For how long?"

"I don't know." Why wouldn't he just go?

He stepped back as if she'd slapped him. "I see. I guess I was feeling something more than you were."

No, no you weren't. If you only knew how badly I wanted to fling myself into your arms and beg you to love me forever, how hard this is for me, you'd cut me some slack.

"I guess this means you won't be keeping your promise to make kismet cookies with Jazzy on Christmas Eve," he said.

Her gut torqued. When it came to that little girl, she couldn't say no. "Of course I'll still make cookies with Jazzy, but let's do it here at the Merry Cherub instead of at your house. It'll give you and Crystal some time alone to talk things out."

"I don't want time alone with Crystal. I want time with you."

"Well you know what the Rolling Stones say about that."

"Huh?"

"You can't always get what you want."

He ran a hand through his hair, looked utterly lost. "Sarah. . .

"Thank you by the way."

He narrowed his eyes at her. "For what?"

She held up the book. "*A Wrinkle in Time*."

"The book was to thank you for helping my daughter. Books are powerful things."

"Yes," she said simply.

"Nothing else you want to say?"

"I'm not your ex-wife. I'm not looking for an excuse to run out on you. I'm thinking what would be best for Jazzy."

"What about you and me? What would be the best thing for us?"

"You told me yourself that you and Jazzy are a package deal. There can't be just you and me. Jazzy is always going to factor into the equation and you know it."

"Are you sure that's it?" His gray eyes darkened to charcoal.

"What are you accusing me of?"

He raised his palms. "Hey, if it's too hot in the kitchen, I get it, but at least have the decency to tell me that and stop pretending you're backing off for Jazzy's best interest."

He couldn't have hurt her more if he'd hauled off and slapped her across the face. This had been an agonizing decision for her and here he was suggesting she was simply running away because the pressure was too much for her to handle.

Could he be right? whispered a dark voice inside her.

She shook her head.

"It's been great reconnecting with you, Sarah. Have a wonderful life," he said, sarcasm tingeing his voice, and then he stepped off the porch and turned away.

Her instinct was to call to him, to ask him to stay, but she squelched it. Squelched it hard. She'd become so adept at squelching her feelings, she didn't know how to take her jackboot off the life-line and allow herself to just breathe.

As she watched him walk away in the darkness, she knew she'd never love another the way she loved this man, but right now, nothing on earth could make her tell him that.

A tornado couldn't have as effectively laid waste to Travis's heart as Sarah's coolly spoken words. Stupidly, he'd thought their lovemaking had meant something to her. Apparently, he'd been dead wrong.

Blindly, he walked back to the square, his pulse thudding erratically. Okay, so Sarah wanted him to give Crystal a second chance? Jazzy wanted him to give Crystal a second chance? Then fine, he'd give the woman a second chance. He'd let her stay at the house and he'd let her back into Jazzy's life, but that was it. He had no feelings left for his ex-wife. All that went to Sarah, and now she was leaving him too.

What the hell was wrong with him that he picked women who couldn't love him back? What did it say about him?

"You love too damn easily, Walker," he growled under his breath. "It's time to take a page from

Sarah's book, stop wearing your heart on your sleeve, and stop expecting to find true love."

Somehow, Sarah made it up to her room in one piece. She got undressed, took a shower, blew dry her new hairstyle, which now felt like a huge mistake, and put on her pajamas. She opened her notebook computer, sat crossed-legged in the middle of the bed surrounded by smiling angels. The Merry Cherub indeed.

She opened the file of *The Christmas Angel* and stared at the blinking cursor. She was almost finished. All she needed was the ending. A Christmas miracle to save her heroine Lily's life.

A knock sounded on her door.

Oh crap, please, please don't let it be Travis. If the man was standing in the hallway outside her door she wouldn't be able to stop herself from yanking him into the room and hauling him into her bed.

The knock came again. Maybe it was Jenny Cantrell or Travis's Aunt Raylene or one of the other ladies from the cookie club who'd just gotten the gossip hot off the grapevine.

She got out of bed, padded to the door, and peeked through the keyhole.

It wasn't Travis. Neither was it Jenny or Raylene or any of the members of the First Love Cookie Club.

Instead, she spied Travis's ex-wife, Crystal Hunt.

Every instinct in her body told her to crawl back in bed, cover up her head, and pretend she was deaf. What the hell did the woman want with her?

Rap, rap, rap.

Sarah thought of Poe's raven tapping at her chamber door. *Go away!*

"Miss Cool," Crystal called. "May I talk to you?"

Sighing, Sarah opened the door, but she did not smile. "How may I help you?"

"Could I come in?"

Sarah stood aside and gestured toward the over-stuffed chair covered in pink angel print. Crystal crossed the threshold and then plunked down in the chair. Sarah closed the door, but remained standing.

"You're her, aren't you?" Crystal said. She wore thick mascara and too much rouge. Her skin was pale and her platinum blond hair was the texture of dried grass. "The girl who interrupted our wedding."

"Yep, that's me. Wedding crasher."

"You're still in love with him." She said it as a statement, not a question.

Sarah shrugged, neither confirming nor denying.

"I thought so." Crystal nodded as if Sarah had said yes.

"What do you want?" Sarah didn't even try to sound polite.

"I just wanted you to know I'm not the villain everyone in this town paints me to be." She stuck a fingernail in her mouth to gnaw at a ragged cuticle. "They judge me. I know they do. Mothers aren't supposed to run off and leave their babies."

"So why did you?"

Crystal blushed, shamefaced. "I shouldn't have. I know that, but I just couldn't deal with Jasmine's illness. She kept getting worse and worse and you don't know what I've been through. No one does."

"Could it be any worse than what Jazzy's gone through?" Sarah folded her arms over her chest. Why was this woman here? Was she expecting sympathy from her?

"Travis was good to me, you know. He was funny, lots of fun."

"He's a good guy."

Crystal nodded, kept working on that cuticle. "He helped me pick up the pieces of my life."

Anger spurted through Sarah; she was surprised at how angry she was at this woman she didn't even know. All she knew was that Crystal had hurt both Jazzy and Travis very deeply. "And you repaid him by leaving him just when he needed you most."

"I suppose I deserve that." Crystal winced. "But you don't know what it's like, sitting there day after day watching your baby slowly dying."

"I don't," Sarah agreed, "but Travis does."

"I'm not just talking about Jazzy." Crystal leaned forward, rested her forearms on her thighs, and dropped her head.

Her words startled Sarah. The woman looked so helpless, damaged. "What?"

"I had another baby. Before Jazzy. Before Travis."

Sarah said nothing, just waited, and the story poured from Crystal's lips. "Most people don't know about this. I wasn't living in Twilight at the time. I don't talk about it much." She hauled in a shuddering breath. "I couldn't even bring myself to tell Travis."

Reluctant sympathy washed over Sarah. She did not want to feel sorry for this woman, but it was impossible to deny how utterly broken she looked. Who was she to say how she might have behaved if she'd been in Crystal's shoes?

Crystal slowly opened her mouth, shut it, and then opened it again. Sarah could see how difficult this was for her. "I got pregnant when I was seventeen by my boss where I worked at the Chicken Shack. When I told him I was pregnant, he said he didn't want to have anything to do with it and for me to have an abortion. He was married with two kids already." Crystal stared off into space. "But I wanted that baby."

Crystal lapsed into silence. Sarah didn't know what to say so she kept quiet.

Finally, Crystal shook herself and continued in a rushed monotone. "Here's what happened. I had the baby on my own. My parents kicked me out. It was hard, but that baby was worth it. I loved that boy more than I loved life itself. He had dark brown eyes and jet black hair. He looked just like this daddy. He'd give me the biggest hugs and his smile was like sunshine. He smelled so good, like cotton blankets and fluffy bunnies. He was my pride and joy."

Pausing, Crystal ran a hand through her hair, then whispered, "His name was Shiloh. Shiloh James."

Sarah felt a stab of pain straight to her heart. *Detach, detach, detach.* But it was too late. Being with Travis had demolished the barriers she'd put up to keep her safe from her feelings. She had no defenses left.

Tears were streaming down Crystal's face. Sarah reached over and handed Crystal the box of tissues from her nightstand.

"Thank you." Crystal sniffled.

"You don't have to tell me any more."

"No, I want you to know. I want you to under-stand."

Sarah suppressed a sigh. She didn't want to know.

"Me and Shiloh lived in government-funded housing across a main street from a park. He loved being pushed in the swings. I'd push him and he'd say, 'Higher, Mommy, higher.' He was smart as a whip, always figuring things out. When he was one year old he learned how to turn on the light switch with the handle of a broom. Then just a couple months shy of his second birthday . . ." She stopped, hitched in another breath, swiped at the tears. Mascara smeared underneath her eyes. "I thought he was in his crib. I'd put him down for a nap. It was in the spring and I had the windows open. I was watching TV and folding clothes, when there was a knock on the door and I open it up and it's a policeman and he's holding . . ." Crystal hiccupped, paused, then finally said, "He's holding Shiloh's little blue striped shirt with the bunnies on the pocket and there's blood on the front of it."

Sarah's pulse was pounding so hard she could feel it throbbing at her temples. She fisted her hands. She did not want to hear this.

Crystal completely dissolved. Tentatively, Sarah reached out and put a hand on the woman's shoulder shaking hard with her sobs. "Shh, shh."

For the longest time there was nothing but the sound of Crystal's sorrow rolling off the walls. Then she sat up, scrubbing her face with the tissue.

"I was so stupid. I'd left his crib near the window so he could look outside. I never dreamed he'd push out the screen and try to go across the thoroughfare to the park."

In her mind's eye Sarah could just see the little black-haired boy in the blue striped bunny shirt toddling toward his beloved swings, oblivious to the danger. She fisted her hand over her heart. This should never, ever happen to any mother.

"The paramedics did CPR and they got a pulse. They rushed him to the hospital, but his head injuries were too severe. He was put on a ventilator. They couldn't stop his brain from swelling. For three days I sat and watched my baby struggle to live and then they told me he was brain dead." Crystal's face was a mask of pure horror. "They asked me if I would donate his organs so another baby could live. The vultures. They wanted to pick my baby's bones clean."

Poor Crystal had been nineteen, all alone, no family support, watching her child die. Sympathy swamped Sarah.

The wave of grief washed over Crystal again, but she was so wrung out of tears all she could do was rock and shake. "But. . . . but then I realized I couldn't let another mother suffer like I was suffering if I could help her. So I signed the papers and they took him off life support and they cut him up. My sweet little baby boy. Don't you see? That's why I couldn't get attached to Jazzy. I couldn't love her the way I loved Shiloh or it would destroy me. Especially after she got sick. I could not go through that again. I could not do it." Crystal wailed a long, keening note of pure sorrow.

Sarah came unglued. She was crying too and hugging Crystal and telling her it was going to be okay. That Jazzy was okay now that Crystal was here to make amends.

And as painful as it was for her, Sarah knew exactly what she had to do next.

CHAPTER NINETEEN

The day before Christmas Eve, Travis met Sarah at the lawyer's office to sign all the papers on the sale of the cottage. They were cordial. He thanked her and accepted the check. She thanked him. They made arrangements about the rent.

"Jazzy's looking forward to making cookies with you tomorrow night," he said.

"I asked Jenny and she said it's fine to use the kitchen at the Merry Cherub if that's okay with you." Her face revealed no emotions. She was calm and detached as usual.

When he was a boy, his mother used to read him a story about an young Eskimo—yes, he knew the term was no longer politically correct, but the book was from another era—who got stranded on an ice floe. It broke off from the main chunk of ice where his family had been fishing and carried the boy out to sea. He still remembered the stark picture in the book with the stunned boy near his own age, floating away from everything he loved into the frosty blue waters, alone and isolated. It had made him feel cold and sad all the way to his bones.

As he looked at Sarah now, he felt the same way he'd felt when his mother had read him the story of the boy lost in the Arctic. Except Sarah was the Eskimo on the ice floe, floating away, a giant chasm of icy ocean stretching between them. Her arms were folded over her chest, her eyes narrowed, but her face expressionless as she pulled inside herself, drifted farther and farther away from him, and no matter how much he wanted her, he could never reach her.

Good. Good. Let her go. It would be easier this way. Saying good-bye.

So why the lonely ache building inside him, layer upon layer like brick mortar? Dammit, he couldn't let her go without at least trying to scale that wall. She might have cut her hair, but Rapunzel had climbed back into her ivory tower.

He put out his hand, touched her arm, and felt her flinch. She might hide it in her face, but her body reacted. "Sarah," he said hopefully. "Would you like to grab a cup of coffee?"

She shook her head. "I don't think that would be a very good idea."

"I still think we should talk about what happened between us in the hunter's cabin. Leave Crystal and Jazzy out of it for a moment and let's just talk about how we feel and if there's a way—"

"Feelings change," Sarah said. "You can't rely on them to stay the same. That's why you should never make decisions based on emotions."

"It sounds logical, but it's a really difficult thing to do. How do you simply turn off your feelings?"

"It's not that I turn them off," she said, "it's just that I accept them as transient. They will change. Joy becomes sorrow. Love becomes hate. Anxiety becomes peace. Feelings are always bouncing back and forth."

Had he imagined it? The love they'd shared in the cabin? Not just the physical love, but the emotional bonding. It had happened. He knew it. How could she so successfully turn it away?

"I want you to know I'm not closing the door on us. Just because Crystal is back doesn't mean you and I can't have some kind of relationship."

In that moment, he saw it, the flicker of longing in her eyes. It disappeared in a flash, but he'd seen it. She was afraid. That's what this was all about. The love she was feeling was so big she had no idea how to wrap her mind and heart around it.

Well, he had the patience of Job. He could wait her out.

After all, he was her destiny. She'd once told him so herself.

Raylene was wiping down the bar at the Horny Toad when Earl came through the door. He had a look on his face like a mule had gut-kicked him. His color was ashen, his eyes full of pain.

"Honey," she said, coming around the bar toward him. Heart attack? she feared, and felt her own pulse rate speed up. "What's wrong?"

Earl stared past her like she wasn't there and glared at the only two customers in the bar at two in the afternoon. "Get on out of here you barflies!" He ran at them like he was chasing off cur dogs. "Go on, git. Shoo."

"Earl?" Raylene was getting a real bad feeling about this. She'd never seen her husband act this way. Fear clenched her gut. "Earlie?"

"Shiiiittt, Earl," drawled one of the drunks. "What's eating you?"

Earl picked up a barstool. "You want me to smash this over your head, Micky? Do you?"

Micky held up both arms in a gesture of surrender and scooted back from the bar.

"Hit the road. You too, Snake," Earl growled.

"I ain't finished my beer," Snake mumbled.

Earl smashed the stool over the bar. Everyone jumped and stared as the stool shattered. Earl wielded the broken bar stool leg at Snake like it was a Louisville Slugger. "I said get out of my bar."

Snake looked impressed and hightailed it out the door right behind Micky.

Earl turned around, the broken leg still cocked over his shoulder like he was about to take a swing and hit something hard.

Raylene gulped and took a step back. She'd never seen her easygoing husband do anything like this. Ever. "Earl?"

His eyes were haunted, empty, like a zombie. "Is it true, Ray?"

Raylene saw that his hands were trembling and so were her own. In that minute, she knew that he'd found out. Probably that damn Crystal had gone blabbing. "Earl, let's sit down—"

"Is it true? Did you sell your own child?"

"It wasn't like that," she whispered, feeling her marriage slipping away from her. In all honesty, this was why she'd never told him. Her terror of losing the only man she'd ever really loved.

The last bit of light vanished from her husband's eyes. His shoulders sagged and he finally dropped the broken bar stool leg. "You did it."

Raylene wrung her hands. "It sounds so bad when you say it like that."

"Did you or did you not accept money for a child you had with Lance Dugan?"

She crossed her arms, uncrossed them, crossed them again. Distress ate a hole through her. "The money was from his family. They didn't want their upper-crust son married to trailer trash like me. They had our Vegas wedding annulled."

"And they kept the baby you had with him and paid you a quarter of a million dollars to keep your mouth shut and go away."

Numbly, she nodded.

"That's called selling your baby, Raylene." Earl shook his head.

"I did it all for you, for us."

"You fucked Lance Dugan for me?"

"I was drunk, in Vegas. I didn't love Lance. We got married by Elvis, it wasn't a real marriage. Besides, you'd broken up with me."

"Because you ran off to become a Dallas Cowboys cheerleader."

"It was a good opportunity."

"Yeah, for you to marry Lance Dugan in Vegas, get pregnant by him, then turn around and sell the man his own damn baby."

"I did not sell the baby." Raylene sank her hands on her hips. "His family just paid me to go away."

"And you came back home to Twilight, never once told me you'd had a child with this man. In fact, you lied and claimed you made the quarter of a million dollars modeling in New York City."

Raylene hung her head. "I wanted you to have your dream of owning a bar. How was I to know that six months later, they'd find oil on your grand-daddy's land and the Pringles would end up richer than God?"

"You're blaming this on me? I don't want this damn bar anymore. It's tainted with blood money. Goddammit, I'll burn it to the ground."

"Don't be stupid, Earl."

"Why not? You've played me for a fool one time too many." Earl shook his head violently. "I knew when you became a Dallas Cowboys cheerleader that it would ruin us. I've put up with a lot from you Raylene, because I've loved you since I was six years old. But there's only so much a man can take. This here's a deal breaker." He threw his arms up in the air.

"Earl . . ." She stretched out her hand to him, but he stepped back, palms raised.

"Don't touch me, Ray."

"Please—"

"If you'd just told me, we could have worked this out. That's why I feel so betrayed. It's because you've lied and hidden this from me. I'm supposed to be the one person who knows everything about you and now I find out I know nothing."

"You say that now, but what would you really have done if I'd come back to Twilight pregnant with Lance's baby?"

Earl plowed a work-roughened hand through his hair. How different he was from blue-blood Lance who'd been born with a platinum spoon in his mouth. "I would have been hurt, yeah. And pissed off, but back then, I loved you more than life itself. I would have done anything to keep you."

"And now?" she asked, alarmed to hear the quiver in her voice.

His eyes darkened. "Now? I don't even know who you are anymore."

And with that, the first boy she'd ever kissed, the first man she'd ever made love to, her husband of thirty-five years, turned and walked out on her.

"I thought you liked my daddy," Jazzy said to Sarah on Christmas Eve.

Sarah paused, wiped her hands on the corner of her apron. "I do. Very much."

"Then how come you're moving back to New York?"

Tread carefully. "Your mother came home."

Jazzy said nothing for the longest time. She just kept spooning kismet dough onto the cookie sheet. The air smelled warmly of cinnamon and vanilla and fragile expectations. "I don't really remember her much," Jazzy whispered.

Those softly spoken words yanked at Sarah's heartstrings. "Give it time. You'll remember her and get to know her all over again."

Jazzy met her eyes. "I like you better."

"She's your mom."

"She ran out on me and daddy just when we needed her most." The child's illness had made her wise beyond her tender years, but even so, Sarah realized she must have heard an adult speak those words. Maybe her Aunt Raylene?

This moment was nothing more than an echo of the future. A future where Sarah didn't belong.

Had she ever really belonged anywhere? Yes, she'd belonged with Gram. But Gram was gone.

"She came back though," Sarah reminded her.

Tears glistened in Jazzy's eyes and it tore Sarah to pieces. She swallowed, put down the cookie sheet, squatted, and opened up her arms. Jazzy tumbled into them, the tears flowing down her cheeks. Sarah blinked hard, desperate to control her own tears. Breaking down in front of Jazzy would do neither of them any good. Later, when she was alone in bed, she'd sob her heart out over everything she could never have.

How could she have fallen in love with this child so swiftly? How could it hurt so badly to let her go when Jazzy hadn't ever been hers in the first place?

She'd tried so hard to hold back her feelings. Struggled to stay neutral. Fought to detach from emotional commitment. How had she ended up so wretchedly involved with this girl and her father? What was she going to do without them in her life? How had they come to mean so very much to her in such a short time? It felt impossible. The enormity of her love. She kissed the top of Jazzy's head and squeezed her tightly.

"Don't leave," Jazzy begged. "Please don't go."

Sarah's emotions stabbed at her, a thicket of thorns, treacherous to navigate, impossible to deny—love, sorrow, regret, emptiness, and aching loneliness, always the loneliness.

"It's okay," she whispered, cupping her palm to the back of Jazzy's head. "It will be fine."

"It won't," Jazzy said viciously.

"It feels like that now," she said, trying to convince herself as much as Jazzy. "But time will pass and you'll soon forget all about me."

"I won't," Jazzy insisted stubbornly. "I'll never forget you. Not ever."

How had it gotten to this? She and Travis had thought they'd been so careful to avoid confusing or hurting Jazzy with their relationship. They'd failed. Quite miserably. Sarah had no idea what to say to her to make it all better.

"Do you want me to tell you the legend of the kismet cookie again? The way my Gram told me?"

Jazzy sniffled, wiped at her eyes, and nodded.

Just as Sarah was finishing up the story, Jenny Cantrell popped into the kitchen. "Hey, it smells great in here. What are you making?"

"Kismet cookies," Jazzy said proudly. "If you put them under your pillow on Christmas Eve, you'll dream of your true love." She held a cookie out to Jenny. "Want one?"

"Since I already married my true love, I'll just eat the cookie instead of sleep with it," Jenny said, and took a big bite.

"Sarah," Jazzy said, "can I be excused a minute, I hafta go to the bathroom."

"Sure." Sarah smiled as Jazzy skipped from the kitchen.

"She's an adorable kid," Jenny said. "I'm just so happy she's finally getting well. The whole town's been so worried about her."

A knock sounded at the back door and Jenny opened it to reveal Travis and Crystal standing on the back stoop. "Come in, come in," she invited.

Sarah told herself not to meet Travis's eyes but she couldn't help herself. She glanced over, saw him standing in the glow of the back porch light, and bam! Their gazes welded.

"Is Jazzy ready to go?" Crystal asked.

"She's in the bathroom," Sarah mumbled. "Let me just pack up some cookies for her." She got out a Ziploc bag and stuffed it full of kismet cookies.

Travis stepped across the threshold. Reached for the cookies. His fingers brushed against hers and she could tell it was no accident. "Thank you," he murmured. "For doing this for her."

"You're welcome."

Sarah stood there being oh so polite, squashing her emotions, when what she wanted to do was the exact opposite. She wanted to kiss him and tell him that she'd made a mistake, to choose her, love her, but of course she did not. She was trapped between wanting to follow her heart's desire and doing the right thing. Nine years ago, she'd followed her heart and ended up bruised. Now she was not following it and she was equally as battered. No matter what she did, it seemed like Sarah was destined to lose.

Jazzy came back to the kitchen, said good-bye, and then they were gone, leaving Sarah wondering just how long it was going to take her to get over Travis this time.

That night, Sarah fell asleep in the empty queen-sized bed, her heart an anchor in her chest. She curled on her side, brought her knees to her stomach, and hugged herself tight. How many times had she lain alone and isolated, secretly aching for that special someone to spend her life with? And just when she thought she'd found him, his ex-wife had blown back into town to reclaim her family.

It wasn't fair.

She didn't want to cry. She was tired of crying. Tired of wishing and hoping and praying for things that could never be. She should just be happy for what she had, a writing career that was back on track, an agent who was her best friend, enough money to make life very comfortable, and her health. Those were worthy things many people did not have. It was greedy to expect more.

After much tossing and turning, she finally fell asleep, and on the night before Christmas, Sarah dreamed the dream again. The one she hadn't dreamed since her fifteenth Christmas. The foolish, sentimental dream that had caused her so much trouble.

The kismet cookie dream where she was marrying Travis.

Sarah jerked awake at the point in the dream where he kissed her. She lay breathing hard, her body covered in perspiration. She threw back the covers, swung her feet over the edge of the bed, and dropped her head in her hands. Why oh why had she had that stupid dream? She'd been in Twilight for almost three weeks and she hadn't dreamed of Travis once. Until tonight. Until Christmas Eve.

She glanced at the bedside clock. One A.M. Ugh. She reached for her pillow, intending on plumping it up, but when she pulled it to her chest, a trail of cookie crumbs fell over her sleep shirt.

Kismet cookies. Underneath her pillow, and she hadn't put them there.

But who could have done so? At once she knew the answer.

Jazzy.

When the little girl made the excuse of going to the bathroom she must have slipped up to Sarah's room and tucked the cookies under her pillow.

Jazzy had wanted her to dream of her one true love. Why? Because she hoped it was her daddy? Or because she wanted to find a lover for Sarah so her daddy and mommy could get back together?

In that moment, Sarah knew how to end her book. She threw back the covers, grabbed her computer, and began to write. Tears rolled down her cheeks; fat, salty tears that hit the laptop with a steady *plop, plop, plop.* How come the only place she could emote was on the page? Why couldn't she express herself in person, in speech, with the heartfelt words that bubbled from her fingertips, through the keyboard, and onto the page?

This then was her fate, spending Christmas alone, interpreting everything from afar, never belonging, never fitting in. Before Travis, she'd readily accepted her fate. Never really fought it or thought too much about it. She'd been happy enough. Or so she believed.

But now she knew better. After knowing Jazzy and Travis and coming back to Twilight, she realized how much she'd been missing, how much she'd lost. How much she'd been holding herself back.

By keeping herself isolated from others, she'd been trying to create clarity in her life. An inner knowing. She'd thought distance would give her a sense of peace born of detachment. But her mistake had been in identifying with her observation of her experiences, rather than the experiences themselves.

You couldn't dissect love and still feel it. Love was deep and vast and you couldn't pull it apart, examine it, and still know it. You could only know it through experiencing it.

It was a moment of pure insight.

She couldn't control who she loved. Love was messy and real and raw. The very things she'd always avoided. Except for the one Christmas Day nine years ago when the fifteen-year-old Sarah Collier had staked her claim on the man who was her destiny.

Just down the road, in the cottage by the lake, Travis dreamed as fitfully as Sarah.

Crystal was ensconced in the guest room; although she'd tried to use Christmas Eve as an excuse to slip into his bed, he'd firmly told her no. For his daughter's sake, he was glad Crystal had returned, but he had no warm feelings left for her. She'd killed whatever attraction there had ever been between them when she'd abandoned their daughter. But she was trying to make an effort to reconnect with Jazzy, so he'd allowed her to stay in the house as long as she obeyed his ground rules and kept her hands to herself.

After Crystal and Jazzy had gone to bed, he'd played Santa, stashing presents under the tree, filling stockings, taking two big bites out of the kismet cookies Jazzy had baked with Sarah and set out on a plate for Santa when she'd gotten home. When he thought of how kind it had been of Sarah to keep her date with his daughter, even after all that had come between them, he felt a deep sense of both gratitude and sadness.

In his dream he was getting married again. He was standing at the altar dressed in a black tuxedo, waiting for his bride to come down the aisle on her father's arm. His heart was pounding. Not with anxiety as it had been in real life when he'd married Crystal, but with thrilling excitement. He wanted this. More than he'd wanted anything other than Jazzy's good health.

Even though he was inside his body, he also felt as if he was outside himself, watching the dream unfold. It was like looking at a pristine scene inside a snow globe. A perfect Christmas Day, a perfect wedding. He was the groom. Jazzy was the flower girl in radiant good health.

And down the aisle, on her father's arm, walked the perfect bride. The love of Travis's life.

Sarah.

Travis jerked awake, his body bathed in sweat, his covers tangled around his legs. He had his hand under his pillow and he had something soft and crumbly in his fingers. He pulled it out, blinked at it in the dark. A kismet cookie.

Had Jazzy put it there? Did she want him to dream of Sarah?

He sat up, dazed and confused. And then he heard a sound that chilled him to the bone and knew it was what had awakened him.

The desperate wheezing gasps of his daughter in the throes of the worst asthma attack he'd ever heard.

Sarah had just fallen asleep after finishing her book, when there was a knock at her bedroom door. She glanced at the clock. It was before dawn on Christmas morning.

Groggily, she sat up. "Who is it?"

"Sarah? It's Raylene Pringle."

Raylene? What was she doing here at this time of

the morning? Had something happened to Travis or Jazzy? Sarah tumbled out of bed and threw open the door.

Raylene looked like hell. Her normally well-teased hair hung in strings around her face, her eyes were red-rimmed and puffy, her clothes were rumpled and stained.

Alarmed, Sarah asked, "What is it?"

"Jazzy. She's in a bad way and it's not just her asthma this time. Her heart's involved. Congestive heart failure or something like that. They've got her on a ventilator. Honest to God, I think Dr. Adams is in over his head. He's scrambling, Travis is freaking out, Crystal is a total mess, the gals from the cookie club are at the hospital chapel holding a prayer vigil. We need a calm head over there. Can you please come?"

Before Raylene got the whole spiel out of her mouth, Sarah was already dressed and had her purse tucked under her arm. "Take me to Travis now."

"Dr. Adams, paging Dr. Adams," came a voice over the intercom.

Travis, who'd been pacing the hallway outside the ICU at Twilight General, swiveled his head looking for Jazzy's doctor. Dr. Adams had been very worried that she'd had a severe reaction to the costly drug they'd been giving her. He'd left to go call a pediatric specialist in Fort Worth. Travis wondered if that's who was paging him.

He clenched his hands. He'd never felt so helpless in all his life. The ICU nurses had asked that only one parent at a time be in the room and Jazzy had wanted Crystal to stay, so even though it had practically killed him to leave her, he'd stepped outside.

The pneumatic doors leading into the intensive care unit opened and the head nurse motioned to him. "Jazzy's asking for you, and her mother asked me to give you this." She handed him a piece of folded notebook paper.

"Crystal isn't with her?"

The nurse shook her head. "She mumbled something about not being able to take it and headed down the fire stairs."

He unfolded the piece of paper and read the simple message scrawled there.

I can't handle this. I thought I could but I just can't. Please forgive me.

Fury whipped through him, quickly followed by sorrow. He wadded up the piece of paper, stuffed it in his pocket. How was he going to tell Jazzy that her mother had abandoned her yet again? Travis swallowed hard. Good. Fine. They'd never needed her anyway. Hunching his shoulders, Travis went back into Jazzy's room.

He stared at his daughter, her chest fluttering as she struggled to breathe. Her skin was the color of dumplings, her cheeks strikingly pink from the fever. Her delicate beauty broke his heart. He couldn't lose her. He wouldn't lose her. She was all he had.

You have Sarah.

No. No, he did not. He hadn't forced Sarah's hand. He'd agreed to give her some space. It was what she thought she wanted, but it wasn't what she needed. When she had space, she withdrew.

Travis smacked the palm of his hand hard against his forehead. God, he'd been such a fool to let Crystal back into his life.

"Ass," he muttered under his breath. He wanted to break something, smash it to smithereens—the expensive monitor mounted on the wall beside Jazzy's bed, the cheap wooden chair a nurse had drawn up for him to sit in, the face of Dr. Adams, who looked so fucking helpless standing there in the doorway.

It was all he could do not to grab the man by the lapel, shake him so hard his teeth rattled, and scream, *Do something, dammit. Save my daughter. Fix her. Make her well, now.*

"Travis," Dr. Adams murmured. "I am so, so sorry."

He knew then that in the pediatrician's eyes, Jazzy wasn't going to make it this time. Travis's anger vanished and grief dropped him to his knees. He barely noticed Dr. Adams backing out of the room, closing the door, useless in the face of such helpless sorrow.

The smell of antiseptic burned his nostrils. His mouth tasted salty. Tears. He was crying. He rested his elbows on Jazzy's bed, clasped his palms together, and bowed his head in supplication. It had been so long since he'd prayed. Years. Not since he was fourteen and he'd prayed for God to save his mother, and he hadn't. Travis had been pissed off at God for a long time. But now, his back was truly against the wall.

"Please," he prayed. "Please don't take Jazzy. Take me instead."

The sound of his anguish rolled off the walls,

washed over his ears. If Jazzy died, he had no reason to live. None at all.

Then a soft rustling noise drew his attention to the doorway. He raised his head and saw her standing there, a witness to the lowest point in his life.

Sarah looked a bit uncertain, holding back a bit, her hands knotted together and held low in front of her. Then her eyes clutched his and she steamed into the room like sunshine.

"She's not going to die, Travis," Sarah said with such certainty, so calm and knowing that he actually believed her. "I have called my parents. They're the best heart specialists in the country and they've asked a top-notch pediatrician to consult. I've arranged to have Jazzy medevaced to Houston. Dr. Adams has agreed. It's all taken care of. They are going to cure her. She is going to live."

Travis stared at her, openmouthed. In that moment, Sarah looked like superwoman—in charge, assertive, unruffled. She was precisely what they needed. He and Jazzy.

Travis knew how difficult this was for her. Taking an emotional risk. Putting herself on the line. Offering all she had to help him and his daughter. He was grateful, so damn grateful.

But there was a part of him, ego perhaps, that felt like he'd failed. He didn't have the money, resources, or influence Sarah possessed. He couldn't pick up the phone and call the best doctors in the country. He couldn't pull money from his wallet and conjure up transport helicopters. He couldn't protect his own child.

"Sarah." He whispered her name and got to his feet.

Their gazes cemented.

He had so much to say to her that he didn't know where to start. Words of regret and gratitude, of apology and thanksgiving crowded his mouth, but before he could find a way to say them, the room flooded with medical personnel.

They were lost in a sea of people, on opposite sides of the room. Doctors, nurses, technicians, respiratory therapists prepared his daughter for her journey. But Sarah's gaze cradled his. He could hear what she did not say. *I'm with you, Travis, all the way.*

Once his daughter was bundled on the gurney, the efficient-looking CareFlite team in jumpsuits propelled her toward the staff elevators that led to the helipad on the roof. "There's not enough room for you to fly with us," said the male nurse, who with his sharp features, no-nonsense stance, and buzz haircut looked like he could have been a marine.

"I can't leave her," Travis said. "She's all I've got."

"We'll take good care of her." The air ambulance nurse's tone softened.

He wanted to demand they all let him go with her, but the longer he argued, the more he put Jazzy's life in danger. He leaned over, kissed his daughter on the forehead, but she didn't open her eyes. Fear sledgehammered his heart. He clenched his jaw, battled back tears. "You're going to be okay, sweetheart; Daddy will meet you in Houston."

Sarah slipped an arm around Travis's shoulder. "I've arranged for a private jet. They're waiting at

the Twilight airfield. We'll arrive close to the same
time Jazzy does."

Travis looked over at her. Her blue eyes shone
brightly as if she was fighting off tears of her own.
He couldn't believe she'd done this. She'd taken
care of everything. He should be grateful. Hell, he
was grateful, but it was hard for him to let go of
the reins, let someone else take over. It made him
feel helpless, useless. What kind of father was he if
he couldn't take care of his daughter's needs?

"I'm going with you," she said, and then added
softly, "That is, if you want me to." She held out
her hand.

He took it, squeezed it, tucked away his pride,
and allowed her to lead him from the hospital, because if it hadn't been for Sarah, he would surely
have gone insane.

CHAPTER TWENTY

On the flight to Houston, they held hands. Sarah could feel the tension in his body. "It's going to be okay," she murmured, and gently rubbed his back.

"Crystal ran out on us again." He pulled a piece of paper from his pocket, passed it to Sarah.

"You've got to let go of your rage toward her," Sarah said. "Crystal has been through more than you can know."

"What do you mean?"

Softly, she told him about the little boy that his ex-wife had lost.

Travis stared down at his hands; his shoulders slumped. "I had no idea. She never told me about Shiloh. I'm still angry with her, but now at least I can understand where she's coming from. Why didn't she ever tell me?"

"It was too painful for her to talk about. She just couldn't cope with Jazzy's illness. What she did was wrong, but, Travis, I do believe she's coping to the best of her ability."

"Yeah," he said. "I suppose you're right. I'm going to have work on forgiving her."

"After this is over you two can have a long talk and come up with a way for her to be a part of Jazzy's life."

"That's assuming Jazzy makes it." His voice cracked.

"She's going to make it," Sarah said fiercely. "Your daughter is a warrior."

By the time they arrived in Houston, Sarah's parents and the pediatric specialists had examined Jazzy in the pediatric medical intensive care unit. Helen and Mitchell Collier stepped into the waiting room just as Sarah and Travis got off the elevator.

"My goodness, Sarah," her mother exclaimed. "Look at you. You're slim and you've cut your hair. You look wonderful."

It was then that Sarah realized exactly how long it had been since she'd seen her parents. She'd lost the extra weight last year when she'd joined Weight Watchers and went from a size fourteen to a size eight.

Her parents had changed as well. Streaks of silver were now heavily threaded through her mother's auburn hair. Her shoulders seemed so small and fragile. Her mother was fifty-seven. How did she continue to manage the long hours in surgery that her career demanded? How much longer would she be able to keep it up?

Her father looked older too, but not in a bad way. He was balding a bit at the temples of his silvery hair and the lines at his eyes had deepened and he was wearing glasses, which gave him a scholarly air.

They both wore green scrubs with white lab

jackets thrown over them and surgical clogs. They smelled of hospital antiseptic and paper scrub masks. Smells Sarah knew well. Some things never changed.

"Turn around." Her mother twirled an index finger. "Let me get a good look at you."

Sarah twirled.

"I'm so proud of you," Helen Collier said. "You must have shed thirty pounds."

It irked Sarah that her mother was proud of her for losing weight and not for her other accomplishments, but she let it go. This wasn't about their past squabbles. This was about saving Jazzy's life.

"I can't thank you enough for agreeing to see Jazzy," she said. "She's very important to me."

"All you had to do was ask," her father said somberly. "We've always been just a phone call away."

As if she was the reason for their estrangement. Sarah let that go as well. The only thing that mattered now was Jazzy. "Let me introduce you to Jazzy's father," she said, stepping back and putting an arm on Travis's shoulder, then tried not to let the jolt of awareness that shot up her fingers show on her face.

"How is she?" Travis asked. "What's wrong? Dr. Adams seemed at a loss."

"We have some good news and some bad news," Dr. Mitchell Collier said. "Perhaps we should sit down."

Travis paled visibly. "Is it that bad?"

"Not now that you're in our hands," Helen said, fully owning her ego. She'd earned the right. "Your daughter has been misdiagnosed for four years. She does not have severe bronchial asthma and this is why her condition did not improve as she got older."

"What does she have?" Travis's entire body was so tense Sarah could see the ridge of muscles bunching along his shoulders. She draped her arm around him, felt him relax slightly. She smiled inwardly at that. To think her touch could comfort him in this time of high stress.

"She's got cardiac asthma, the treatment of which is completely different than it is for bronchial asthma."

"But I don't understand. We took her to several specialists. Why didn't anyone discover it before now?"

"There's several reasons," Mitchell said. "For one thing, Jazzy's symptoms were atypical for cardiac asthma. Then there was your mother's history of severe bronchial asthma. Bronchial asthma can be hereditary and that probably predisposed doctors to look there first."

"What's causing it?"

"That's the bad news, Jazzy has a congenital malformation. She needs surgery and she needs it right away." Sarah's father and mother proceeded to go into in-depth medical detail about Jazzy's condition.

"Are you certain?" Travis said. "She was doing so well on that medication Dr. Adams prescribed."

"That drug was merely masking her symptoms. It wasn't helping her," Helen said. "Surgery is the only option."

"The good news," Mitchell interjected, "is that Jazzy should make a full recovery."

"So when are you doing surgery?"

"She's being prepped right now. We just need you to sign the paperwork."

Sarah stood back, watching her parents interact with Travis. She'd never been on this side of the equation before. She'd always been the kid being stood up by her parents on Christmas Day. But now, she was with the kid they were spending their Christmas with. A sick child who desperately needed them.

Suddenly, she saw her folks in a whole new light. She wished they'd brought her to the hospital to see the kids they helped. Maybe she wouldn't have resented Christmas so much. But it didn't matter. The past was behind her. She remembered something Travis had said to her when she told him about her scar. *Scars are just evidence of where you've been, they're not markers of where you're going.*

Everyone had things in his past he'd like to change. Some kept secrets and those secrets could eat your soul, lead to loneliness and isolation. Like Travis's father and Crystal. But others were wise enough to open up, to take the emotional risk of sharing their secret pain to find love and acceptance.

Deep inside, Sarah felt a hundred different things all at once. Felt them and let them unfurl inside her. Surprise, joy, relief. The resentment she'd been holding on to slipped away. She canted her head and studied her parents. They were brilliant, accomplished people who made a real difference in the lives of others. They weren't perfect. They made mistakes, but they tried.

And they loved her, in their way. She could see it

in their eyes when they looked at her. Funny, she'd never been able to see it before.

"Sarah," her mother said as they got to their feet, "can I speak to you in private for a moment?"

"Sure." She turned to smile at Travis. "I'll be right back."

She went down the hall with her mother, pleased at the lack of tension that was normally in the air whenever she was around her. Maybe she'd been as much of the problem as they'd been.

"This is him, isn't it?" her mother said when they were out of earshot of the waiting room. "The one you had the dreams about when you were a kid."

Sarah nodded.

"He makes you happy."

"How can you tell?"

"A mother knows when her child is happy. He loves you, you know."

"What?"

"He can't stop looking at you. It's the same way your father looks at me."

"I thought you didn't believe in soul mates and destiny and stuff like that."

"Maybe not," her mother said, "but I do believe in the healing power of love. I see it in my practice every day. Hang on to him, sweetheart." Then in a very uncharacteristic gesture, her mother kissed her cheek. "He's the one."

Sarah sat with Travis throughout Jazzy's surgery. They didn't talk, just waited, holding hands. She fell asleep curled next to him on the couch. He'd almost fallen asleep himself when he saw her parents step into the waiting room. He stood up, stretched his legs, his heart thumping crazily.

They smiled.

Relief flitted around him. Smiling was good. Travis wanted so badly to believe in a Christmas miracle. No, not a miracle. Sarah had done this. He'd been forced to swallow his pride and let Sarah help him, and thank God for that. Just admitting that he needed help, that he couldn't do it alone, caused a huge weight to roll from his shoulders. It felt good.

"Your daughter came through the surgery with flying colors," they assured him.

"We'll keep her here for a few days," Helen said. "But we anticipate a full recovery and more than likely you can take her home by the middle of next week."

"I can't thank you enough," he said.

"Go get some rest." Mitchell Collier clapped him on the shoulder.

"I need to be with my daughter."

"She's still under sedation," Helen said, and glanced over at Sarah, who was still sleeping on the couch.

"Your daughter seems to have taken quite a shine to mine," Helen murmured. "All Jazzy wanted to know was if you two were here. Oh, and she wanted me to make sure her Isabella doll and that *Magic Cookie* book would be here when she woke up."

"We've got them," he said, realizing he was talking about himself and Sarah as if they were a couple.

Helen smiled as if she understood everything that was churning through his mind. "You're a great parent," she said. "A far better one than Mitchell and I ever were to Sarah. We've got a lot to make up for."

He saw the pain and regret in her eyes. "There's plenty of time. Sarah wants a real relationship with you."

"Does she?" Helen looked surprised, but hopeful. "Really?"

"She might not be able to say it, but that's what she wants more than anything."

Helen shook her head. "You're what she wants more than anything. I see the way she looks at you."

Could it be true? Travis shook his head, wanting to believe it, but afraid to get his hopes up. "When can we see Jazzy?"

"Mitchell and I are going to check in on her to make sure everything is on target, and a nurse will come get you when she's settled."

Travis looked over to see Sarah had awakened and was standing with her arms folded over her chest, holding herself apart.

Her parents departed, leaving Travis and Sarah alone in the silent waiting room. His eyes stared straight into hers.

Travis reached out and took her hand. "I was a fool," he said. "A damn fool to let you talk me into giving Crystal another chance."

"She's Jazzy's mother; I had to convince you try to fix things with her. And you weren't a fool. Crystal is hurting. She needs a little compassion."

"You've been more of a mother to Jazzy in three weeks than Crystal ever was."

"But that doesn't mean we can't sympathize with Crystal's plight. She tries her best, even if it's not good enough. Some people just aren't cut out to be full-time mothers."

"You're thinking about your own mother," Travis said.

"I'm not blaming my parents for who they are. I understand them better now than I ever did before and I think they understand me a little better too. But you really should give Crystal another chance to make amends."

"I'll try." He nodded. "There's another reason I was a damn fool."

"What's that?"

"I got my feelings hurt."

"I hurt your feelings?"

"Damn straight. When you told me what happened between us in the cabin was nothing more than a good time. While a guy likes to know he's able to please his lady, that doesn't mean he likes to be treated like a sex object."

"Poor baby."

"That's right, be glib about the knife you stabbed in my heart."

Sarah sobered. "Did I really hurt you?"

"I felt like you ripped out my heart and stomped it with those stiletto boots of yours. In my pain, I couldn't see the truth. That you were hurting as much as I was."

"Jazzy knew best." Sarah smiled. "She put a kismet cookie underneath my pillow on Christmas Eve."

"She put one under my pillow as well."

"Did you dream of your one true love?" Sarah asked.

He looked deeply into her eyes. "I could ask you the same thing."

"I dreamed of my wedding day."

"And who were you getting married to?"

"My soul mate."

"What did he look like?"

"How do you know it was a he?" she teased.

He smiled. "It was me."

She swatted him lightly on the shoulder. "Look at the ego on you."

"You told me nine years ago, but I was in no position to listen. You were only fifteen."

"But you liked me?"

"Yeah, but how could I admit that? You were a kid and I was getting married to Crystal. I attributed the feelings to cold feet, but part of me knew there was something there. Something I could not admit."

"Really bad timing on my part."

"But I'm no longer married to Crystal," he said, "and you're no longer a kid. I've been with a lot of women in my time, Sarah. It's not something I'm particularly proud of, but I've never . . . no one has ever . . ."—he paused, searching for the right words—"impacted me the way you have."

"Right back at you, big guy."

"I love you, Sarah Collier. You might not be able to say it back to me right now, but I know you love me too. You told me once upon a time that I was your destiny and you were correct."

He stopped, realizing that she needed time to process. He had to take a deep breath and step back and just give her the time she required. He couldn't push her into this. She had to come willingly into her emotions. He'd let her know how he felt. The rest was up to her.

He had to fist his hands at his side to keep from

moving toward her. He met her gaze and waited. What would she do?

Sarah caught Travis's gaze and her heart swelled.

She was attracted to his openhearted generosity. The way he willingly gave of his time to others. He had a provocative way of engaging with people and activity, submersing himself in life. Their communication styles were completely different. He loved parties and people. He went out and tried new things while she moved away to analyze and think.

But their differences melded perfectly. He balanced her, pulling her into life with rich gusto she lacked; and she balanced him, by suggesting he step back, take a deep breath, and think things through before jumping in willy-nilly.

He'd finally said the words she'd wanted so badly to hear and yet was so afraid for him to say them because she didn't know if she could say them back. She felt love for him vibrating to her very core. She'd never experienced anything so expansive, so filled with possibilities. Part of her wanted to withdraw, to go off by herself so she could think this through, set the stage, and come up with the perfect reply.

But here he was looking at her with such hunger in his eyes, as if he was just craving to hear her tell him what he so badly wanted her to say. And he was giving her space, keeping his distance, letting her process what he'd said. His actions—or rather lack of action—told her what she needed to know. He was willing to temper his natural tendencies in order to give her what she needed. If he could do that, then so could she.

Declaring her love would mean opening herself

up to pain. If she committed herself to love, she was committing herself to a lifelong struggle over the security of being alone. To choose him would be to choose uncertainty. Loving him meant admitting the possibility of losing him.

She looked into his eyes, so honest and true, and felt something shift inside her. He was worth the risk. This relationship was worth facing the dreadful gap between the ideal fantasy and the real man. He was worth the price.

Sarah shut down the part of her brain that thought too much. She closed off the internal filter that had kept her locked in a metaphorical tower. She allowed the feelings bubbling in her heart to overflow.

And she just went with it.

She stepped forward. "Travis."

He opened his arms wide, his smile was tentatively hopeful, but he waited for her to come to him. "Sarah."

She rushed to him as surely as the river rushed to Lake Twilight, headlong, heedless, *happy*. "I love you, Travis," she cried exuberantly. "I love you, I love you, I love you."

He caught her in his embrace, squeezed her tightly, and spun her in a complete circle. His broad laugh echoed around the room, and that's when Sarah Collier realized that finally, at long last, she'd come home.

FROM

**LORI
WILDE**

AND

Wm

WILLIAM MORROW

DISCUSSION GUIDE

1. This novel explores the "wounds" that hold people back in life. Are Sarah's emotional wounds understandable? How does her physical wound complicate her emotional healing?

2. What are some of Travis's wounds? How do his wounds differ from Sarah's? In what ways are his coping mechanisms more effective than hers?

3. The community is a strong influence in this story. What do the members of the First Love Cookie Club teach Sarah? What do they offer Sarah that her own family did not?

4. The annual Dickens Christmas event is very important to the town of Twilight. Why do you think the author chose Dickensian symbolism? In what way is it a metaphor for Sarah's emotional journey?

5. Secrets are an important theme in this novel. Sarah has a secret scar. Travis's Aunt Raylene has a dark secret. Even Travis's ex-wife Crystal has a secret. How common are secrets in families? Have secrets been kept in your family?

6. Sarah grew up isolated from her brilliant heart surgeon parents. She learned to live in her own head and spun stories to comfort herself. These stories led her to be an author of children's books, but her coping mechanism of withdrawing has kept her from fully embracing life. Do you believe Sarah has learned better coping skills?

7. In order to deal with his grief over his wife's death, Travis's father isolated himself from others. How is Sarah's isolation different from that of Travis's father? What important lessons did she learn that Travis's father did not?

8. Christmas cookies are an important element in *The First Love Cookie Club*. Cookie swaps are a popular holiday activity. What is it that the cookies offer to Sarah and the ladies of the Cookie Club? What do the cookies really represent?

9. Travis tells Sarah that "Scars are just evidence of where you've been, they're not markers of where you're going." What are some examples of this throughout the story? How have people allowed scars to hold them back? Who is the one person who doesn't let anything hold her back?

10. Raylene has a dark secret that once it's exposed damages her marriage. Did the secret change your feelings about Raylene? The author purposely chose not to resolve Raylene's story line. Would you have liked more closure for that character? Or do you appreciate that life is more fluid and things can't always be tied up with a pretty bow?

11. Finding out Crystal's secret makes it easier to understand her behavior. Still, she is a mother who abandoned her child. Does she deserve a second chance at being Jazzy's mother? Or are there some actions that can never be redeemed?

12. *The First Love Cookie Club* teaches us that it is possible to heal old wounds. Through loving Jazzy, Sarah comes to understand her parents better and they are able to take steps toward bridging the gap between them. What has this novel shown us about love, belonging, community, forgiveness, and healing?

FABULOUS COOKIE RECIPES

GRANDMA MIA'S KISMET COOKIES

½ cup white sugar
½ cup dark brown sugar
½ cup butter, softened
½ cup coconut oil
1 egg
1 egg yolk
½ teaspoon vanilla
1¾ cups flour
½ teaspoon baking soda
½ teaspoon cream of tartar
½ teaspoon salt
½ cup rice cereal
½ cup oatmeal
½ cup shredded coconut
½ cup dried cranberries
½ cup chopped macadamia nuts

Gently combine sugars, butter, coconut oil, egg, egg yolk, and vanilla in a sizable mixing bowl and mix thoroughly. Add flour, baking soda, cream of tartar, and salt; mix until fully integrated. Add cereal, oatmeal, coconut, dried cranberries, and macadamia nuts and stir. Shape dough into 1-inch balls. Ease onto greased cookie sheet, 1 inch apart, and flatten with a fork. Bake at 350 degrees for 10 minutes, then let sit for a few minutes before removing from cookie sheet. Cool on a cookie rack. Sleep with them under your pillow on Christmas Eve and dream of your one true love. Yields 5½ dozen.

CHRISTINE NOBLE'S PECAN SANDIES

1 cup butter, softened
1 cup powdered sugar
2 teaspoons vanilla
1 tablespoon water
2 cups flour
2 tablespoons cornstarch
1½ cups finely chopped pecans
Powdered sugar, sifted

Take your time. It's not a race. Enjoy the process. Savor each step. Take pride in the fact that you're creating something delicious to share. Cream butter and sugar. Add vanilla and water. Add flour and cornstarch. Mix well and add pecans. Roll spoonfuls of dough into balls and place on an ungreased cookie sheet. Bake at 300 degrees for 20 minutes, or until delicately browned. Cool slightly, then shake powdered sugar on both sides of cookies. Yields 3 dozen.

RAYLENE PRINGLE'S SPICE COOKIES

1½ cups real butter, softened
1 cup sugar
2 cups brown sugar
3 eggs
1 cup chopped pecans
1 cup chopped walnuts
4½ cups flour
1 teaspoon salt
1 teaspoon baking soda
1½ teaspoons cinnamon
1 teaspoon nutmeg
⅛ teaspoon ginger

Grab a mixer and cream the pants off the butter and sugars. Whip up on those eggs. Stir in the nuts. Sift flour with salt, baking soda, and spices; add to mixture. Shape dough into two balls. Chill dough and then shape into two 10- or 12-inch rolls that are about

2 inches in diameter. Wrap in wax paper or plastic wrap and aluminum foil and store in freezer. When frozen, slice thinly and bake at 350 degrees for 8 to 10 minutes. The rolls may also be prepared and kept for months in the freezer. Yields 2 dozen cookies per roll. They're gonna be spicy. This recipe ain't for wimps.

SARAH COLLIER'S PEPPERMINT COOKIES

1¾ cups flour
2 teaspoons baking powder
¼ teaspoon salt
½ cup butter, softened
1 cup sugar
1 egg
½ teaspoon peppermint extract
½ cup peppermint pieces
Dab of milk
Peppermint Icing (recipe follows)

Take the isolated ingredients of flour, baking powder, and salt and mix them together. In a large mixer bowl beat butter. Add sugar and beat until fluffy. Add egg and peppermint extract and beat well. Add flour mixture and beat until well mixed.

Divide dough into fourths. Form each quarter into a 12-inch roll. Place two rolls 4 to 5 inches apart on an ungreased cookie sheet. Flatten until 3 inches wide. Repeat with remaining rolls.

Brush flattened rolls with milk and sprinkle with peppermint pieces. Bake in a 325-degree oven for 12 to 14 minutes, or until edges are lightly browned. While cookies are still warm, cut them crosswise at a diagonal into 1-inch strips. Cool and drizzle with peppermint icing. Yields 4 dozen.

Peppermint Icing
Stir together 1 cup powdered sugar, ¼ teaspoon peppermint extract, and 3 to 4 teaspoons milk (enough to make the icing of drizzling consistency).

Coming Fall 2011

Lori Wilde's

Christmas Cookie Chronicles

Three mouth-wateringly delicious e-original novellas
from Avon Impulse

Available:

November 15
November 29
December 13

Find Lori on Facebook and Twitter!

www.facebook.com/loriwilde

www.twitter.com/loriwilde

AVONIMPULSE

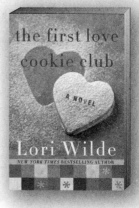